Voices from Viet Nam

#3

AGAINST THE FLOOD

by
MA VAN KHANG

translated and adapted by
Phan Thanh Hao
and Wayne Karlin

with an afterword by
Wayne Karlin

CURBSTONE PRESS

FIRST EDITION, 2000
Copyright © 2000 Ma Van Khang
Translation copyright © 2000 by Phan Thanh Hao and Wayne Karlin
All Rights Reserved

Printed in Canada on acid-free paper by Best Book Manufacturers

Cover design by Susan Shapiro
Cover art:
Nguyen Trung (b. 1942), "Moonlight", 1999, oil on Canvas, 100cm x
100cm. Galerie La Vong, 13/F, One Lan Kwai Fong, Hong Kong

This book was published with the support of the
Connecticut Commission on the Arts, the National
Endowment for the Arts, and donations from many
individuals. We are very grateful for this support.
The publisher also thanks Jane Blanshard for her help
in preparing the manuscript for publication.

Library of Congress Cataloging-in-Publication Data

Ma, Van Kháng.
    [Nguoc dòng nuóc lu. English]
    Against the flood / by Ma Van Khang ; translated and adapted
by Phan Thanh Hao and Wayne Karlin ; with an afterword by
Wayne Karlin. — 1st ed.
    p.cm. — (Voices from Vietnam ; #3)
    ISBN 1-880684-67-5
    I. Title. II. Voices from Vietnam ; 3.
PL4378.9.M25 N4813 2000
895.9'22334—dc21   055556

published by
CURBSTONE PRESS   321 Jackson Street   Willimantic, CT 06226
phone: (860) 423-5110   e-mail: books@curbstone.org
www.curbstone.org

"Darling, to you I offer our century,

where swiftly pass such joys and sorrows."

— Te Hanh

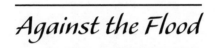

Against the Flood

Chapter One

THE SEA

Khiem stretched himself out on the beach.

The waves rolled onto the shore in a measure as regular as the breathing of a giant. The water slowly inundated the edge of the sand, licked at his ribs like a puppy. His eyes half-closed, he let his muscles relax, let himself become part of the dream of the beach. First light was opening the sky like a door. A long purple cloud shaped like a sword lay low over the horizon. It elongated, and the sunlight glinting beneath it clarified its shape and reflected down onto the sea and then onto the shore where it lay like a moment at the creation of the world: a strange, vaguely dewy light that trembled between the new day and the slow melt of the darkness.

Dawn as an opening book. The faint, bass voices of breezes. The sound of waves swelling, falling, slowly withdrawing, their frothing white foam impregnating the dry sand, leaving white, crooked traces. The soft shuffling footfalls of the all-night fishermen as they moved backwards up the beach, drawing their dripping nets towards their chests. The fierce flapping of the desperate fish caught inside.

Under these sounds, a worshipful silence. A temple, well and cleanly kept. The salt taste of the sea, permeating his senses, smoothing the chaos of his life. Silence as the melting of all the noises and troubles eroding him and the vague

1

sense, somewhere in it, of the true form of his life, fastened to the shapes of sky and sea in the early dawn.

The sun, like a red egg yolk, like hot iron, rose above the horizon. Khiem squinted at the huge form that carried in it the memories of millennia. Here on the smooth sand, he felt suddenly that he was lying in a false calmness. He stirred, as if half caught by an idea that had just come to him, or a desire just out of his reach.

The cadence of the waves until now had sounded like hesitant footsteps, reluctant to destroy the dawn's silence, gently rattling the shells left like night gifts on the shore. The footsteps suddenly grew louder now, rushing, the stampede of a horde released from cages, dashing into one another, pouring out. Some inner force seemed to be building in the waves; they threatened now, roared, threw themselves onto the beach, overran the dry zones, boiled up like water thrown onto a metal stove. Waves smacked into Khiem's flesh. He felt the sand washing out and collapsing under his back in stages, his body being pushed and drawn, and suddenly he was sliding out of the place where he'd been lying. He closed his eyes, enjoying the sensation of lightness, of slipping away from the complications and troubles of his days in a haze of nebulous longing, floating towards her, the woman who had asked him to come here.

After a while, he opened his eyes. The landscape around him had changed. The sun was higher. The ceiling of cloud was high now too, hanging over an immense expanse of blue sky. The curve of the beach separated itself from the sea and the empty sky; behind the rows of sea pines, the shore was crowded with guest houses, hotels, and hostels of all styles, each competing with the other to push close to the water. Nearby, the squares of the salt-production fields sparkled like segmented glass, and down the coast he could see villages here and there behind the sea dikes, their houses white as crumbs of rice powder cake.

A faint worry rose in him, here in front of this immensity which seemed a symbol of absolute power. Yet at the same time he felt a sense of joy, a lingering of the serenity he had just touched.

He had seen the sea for the first time when he was twenty years old.

In the summer of 1965, after their wedding, he and Thoa had received a honeymoon leave from her trade union—she was a skilled textile worker—and had gone for some days to Sam Son Beach. He was a citizen of a country with more than three thousand kilometers of coastline, and a social science teacher as well, yet until then he had been like a person living in a house who had never seen its façade. Nguyen Tuan had written that a person should know the geography of his country the way a child knows his parents' names, and Khiem had always felt remiss. But that first visit to the sea had been cut short when the Americans began bombing along the coast; it was the beginning of their war of destruction against Vietnam. The managers of the beach guesthouses had quickly chased their guests away, so they could close their doors and evacuate themselves from the area.

Khiem had become a teacher in the northern highlands. Because he was responsible for his students' safety, the idea of asking for a holiday had seemed shameful. Those were years of difficulties and uncertainties, and all individual needs had to be subordinated to the demands of the war. Later, as the fighting became worse, Khiem joined the army and fought for five years. When he returned, his relationship with Thoa was on the verge of collapse, and the last thing either wanted was a holiday together at the beach. Moreover, it was a time when a need for creativity had started to burn in Khiem. He had written some stories now and then when he was twenty, but had never really had the time to devote to that work. But back from the war, he felt both the inspiration and the need to write. It was one of the most exciting periods to be a writer in Vietnam, and his work and those times had consumed him. In all the decades since, he had never returned to the sea.

But that brief, long-ago meeting had left impressions that had never gone away, and he sensed in those memories, that feeling, a piece of the Creator within himself. Humankind came from the sea; its salt still traceable in their blood. He had read that somewhere; he remembered it forever, and he'd inherited the elements of the ocean in his own body. His ancestors were the children of the Lady of the Nation, Au Co, Mother of the Hundred Eggs that became the Hundred Children, fifty who went to the forests, fifty who went to live by the sea. His forebears were tattooed fishermen, pearl divers, strugglers against the fierce creatures of the ocean, its waves and its wind. Their lives and legends had burned like stars in the firmament of his childhood imagination. He'd loved those stories in which people had to put aside their own safety, struggle with terrible creatures and poisonous snakes when they were forced to dive for pearls under the terrible Chinese Ming dynasty—their suffering imprinted on his boy's mind when he read Uc Trai Nguyen Trai's proclamation of victory over the Ngos. He'd loved the passions and treachery told in the story of My Chau's love and betrayal by Trong Thuy, her beheading by her father, King An Duong, as she was sitting on horseback by the sea. Her innocent blood dripping into the sea, caught by oysters, transmuted into pearls.

The sea. In that first meeting with it, Khiem had come face to face with something invisible and magnificent that stood outside of time and whispered to him the secrets of a divinity.

In fact, he hardly understood the sea. He'd come here now for a summer holiday, both for his health—he'd been working too hard—and to meet secretly with the woman he loved. He was sharing a hostel room with two other people: the retired head of a dairy collective named Biu, and a naval engineer, Coc, who was taking leave after a long voyage. As for Biu, he was enjoying his stay in the guesthouse immensely. Hot water in the bathroom, air-conditioning in his room, and constant, caring service from a staff of pretty girls: Miss Duyen, Miss Xuyen, Miss Phuong, Miss Loc, Miss Vui, Miss Hoa. Bui had done what men of his generation did whenever they were very moved: composed a poem. It wove each of the young women's names into a single sentence.

"Hey, writer," he called to Khiem, when he'd finished. "Listen to my poem and let me know what you think."

For most of their stay, it had been Bui's poem that had defined Khiem's relationship with the retiree. He would have liked to ask Bui about his life: he'd heard the man had taken wild buffaloes from the forests, trained them, and transported them to the Mekong Delta—a possibly interesting topic to write about later. Instead, day by day, line by line, word by word, he would listen and suggest, suggest and listen, probably until the day he would take the old man to the bus station. By then he would know the poem, with its old folkloric style, by heart; he would know the stress on every syllable of each of the girls' names.

But it was Coc, the naval engineer, who pointed out Khiem's ignorance about the sea and appointed himself Khiem's teacher.

"Do you know what Tsang-tsu said the sea means to Vietnam?" he'd asked. "'If one has a house with a façade on the main road, one can be a wealthy man.' That's Vietnam!"

Coc had laughed triumphantly, his teeth white against his tanned face.

But what about the life behind the façade? Khiem had thought. Was it as cheerful as the former head of the dairy collective's poem? Coc faced the sea, but there was so much he didn't see behind him. Like himself, Coc was a veteran of the American war. He'd studied and graduated from a university in the former Soviet Union but knew nothing now about what had happened there after its collapse. He was like a man with only one woman in his life. He knew only the sea. His life consisted of a series of journeys, each twenty days long and spent on a boat that traveled eleven nautical miles every hour and then stopped to mark its position on a chart.

Yet he brought a methodical passion to his work that Khiem admired. At every anchorage, Coc would observe the weather, the chop of the waves, the wind speed, the temperature at various depths; he would take samples of the water for chemical analyses. Then the boat would start again, slowly, taking specimens of sea life, cataloging the ephemera, studying them. Nature is more abundant than anyone can imagine, he enthused to Khiem. In the waters off Vietnam there was a type of squid as small as his thumb, and flying fish that changed the color of their scales, and porcupine fish with spines as hard as wood and as long as two fingers. There were seahorses that carried their unborn in their bellies, and crooked-back salmon that swam back up the rivers where they were born to breed and give birth and die in the same place, as their offspring swam back downstream to the sea. There were devil fish, with long beards, and bodies glowing with luminescence, and leaf-shaped fish that stuck themselves into cracks and crevices from which they couldn't be removed, and crawfish that jumped like Russians dancing. There were toadfish that could swim backwards and had poisonous skins, and tough, fierce tiger-pointer sharks who feared tiny fish that wiggled into their mouths and gills and ate their mucus, sapping their vitality.

Once Coc's boat was caught in a storm for three days, blown here and there like a bamboo leaf in the water, bringing him right to the brink of death. Afterwards the sea smoothed back to calmness and lay still, "as spent," he'd said to Khiem, "as a man after orgasm," reflecting sky and cloud so clearly he felt as if he were floating in a vacuum between heaven and earth.

He had been sitting with Khiem here on the beach last night, next to the ocean he was describing. They had rented canvas chairs and stretched out their legs, and the waves lapped against them, making the two men feel as if they were floating. Night and sea had flowed into each other. Behind them, the white sand dimly reflected the sparkling of the stars. In front of them, waves pulsated and boiled on the immense black ocean. Staring at it, Khiem had remembered why he was here. The sea has always been a place for love affairs. What could be a more powerful reminder of the storms of life that will buffet the lovers, that they will innocently swear their love will withstand?

The sea and the sky mirrored each other in the night, the sea appearing as old as the sky protecting it, sheltering Khiem and Coc as well, stretching out over their heads, fastened by the silver nails of millions of stars. Khiem had stared at their vast numbers. Which star had written its characteristics on the hour of the Rat, the day of the Tiger, the month of the Pig, and the year of the Rat that marked his birth, his unique fate? He felt a sudden, giddy kinship to the stars. Coc fixated on aquatic products, and Biu composed poems to hotel maids. But writing was Khiem's daily business; his fate, it seemed was to try to find substance and pattern and order in the dark and chaotic universe around him.

It had grown later, and Coc had left, had been gone a

long time. But Khiem had stayed until the sky began to lighten.

He was alone on the beach, in the dawn. But soon a couple collecting seashells increased the human presence to three. Next a family of four appeared. A dozen young girls on summer holiday. Then a team of young men playing ball multiplied the population to about fifty. Old men in t-shirts and shorts powerwalked by, their arms rising and falling in rhythm with their breathing. More people appeared, then more. Cars and buses, the sunlight now reflecting off their bright colors, beeping noisily as their drivers searched for parking spaces under the canopies of the pine trees. Now the guests from the government hotels and the private guest houses rushed out, flowing into the crowd, multiplying it, until it was uncountable.

Eight o'clock. Needles of sunlight glared off the crown of each wave. The beach was now jammed with thousands of people.

The small inns and restaurants of the resort town had covered the entire shoreline, Coc's façade. The beach itself, which used to be empty, had become the façade of the façade, cluttered with small jury-rigged huts roofed with plastic, palm leaves, canvas, or, sometimes, only a big umbrella. The concessions sold wine and beer, rice and noodle dishes, dog meat, and other snacks that went with the wine and beer—a new custom Khiem had heard called "instant noodle lifestyle." Or they offered inner tubes, canvas chairs, or bathing suits for rent. Or massages. Or freshwater showers. Moving aggressively through the pressing, pushing crowd were the old women and children who lived hand to mouth, selling cheap gifts and snacks: barbecued squid, fish with chili sauce, rice cakes with fish mixed with hot chili.

It occurred to Khiem that the crowd boiling around him on the beach was like an instant nation whose laws and rules of behavior were determined only by the whims and needs of the moment. There must have been five or six thousand people gathered here now, all squeezed onto this narrow strip of sand, all intent on swimming, eating, enjoying themselves. The teenagers played football wherever they could. People sat, ran, jumped, shouted, or screamed, as they pleased. Nature was for everyone, wasn't it? People had the right to do whatever pleased them, didn't they? Khiem could still remember a time when husbands had to persuade their wives to put on bathing suits instead of standing and contemplating the sea in full black trousers and white blouses. If the husbands nagged too much, the wives would just say they were menstruating and beg off. Only the boldest would wear bathing suits under their clothes, which they wouldn't remove until they reached the water.

Now women displayed their bodies in their bathing suits as soon as they opened the doors of their hotel rooms and strode proudly to the beach. That exhibition had become another part of the show: who had the fanciest, most colorful swimming costume, who would expose the most flesh to the sunlight? Men followed, taking photographs. After all, hadn't the female body always been the subject of art? The beach served up anything anyone could desire. For five thousand dong, one could be a Tanzanian riding a zebra. The deputy director of an accounting department could transform himself into a gallant chevalier in a plumed, wide-brimmed hat and black tights, while his wife, a girl from the village, could magically become a Spanish duchess sitting in her carriage, regal in a flowing white gown, half her face veiled, black velvet gloves on her hands. Compared to the magic of karaoke that could turn an itinerant locksmith into a famous singer, it was nothing to paint a few black zebra stripes on an old nag, or to fashion the baroque European costumes the photographers would rent to their customers. Or, if someone really wanted to feel like a king, he could always rent the services of a "hugging swimming partner": fifty thousand dong for a young woman who would take care of his needs and make sure he enjoyed himself underwater with her. What more could anyone ask?

All around Khiem, people, most of them domestic tourists, were jammed together on the sand like a living representation of the country's economic recovery. The beach was no larger than it had ever been—it hadn't been stretched to accommodate the onrush—and the sea in front of Khiem was black with bobbing human heads. Four girls clinging to a rubber tube, a poor gray-haired old husband pushing an inflated rubber mattress that displayed his plump and attractive young wife, desperately trying to chase away a gang of young bastards making fun of her. Everything and everyone together, tumultuous, noisy, taking over a whole corner of the sky and sea.

Khiem moved along the edges of the anonymous crowd, the gathering horde of autonomous individuals drawn here casually, temporarily, from everywhere, unified by a kind of mass hilarity, as if all its discrete joys and expectations had wrapped themselves into a communal soul, a common face, a single noise. He sensed the potential of it, a compacted, seductive energy that could mesmerize him, overcome him, absorb him until he became it, became the crowd, felt his uniqueness drip away and disappear like a discarded shell.

And what else?

He remembered talking to his closest friend, Thinh, a doctor now working in a fashionable private hospital, about how the gap between rich and poor was growing more flagrant in their society. "Do you know how much a construction worker—you've seen them around the city, digging foundations for new buildings, mixing cement—do you know how much workers like that earn a day?"

"How much?"

"Eight thousand dong. The cost of a can of beer."

Thinh had shaken his head in disbelief. "I've seen people drink twenty cans, one after the other, pile the empties up as high as a wardrobe. Yes, it's terrible, but what can you do? You have to look out for yourself."

Thinh. He was an excellent doctor and an intelligent man, could speak four foreign languages, had a rich knowledge of history. When he was a young man, his passion had been literature; he'd loved it dearly. If a man forgets poetry, he'd say, a man has forgotten himself. He once published an eight-sentence poem. But instead of gaining a place for him in the firmament of letters, those eight sentences had broken his wings and cast him down. The poem was attacked by the Province Department of Culture and Ideology. Thinh's poem, it was decided and declared, was antipolitical and didn't present a clear ideological message. Poor Thinh. In reality, Khiem had thought the poem rather mediocre, except for its last line, which read: *No one wonders about the coldness in the foot of the pillar.* It was the poem's best line, and it was exactly that line which got Thinh into trouble because of its being—in the view of the Department of Culture and Ideology—"unclear, equivocal, and tricky."

That was during the sixties. Thinh's punishment was to be immediately drafted and sent to the front. Since that time, he had bidden farewell to what he called the "Poetic Disease." Before he left for the battlefield, Thinh and Khiem had a long conversation about life, science, and literature. The latter, Thinh said, was shaped and evaluated too much by the fashions and exigencies of the times in which it was written, by what was permitted and what was forbidden. No, Khiem had said: he wrote as if he were simply tossing a stone from his hand, letting it fall where it might. Maybe, but medicine was a simpler, more clear-cut profession, Thinh replied. All a doctor saw in front of his eyes were human bodies, differing only in age or sex. They got sick or they healed according to the laws of science, no matter how much any district politician might want to interfere. But literature was like a vegetable garden where anybody could plant whatever fatuous things he wanted. Anyway, Thinh had laughed, *Tout cherche tout, sans but, sans repos*—everything searches for everything, without aim, without rest. Khiem's talent was just ripening—they'd see where it went.

Khiem, jostled, turned his mind back to the crowd on the beach. A foreigner looking at them would find his stereotype of Vietnamese as poor and thin contradicted. The people around him all looked plump and healthy and prosperous. He remembered the time the late writer Nguyen Tuan had visited Bulgaria, when it was still a socialist country. His hosts had invited him to take a swim in the Black Sea, but Nguyen Tuan had refused, and had even asked them to allow him to go home before the end of his scheduled trip. Upon his return, he'd said that he'd been ashamed because he didn't have a bathing suit and his legs were too skinny. Khiem understood: He was a poor man from a poor country, was what he'd really been saying. At that time nearly everybody in Vietnam had felt they were in the same boat. To be happy and rich, to swim like a wealthy bourgeois, when everyone else was wearing tattered clothes and going hungry, was indecent. The mark of a rich person at that time was owning a bicycle with a German trademark, a Mifa, or a Russian sewing machine. If Nguyen Tuan were resurrected now, Khiem wondered, how would that poor wandering soul of a writer feel standing on this beach?

The *nouveaux riches* were everywhere now. They drove here in their private cars. They stayed in air-conditioned luxury hotels for 500,000 dong a night. They ate special dishes and washed them down with foreign brandy, spent a million dong for a meal for three people, when the price for a kilo of crabs had gone to 80,000 dong, ten times what a laborer could make in one day. The last time he had come to the shore had been with forty-two other people jammed into an old Russian van. All the men had gone swimming in their dark blue shorts. Everything had been simple and monotonous. But there were no beggars on the streets, no one like the old woman in a tattered conical hat, skinny and trembling, holding her hand out to a group of men drinking in front of Khiem. Begging them for a few hundred dong. The men, all with gold chains around their necks, laughing at the old lady as they downed cans of Heineken and Tiger beer, egging each other on to go bottoms up, red-faced, their eyes rolling. "Get away from here, you old bitch—stop bugging us!" one of them yelled, twisting his face into a kind of comic maliciousness. "Are you from Thanh Hoa, granny? I heard that in your province there's a commune of professional beggars, each so rich they build brick houses for themselves. Tell me the truth, old woman, and I'll give you something."

A teenage girl, her breasts just starting to bud under her blouse, suddenly pushed a tray of sunflower seeds under his nose. "One hundred dong a packet," she chanted. Khiem bought ten.

"Why aren't you in school?" he asked her.

She shrugged. "My grandma is blind and stays home weaving baskets for about 500 dong a day. I can make over a thousand doing this. What else can I do, uncle?"

"Come on under those trees with me and I'll show you what else you can do," one of the gold-chain men leered at her. "Or under the blanket, right here. Those two perfumed mushrooms of yours are looking just about ripe now—let me have a look and I'll show you how much money you can earn." He laughed, baring his teeth, and his friends joined in, all of them laughing, Khiem thought, at this little girl. Looking at her, he felt something wrench his heart, something pulled away from him, something lost.

He turned away, troubled. Feeling in spite of his sadness

and disgust, the seductiveness of the mob tearing at him, as if pulling apart the very yin and yang, the male and female elements of his nature: the strength of this crowd to assimilate him, to take him into itself, to make him someone he was not.

At that moment he heard someone call his name.

He heard it clearly in the chaotic uproar; he heard it emerging from the anonymous noise of all the people around him. He heard it distinctly, as if called from the depths of his own subconscious. His heart beating faster, he squinted at the sun-splashed sea, thick with the bobbing heads of the swimmers, and saw Hoan, swimming towards the shore. Hoan, whom he could never mistake for anyone but herself, even in this milling crowd, swimming straight across the waves to him.

She was using a breast stroke and swimming as if she were alone in the sea, making a path for herself. When she reached the shallows, she stood, the waves splashing against her legs, and waded towards Khiem, waving. The synchronicity of the event filled him with a kind of giddy elation: Hoan wasn't a ship with a compass; he, Khiem, didn't possess a special scent to attract a female—how could they have found each other?

Looking at her, he thought: each human being is a universe. He had come here at her invitation, finally at her insistence: his passionate love, his bitter sadness. Her face was round and her neck long and her breasts full and virginal and her body lovely in the black swim suit. She stood as real and beautiful and solid as truth, and at the same time was still something of a mystery to him. Yet he felt tied to her. Their mutual attraction and where it could take them had so long been a living part of both their imaginations that it allowed them to feel they had loved each other all their lives.

In reality, even though they had known, and loved, each other for the past ten years, they had only managed brief, furtive trysts in the city, had not allowed themselves to fully consummate the relationship. Khiem was the director of the Cultural Affairs Division of General Department T, Hoan a proofreader. The division's main function was to publish annually the speeches, resolutions, and internal documents generated by the General Department's leadership. Although the operation was subsidized, it needed to generate its own income through the publication of novels, short-story and poetry collections, and plays—in short it was a publishing house. Hence Khiem's directorship. He was the only real writer there: the other editors were drawn from the workers or administrative staff, and the writers and poets the division published were mainly those who had won prizes in worker competitions for stories about exemplary people performing "good" deeds. Khiem's deputy was an old trade unionist who'd trained as an interpreter in Guangtung and had only finished the seventh grade. His head of distribution was a fifty-six-year-old man who was always flirting and chasing after the younger female workers. His bookkeeper was a young man who had received a certificate for completing a short accounting course—a stuffy, eccentric person. Many of the staff worked at outside jobs and were indifferent to literature. In general, Khiem found the atmosphere deadening and the office politics vicious.

He had wanted to leave this position for a long time. But when he broached the subject to his wife, Thoa, she had called him a fool. Only when wolves stop eating meat should anyone give up such a secure directorship, she'd said. Hoan, on the other hand, had always understood his feelings of isolation.

Since he had reached his fifties, Khiem had come to understand that alienation was the central condition of his life. He was disgusted by his colleagues' ignorance, the way they pretended to obey him, kissed up to him. His own boss, Nguyen Van Pho, the General Director, was an arrogant and narrow-minded man. The tension between them had become extreme. At the same time Khiem felt their arguments were trivial, and worse—only sapped energy from his writing. He realized suddenly how exhausted he was, how tired of the fierce disputes between himself and Pho, of the divisions these had caused within his section. Lately he'd begun to see that his staff, even those who once swore they'd always be faithful to him, had sensed he might be in danger of losing his job and had begun carefully distancing themselves from him. He was sick of it. He was fed up with the self-important, self-serving babblings of meetings and seminars whose only function seemed to be to produce resolutions that were treated as if they were sacred texts. He was appalled at the cunning, the dirty tricks, the constant jockeying for power that life seemed to have become, an endeavor no different from the constant struggle for profit, for prestige, for amusement he saw everywhere, even on this beach.

Only Hoan had always, silently, shared his feelings, been a refuge for him.

Now, finally, she had invited him to meet her here at Thinh Luong beach, during the festival of the Princess My Chau.

Now finally, after ten years of reining in his desire for her, he had agreed to come.

He had taken the train here; he had taken his room with Coc and Biu; he had taken his meals in restaurants as expensive as Hanoi's. He had walked up this beach, surrounded by multistoried hotels, guest houses, mini-hotels all jammed against each other, surrounded by the milling crowd, and all the time he had wondered how he would ever find Hoan in this place.

But here she was, as if drawn by the invisible thread strung between them.

Hoan was in her forties, her body ripened to a harmonious and lovely maturity. A V-shaped bit of lace lay smoothly over the top of her full breasts, the mysterious shadowed valley between them. Her legs were straight and smooth, her skin white in the sun, her face opening to him now with a radiant smile. A shiver ran through his body: he pictured how he would embrace her, envelop her, press her to him. But, suddenly, he was overcome by a deep sense of exhaustion. It had taken him so long to get here, so many years to get here, years that had taken him through the Agent Orange defoliated jungles of the South and of Laos, through suffering, hunger, thirst, through the fear of death and the pain of betrayal. It had been a long journey, and so hard, to this beach, to this place, to this person.

Hoan smiled at him and raised her hands to the back of her neck to push up her hair, the motion thrusting her breasts out, making him ache with desire. Then the spell was broken.

"A photo to memorialize this moment, dear sir and madam!" a voice calls.

A street photographer in ragged cutoff jeans grinned at them and raised his black Pratika camera. Another photographer appeared next to him, then another. But it wasn't only money they were after, Khiem smiled to himself; who could blame them—these were men who searched for beauty. He put a hand on the first photographer's shoulder. "We'll take a picture together another time," he said. "For now, please just take hers." He gestured towards Hoan.

Looking at her now, as if with the photographer's eyes, Khiem was struck again by her beauty and grace, by his good luck. Born in 1953, in the year of the Tiger, Hoan was self-confidant and blessed with a sense of humor that he knew helped her deal with people. He loved that about her, and her poetry, and that she read widely and well: he loved her thirst for knowledge. He loved her faith in the ability of the stars to chart people's destinies, her faith in prayer, the way she could read people's character in their faces; he loved the way she threw herself wholeheartedly into her work.

He'd been surprised when she had first come to work for him as a proofreader: she seemed very overqualified for the job. "It's what I wanted," she told him: she'd asked her uncle to help her get a job in the city, and the position as proofreader was the only one available. "I was too restless, had too many problems at home. I wanted to get married, but at the same time I didn't. When this job came up, I said yes immediately." Later, after they had gotten to know each other, she had confided that she really didn't know why she had taken the job. Maybe it was her karma. "To be truly happy," she said, smiling, "one has to be a little stupid." Khiem had wondered if her words were aimed at him; she was always sharp-tongued about the people around her. Her colleagues, with their seventh-grade educations, were the "worker-peasantry." Lieu, who always hovered around Khiem, was Flatterer. Quanh, Khiem's deputy, was the Squint-Eyed Toad, both for his looks and for his cruelty. Nghiem, the half-crazed flirt who wouldn't leave the female staff alone, was Sleepwalker. He'd been convinced Hoan found him a handsome man until the day she told him that she loved the way he tightened his belt so much that it made his skinny body look like a segmented stalk of bamboo.

She was sharp that way. Perhaps too sharp. Khiem's own relationships with the younger editors like Lieu, Khoai, and Phu were, he felt, collegial. He respected and sympathized with the fact that they had come up from the working class and hadn't had the chance to get a proper education—even though he recognized that he could indulge the luxury of such feelings because he was in a higher position. Hoan, on the other hand, while not criticizing their professional skills or backgrounds, was scornful of their behavior. Besides naming Lieu Flatterer, she was also suspicious of him as the younger brother of a man notorious for having "put on the other's shoes," that is, betrayed his comrades-in-arms and defected to the French during the French war. Phu she called Thunder, to describe his rudeness and foul temper. And Khoai, the young editor who had just been promoted to deputy head of the accounting department—a handsome, loquacious, cheerful man who often told humorous stories —was Horse-Eating-A-Cake.

He was also not sure if it was because of a natural antipathy, or because of his problems with them, that she hated Department General Director Pho; Duc, in charge of Cultural Propaganda; and Hien, the Chief of Staff. Her name for them was the "Three Cards." Khiem wondered if her bitterness towards them might also have something to do with her uncle's. He had once been Director of Personnel, and Khiem knew he had despised all three men.

Hoan, he knew, was someone who would always swim against the stream. She despised most of the men in the office, and was somewhat uncomfortable with the women staff as well, though her nicknames for them were affectionate: Ms. Tam, the Jackfruit Seed; Ms. Chuong, the Skinny; and Ms. Tuyen, the Fat. Hoi, the cleaning woman, who was small and slightly deformed, was Twisted Fetus, or Tiny, though Hoan felt sorry for her and had taken her under her wing, teaching her proper ways of speaking and applying makeup, giving her clothes, now and then taking her to lunch.

From the beginning, Hoan had always worried him. He was afraid her sharp wit would make her the object of hatred and jealousy. At first, he wasn't sure why he was so concerned, since there was no link between them. Then one day his wife, Thoa, had to go to Lang Son on business—she had just been promoted to the position of inventory manager for a department store. Khiem had had to take care of their daughter, Hong Ha, who was then four years old. He'd brought her to work, but had to leave her alone, playing with his potted plants, when he went to a meeting. Everyone else was busy and ignored her, except Hoan. When she came into the room and saw the little girl, she ran over to her, her face creased with worry. "What are you doing here, little one?" She picked Ha up, combed her hair, sewed on a button missing from her blouse, clipped her fingernails, and even brought her some cakes. There hadn't been any special sympathy between them then—she hadn't known whose daughter Ha was—and Khiem had been touched by her actions, particularly since she clearly wasn't trying to kiss up to him. Under her toughness, he sensed a sensitive person, easily touched, sincere—and yet sharp in her assessment of people. Later, Khiem would tell himself that what he saw that day created the first feelings of silent connection he felt towards Hoan. True lovers always suffer from contradictory emotions inside themselves.

***

And now, her bathing suit replaced by a light, peach-colored dress, Hoan was holding his hand and looking at him, and he understood they were finished with hesitation and caution. They had moved away from the beach and the guesthouses and hotels and were walking on a dike towards the fishing village hidden under a canopy of trees past the edge of town. The breeze brought them the sharp tangy smell of salt and ruffled the sea grass clinging precariously to the sand. On their left, the ocean stretched off to the horizon, small boats with bat-shaped sails skimming effortlessly along its surface like a swarming flock of birds stretching their wings against the wind. White clouds floated endlessly above the two of them, the sky echoing the strange emptiness of the salt-drying fields to the right of the dike. It was as if they were alone: everyone else busy with their joys, their homes, their fields, their salt, their fishing, their sails. Their lives. Khiem felt choked with a sudden, giddy happiness. For so long now, since they had fallen in love, he had pictured this day as a final reward for their long patience and forbearance, a moment reserved for only the two of them. For Hoan and him. For Hoan and him only, in a separate world. In the world they had entered now, Hoan holding his hand, so that he felt the reality of her flesh and yet was still walking in a dream. Until the moment Hoan pulled him after her off the dike and they walked down the steep path to a house at the beginning of the fishing village. He stopped and stared at her.

She smiled at him. "Do you think I'm still teasing you? This is my uncle's house."

Khiem let go of her hand. They were standing in a small yard. In front of him was a thatched house covered with sugarcane leaves: it had the usual larger section, with an extra room attached to one side. To the left of the door was a storage basin for fish sauce, covered with a concrete lid, and on the wire clothesline nearby he saw a light brown skirt, a pair of white panties, and a bra, flapping in the wind from the sea.

Everything was real. The salty smell of the fish sauce made the air seem thick and sticky. The sugarcane leaves on the roof looked as if they were beginning to rot. The thin plume of smoke from a fire still smoldering under ashes in the firepit hung in the air as motionless as a drawn line. Everything was hot and very still, like the atmosphere just before a storm.

And yet everything still seemed unreal to him. Hoan took his hand again and silently drew him after her, to the attached room. It was small and simple and a little messy, a few of her things scattered about. The bed consisted of two planks of unpolished ironwood, an old mosquito net draped above it.

The air was hot and still inside, and the light dim. Khiem felt suddenly nervous and strange. To finally arrive at this scene, this unpredictable turning point in his life. Yet his sense of strangeness was undermined by the intimate familiarity of Hoan's scent in this closed place, emanating from her dark blue overnight bag, from her yellow t-shirt hung over the mosquito net.

He heard the sound of the bamboo door being closed behind him, and turned around to see Hoan quickly drawing her dress over her head.

She stood in front of him, wearing only a pair of violet panties. She seemed vaguely shy, seemed to him still to be both very real and yet part of a dream. As if sensing this feeling in him, she took his hands and put them on her shoulders, and stared into his eyes, as if she wanted him to say something, as if she wanted to ask him if she pleased him. She raised herself slightly onto her tiptoes and pushed her lips against his. Then, suddenly, she took his hand again and pulled him to the bed. The excitement he'd repressed in himself until this moment suddenly seized him and he pressed his lips to hers as her hands fumbled frantically at his clothes, unbuttoning, undressing him, helping him pull away the last piece of clothing covering her body.

He looked down at her, trying to freeze the image of her in his mind. She stretched to her full length under his gaze and then, holding him, pushed against the wall with her feet, moving them to the center of the bed. The sound of her flesh against the wood, the dimness of the air, the small moaning sounds she was making now increased his passion. He pressed his lips against her breasts and she lay still, caressing the sides of his face. Suddenly she pushed him slightly away and looked at him. "You have a beautiful body," she whispered, smiling shyly, and lay down again, and took his sex firmly in her hand.

He looked at her face. He'd never seen her like this, her skin flushed and lovely with passion. He smelled the perfume in her hair, felt the impossible smoothness of her skin under his touch. "Don't worry, my darling; my horoscope says there are no unexpected traps awaiting me today," she whispered. He felt her nipples stiffening and she sealed her mouth to his, her tongue moving in his mouth, her body rising up under him, until she let out a single cry and she shuddered and he felt that shudder move into his own flesh and he was dissolving, disappearing into her, becoming her.

"Are you pleased, my love?" she asked, her eyes lidded and heavy. She clutched at his shoulders, as if she wanted him to slow down, not become too excited. A little ashamed, he pushed his face into her shoulder, trying to regain control.

"Love me," she said, and then said it again, and again the tide was rising, pushing them into a rhythm, both of them bucking against each other, yelling, twisting into the strange entwining configurations love pushes bodies into as it does souls.

After a time, he asked: "What is it, darling?"

"Do you hear something?"

They both did. When she turned to look at the door, he saw tears of happiness in her eyes. Then heard the sound of rising waves pounding against the beach as if against their skin, and the wind whipping against the earth, against the sides and roof of the house. They listened to the sea pines rustling fiercely outside, and the sudden wind rattled the frame of the thatched house, rocked it, moved into them. They got off the wooden bed and down on the tattered jute mat on the floor. Hoan was shrieking, shaking with desire; she pushed him down, controlled him, urged him into her with her hands, the wind outside sparking the fire in her into a conflagration.

Khiem felt himself becoming someone else, someone different from himself in every way: a man with no complexes, no hesitations, no pretenses. He struggled with Hoan until he took control, leading her into the sex, moving with her, and they reached the moment together and a scream of release burst from both their mouths and they fell together into the abyss.

Hoan held him tightly, as if she was sheltering against him from the storm outside. His hair was pasted to his forehead with sweat. He closed his eyes and let himself wander and didn't let himself hear her when she asked him if he had made love to Thoa in the same way.

When he opened his eyes a half-hour later, the first thing he was aware of was her face against his chest. Her hair was also damp with sweat, her body loose and relaxed. He put his arms around her shoulders, and felt her shivering. Her previous question about Thoa came back to him then, like a distant memory. The truth was it had been more than two years since he'd slept with his wife: he had always been something of an idealist about sex, could not regard it as only an act of physical release, and there was a spiritual gap now between him and Thoa that he just couldn't overcome. Again Hoan asked him a question, and again he heard it from far away, as if it was an echo: Darling, what if we've made a baby?

Outside, the wind had died down. He sat up, feeling empty and blank and deeply content, and looked at Hoan, leisurely and lazily now, the sweet, ripened maturity of her grown woman's body. She smiled at him and wiggled into her panties and he told himself that he would hold this image and this moment forever in his mind, the gift of this woman. Looking at the violet panties, he smiled at the way they recalled his initial excitement and anticipation when he saw her other pair hanging on the clothesline outside. As if it was a year ago. He reclined full length again and embraced Hoan, her back to him now, pushed himself against her. She took his hands and placed them over her breasts.

"For you," she said, and pressed her back against his chest, her breasts full and heavy and smooth and slightly sweaty under his hands. "What do I look like now? Like the ship in the storm in Du Thi Hoan's poem?" She looked over her shoulder at him.

> I am like a ship in a storm
> The coral at the bottom of the sea
> No time to drop the anchor
> the coral at the bottom of the sea
> I am like the ship in a storm
> on my wedding night

She snuggled against him, and they talked easily, sleepily, Hoan telling him about her grandmother, whom she'd lived with until she was sixteen. "Until I was that age, she still helped me shower...she felt so sorry for me, after my parents died. I'm sorry, darling, for talking so much. Are you tired?"

"No, not at all. Tell me more about your grandmother."

His eyes half-closed, Khiem caressed her breasts, her voice carrying him back to his own childhood, and then to the first time he had met her. She had worn, he recalled vividly, a brown blouse with a heart-shaped collar. When she looked at him and said, "Hello, Mr. Khiem," he'd been surprised that she knew his name, had felt the same sense of grateful inevitability he'd felt that morning: how had she found him, come straight to him, among the thousands of people on the beach?

She rose and they dressed. Just as they finished, Khiem glimpsed a shadow outside.

It was Hoan's uncle, returning from the sea. Mr. Tuy was sixty-five, a sturdy, well-built man, who looked just like what he was: someone who had spent his life on the water. His eyes were narrowed in a permanent squint, the prow of his head bald, as if worn from constant exposure to wind and water.

"We've had rough seas for the last four months," he told Khiem, shooting out his words rapidly. "It wasn't until the day before yesterday we could finally get out. We were lucky, though, and ran right into a large school of fish. Unfortunately, we got so excited we forgot what we should have remembered and followed them into an area that has many large, underwater rocks. It's also haunted by a ghost. That ghost led us around in circles for a while, until we didn't know where we were, and fell into a kind of trance. When we finally snapped out of it, we just let the waves carry us in to shore—then we got caught in the storm."

Khiem enjoyed listening to the old man, watching him efficiently kill and scale the fish he'd brought back with him. He'd never given much thought to the amount of skill and knowledge and creativity a fisherman needed, the different techniques involved in catching fish, or squid, snail, shrimps, oysters...

Hoan helped her uncle, squatting by the small fire they'd kindled in the brazier. A plume of white smoke rose to the thatched roof. The ghost, Uncle Tuy explained to Khiem, comes in the shape of a silent boat. The fishermen told each other that if they saw that boat, they must pinch their cheeks to keep from falling under its spell and following it into the rocks; they must pray hard to Buddha to protect them. If they could see the mountains on shore, that would mean they had broken away from the ghost's lure, and could make it back home. Khiem was struck by the difference between this old man's relationship to the sea and Coc's.

"But the sea is the same everywhere," Uncle Tuy said: "it is never totally calm."

Khiem pressed him for more details about his life. Uncle Tuy was very poor, and didn't own his own boat. He took forty percent of the catch when he went fishing, and the boat owner got the rest. Yes, of course fishing was a very risky job, but that was normal in life. One June, on the 25th day of the month, he said, the people in his village got reports of a large school of anchovies offshore. On that day, over a hundred boats went out in pursuit, a hundred boats with two hundred and forty-eight men on board, most of the men in the village. They found the anchovies, but in the middle of the frenzy of fishing, a bad storm came up, a Force 12 wind—did Khiem know what that meant? Waves as large as houses hammered the boats, swamping them, raising their bows up like arrows pointing at the sky before they sank. Every boat went down. Almost every fisherman drowned. There were only eight survivors; he, Tuy, had been one of them. He was seventeen years old at the time, and he had never understood why he had been left alive when so many others died; why he had found the plank he'd held onto and hadn't drowned, hadn't become food for the fish. It was strange, he said, shaking his head. But did Khiem know what was stranger? Neither he nor any of the other survivors were afraid of the sea after that. As soon as they were rescued and brought to shore, their eyes had swung out to the sea again like magnetic needles, as if they knew they had an appointment to keep with it. So it was. The sea was capricious; one day it could be deadly, the next it could be generous. He and the others had gotten into their boats and gone out again. They lived by the sea and they would die by the sea.

"The two riskiest ways one can travel in life are by horse

and by boat," old Tuy said. "I know that. But to be alive is to seek risks. That's what it is to be a human being."

Khiem bit his lips. Tuy's simple words resonated straight into the heart of his own situation.

"Are there big fish in the waters around this area, uncle?" he asked.

"Oh, yes, even whales. Listen, I came back here when I was discharged, after the three years of my last enlistment. It rained for three days. I was getting ready to take the boat out, and scanned the sea. But my view was blocked by something. It was so large, at first I thought that a pagoda was somehow floating by, or had emerged from the water. Uncertain what it was, I took a sampan and went out to it. My God, what a whale! For some reason, he had chosen to come to my village in order to ascend to heaven. But now I could see he was terrified—a horde of hungry sharks were swarming around him. I returned and called the whole village together and we set up an altar and prayed for the whale. Soon after, a large swell came up and carried him in to the beach."

"So there are sharks here as well, uncle?"

"The sea is like the mainland, like life everywhere. It contains good and bad, kind and cruel. All come from the Creator. Yes, there are many kinds of fierce fish in these waters. If we're born on this earth, it's our fate to deal with such things."

He continued telling his stories to Khiem: memories of seeing other whales and frolicking with them in the sea, of encounters with sharks. Once he'd caught a fish that was shaped like a dragon and must have weighed half a ton. Fish weighing up to a hundred kilos were plentiful in the area. Sometimes he would catch too many to sell, and would string them together through their noses and keep them following him under water as if they were a herd of buffalo.

Outside the entrance, along the path that ran next to the fence of thorny bamboo, Khiem could see the shadows of people passing in the violet light of dusk. The voices of mothers calling their children for dinner drifted into the room. Hoan placed a fruit-shaped bronze pot on the heap of glowing charcoal, to cook the rice. Another pot of fish soup was simmering in the kitchen. She turned towards them.

"Uncle, is that the whale's shrine, near Princess My Chau's?"

"Yes, that's it. But the festival begins in the communal house, before going on to the pagoda. Do you know what they say about the princess—'right in love, but wrong in reason.'" He chuckled.

"What a saying!"

"Isn't it true, though? In reality, her execution was an injustice. When she fell in love and married the Chinese prince, she never imagined he was scheming to steal her country's sacred weapon. But who can love and remain careful and vigilant at the same time, right?" He smiled slyly at the two of them.

"I believe that," Hoan smiled back. "To love and to remain careful isn't really love. Love doesn't stop to consider consequences."

"That's why the princess is so adored by the villagers. Well, her festival is tomorrow. Whatever we're doing, even if we have to abandon a huge school of fish, we'll come to commemorate her, to show our respect for the past."

He stretched against an ache in his back, and looked at Khiem, nodding as if he had just recognized him.

"You were a soldier, weren't you? On the Truong Son Trails, right? And in Laos? I can see it in your face. One soldier always knows another." Khiem touched his own face, as if trying to feel the vestiges of his hard past on his flesh. Tuy looked away, seemed sunk into deep thought. "'Love doesn't stop to consider consequences?' is that what you said,

Hoan? There were five of us in our squad," Old Tuy said, his voice still distant. "Once, we strayed off the trails and were lost in the jungle. We ran out of water and were so thirsty we had to dig down into the jungle floor and find an underground stream. After that, the other four men all died, all poisoned by the Agent Orange defoliant the Americans used. Now I'm the only one left. But what am I complaining about, right? Living means moving on, doesn't it?"

Khiem shuddered, a sudden chill passing through him. He stood up and held the old man's hands.

***

The sound of drums and gongs filled the air and echoed back from the sea. Khiem stood entranced before the immense tide of colorful flags, flapping, brightly recalling the yellow sunshine that at that moment was sparkling off the sea. Flags, he thought. When did humankind develop its need for flags? Triangular flags led the procession, and then the ancient national flags bearing the five characteristics of the universe: gold, wood, water, metal, and fire, each symbolized by its color: yellow, brown, white, black, and red. After these came the Eight Trigrams and the four sacred animals: dragon, unicorn, turtle, and phoenix; the four directions...on and on, a moving, undulating ocean of silk floating over the festival, held steady by the proud hands of the flag-bearers. The latter wore small conical hats and the traditional blue shirts and tight black trousers bound with silk sashes, with small mortars attached to their fronts to support the flagstaffs. The bearers walked slowly and solemnly, as if self-conscious about being the symbols of the festival.

Directly behind them came a huge drum carried by two men and shaded by a gigantic yellow umbrella. They were followed close at heel by a wooden statue of an elephant, as large as the real animal, rolling down the rutted road on a plank with four wheels.

Next in the procession were men bearing ancient weapons and dressed in the black-and-red-striped uniforms of ancient warriors. They marched before the dragon-shaped palanquin of the Emperor, borne on the shoulders of thirty-two powerful men, their faces deadpan serious. After them came five more flag-bearers, leading the phoenix-shaped palanquin of the Empress. These were the two palanquins of the fishing commune. On each was a large tray heaped with sticky rice, a boiled pig's head topping it, surrounded by huge square cakes. Rows of white candles stood on each side of the tray, their flames like white banyan buds. As they moved, the two palanquins were jerked forwards and backwards to the pounding beat of the drums, sometimes quickly, sometimes slowly. To Khiem they seemed connected to the emotions he'd had since being here with Hoan; that is, they were both indisputably real and yet still seemed part of a dream, as if he were floating, unmoored from time.

The procession continued to flow past him: eight more villages and their connected clans following one after another, each with its own two palanquins—one bearing the god of the village, the other bearing offerings. Eight young men bore each one, and they too marched with dignified and self-conscious solemnity, following an exacting ritual which decreed that each step they took should cover precisely one foot of ground.

The crowd here was huge, no fewer in number than the crowd he had been engulfed by at the beach. But what was around him now was marshaled and ordered by sacred belief. There was nothing chaotic here, nothing out of place. He noticed that even the noisy children who sold incense sticks and spirit currency knew to keep away from the procession and the communal house, not to disturb people, as if they had an unspoken sense of what was proper in this place and what was not. He remembered—the kids' self-imposed absence somehow bringing him there—the way condoms had been distributed free during the campaign against AIDS. In that, he supposed, was a kind of official acknowledgment that young lovers were having sex casually and carelessly, everywhere, even in public parks. Yet even so, they would never make love in the forests around the shrines of the Hung Dynasty, the founders of the nation. They somehow still felt linked not only to themselves, to their own needs, but—like the people here—to the community and to its history. Yes. The feelings that cemented human beings to each other were neither chaotic nor dictated, but grew naturally from the same sense of spiritual reminiscence he saw all around him.

The procession was gathering in the large square in front of the communal house, its entrance guarded by two ancient banyan trees. The center of the square was marked by two rows of mats: the villagers knew not to enter that area during the course of the ceremony. The offerings that had been on the palanquins were removed and placed now in rows on the mats. Ancient wooden weapons, newly polished and lacquered, had been set in front of the door to the communal house. An old man, dressed in a yellow tunic embroidered with blue dragons, walked out of the doorway: this was the master of the ceremony. Behind him were his four assistants, each dressed in a red tunic with white seams. They clapped their hands slowly and solemnly in front of the altar. Other old men, the heads of the different clans, stood a short distance to the side. To their left, on two benches, was a traditional orchestra.

Three drum rolls split the air. Over the noise, the master of the ceremony raised his voice and called for the gongs. These were struck three times, and then the musicians began to play the traditional instruments. Each step in the ritual was done with care and deliberation, and the people watched in silence, motionless, contemplating every movement made by the master of the ceremony and the other village elders. It wasn't until a troupe of graceful young dancers entered the square singing, that the crowd began to stir and whisper.

Taking advantage of that sudden movement, Khiem edged closer. To his surprise he saw that the master of the ceremony was Old Tuy, Hoan's uncle. He only recognized Tuy from some of the facial features he remembered, though they seemed to him at the moment merely the lines of a mask. What he saw truly was a Tuy stripped of his fleeting physicality: a strong, sincere spirit, serious and calm and innocent, that embodied the ceremony. That was the old man's essence. Old Tuy, he thought. Old Tuy, the master of the ceremony to commemorate Princess My Chau. The old soldier from the Truong Son Trails, the fisherman with his tough and rude life, was in reality a soul elevated by a celestial belief.

Khiem smiled. He was fifty years old and had faced troubles and death, and thought of himself as an experienced person. Yet there were still so many things about his own country he had yet to understand. How strange, to come here and find these people who live with difficulties and suffering but don't complain or seem afraid of life, seem instead imbued with its beauty. The blood of the beheaded princess had truly been transmuted into pearls.

Feeling somewhat dazed, he saw that the ceremony was coming to an end. Again, he was caught by surprise—the lead dancer in the group was Hoan. His beloved Hoan, astonishing him once more.

She was beautiful in the traditional green turban, yellow tunic, and rose-and-white trousers, dancing like a dream in front of him. Turning, her eyes met his, and her body arched towards him, and, as she sang, he felt the silk threads that tied him to her shiver inside himself.

Goosefeathers spreading on the wild meadow,
Cau river stretching along two sandy banks
Floating in the dying dusk
Oh, for whom is this bracelet of pearl?

It was the song of Princess My Chau. After the Hung dynasty, King An Duong Thuc Phan came to the throne and began building the country under the name Au Lac. But his citadel kept collapsing. When the king prayed for guidance, the genie of the Turtle appeared to him and helped him chase away the devils that were preventing the building of the citadel. Afterwards, the genie gave the king a magic bow that would kill thousands of enemies whenever it was used. At that time, the Chinese emperor Trieu Da wished to invade Au Lac, but was afraid of the celestial weapon. Instead he sent his son, the prince Trong Thuy, to ask for the hand of the emperor's daughter, for My Chau's hand. The princess fell in love with Trong Thuy, and, trusting him, showed him the celestial weapon.

And so he betrayed her and stole it. But before he left, he asked My Chau how he could find her if anything ever happened. "I have a coat made of goosefeathers," she told him. "Wherever I go, I'll leave a trail of feathers for you to follow." Soon after, Trieu Da sent his army to invade Au Lac. Thuc Phan had to flee south, carrying his daughter on the back of his horse. As they rode, she plucked feather after feather from her coat, and Trong Thuy followed the trail she left. When they had come to this very beach, the genie of the Turtle heard Thuc Phan's prayers and appeared to him, telling him that the enemy who had betrayed him was sitting behind him on his horse. Angrily, the king drew his sword. Before he struck, Princess My Chau raised her hands in supplication and said: "If I intended to betray my father, may my body become dust. But if I am faithful and have been deceived, may my blood become pearls and wash away my shame."

***

Hoan still seemed otherworldly to him, even after she was dressed again in her everyday clothes. She had changed after the dance and had come to him looking harried, insisting that they go immediately to the beach. Literally pushing at him when he hesitated, like the strong wind pressing at his back now. They were walking hand in hand along the shore. The sea grass rustled around their legs and gray clouds flew overhead. There wasn't a sail on the sea, and the beach itself was completely empty—everyone had gone to the ceremony. They were completely alone, and the wind pushed against Hoan, revealing the curves of her body under her silk dress.

"What's the matter?" Khiem asked, concerned about her urgency to get him away. But his words were carried off by the wind. Hoan ran forward, pulling off her dress, motioning for him to follow her. She walked into the water, raising her arms to welcome the wave that crashed into her.

It was almost dusk now and the tide was coming in, the surf roaring in their ears. Khiem undressed and followed her in. The last light of the sun was sparkling on the water. He felt a sudden wave of fatigue and a chill. He was usually a healthy man, but the intense introspection of the last few days, the excitement of his time with Hoan seemed to have exhausted him. Or maybe, he thought, it was Tuy's story about the death of his four comrades-in-arms that had awakened the sickness that always dwells in an old soldier's heart. A wave nearly knocked him off his feet. He wiped his eyes and saw Hoan surface and swim to the beach. She opened her hand and showed him the oysters she'd gathered.

"Aren't they beautiful?"

"Princess My Chau's blood turned into rosy pearls—but they weren't inside oysters."

"I know the story," she said, smiling back at him.

She shook the water from her hair and stretched out on the sand. Khiem held the two oysters in his hands, their elongated wedge shapes thick with yellowish encrustations, beautiful against his palm. Hoan was lying on her side and looking down at her long, smooth legs. Khiem bent to her, wanting to say something warm and loving. But a sudden chill seized him again, and he shivered. The oysters suddenly seemed to contain the worries that had been racing through his mind.

"Are you all right?" Hoan stood up, her face concerned. Khiem put his shirt on and shook his head.

"Actually, it's you I'm worried about. Something seems to be bothering you."

"Lieu," she said.

"Lieu? You mean from our office? Where did you see him?"

Hoan brushed her hair back from her face. "When I was dancing. He was standing to your left, looking shifty and nervous. Be careful—he's ready to betray you."

"I wonder what brings him here."

Hoan put her dress on, holding onto his arm. "Let him be. Let's go back. My God, why are you trembling?"

"Maybe I'm thinking of Lieu."

"Forget him. I think you're catching a cold. Let me walk you to the guest house."

They walked across the beach, feeling the heat evaporating from the sand under their feet. They could hear the rising noise of the crowd, over at the festival, and the sound of the waves seemed to be louder also, echoing it. It must have been the time to give awards for the palanquins and to receive the offerings from the villages. They could see people walking towards them from the far end of the beach. The boats anchored close to the shore were bobbing mani-acally in the surf.

"Khiem—if we have to separate later, how shall we find each other again?"

Khiem was so shocked at the question, he forgot his chill. He turned and looked directly into Hoan's worried eyes. Why had she asked him that so suddenly? Maybe she really had recognized some danger in spotting Lieu here. Had something happened in the office during his absence? Had Lieu been scheming to support someone trying to replace him? He wanted to ask Hoan, but she just shook her head and pushed him forward. Once again, he felt exhausted.

"I was just thinking how Princess My Chau knew to drop goosefeathers and leave a trail for her beloved," she said. "The ancient people knew what to do—why don't we? Come on, darling, lean on me. I'll take you back and rub some tiger balm on you."

Putting her arm around his waist, Hoan let him lean against her, took his weight. As if, he thought, she was a seeress who had predicted his destiny and now wanted to protect him from her own prophecy.

Chapter Two

THE TRAUMA

When Lieu was sixteen years old, a skinny but strong boy, he dropped out of school and joined a gang. Most of the others in it were kids whose fathers were small-time locksmiths or tinkerers, men who found work fixing fountain pens, flashlights, glasses. The gang hustled all kinds of odd jobs also, but gave themselves the grandiose name "Samurai Knights," and tattooed dragons' heads on their left arms. Later in his life, Lieu came to regret the tattoo as a brand on his flesh that would always reveal his delinquency.

His own parents were both petit-bourgeois: his mother had a small shop where she sold secondhand clothes; his father was a clerk under the French administration. They were both ambitious, but without either the capability or the energy to achieve any real success. They possessed enough cunning and greed to make a bare living, but no more than that.

During his childhood and teens, Lieu had evinced neither a particularly bad nor a particularly virtuous nature. Occasionally, he showed a sweeter side of himself and was praised for helping classmates who got sick or forgot pens or rulers; once he helped repair someone's bicycle. Now and then he got into trouble—but always as a follower, not an instigator. He was good in mathematics and literature—

probably the latter was his best subject. He showed promise as a student. But when he reached seventh grade, he left school and took a job as a horse-cart driver for the cultural affairs division's print shop. It was a simple job—all he had to do was whip the horse's rear end, bring paper from the paper mill to the shop, and transport books and other publications, as well as the occasional pig or chicken, from it.

Afterwards, Lieu always cultivated a feeling of ironic bitterness to comfort himself when he thought of the other kids who had stayed in school but who weren't as bright or intuitive as he had been. He felt the same sense of secret superiority towards the other workers in the print shop. Even though he was only a horse-cart driver, he knew they would never understand the ideas and sentiments in the books they printed as well as he would. They no more understood him than they understood his horse. In their eyes, the horse was simply an ordinary brown nag with a white star on its forehead, pulling an old wooden cart. But not in his. Once he had taken it outside the city and climbed onto its back. The horse, not used to being ridden, had bucked and kicked, then turned and bitten him. Lieu had dismounted and whipped the animal to its knees. Then he'd helped it up, climbed onto it again and rode it until it was used to him and would obey him. After that, Lieu became gentle again. He loosened the reins and rode slowly along the dikes of the Red River, imagining himself a soldier returning from battle. The breeze blowing off the river filled him with a poetic sense of harmony between himself and the animal, between himself and nature, between reason and passion, excitement and desire. At that moment, he felt life was good and he could be truly satisfied as a working man. Soon after, he married a girl who sold sugar cane in the market. His cart was their wedding chariot.

He had deliberately fashioned himself into a real

member of the proletariat, a useful contributor to society. Years later, when the Party cell at Khiem's division met to discuss his application for membership in the Communist Party, the question of his motivation in becoming a horse-cart driver was raised. Why had he dropped out of school and taken on that kind of work? Did he think of his family's needs—he had six younger sisters, aged 8 to 14. Was he restless in school, dreaming of adventure? Or did he accept the fact that he'd never have the opportunity or talent to enter the gates of higher education?

The truth was, his family's stained political and class background had made him feel he had little choice about taking on that type of work. What had ultimately been responsible for his decision were the posters that hung wherever he looked, always displaying four main figures: the Worker, the Peasant, the Soldier, and the Intellectual. In the foreground, the worker grasped a hammer or a pick. Behind him, a female peasant cradled a sheaf of paddy. After her was the soldier with his rifle, and then finally the intellectual, with his thick spectacles. Each era has its own heroes, and it was these figures seen hanging everywhere that young people in Lieu's day were encouraged to emulate. These were the heroes who would finally dig the grave to bury capitalism. These were the symbols of the new means of production, the symbols of communism, of hope for the future of mankind. An ordinary worker could feel himself elevated to the status of a mythological being: he was the dream itself, the reason for history, motivated by the vision that now the children of the exploiters would have to kneel down and humble themselves and hope to be granted a place next to workers like him.

This was the role Lieu sought to assume. He had planned out his future with a precocious cunning that sprang from a deep hatred for his elder half-brother, the son of his father's first wife. Kien was sixteen years older than Lieu, and it was his tainted heritage that had cursed Lieu's existence. Lieu had grown up during a time when each person was defined very clearly and simply by the question, "Whose side are you on—ours or the enemy's?" The relatives of anyone who had betrayed the revolution had to demonstrate very clearly how different they were from such a person. From such a person as Lieu's half-brother. He was the real reason Lieu had to stop going to school and had joined the working class—all of it a way to show his rejection of his brother, a way of distancing himself from a traitor.

Once, Lieu had spoken confidentially about his feelings to Khiem. "Since I consider you my true brother, I have to tell you that truly there were times when I hoped that the one I am forced to call eldest brother would die. Not only was he a traitor to the revolution, he also abandoned his wife and had an affair with a trader in Phu Ly. I still remember the night his wife found out and put the edge of a sharp knife blade to her own neck and shrieked: 'Now you decide—if you want to go and marry that whore, I'll kill myself and get out of your way.' You have no idea how hard my life has been because of that man. While all my former classmates could go to university and become engineers, doctors, managers, I had to become a horse-cart driver, just because I had a brother who betrayed both the revolution and his own family! But I'm lucky—I'm not like him, don't you see? I'm a hundred and sixty-three centimeters tall while he's only a hundred and fifty-one! And I'm so healthy I can whip my horse's rear end a hundred times. Oh, how I wish he wasn't my brother!"

***

Khiem knew these things about Lieu's half-brother:

In 1944, Chuong Kien was eighteen years old and worked repairing shoes on Sinh Tu Street in Hanoi. That year he married Hue, who sold secondhand clothes in the free market. Kien had earned a diploma from a bilingual French-Vietnamese school and so was considered to be an intellectual. On the 19th of August, 1945, when the general insurrection started in Hanoi, he at first remained merely a spectator to those occurrences. But Kien was clever enough to see that what was happening was completely different from the small coup d'état that occurred on March 9, 1945, when the Japanese chased the French away and seized control of Indochina. He understood that the uprising would transform both the substance and the form of his whole society—he saw everyone calling each other comrade, greeting each other with the clenched-fist salute, and he knew that a new order had been born. The August Revolution was truly a magical time, its energy and resolution drawing the people together. Kien immediately began to grow a mustache, bought himself a Japanese sword, and volunteered for the national defense force, marked by its symbol, the square star. He became one of the thousands of resistance fighters willing to sacrifice their lives to bring about the birth of the nation. He participated in the sixty days of fighting that kept the French out of Hanoi, and later he was part of the withdrawal, which in Khiem's mind was always evoked by the words of Chinh Huu's famous poem:

> *The night we departed, both sky and earth*
> *were on fire*
> *and behind our backs*
> *the capital burned*

Departing with Kien that night, as the capital burned, was a nurse.

It was difficult to pin down Kien's true motives, Khiem supposed. Who can say if his participation stemmed from a true sense of patriotism or whether it grew simply from his adventurous nature? But, in any case, he was a clever man and spoke French well, and even though he was known as a womanizer, he was soon promoted to platoon leader.

After two months of combat, Kien requested a transfer to the propaganda section in charge of persuading Vietnamese fighting for the French to defect. His request was granted, but after a bout with malaria, he again asked to be moved, this time to the economic affairs division in Phu Tho province, where he was assigned as an accountant. At that time, there were very few educated people in the resistance forces.

"My father was an old civil servant who married my mother when she was a young street vendor," Kien told his officers. "Since he always wore a beard, which was the symbol of resistance, his French boss didn't like him, and he was reassigned to the mountains. In reality, he was exiled. He died when he was 47 years old, from malaria. I was the poor one, among all my rich classmates from Silk and Silver Streets, and so my only choice was to study harder than any of them. That's why I've always done well in school."

Thus Kien portrayed himself as a poor worker from the slums and gave himself the right class background to be promoted to head of his department. Yet in the winter of 1950, along with his lover, the nurse, he stole away from the resistance base on a boat, then walked the rest of the way to Son Tay, some fifty kilometers from Hanoi. It was there that he went over to the French, and so became a traitor to the resistance and his country.

And yet, Khiem thought, many people who couldn't stand the difficulties and hardships of the struggle finally left the resistance—it was difficult to call all of them traitors. Not everyone can become accustomed to hunger, thirst, sacrifice, and death overnight.

Back in Hanoi, Kien lived openly with the nurse, while his wife and two children remained in Thanh Hoa with his parents. The nurse began to work at a French military hospital, and Kien applied for a job as a primary school teacher.

This was the curriculum vitae that Khiem had to report to the Communist Party cell meeting at the publishing division, concerning Lieu's application to become a member of the Communist Party. It was the late eighties, and he was still a horse-cart driver. In summing up the record of Lieu's half-brother, Khiem had said the following:

"Once, Ms. Hoan remarked that it was strange that a traitor's brother had requested to become a member of the Party. But I believe that if Mr. Chuong Kien has truly betrayed our country, it doesn't mean that Lieu's character is stained, as Hoan suggested. Our Party struggles for communist ideology; it is an organization of people who fight with determination against oppression and exploitation, and who have sacrificed all for our national independence, freedom, and reunification. The family history of someone who has volunteered to stand with us under our glorious flag is only significant as an anecdote to help understand that person's origins, in order to influence the way we can direct and train him. It is not a condition that necessarily predicts his future behavior. Among the founders of Marxism were many whose families were exploiters of the proletariat. As for Kien, we can see his actions either as an unconscious betrayal, or as the calculated act of a selfish coward, a slick opportunist who schemed for his own petty gain and dirtied his reputation. Which was it? Lieu has told me that the malaria epidemic in Yen Bai reminded Kien of his father's death while he was working in Lao Cai, and that frightened him. Besides that, he was also pressured by his mistress, who had been born to a bourgeois family. He wanted to divorce his wife in order to live with her, and so two years after becoming a teacher, he decided to enter the Thu Duc Military Academy. This was an important turning point in his political life. I know most of you are familiar with the events of those years, but please be patient with me if I reiterate them—to understand Kien, we need to remember clearly the history of that time."

Khiem cleared his throat and continued:

"After our victory on the Chinese-Vietnam border in the autumn and winter of 1950, the fighting spirit of the French forces wavered. That December, their general staff held a special meeting in Paris to map out their plans, and they sent Jean de Lattre de Tassigny to Indochina to replace General Carpentier. De Tassigny, you'll remember, had an impeccable reputation; he'd been promoted to general even before De Gaulle, and was known as an experienced strategist. He arrived in Vietnam on December 17, 1950, along with his deputy, General Salan, and they began vigorously to reorganize their European and African troops and strengthen their Vietnamese forces in order to secure the areas they'd already occupied. Any man who lived in the French-controlled areas was eligible for the draft, without exception. Every male from 18 years old up had to register, even the bureaucrats, teachers, and artists who had been exempted before, though these received the privilege of being sent to the officer-training academies."

Khiem had paused then, waiting to see if anyone had anything to add.

"The fact that Lieu's brother Kien became a cadet at the Military Academy of Thu Duc near Saigon and later became a lieutenant in the traitors' regime, was due to a twist of fate and the irony of the history of this land. To give it its proper name, Kien was the product of an historical trauma. And Lien is a victim of that trauma as well."

***

The training course had lasted eighteen months, and the pressure, whether in the classroom or in the field, was constant; its goal was to weed out the weak and the cowardly. In addition, the cadets were taught all the usual military skills: weapons training, attack tactics, organization, and intelligence. For the graduation ceremony, all the cadets wore white dress uniforms and the French military cap, the kepi. The new officers marched proudly down the Rue Catinat in the middle of Saigon, their steel taps echoing against the pavement, as the curious Saigonaise girls stared at them.

Kien was one of them. He had enjoyed his leaves in Saigon, with its expensive jewelry shops and luxury brothels. He had broadened his experiences and widened his circle of contacts. He had had the same "slow-twist" prostitutes the other officers relished, adopted wholeheartedly the soldiers' philosophy of Eat, Drink, and Make Love. Love was carnality. Friendship was the willingness to lend money. And Brotherhood meant not only becoming part of the history and tradition of the French army, but also adopting its attitudes. Kien smoked Filipino cigars, drank Martell cognac, watched the cock fights, and slept with all the sweet Saigon girls he could. He became enamored of the old French soldiers' mottoes: "Kill or be killed," and "Never surrender what you hold in your hands." Thu Duc Academy had given him a new and robust self-confidence, as it had the others marching on that graduation day. There was nothing and no one these cadets would fear: They were privileged young men—life for them was a market full of stalls from which they could take anything they wished, and death in war was glorious. And if they died and went to heaven, they wouldn't hesitate to booby-trap and mine the clouds and behead the so-called God Himself! Hey!

The formation of graduating cadets marched to the

center of the square in the middle of the city. In the reviewing stand were some of the famous generals who had originated the philosophy of war that now inspired these young men. Kien's company halted en masse. Then Kien continued forward alone, holding himself tall and straight as he marched towards the commanding general himself. He had thought he would tremble, but he found himself calm, and even more self-confident than he'd been during his final examinations. He stopped, came smartly to attention, saluted the general and the flag, and then knelt.

"My dear general..." he began.

"Greetings to the top graduate of the class," the general boomed, beaming and returning his salute. "You represent the future of this nation. A great career awaits you, my boy."

Now Chuong Kien did find himself trembling, as if seized by the sacred nature of the moment. He felt the hallowed sword of the King, the symbol of the glory of France, touch his left shoulder, and he became dizzy with happiness, envisioning the bright glory of his future. He lifted a corner of the French flag and raised it to his lips. Then he stood to attention and recited the words of the cadet's oath, which he had learned by heart, with true passion.

***

Khiem had continued his report to the Party cell:

"However, while it is true that Chuong Kien was chosen to represent the entire class in the recitation of the oath of loyalty, to be fair, this did not mean that he was picked for his determined anticommunism. He was simply the top trainee. He had studied in the artillery school, his French was good, and he had always done well in mathematics and physics when he was in school, which ensured his high grades. He was graduated as a second lieutenant, not as a full lieutenant as some have maintained. Since he was at the top of his class, instead of being sent into combat, he was assigned as acting chief of the French army's artillery logistics office, replacing someone who had died. Another reason for that assignment was that, at the time, our forces and our Laotian allies had launched a campaign in upper Laos. The French and their Vietnamese agents there were in danger and needed supplies desperately."

After the meeting adjourned, Khiem told Lieu what he'd said to the others. He'd added, "Some in the Party Cell weren't aware of the latter part of your brother's life. It was hard to explain to them how he had been responsible for supplying the French in Laos. They did know that in 1965, when the Americans began escalating their air attacks against the North, he was sent to a reeducation camp."

"I totally agree with the Party's judgment in that matter," Lieu said quickly. "I only hope that you'll feel pity for someone who has suffered as much as I have because of it. I recognized the crimes of my traitorous brother long ago, and I've always been determined to rid myself of that guy and to transform myself into a worthy person." He swallowed hard, his eyes glistening with tears.

"I visited the prisons in Lao Cai, Ha Giang, and Thai Nguyen, where your elder brother was held. I read all the reports and interviewed the prison authorities there. Luckily for your case, they all agreed that Kien had done nothing negative while he was there—he usually obeyed the rules and worked hard. In Phu Son, he was trained as a carpenter and a rock carver."

Lieu blinked rapidly.

"Thank you very much. But I would like to report to you, and through you to the Party cell, that I never once visited him during the entire period of his imprisonment. I never even went to see him later when he was released after seven years and was living alone, since his mistress, the nurse, had abandoned him. I didn't even care if he got sick. Once he carved my likeness on a piece of stone and gave it to me as a gift, and I threw it away. I feel nothing towards him, no kinship, no brotherhood. He disgusts me, that guy. I'm determined to hate him."

Khiem, to his astonishment, saw that Lieu was clenching his yellowed teeth. Two threads of spittle ran down from the corners of his mouth. Kheim put a steadying hand on his shoulder. "Don't talk like that, Lieu."

Lieu shook his head vehemently, his eyes bright. "No, let me speak. I dropped out of school and became a worker, and then I was able to become a clerk in your office as well, and now I've been promoted to be your assistant—it all came about because I decided to rid myself of that guy. Becoming a true member of the working class has rescued me from his influence. I remember once when I was still living at home, he said to me, 'only help someone if you see you'll gain from it later. Carefully calculate your every action before you take it—no one in this life does anything without thinking they'll get something in return.' How disgusting! I'm determined to have no links to that guy. I hate that guy! I curse him! I denounce him!"

"Don't be ridiculous!" Khiem blurted out. He wondered if he'd made a mistake with this young man. From the beginning of their talk, Lieu had kept referring to his brother as "that guy," had wished him dead, had continually and vehemently declared his hatred towards him, his wish to get rid of him. It couldn't be clearer that Kien had committed crimes against the nation. It was certainly correct for Lieu to choose a different path from his elder brother's. But Kien was still the young man's blood-relative, and there seemed something unnatural, exaggerated, and cruel in his hatred. Khiem had been uneasy, unsure how to feel towards Lieu.

***

These days, Lieu himself often felt surprised that his work as a horse-cart driver, and later as a clerk, had brought him so much success. Yet when he'd joined himself to the working class in order to be rid of the stain of his brother's political history, he unconsciously followed the lessons his brother had put into his head: never make any decision or take any action without thinking what gain it could bring.

In 1975, while still driving his horse-cart, he had written some well-received poems about model workers, and so won a prize from the Municipal Trade Union and had been sent to a media training course. But all Lieu had done was teach himself to imitate the kind of writing he saw was acceptable. He also made as many contacts as he could in the Trade Union's department of cultural and ideological affairs. As a result of the prize and the course, he was taken from his horse-cart driver's job and promoted to the editorial staff of Khiem's division. His mother had been very pleased. "Your brother brought harm to you," she'd said, "but you see, you're still blessed by Buddha." But Lieu had no real writing talent, and only a low-level education, and he found that the work was beyond his capabilities. Being realistic, he decided to apply to become a clerk again, but at the same time go back to driving his horse-cart. He was convinced this would be the way to bide his time until he was able to effect a brighter future.

He had met Khiem after Khiem had decided to move to the capital—a decision partly brought about by Thoa's affair with a photographer, a man with a crooked mouth. She had carried on with him shamelessly while Khiem was off fighting—three times she'd been caught by the home guards making love with that man right in her shop. As punishment, she was demoted to storage keeper. Khiem didn't feel they could stay in the same place. Hanoi was crowded, and people didn't seem as concerned as they did in the provinces about a person's private life. He wasn't proud of having a wife who'd cuckolded him. But he'd decided to try to keep his family together.

It was at this time that Khiem's passion for writing had flared to its full force. When he was writing, he could forget everything else, wrap himself totally and obsessively in the story, body and mind and heart. He worked like a madman, had felt that the creation of even one perfect short story would justify his existence as a human being.

He'd published three collections and three novels, all well received by the public, and was already a well-known writer when Lieu first met him. Lieu had presented himself as Khiem's biggest admirer, his would-be apprentice. "There must have been a lucky star in my horoscope, to get you as my boss, brother Khiem," Lieu said. "We're very alike, you know—we're both very determined men. You always present yourself as very easygoing on the outside, but I can see that inside your will is as hard as ironwood. That's how a real man is, right?"

The others at the cultural affairs division in fact regarded Lieu as a cunning kiss-up, a man who would wash anyone's feet, lick anyone's ass, if he thought it would do him some good. He had insinuated himself with the top men in the General Department, the "Three Cards." If one of them caught a cold, Lieu would be there immediately with sugar or milk for their tea, sympathy for their pains. He often embarrassed Khiem with his exaggerated adulation. Khiem understood that Lieu was a blatant suck-up. But he also felt that really had no bearing on how well he did his job. Lieu was responsible, hard-working, and eager. There was no reason why he shouldn't be promoted. After all, Quanh, the man Hoan called the Squint-Eyed Toad, also had a reputation for being cunning, greedy, and scheming. But still, he'd been a book editor for thirty years and had a good

deal of political experience, and Khiem had no com-
punctions about promoting him to the position of deputy
director. He was always reluctant to judge a person too
harshly.

***

It would have been easy for Lieu to fall into the manners
and patterns of behavior of the other horse-cart drivers
when he'd done that work. They were a crude and unruly
bunch. Whenever and wherever they gathered to wait for
jobs, they would play cards, gamble, curse, gossip, and tell
dirty jokes. They saw themselves as being at the bottom of
the heap, with no particular reputations to protect. They
didn't give a damn. They gossiped about everyone, even the
highest officials, and usually saw things with the clarity of
people who have nothing to lose. That guy is so cheap that
when he came back from France, all he brought his driver
was a lousy piece of rock. And that one was promoted to
head of the department because he faked some documents
that proved his rival was an agent of the Americans in Hue,
in the 1968 Tet offensive. The only reason X keeps his
position as chairman of the Trade Union is his wife's little
mushroom. Right. Life is shit. The big shots eat big, and the
small fry eat little. Mr. Y has three or four villas. Mr. Z has a
dozen mistresses. And the thing is, their women are either
smugglers or nymphos. Hell, they're young and these guys
are all seventy years old. Only thing the women can do is get
in the back of the car, unzip themselves, and take care of
their own needs quick and nasty, that's the modern way. That
one's like the Chinese Queen Vo Tac Thien. The other—she's
the modern version of Lady Giang Thanh. I took her out of
town once and made her come until she screamed. You know
you don't even need a marriage certificate to get into the
hotels any more.

And so on.

Hearing the other cart drivers speak had widened Lieu's experience of the world. But he kept himself aloof from them, and refused to gamble or gossip. He had no intention of remaining a laborer all his life. He knew how to plan, to calculate, to play the angles. He knew where he was and he knew life was short, and what a person had to do was jump onto his charger and gallop to his goal.

And his job as a horse-cart driver also brought him concrete benefits. At times, he was able to do favors for other people in the division. In the late eighties, he began his campaign to become a Party member. He had cultivated Khiem, and felt it was time to move up to an editorial position again. When the Party cell met to consider his application, he had strong support from several people. Ms. Kim Cuong, for one, was a woman who had been in the Party since 1948, when she had been a village militia woman. Her husband was the chairman of his district and later had been promoted and transferred to Hanoi as an expert on personnel administration. It was for these reasons that she had been given her position in the office, though she had only a fifth-grade education, My mind is like a cauliflower, she often said, and it was true she had never been able to stop using the Thanh Hoa dialect, and often misspelled words, using the wrong accents on letters. In recommending Lieu for membership in the Party, she said:

"Lieu has a high spirit of class solidarity. Last winter, my mother caught cold and needed to be sent to the hospital. I went to his house and, in spite of the freezing weather, he immediately drove my mother to the emergency room."

And Ms. Hoang Chi, who had been a clerk on the resistance base at Viet Bac, and who was also a senior member of the Party, said:

"I agree with Ms. Cuong's recommendations. Lieu is a very responsible worker, and is very modest when he speaks to people. He calls his elders 'big brother' or 'big sister,' and is sweet to those younger than himself, calling them 'younger brother' or 'younger sister.' He doesn't gamble or take drugs, nor has he committed adultery—he is always faithful to his wife. Also, even though his wife used to be a sugarcane vendor, he has gotten her a job in the rubber factory, so that both are members of the working class now. He uses his time well—I've observed that whenever he has a break at work, he is either reading or writing. He is also very keen about writing poetry, although it's not certain whether that is something at which he'll succeed!"

Only two people in the Party cell, Mr. Thieu and Mr. Dang, disagreed with the two female comrades. The first was a graduate in law from the time of the French colonialists, and the second also had a university degree. Mr. Thieu argued that the only book he ever saw Lieu read was *The Tale of the Three Kingdoms*, and, although he only had a seventh-grade education, he styled himself a poet. As for his way of addressing others, what did that matter? It was how all ill-educated people spoke, and, anyway, someone who flatters you one day can insult you the next. The two female comrades bristled at these remarks. *The Three Kingdoms* was a book, wasn't it? And why should Mr. Thieu criticize the use of working-class language? The Party had to show its solidarity with the working class above everything else.

That silenced Mr. Thieu.

But there were other areas of Lieu's life that disturbed people. It was common knowledge in the office that he often insulted his wife. There was even talk of his threatening his father-in-law, the director of a vocational college—a story Ms. Cuong related to everyone. Lieu's wife had disobeyed her parents and quit school, and then had started selling sugar cane in the market to support herself. It was said that the reason she'd left home was because of her passion for the horse-cart driver. Her father had forbidden her to see Lieu—

he couldn't bear the thought of a horse-cart driver as a son-in-law. But it was useless, Ms. Cuong said, "Lieu had already 'used' his daughter many times, and they were even living together." Still, her father had called her home and begun to beat her. Lieu, hearing her cries, ran in, stuck his finger in her father's face, and cursed him foully, screaming that he had no right to beat his wife. The director was dumbfounded, never having been in such a situation. It was a horse-cart driver's way of behaving.

A horse-cart driver's way of behaving. And then there was the way he had rejected his own brother. Everybody stopped when they thought of that. And then Quanh raised two more issues concerning Lieu's personality. First, he'd heard that during the war Lieu had injected his arm muscles with Vitamin C so they would shrivel and he'd get out of the draft. Second—he hadn't really finished seventh grade, even though he said he had. Serious issues, it seemed, but Ms. Chi dismissed them easily. "People always gossip. Lieu told me about his arm—what happened was he was so angry with himself for getting the gang tattoo dragon's head on his arm, he tried to erase it. It was a youthful mistake, and we should tolerate it. As for faking his diploma—well, he isn't the first person. We know several other cases like that, where people who never even finished school were given diplomas. I'm even told there's a certain professor who never really graduated from the university!"

By this time, the meeting was in an uproar. Mr. Dang turned and whispered into Khiem's ear: "What do you think?"

"I don't know. How about you?"

"I'm about to retire. But you're the director and have another twenty years ahead of you. Remember that some people, particularly young people, are more cunning than we are. Be careful."

Khiem had felt a chill. But still, he voted for Lieu's Party membership. In the end, among the seven in the cell, only Quanh, the Squint-Eyed Toad, had disagreed. The others kept their unease about his behavior towards his brother and the other stories to themselves. Lieu was praised for his revolutionary and class principles, and brought into the Party.

***

It had been very different during Khiem's youth. When he had been selected for Communist Party membership, during the time of the struggle against the French, all communist activity was clandestine. He had been head-master of a secondary school. One day a cadre from the Provincial Department of Education came to meet him, and introduced himself as the Party Secretary. "We've noticed," he said, "that your activities and your ideology indicate a clear communist orientation. Would you agree?" Khiem did, and shortly thereafter joined the Party, feeling the act was a spiritual necessity for him—something that grew naturally from his beliefs but was also a sacred commitment. The night he was recruited, he'd stood in the dim light of a kerosene lamp, in an attic at the end of an empty street in Lao Cai Province, and had taken the oath with seven others. Tears had run down his cheeks, and he'd felt a sense of great happiness and fulfillment at having joined the struggle to achieve a great ideal, the struggle to bring humankind to its true potential. There had been no thought then of joining the Party in order to be promoted, or to gain privileges.

Lieu's family on the other hand had been delirious with happiness at the news of Lieu's glorious victory because of the way they saw it changing the family's luck and fortune. No one mentioned the traitorous elder brother, who, rejected by his stepmother, brother, and sisters, now lived in a small village near a railroad station thirty kilometers from Hanoi.

Lieu himself lived in a separate flat with his wife and son, but on that day he brought them over to celebrate with his mother and five stout younger sisters. They all looked at each other significantly and proudly, as if one of the family had ascended to a high office. The two sisters closest to Lieu, both in their twenties, played their guitars loudly and serenaded their successful brother.

***

At that time—during the eighties—life was very difficult. Every afternoon, when Thoa, Khiem's wife, finished at the storage facility where she worked, she would go furtively to the open market and sell a blouse, some trousers, a piece of cloth, or a bar of soap that had been "distributed internally" by her colleagues. Afterwards she would take the money to the railroad station and buy some cassavas to mix in with the family's rice ration. The nine-square-meter room where they lived was inhabited by four people: Khiem's seventy-year-old mother, Khiem and Thoa, and their daughter Hong Ha. Khiem, distraught over the atmosphere at home, had even taken to bringing his daughter to work with him. The situation wasn't an easy one, and Thoa complained often. Their hardships had accelerated the disintegration of their relationship.

***

Lieu's celebration of his Party membership went on for a week. All of his relatives came to congratulate him. When he invited colleagues from the office, Mr. Dang and Mr. Thieu both begged off, telling him they were sick; Mr. Quanh said he had a toothache and couldn't attend. Only Khiem showed up. The food was Western—rabbit ragout and steak with bread—a luxury in those days. Lieu was wildly happy that Khiem could attend, unconcerned about Dang and Thieu, since they were almost retired anyway. As for Quanh —well, he wasn't a very important man anyway.

The happiest person there was Lieu's mother, the seller of secondhand clothes. She regarded her son's triumph as a way of thumbing her nose at the rotten legacy her husband had left her. "Please share our happiness," she beamed, as she shoveled yet another helping into Khiem's bowl, "My whole family and I are grateful to you for the new chance at life you've given us." Khiem started to protest that he was only one member of the Party cell, but she didn't give him a chance to get in a word. "Without your support, Lieu would never have amounted to anything, even though he joined the working class on his own. But we know it would have taken him forever to become a Party member! We know you're the one who has removed the stopper so the stagnant sewage can flow at last. My family is what I mean, sir." She flapped her hand towards Lieu and the others, and raised her voice. "Do you hear me, children? Mr. Khiem has removed the weight of bad luck from us. From now on, you are free to fly. From now on, if you don't get into the university, don't get permission to go abroad, don't get a promotion, you have no one to blame but yourselves." Her face tightened. "Oh, that piece of garbage elder brother of yours," she spat vehemently.

The food suddenly tasted bitter in Khiem's mouth. He wasn't naive; he understood that what people valued didn't remain the same. The Party membership that had meant so much to him and to people of his generation, that had been a sacred commitment to the people, was now considered little more than a step towards success and promotion. He knew that, wasn't blind—but seeing it so nakedly celebrated here galled him. He put his bowl down, feeling he was choking.

***

Since then Lieu had stuck to Khiem like his shadow. The female staff in the office would whisper to each other: "He pastes himself onto Khiem like an old man on a young girl." Lieu's constant stream of praise made Khiem uneasy. "Mr. Khiem saved my life—he's allowed me to be reborn," Lieu would gush. "Mr. Khiem's talent and integrity are rare things in our society. A man with his capabilities should be General Director, not just the head of our division. Mr. Pho is nothing compared to him, only worthy to be his slave." If Khiem made a suggestion to someone, Lieu praised his profundity; if Khiem was angry, Lieu nodded and asserted that a good general always should have his sword drawn. He liked to compare Khiem to a general whenever he could. "Big Brother, you're like a general who never reveals his own thirst until a well is found for his soldiers, or his own hunger, until his soldiers have been fed. You make people follow you, not only by your example, but also because they can see your heart. You're the exact opposite of those who are outwardly kind, but cruel inside. Big Brother, excuse me, but once when your shirt came up, I saw a pattern of red beauty spots on your back—they mean that you will be rich, powerful, and successful!"

Khiem, bemused, felt like the rooster being flattered by the fox. Often, he remembered Dang's words about Lieu, and wondered if he had made a mistake. Was Lieu a scheming sycophant, or simply a sincere but immature youth? "Listen, Lieu," he'd said, just last month. "You're really making me uncomfortable. I want you to stop praising me in front of the other staff."

Lieu flicked his cigarette and smiled. "Big Brother, I understand you—your name means 'Modesty.' But you aren't using your position as effectively as you could. My elder brother, it's true, is a piece of trash. But I have to admit he was someone who knew how to take advantage of opportunities."

Khiem looked at him, astonished. "Your elder brother?"

Lieu flushed. "No, no, forgive me. I didn't mean to bring him up."

"Lieu, all I try to do is to live consistently with my own beliefs."

"Big Brother, I don't disagree with you. Believe me, nobody understands you or appreciates you as I do. Once I told Ms. Thoa she must be wholeheartedly grateful to have a husband like you. Where would she and her two children be today without you? And Ms. Hoan—how lucky we are in the cultural division to have a leader like Big Brother, I told her. Anyone who loves you must be truly happy. Believe me, I've studied you and your success. Sixteen years old when you went into the armed forces and fought against the gangster enemies, and then worked in the mountains, helping develop the rural areas. Only eighteen when you were selected for the Party, and already headmaster of a secondary school. Then editor-in-chief of a newspaper. Then an officer during the American war. Then a talented writer...there aren't many people like you, Big Brother. But listen, the only thing is...you need to promote yourself more, plan better, both in your private life and in what you write. You need to think about yourself more."

What he needed to think about, Khiem mused, were the two important facts he'd learned from Lieu's little speech. First, Lieu had met Thoa and might have unknowingly poured more kerosene on the fire of their domestic tension. Second, and more worrisome, Lieu, with his horse-cart driver's nosiness, had found his weak point: his secret love for Hoan. He knew Lieu disliked her, that he was aware of her calling him the Flatterer.

But really, he didn't care. He had more things on his mind these days. He was fifty years old and had gone through too much in his life, had faced many complicated situations, and had always acted as he felt he should, both physically and spiritually. He'd never been a coward. His true life was in his writing. His task was to create something true and beautiful, and as long as he did that, nothing else disturbed him, affected him. He'd never felt the need to "promote himself" as Lieu suggested. Writing was like tossing a stone from his hand; it was as natural and necessary to him as breathing. He'd just finished the novel that he regarded as the best work of his life. *The Haven* contained and embodied everything he'd learned, everything he'd lived, everything he'd loved. It was the great work of his life. Hoan had read the proofs just before the book had been printed and had been stunned by it. But every copy of the book was still stacked in the storage warehouse of the print shop. The General Director, Nguyen Van Pho, along with his deputies, had made the decision not to release it; nobody knew why, or what the fate of the novel would be.

That was what had been sticking in Khiem's mind like a knife. It was one of the reasons he'd taken some time off and had gone to the beach at Thinh Luong, at Hoan's urging.

He had been preparing for that trip when Lieu had shown up at his flat, bringing Chinese apples for the children and some fabric for a new tunic to Thoa. He'd asked Khiem to go out for a beer with him.

Khiem went, wondering what Lieu's real agenda was. Lieu toasted him, then bit his lip. "I must tell you something, Big Brother," he said. "Yesterday, on Sunday, I had the chance to see a copy of *The Haven* and to read a few paragraphs. Your writing brought tears to my eyes."

"Please change the subject."

"OK, OK! Bottoms up!"

Lieu drank, put the glass down, wiped his mouth, took out a cigarette, and then swallowed nosily.

"Big Brother, I remember once my elder brother told me

a French saying. It went something like, 'if you're not prime minister by the time you're forty, you're nothing.'"

"I've heard it."

"It's true," Lieu said. "It fits you, Big Brother. You're truly a success. You're a general of literature. You're loved by the staff." He began to name them. "No need to think of Ms. Tam or Ms. Chuong...but among the men, Khoai and Phu adore you. Only that Quanh, that nothing with his Guang-tung dialect, that Squint-Eyed Toad as Hoan calls him—only he is against you and is secretly trying to harm you..."

"'Nothing to fear when you're not greedy; nothing to worry about when you've done nothing wrong,'" Khiem recited. Lieu licked his lips.

"I know you're powerful. But Big Brother, don't neglect this."

"Neglect what?" Khiem said derisively.

Lieu moved his chair closer. "Don't worry, Big Brother. But don't look down on me. I wouldn't care if there were three Quanh's, or even if he were supported by the three big shots in the General Department. But please remember this, Big Brother: Trieu Tu Long, the Chinese general in *The Tale of Three Kingdoms,* is only powerful because he has his magic lance. Or a writer, as you often say, can only succeed if he has material for a story, and not just the inspiration to write one. What I mean to say is...I'm too weak to be a good ally for you if I'm only an editor while Quanh is a deputy director. Better if I'm chief of the editorial section. And remember, I'm a Party member."

It all became clear to Khiem. He had vaguely sensed that an alliance was being put together against him, and that his novel might be used as their weapon against him. Now here was Lieu, taking advantage of the situation to ask for a promotion. Yet Khiem considered it seriously. It wasn't that he couldn't use an ally. And Lieu was certainly capable and knowledgeable enough to do at least an adequate job. He'd worked as a clerk in the administrative section for ten years before becoming an editor, and the other people on the staff were relatively new and had not yet matured. Khiem could sign the promotion immediately. But why was Lieu pressing him to act so quickly?

Looking into Khiem's eyes, Lieu put down his beer and leaned forward, his voice wheedling. "You must trust me, Big Brother. You've given me everything. If you tell me to live, I'll live, and if you tell me to die, I'll die. And if anyone wants to touch you, I'll ruin his life."

Khiem smiled. "Thanks. But is it really all that serious?" he said teasingly.

"Yes, it is," Lieu said. "Big Brother, I will swear an oath to you. I swear if you're dismissed because of *The Haven,* and Mr. Quanh is given your position, then half an hour later, I'll quit and go to work with my wife. Did you know she's raising dogs to sell as pets these days?"

Once he'd said this, Lieu brought his cigarette back to his lips, and smiled faintly.

***

The two trucks had slammed into each other on the curve near Tam Diep pass, near the Dong Giao state farm. The road is narrow there, and both drivers were drunk and going full speed. They were killed instantly, their bodies taken to Ninh Binh hospital. The wreckage of their trucks, the front ends twisted, the trailers upside down, sat in a heap in the middle of the road.

When Lieu left Thinh Luong beach, it was already three in the afternoon. The traffic jam he was in now backed up for a kilometer. He looked at the various vehicles in the line, noting their make and to whom they belonged: Vietnam Airlines, Vietnam Textile Industries, the Youth Theatre, Trade Union Tourism Company. A GMC packed with bamboo crates. A Kama loaded with cement from Thanh Hoa province. A petrol truck. Buses. Several ugly minitrucks that looked as if they'd been fashioned from tractor parts. But also Nissans, Toyotas, Dawoos, Mekong Stars, Peugeots, Fiats...all belonging to the big shots and the *nouveaux riches.* Looking at them, Lieu saw the same people, the new, privileged class he'd seen crowding Thinh Luong beach. A wave of self-pity washed through him.

Khiem had signed the order promoting Lieu to section head. But Lieu still didn't feel truly secure. He'd planned to find Khiem at the beach and speak to him about saving his, Khiem's, job. He would speak frankly to Khiem; Khiem liked that. He'd tell him, Big Brother, swallow your pride and beg Pho's forgiveness. You're an honest man, he'd say, don't waste your time fighting these worms who walk upright and pretend to be human. Just let it go. If you're too stubborn, they'll hurt you, and it will be hard for me as well. We've been close colleagues for a decade. If you're gone, I'll lose someone I can rely on. And it will be even harder to know how to act towards you if you're no longer in the same position. I couldn't really associate with you anymore—whoever replaces me would get suspicious that I wasn't loyal to him. And then...

And so on. Lieu had run what he'd say through his mind over and over. But then he hadn't been able to get any time with Khiem. He'd spotted Hoan among the dancers in the Princess My Chau festival, but she and Khiem had disappeared after the ceremony.

He got out of the car and walked up along the line of backed-up traffic, looking at the clusters of chatting people he passed, hoping to spot Khiem—a little while before, he thought he'd seen Hoan out of the corner of his eye. In front of him a crowd hovered around a tricycle police van with a German shepherd in the back, and he asked someone what was going on. The man whispered that the police had been following a truck transporting drugs, but now had gotten stuck here. Lieu saw the dog pacing back and forth, its tongue hanging out. It panted and let out small yelps and whines now and then, as if frustrated at losing an opportunity to work. He'd heard the police say the smugglers had nearly twenty kilos of opium, the man whispered to Lieu. If they were caught they'd be sentenced to death.

Lieu walked on. He passed one group passing snuff to each other, and another playing chess. Past them, he saw some drivers playing cards. He felt as if he were meeting old friends.

"Hey, brothers—planning to sleep here?"

A curly-headed guy threw down a card and turned to Lieu. "Why not? Only the big shots get uptight about being stuck. As for us, we can sleep wherever we find ourselves— one bed's as good as another."

"I heard the deputy minister in this place used to be a driver—that right?" one of the others asked the first man.

"Yeah, for a year, before he got promoted to Secretary of the Youth Union. After that, he rose like a kite. But he's a fucking bastard. There was one time, on a stormy night, a clerk in his office had appendicitis and was in agony. There was a car, but that fuck refused to drive him, had someone call a taxi instead. By the time the taxi arrived, the guy's appendix had burst."

"What a dog."

"Hey—speaking of dogs, I heard you can buy one cheap now."

"Hey, you," the curly-haired man said to Lieu, "want to play? You do, better put down some money. You too cheap to do that, better be on your way."

Lieu scratched his unshaven chin, as if he felt insects crawling there. He felt vaguely depressed, finding himself in this kind of company again. How dare these people think of him as being on the same level as themselves? But his ears had pricked up when he heard the one driver talking about the price of dogs, and he pulled back the knees of his trousers and squatted down.

He noticed now that an old man, about the age of his disgraced elder brother, was sitting next to the curly-haired man. He was stout, with salt-and-pepper hair and beard, but was well-dressed and wore a stylish hat. The curly-haired man spat and then glanced up at the man. "There's dirt and thugs everywhere. You're from the South, right? Be careful who you get friendly with..."

A man sitting opposite him picked up his cards and fanned them. "Remembah—doan' trust nobody," he said, in a fake Southern accent.

The old Southerner shrugged. "What can anyone do to me? I was a general in the Saigon army and I spent time in a reeducation camp. I've come up here now to look up some former colleagues. I knew one man from Hanoi—we were together at the Thu Duc Military Academy, back in '53. He graduated top of his class. I'd like to find him, but at the same time I'm afraid of causing trouble for him. Is it true that people in the North still take your record during the war seriously?"

"Not any more," another man said.

"That's not true," said curly-hair. "People are forgiven anything, except if they defected to the enemy and betrayed us."

"No, that was in the past."

The curly-haired man licked his thumb and spread out the fan of cards slowly, "Just five years ago," he said, "there was this guy in my factory who was just crazy to make foreman. The problem was, his old man was a police chief during French times. One day, his father, who lived about thirty miles from Hanoi, was killed, hit in the back of the head with a pestle."

"It'd be easy to figure out who killed him."

"Nope. Even though the cops were wise to him, the night the old man was killed, his son was working in the factory. He had a bunch of witnesses."

"So who did it?"

"Oh, it was the son all right. This is how clever he was: at nine, he went to bed, then at ten got up, ran three hours to his father's house, killed him, then ran back, taking another three hours. He was back in bed by 4 AM, and got up at five to do morning calisthenics with his co-workers."

"Was he arrested?"

"Hell no. It was what people figured happened, but there was never any proof."

"Man, that guy could win a marathon!"

"But to kill his own father over a job. What a son."

"I bet he had to train every day to run that far."

Lieu felt the eyes of the former Saigon general on him. A chill ran up his spine. He shook his head and unconsciously wiped at his face, as if erasing any traces of resemblance to his brother. Could there still be any similarity? He, Lieu, was forty-five now, and thought of his face as polished by time, firm, determined, and full of energy. His straight eyebrows, thick beard, and high nose made him look fierce, though he knew his teeth were brown-stained and terrible from too many cigarettes.

"Hot today," he said casually to the ex-general. Trying to look relaxed, he pushed himself off the ground and stood. It was close to dusk. The hills and mountains were outlined against the darkening sky by a rim of yellow light. Everyone on the road was looking up towards the front of the line of traffic, fanning themselves with anything they could get their hands on. He heard someone say that the cranes to move the wrecked trucks wouldn't get there until tomorrow. Old women and children from the nearby villages began selling tea, sugarcane, and papayas to the stuck motorists, their shrill cries adding to the din. The three-wheeled police van, with its big German shepherd in the back, gunned its motor, as if angry at being held back while its prey escaped. Lieu walked down to the end of the traffic queue. He saw several clusters of people who had broken out cases of beer and canned foods, yelling to each other happily. A cassette recorder blared out romantic tango music. Lieu stood still for a moment, feeling sad and lonely.

"My God, will somebody help me? Stop! Stop!"

He spun around and saw a cloud of dust rising from the middle of the line of cars, people shoving each other to get out of the way. Then he saw why. A horse had broken away from someone and was galloping frantically, heading right for Lieu, an old cart with a splintered frame bouncing along behind it. It tossed back its head, its eyes wild and gleaming with a bluish light: a small, brown, beautiful animal with a white spot on its forehead, just like his old horse. His eyes brushed over the compact body with its broad haunches, the high-stepping hooves and silky coat, the arrogant toss of the head—it truly did look like his old horse. It must have been standing and waiting so long in the heat that it had become frustrated, Lieu thought sympathetically, and now it was galloping and rearing like a whirlwind, breaking free of anyone trying to stop it. The horse was on the side of the road, charging through the frightened, shrieking people, the tea vendors abandoning their pots and glasses and jumping aside, others hiding behind their cars.

"Stop! Stop! Oh you damn horse!" screamed a thin bare-chested, barefooted man, his long hair coming down over thin shoulders. He rushed after it, looking terrified.

Later, thinking about it, Lieu couldn't explain to himself why he had stepped in front of the runaway horse. It was clearly not an action he had calculated. Was it to prove his courage, some macho need for heroism? An automatic reaction, because of the work he used to do? Or a throwback to his unselfish behavior when he was a kid and liked to help his classmates?

Whatever the reason, there he stood in the horse's path, his arms and legs spread, looking face to face at the fierce animal rushing right towards him. The horse rolled its eyes and galloped straight forward. Lieu heard someone scream, people yelling to each other to get out of the way or be trampled. He stood perfectly still until the horse was almost on him, then, at the last second, he stepped aside, grabbed the bit, and swung himself up onto its back, yanking the reins hard. The horse reared onto its hind legs, and, as it did, the lines holding it to the cart poles snapped and the cart tumbled over backwards, its two poles sticking up in the air. The horse stopped.

Around him, Lieu heard people cheering, exclaiming over his feat. The owner of the horse ran over and grabbed the reins. Lieu dismounted, people crowding around him, patting him on the back, applauding. The long-haired man secured the horse and thanked Lieu profusely, asked him to come over for a beer at a nearby kiosk. Lieu noticed that the Saigon ex-general had also come up next to him. The man put a hand on his shoulder. "You're a brave man," he said. "Let me ask you something—do you have an older brother who was once at the Thu Duc Military Academy? No? Forgive me, but you bear a strong resemblance. Never mind..."

***

Lieu untied the string and dumped the oysters out of the bag. They lay like a heap of stones on the floor. His thirteen-year-old son Toan rushed out of the other room. "Daddy, the dog had its litter already! What's that?"

Lieu pushed him away. "Don't touch them or you'll get

dirty. They're oysters." He bent down, looking at the pile of fan-shaped shells. He'd gone looking for a pearl, for Khiem, but had come back with only these. Anyway, better than nothing. His wife always insisted that every action needed to show some measurable profit.

He noticed that Thuc hadn't come out to greet him and wondered if she was angry. He could hear the new puppies whimpering inside. He remembered his wife saying that raising puppies was as hard as raising kids, needling him about not helping her enough.

Their marriage, he admitted to himself, was no longer a happy one. After Thuc had given birth to their first child, she had applied for early maternity retirement from the rubber factory and had started a cloth-trading business. The innocent, attractive girl who had made him drunk with love disappeared, along with her breasts, which seemed in Lieu's view to have flattened to nonexistence. His wife, his love, had turned into a dried fish with a thirst for other men and money, mostly the latter.

As for Thuc, she was dissatisfied with Lieu as well. Her husband was no longer the man she had dreamt about when they were first married. Better for her if he had stayed a horse-cart driver. When that was his job, at least he'd come home every day with two pockets full of money from his passengers, a packet of dog meat in one hand and a bottle of rice wine in the other. They'd eat a long dinner, put out the lights, and he'd pull her pants off and they'd roll around together until they were both so spent they'd lie still as corpses. But no—he had to have it all, had to have both a big reputation and money, and so far he had neither.

"Stop kidding yourself," she told him now, as they got ready for bed. "You were a horse-cart driver. You took things from one place to another. At the end of the day, my husband, a cat will still be a cat. Literature and poetry are for people with talent. Face it—you don't have any education. The people who are encouraging you are just making fun of you behind your back. You believe all that nonsense that being a worker gave you a strong and determined character? You think just because you traveled to some cooperatives and listened to the peasants talk, and got a few hints from the writers at work, that's enough? Look around you, look at all those people dying to be famous. They work eight hours a day, then sit at their writing tables and scratch their heads and pull their hair and cover the floor around them with their cigarette butts, just to write some silly, so-called poems that stick in your ears like wet clay. Who's going to buy their poems? My husband, becoming famous isn't easy. Give it up!"

"Look," he said, "if I hadn't written those poems about model workers and been named a Workers' Writer, I'd never have gotten my job at the cultural division in the first place. That's how life is. If you understand how to create an opportunity for yourself, then you'll have one. It's like...these oysters. Or your puppies. Nothing is meaningless if you know how to find some advantage in it."

"Really, I think you're in love with your so-called big brother. You go chasing after him to the end of the world."

She put on her nightgown. Lieu didn't reply. Instead he squatted in front of the puppies' cage and caressed their fur, cooing at them. "How beautiful," he said.

"You even know how to kiss up to my dogs, don't you?" she said.

"You don't think they're beautiful?"

They were beautiful, he thought. A dream come true. He had chosen the bitch carefully, examined its pedigree, visited the former owner several times before finally bringing it home. Once the hour was auspicious, but the day was ill-omened. Another time the hour was too early, the next too late. He refused to leave anything to chance. The dog cost ten million dong, the equivalent of a Honda Cub. Each time it caught cold, the whole family was agitated and there was an uproar in the house, his wife yelling at him, he screaming at his son. But now it had all paid off, and Heaven had blessed them.

Actually, Thuc was delighted with the puppies, but furious with her husband. The night before last, she had sat breathlessly and watched them being born. First a male. And the next. She began to get worried. But when the third emerged, she jumped for joy and called to her son. "Toan, come look. It's a white female." The next was also female, and the fifth, and the sixth. But by then Thuc had begun to curse the absent Lieu as she had when she'd given birth to their son and he hadn't been there either. "Damn your ancestors, Lieu," she said then, "you enjoy yourself, and now I get to suffer." He'd been away during their son's difficult birth, and now he'd been away again, at the beach, looking for his so-called big brother. He never had any consideration for her.

"How beautiful," Lieu said again. He put his hand into the puppies' cage, fondling them. One, two, three...six puppies. Two spotted, four white. They were a special short-haired breed with pug faces. In a month, the dog sellers would be vying with each other to put down their deposits. He was sure each was worth at least as much as a Honda Cub, or two ounces of gold—no less than that.

"We'll be able to buy some motorcycles now, honey."

"It isn't so easy." Thuc raised her voice. Her son put his arms around her neck, clinging to her. "Making money isn't like drawing oysters from the sea. You can't just reach in with empty hands and pull it to you." She pried her son's hands away and stood up, shooting her husband a dirty look. "Starting tomorrow, I'm going to be busy with my contact from Saigon." Her voice rose shrilly. "Try to reduce your workload at the office, so you can take care of these puppies. Or don't you think you had enough pleasant days at the beach yet?"

"It wasn't that I wanted to go."

"So who forced you?"

Lieu raised his voice. "You never understand anything. The Trade Union gives us summer vacation allowances. If you don't find some pretext to use it, they just take it back. Anyway, I had to find Mr. Khiem and talk to him. The situation now is..."

"Bullshit. You have to take care of your own life, not everybody else's. Why are you bothering so much—you're not in debt to the man. Anyway, if someone is in debt, the best way to handle it is to pay it back in cash. In the end, that's the easiest way."

"I know what I'm doing."

"When Tiny Hoai was here, she said you'd declared that if Mr. Khiem were fired and Mr. Quanh were promoted to director, you'd quit within half an hour and go home and help your wife raise puppies."

Surprised and worried, Lieu said: "When was Tiny Hoi here?"

"Three days after you left. Did you really say that?"

"Rubbish."

"What do you mean—rubbish! She's small but she's a lot smarter than you. Don't you know why the big shots don't like your so-called big brother Khiem? Well, the saying is true: 'Cleverness has limits, but stupidity knows no borders.' Know who said that? It was your precious older brother. That reminds me, he sent a message from Song Van asking for some money for the medicine he needs. Listen, if you have your own money, you can give it to him. But don't ask for a dong from me. I'm broke. I need money. Give me some damn money!"

Gloom settled on Lieu. He mumbled something, then

went over to the window and looked outside, to the road. A moment later, he turned around.

"What else did that fool Tiny Hoi say?" he asked. He stroked his beard, feeling stunned. Why did his elder brother keep popping up everywhere, as if to haunt him?

He remembered stopping the horse in Tam Diep, and the old Southerner, and he sighed and thought: *every mistake has its own history.*

Chapter Three

THE LINK

Morning at the Division of Cultural Affairs usually brought a slow, cumulative gathering of the staff. One by one, each individual personality added itself to the totality: a process not unlike the crowd assembling at Thinh Luong beach. Usually the first to arrive was the lowest in rank: Tiny Hoi, as diminutive as a schoolgirl, responsible for unlocking the door and general cleaning. But this morning, and over the last few days, the person who opened the door and aired out the stale offices was the deputy director, Mr. Quanh. He flung the windows wide, switched on the ceiling fans, and then sat at his desk, opening files, reading intently, taking notes.

Quanh had been born in the impoverished village of Thanh Hoa, and still had the dry, weathered appearance of a peasant. Although already in his late fifties, he still followed the ways of his youth and would eat only one meal a day. Each noon when his colleagues went out for noodles or rice, Quanh would close his door tightly. Sometimes a secretary felt sorry for him and bought him some sticky rice, but he would give it back to her, untouched. It wasn't that he was cheap, only that his stomach rebelled at the idea of lunch. Hard work and frugality had been imprinted on his genes, as much a part of him as the paddy mud which for ages had stuck to the feet of his ancestors, or the squint into which his right eye was perpetually frozen. In Vietnamese folklore, squinty people are always seen as schemers and plotters— thus Hoan's nickname for Quanh of "Squint-Eyed Toad." But her description wasn't simply because of his eye. At times there seemed something weak and equivocal about Quanh. In the beginning, Khiem had called him Quinte, a Balzac character who never spoke directly, only hinted about what he meant. But nobody got the reference, and after a while, Khiem realized that no one else at the Division of Cultural Affairs read Balzac, and gave it up.

Quanh had finished seventh grade in 1954, and been sent to a six-month Chinese language course in Guangtung. After completing his studies, he was appointed temporary interpreter for the General Department, with a year-long tenure. But six months is only enough time to learn a little colloquial Chinese, hardly any of the written language, and when it became clear that Quanh was unable to translate documents, he was transferred to the print shop. A few years later, he was stricken with epilepsy. Periodically, he would be seized by a fit, fall under the table, and remain unconscious for a while before coming back to himself. After this had happened a number of times, the personnel department reassigned him to Cultural Affairs. This last year, since he'd turned 59, he sometimes got the shakes and seemed depressed. Since he would retire at 60, Personnel, as a reward for his service, had ordered Khiem to take him as his deputy director, in charge of administration. Khiem hadn't minded. He'd heard Quanh described as a snake who hid his cruel and cunning nature under the skin of an eel, but he thought the description exaggerated. In any case, Quanh only had a year left and seemed to Khiem to be responsible, serious, and hardworking, though, true, also at times opportunistic and deceitful, the epitome of the sly, greedy peasant. In fact, Quanh's personality fascinated him. For a long time, Khiem had planned to use him as the basis for a character in a novel he wanted to write.

This morning, however, Mr. Quanh seemed completely transformed. His long face didn't have its usual mournful expression. Instead of his blue shirt, worn khaki trousers and torn plastic sandals, he was wearing a shirt with a Scottish plaid design, a tie, and new, expensive trousers. His mud-stained feet had been squeezed into white socks and shiny brown shoes.

To the others, glancing at him through his open door as they arrived, he seemed ten years younger, eager and excited. The next to enter the building was the skinny typist, Ms. Chuong. "Hey," Quanh called to her, "have a good time with that guy with the thick specs last night?" When Ms. Tuyen, the plump supply clerk, showed up, he asked if she'd enjoyed herself with her boyfriend at the Thu Le Zoo. After her came Ms. Tam, round as a jackfruit seed. "How pretty you look this morning!" Quanh told her. The women rushed into their office, looked at each other, and burst into laughter. "The old toad has gone crazy," Tuyen said.

Four people had arrived by now. The three women started chatting about their personal affairs, but changed the topic when the fifth, Mr. Nghiem, peered into the room. Nghiem, whom Hoan called the Sleepwalker, was a fifty-five-year-old with effeminate mannerisms; he flitted around the women, trying to clasp their hands or shoulders, making them shriek with laughter. The subject turned to the price of gold and the dollar. Suddenly, Ms. Tuyen cackled, "Hey, did you hear that Lieu's wife is in trouble? China has banned the importation of pets, and the price of dogs has fallen through the floor."

"Something juicy?" asked Khoai, a slim, handsome man of forty-five, grinning as he entered. The sixth person. As he did every day, he threw away the old flowers in the vase on his desk, and tacked a new photo from his favorite magazine onto the wall, among the others already covering it. His office looked like a barber shop.

The seventh and eighth persons arrived, and then twenty more filed into their offices, a swarm of bees entering a hive, each knowing its niche. But once their bottoms had found their chairs, the staff stared at Khiem's door, wondering why he hadn't shown up yet. The conversations about dogs and dollars slowly died out. Unlike the chaotic crowd at the beach, the staff had always had a stable center that unified them, and he was still missing, his future uncertain.

Khiem was on Quanh's mind as well. "What's this?" he asked Phu, staring at the document the new deputy head of administration had just put on his desk: a report of last quarter's publishing plan. Phu stood stiffly behind him, breathing down his neck. Quanh quickly pushed the paper away and shook his head. "Let's just wait until Mr. Khiem arrives." Phu chuckled, picked up the pen, and put it into Quanh's hand. "Sooner or later it will be you who signs," he said, and then Quanh did, quickly, without further resistance.

He stood up and stretched, unable to contain his excitement. The act of signing the report made him feel important, and a sudden thrill of anticipation ran through him. He knew that Pho, the General Director, didn't trust Khiem. Not that he, Quanh, respected Pho greatly either—he'd worked with him in the print shop. Pho had started as a railway worker and had been promoted to deputy director after being chairman of the province's trade union. The luck of heaven fell on his head when the former General Director was killed in a car accident, and Pho had been moved up to take his place. He soon forgot his own origins and had turned into an arrogant and overbearing tyrant who often screamed at his colleagues for nonsensical reasons. Once Khiem had been forced to admonish him not to behave like an uneducated person, to remember who he was talking to.

That comment was occasioned when Pho, Duc, and Hieu had called upon Khiem to complain about the publication of a book which contained some mild depictions of extramarital love affairs. At that time, Quanh had agreed with Khiem. But afterwards, he'd told Khiem that he'd been too stubborn and tough on them. "It's true, they threatened you a bit, but after all they are our leaders," he'd said. His excitement these last days stemmed from a meeting he'd had with Pho. The general director had asked him to check into Khiem's *Haven* to see if any official procedures or policies had been violated in its publication. Pho couldn't find the tiniest sin for which to criticize Khiem himself. That night, Quanh had told his wife about the remark. "Khiem must really be in trouble," he commented. He knew very well that Khiem's problems would mean opportunities for other people. So did everyone else in the division. Quanh hadn't been very surprised, the day before yesterday, when Tiny Hoi called out, "Good day, Director," as he passed her. That little rodent was good at sniffing out the way things lay; he was sure she knew of his meetings with Duc and Hien, as well as with Pho. He was thrilled also at the unusual eagerness Ms. Tuyen, Ms. Chuong, and Ms. Tam had displayed when he went into their office and checked over their work. "Why did you come in so early today?" Ms. Tam asked him cheerfully. "Didn't your wife feed you properly last night?" Chuong added. They had never been that friendly before. "Don't be stupid," Ms. Tuyen said. "This man is going to be our director. Don't you see how good he looks in that tie?" Then the big-mouth asked him directly whether it was true that Khiem was going to be fired. He was spared the need to reply when a voice from the corridor interrupted them with a burst of song:

As soon as I return, adventures lure me away again
This side of the meadow is filled with young grass,

the other with dreams
Whether we go to the mountain
or to the immense sea
no generous arms welcome us
and the wild breezes blow away
the last days of spring.

And Nghiem appeared in front of them. "Aha, caught you eating on the sly, Mr. Quanh," he crowed, his balding head and beaked nose rapidly bobbing. Narrow-shouldered, with his short-sleeved white shirt tucked into his trousers, he seemed a strange combination of malnourished child and fading old man. The son of a village schoolteacher, Nghiem was an autodidact who'd burdened himself with an immense collection of useless knowledge. Once he had been considered a rising star in the Division of Cultural Affairs. But when he reached his fifties, he began behaving strangely. One night he woke up his wife, pointed at his eyes, and demanded: "Do you see anything in here?" When his wife stared at him in astonishment, he slapped her. She came to work sobbing the next day, telling people he had beaten and screamed at her for no reason. "He told me he was the Prince Kamasutra and broke all the dishes and plates." The next day, he climbed to the roof, opened a book, and read it aloud backwards, from end to beginning. People speculated that his brain had become overloaded with words. Soon after, he was committed to a mental hospital. Upon his release, he became a silent shadow of himself, avoiding people, acting as shy as a teenage girl. At work he concentrated on his editing and reading and hardly spoke; when he did, it was always slowly and softly. Then last year, he'd changed again, suddenly becoming very bold around women. Whenever he met a female in the hallway, his eyes would sparkle and his hands would reach eagerly to touch her hands or shoulders. Chuong, Tam, and Tuyen, all single women, complained one day that the man had knocked at each of their doors and demanded to share their beds. He also pursued Hoan, asking her to lunch every day and giving her presents every week. Hoan attributed his behavior to male change of life, the obsession with sex that sometimes seizes aging men. Nghiem did his dirty-old-man act for about six months, and then again returned to being a silent shadow, a person who would not utter a word all day. Now he was back to his agitated stage, talking to everyone he met, sometimes startling or shocking them with his words.

"Hey, hey, Mr. Quanh—there you are!" Nghiem glanced at Quanh and then brushed his eyes over the three young women. "Listen, everyone—when I was reading last night, I ran into the word *thiem thu*. Would the interpreter graduate of the prestigious Gaungtung Language Institute kindly tell me the meaning, please!"

Tam's face brightened, as if she had remembered something. "Yes, when my cat gave birth to three kittens, my mother said one was like *thiem thu*. I don't know what it means either."

"Hence we must ask our deputy director," Ngiem said. "He must know. He's our last chance, since I already asked Mr. Khoai, and Lieu, and Phu, and they couldn't explain it either."

"*Thiem thu?*" Quanh knitted his forehead. "What the hell kind of animal is that?"

"'What the hell kind of animal is that?' Can it be correct that out of this whole division, only Mr. Khiem and I understand what that word means? I suppose so. I suppose a peasant who only went to seventh grade in a village school can't manage derivatives and integral calculus." Nghiem hawed loudly. He spotted Tiny Hoi carrying two thermos bottles to Khiem and Quanh's offices, and grabbed her by the shoulder. "Hoi!" he cried. "Hoi, how do you know when a toad turns out to be a human being? What happens, Hoi, when a toad opens its mouth?"

Hoi shook her head. "I don't know what you mean," she said carefully. She put down the thermos bottles.

"A busybody corner-ghost like you doesn't know! Why should you bother to hide your knowledge from me? From poor old me?"

"Really, I don't know anything! Please believe me."

"You don't know that *thiem thu* means toad?"

"I do now."

"So you do, so you do. Do you also know, that even though someone can give someone else a high position, no one can give another person talent, intelligence, morals, and beauty? Those are only dispensed by Heaven. Do you understand me, Tiny Hoi? Do you know what it meant when Mr. Khiem put the word 'tiny' in front of your name?"

***

Tiny Hoi bent down and picked up the two thermos bottles. She knew that Nghiem had never respected Quanh, was attacking him for taking Khiem's position. Khiem. Like everyone else here, like soldiers to their commanding general, like Christians to Christ, she knew the fate of all of them was linked to whatever happened to Khiem now. She wondered who would finally come out on top.

Hoi's surname was Nguyen and her middle Thi—both commonplace names. But her given name, Hoi, meant pig, both the ordinary village animal and one of the twelve symbolic animals in the lunar calendar. Pig also of course connoted gross and fat, characteristics Hoi was completely lacking. Her nickname, Tiny, had been coined by Khiem, out of sympathy and to avoid crueler nicknames. She could thank Khiem for that. Even Hoan was occasionally cruel— Hoi knew she sometimes called her the "deformed fetus." Nghiem, of course, called her a corner-ghost—a busybody, and to Lieu she was "the dwarf." She didn't really care.

She was twenty years old, but skinny and flat-chested and as small as a ten-year-old girl. Her parents were both road-construction workers, both robust, and people said it was strange and ironical that they had brought this little rat-like person into the world.

Others at the division also felt pity for Hoi: not only was she small and skinny, but also had a small, upturned pug nose and wore a permanent idiotic expression, her mouth hanging open a little, her eyes dead and empty, void of the vitality one would expect in a twenty-year-old. It didn't seem as if life had done her any favors at all. Usually, unattractive people were blessed with strength, but Hoi didn't even have that. Whenever she had to carry a bucket of waste water downstairs, she would nearly collapse. Even now, having just brought two thermos bottles to Director Khiem and Deputy Director Quanh's offices, she was out of breath, panting like a water buffalo after a day of planting.

She had been there for a year. At the end of her six-month probationary contract, several of the women in the division—there was a strong antipathy to her, particularly among the women—demanded that Khiem dismiss her. The first to bring the matter up was Ms. Tam, leader of the trade union. She began to spread rumors about Hoi through the division, until they became common wisdom. When the complaint was brought to him, Khiem, as usual, was absorbed with his own writing but had felt he had to intervene. He set up a meeting with the complainants. It soon turned into a bitching session.

"She's dishonest," Tuyen had said bluntly. "For example, last October, you gave her a million dong to reimburse my expenses, and she was short fifteen thousand that I never saw..."

Khiem knew his decision on Hoi would be the last word, and his sympathy was with her. But he was surprised at what Tuyen said and had felt he needed to hear more.

"In that case, I was responsible for the shortage, since Hoi didn't count the money again when I gave it to her..."

Chuong interrupted abruptly. "Please don't try to protect her—we're not stupid. Anyway, Tiny Hoi is an ignorant person. It isn't right that she works in a cultural affairs division like ours."

"She isn't as ignorant as you might think."

"Do you hear the way she substitutes N's for L's?"

"She finished primary school, and was going to be a nursery school teacher. But her appearance disqualified her."

"She puts on airs, acts like she's your secretary. Her job is to clean the offices and the toilets. Why does she come into the lounge and sit there like a boss?"

"I heard about that incident also. What happened was that whenever Mr. He from the Polytechnic University called and asked for our monthly plan, he'd address her as 'Dear Mr. Khiem's private secretary.' She reminded me of that, but has never dared to refer to herself that way." Khiem shook his head slightly. "Ah, Tuyen, dear friends. Let's just give her the benefit of the doubt. She works continuously from 7 AM until late afternoon. If now and then she comes into the lounge and relaxes, it's understandable. Think of her as your own daughter or sister, OK?"

Tam shot him a dirty look. "One day you'll see your little daughter taking your place."

"Don't exaggerate."

"Just be careful. Otherwise, you won't even have time to feel sorry for yourself," Chuong said. "Haven't you looked at her, can't you recognize how ungrateful she is to you? You want to protect her—but one of these days I'll make a list of all the things she's done, so you can protect yourself."

Chuong pursed her red lips and flipped through the pages of her notebook. Khiem watched her with some astonishment: She'd taken the time, even while doing her own typing, to observe Hoi's activities and take notes. She read her catalog of Tiny Hoi's misdeeds. Boasting. Lying. Rudeness. Answering visitors' queries casually and curtly. Often late. Terribly dishonest. If an orange juice cost one thousand dong, she claimed one thousand five hundred. Making out with a motorcycle driver in front of the office. Quarreling with the tea seller in public.

The others had chimed in, all demanding that Khiem dismiss Tiny Hoi. Not only had she done all of the things on Chuong's list, her unattractive appearance made a bad impression on visitors. Besides, could someone of her family background really learn to be faithful to her colleagues? When a person is so untrustworthy and dishonest, how could they ever accept her?

Khiem understood there was little he could say to change their minds—there was too much hatred here; he wasn't going to make anyone love Tiny Hoi. He remembered the old saying: if someone wants an excuse to whip a dog, it's enough to say he ate the frying pan.

"Look, I appreciate what you're telling me and don't want to contradict you. But think of it this way. Even though Tiny Hoi has made so many mistakes, she comes from an unfortunate background. That's why I look at her as my child or niece and feel pity for her. If I fired her, nobody else would give her a job—what would become of her?"

The women, recognizing that Khiem's mind was made up, all stood at once. "All right," one said, "it's your decision; you'll have to bear the consequences. Just don't forget we told you what would happen." As they left, another turned and said, "Just remember, that tiny little thing is very cunning. And not only that—Hoan hasn't been wrong in naming Quanh the Squint-Eyed Toad and Lieu the Flatterer. She knows how to read character in a person's face. Boss, you have an empty glass in your hand and you think it's full. Be careful!"

Later, alone, Khiem had smiled. He recognized the

women's sincerity, but in his heart he really didn't believe there was true malice towards him, not on Tiny Hoi's part. And without his help, Lieu would never have gotten Party membership, or promotion. Besides his brother's background, he would never have been able to explain away mutilating himself to avoid military service, or lying about his educational level. The same with Quanh, who'd been under suspicion of taking bribes as well as being too tight-fisted. No one was perfect. Some of his staff did work under the table, others pretended to positions that weren't theirs, faked signatures, produced false documents, cheated each other. But the only way people could live together was by understanding and forgiving each other. "Nothing is more human than kindness," the ancestors would say.

And he was certain Tiny Hoi wasn't that bad. "Ugly woman, good character," as people said. She knew she wasn't attractive and as a result worked harder than anyone. From the hottest day of the summer to the coldest day of the winter, she was always the first to be in the office and the last to leave. Her duties were not too mentally demanding, but she had to deal with all the dirty work, the details, and was busy continuously, morning to night. Cleaning the floors, dusting the furniture, making tea for seven different sections, acting as a telephone receptionist, and whatever other jobs the staff found for her to do. True, sometimes she went too far. But she was young and from a poor family, and now she was working in a cultural affairs division and it was hard for her not to put on a few airs with the street vendors. Yes, sometimes she was curt and impolite. Sometimes she did neglect her work. And yes, she did seem to be having an affair with that motorcycle rider who hung around outside, groping her. But when he had invited the man in to ask about the relationship, the man had just snickered. "Brother," he'd said, "as tiny as her body is, what she has down there would be small as a bamboo leaf. No way I want to touch her. Be careful, brother—if she said she's having an affair with me, she could accuse you next." Just by listening to him, anyone could tell what kind of guy he was. Besides, if something was going on, it wasn't that Tiny Hoi had seduced him, but more likely they were both just having fun. So what?

He had run it through his mind again. Tiny Hoi worked hard, and she also liked to help others. He didn't think she had stolen the fifteen thousand dong. She was poor, but had never seemed obsessed with money. If any other worker in the office got sick, she would always visit, often bringing a whole kilo of pork which he knew had cost her twenty thousand dong. When people asked her how she could dress so well, she would just laugh and say: "I save and I don't eat." Also, she was clever, and outside of her cleaning duties, would often assist him in other work. She had a very good memory and rarely made mistakes, remembering hundreds of telephone numbers of the division's stringers. A lot of the other female clerical staff just sat on their seniority, wrote sloppily, spent the day thinking and talking about boyfriends, family complications, shopping, prices in the market, and so on. But Hoi always seemed to be organized and to get her work done. Besides, she had beautiful handwriting, even though she always transposed N's and L's.

And she did, he knew, have certain blessings as well—life hadn't been totally cruel to her. She had a good sense of humor. And sharp, almost as sharp as Hoan in her ability to name people according to their characteristics. Khoai was the Rooster, since he was handsome but stupid. Phu, big and fat, was Mr. Farmer. She described Nghiem's sudden liveliness whenever he was around the women in the division as being like a medium waking from a trance. She was equally adept at recognizing bad poetry and pretentious poets.

Anyway, that meeting had taken place six months before. He was sure Tiny Hoi knew he had protected her, as if he were an uncle or a father, and out of compassion for someone not as fortunate as other people. In turn, she had treated him as if he truly were her own father. Chided him when he didn't dress warmly enough in cold weather, made instant noodles for him when he forgot to go out to lunch, nagged him about his smoking. When the office bathroom was equipped with an electric water heater, she chirped excitedly, "Uncle, you have to take advantage of this and take a hot shower during the day. In your fifties, it's very healthy to do that." Or she would scold him about riding a motorbike, insisting that traveling by bicycle was safer.

***

Tiny Hoi wandered like a mouse through all the sections of the division, hearing everything, aware of every faction and issue among the staff. That's what worried her. She did like Khiem. But a small woman had to look our for herself, didn't she?

On this morning, though Quanh assumed he had been the first to arrive, in reality it had once again been Tiny Hoi. Her flat was far away, and she liked to get up early and avoid the heat and the traffic. Also, she liked to take a shower at the office, and needed to make tea for the staff. By six a.m. all the thermos bottles were filled with hot water and the halls and offices were clean. She locked the door and went out to the banyan tree by the front gate to wait for Hoan. She'd been there all morning.

She liked Hoan too. Why not? Hoan, for the most part, had treated her like a younger sister. She gave her money occasionally, when Tiny Hoi needed it, as well as some of her clothing, and coached Hoi on ways to dress and behave. Ostracized as she was by the other female staff, Tiny Hoi had come to rely on Hoan to help her feel less lonely. And she had become, she knew, someone Hoan relied upon as well. None of the men—Quanh, Lieu, Phu, Khoai, and Nghiem—

liked Hoan. Neither did the women in the office. Hoi knew they were jealous of Hoan's good looks and intelligence. Hoan was isolated in her own way: a single woman, with no executive position in the division or even in the trade union, and not even a Party member like Ms. Tam, Ms. Chuong, and Ms. Tuyen. In spite of all that, Hoan always seemed proud and conscious of her superiority to them. Tiny Hoi hoped she and Khiem would come out of everything OK. For their sake and for her own.

But how long would he stay in power? She was nervous. She really needed to speak to Hoan. She knew all about the tension between Khiem and his wife, had kept her knowledge of the love affair between him and Hoan secret. She knew very well that during their ten days' leave, though one had gotten permission to go to Bac Thai and the other to visit relatives in Mong Cai, they had been together, somewhere. But it seemed that the Squint-Eyed Toad had discovered something about their affair. She pictured Hoan's arrival now, ran what she would say to her through her mind: *Auntie Hoan! What took you so long—I've been so nervous. You look so different. Did you bring me a present? I've missed you so much. Did you know that yesterday Uncle Khiem's wife called and said he'd caught a cold and would be out for several days? So much has been happening. Mr. Hien and Mr. Duc have been meeting constantly with Mr. Quanh. I haven't heard a thing they've said—they always keep the door closed. And Mr. Lieu came back but disappeared at once, and Mr. Khoai said he was upset because the market for pets was falling, and dogs that used to sell for ten million dong now sell for five hundred thousand, and no one wants to buy anyway. And the other day I saw Mr. Lieu and Mr. Quanh drinking together in the bar across the street, and Mr. Khoai and Mr. Phu were there too. Auntie, you can measure the depth of a river, but not a human heart. Oh, and I got in trouble yesterday because I opened the door to bring some hot water into Mr. Phu's room and they were having a meeting. All of them. They were signing some sort of proposal to bring to the General Department. Auntie, I'm so worried for Uncle Khiem. And I heard Mr. Quanh talking on the telephone to Mr. Pho and Mr. Duc and Mr. Hien in the General Department, and they're planning a big meeting, Auntie. What should I do? I'm so worried.*

All of this raced through her mind, as she waited for Hoan to return. But suddenly she saw her motorcycle rider gesturing at her to come over. And when Hoan arrived on her German Diamant bicycle, Tiny Hoi never even saw her walking into the building, as easily and confidently as she had strode towards Khiem when she'd met him on the beach at Thinh Luong.

***

Hoan put her bike under the staircase and slowly walked up to the first floor. To her relief, there was no one in the corridor. She hurried towards her office, thinking she would unlock the door noiselessly and sneak in before anyone knew she was there. Then she stopped. Nghiem and Quanh were walking together in the hall. Both saw her at the same time, and stopped in their tracks as if stunned.

She was a beautiful woman, but today, this morning, her beauty seemed more vibrant and alive than either man had ever seen before. A faint aura seemed to glow from her skin.

She felt completed, felt like a newly tilled furrow that held a fragrant, germinating seed. She had been gone only a few days, but seemed transformed, possessed by love. Since her return she had felt slightly dizzy, slightly seasick. Her tanned skin seemed firmer, her face flushed, the rings under her eyes smoothed away. Now and then something itched in her breasts, as if the blood were coursing faster in her veins.

"Oh, Ms. Hoan! You were gone only a short time but I hardly recognized you," Quanh sputtered, like an old engine trying to get started. Nghiem stood, motionless, struggling to find words. "Your beauty devastates me," he said finally, forgetting that he usually called Hoan "Ms. Tough."

Hoan ignored them both and kept walking towards her door, her shoulders thrown back. But her heart was pounding. Entering her room, she took off her hat, put her handbag down, sat down at her desk, piled with galleys to proofread, and slowly let out her breath. Her office was at the far end of the hall, away from the others, and with its windows latched and its door locked, she felt at last that she was safely alone.

Alone in her room. Away from everybody. Since her return from Thinh Luong she had sought these moments of quiet, when she could remember and savor the events and emotions of her days at the beach, the echoes of those days that seemed now to have taken place in a dream.

They seemed to her now as lovely as a painting in a golden frame. Each moment preserved in her mind. The beach, the sea dikes, the surface of the water riffled by the breeze, the rustle of the pines, the smell of salt fish and smoke from the incense sticks during the festival of Princess My Chau, all blending with the beat of drums, the blare of trumpets, the brightly colored flags flapping in the procession of the palanquins, the answering leap of the ritual dancers. All of it gathered in her mind, a resplendent backdrop for her time with Khiem.

But the backdrop for the first time they had made love was the wild wind blowing from the sea. As if nature had been reflecting her own turbulent emotions. Every movement, every moment was carved in her mind. But what was strongest, what stayed with her the most, was how she had felt when they had offered themselves to each other. The memory was so strong, for a moment she felt she was choking, and had to reach around to unfasten her bra, to ease herself. Her blood was racing through her veins, all of the images of that time running before her vision, and she felt tears course down her cheeks, and she wanted to scream out Khiem's name. But controlled herself. Whispered it.

She had never experienced love like this, had never believed it possible. Their love-making had flooded her with complex feelings. It had been at once carnal and sacred, at once nakedly sensual and earthbound, and yet had floated her into an immensity without border or form.

In her journal she wrote:

> *Please stop, oh my darling, oh storm*
> *Oh the whirling wind in my life*
> *bringing me the sweetest passion*
> *erasing all the years when the roads*
> *I traveled were spread with thorns*
> *Oh darling, a thousand times my darling*
> *I call you silently from my loneliness*
> *We are like two banks of a river,*
> *when one slides into the water,*
> *the other fills with sand*
> *We will have each other at the end of our lives*
> *it is the will of Heaven*

It was her habit to try to put her strongest emotions into poetry. Khiem would tease her about her sentimental, old-fashioned style. But she was not a poet, did not want to be a poet. She was in that way like Mr. Bieu, the retired head of the dairy farm—all she wanted to do was express herself, for herself.

And she sat by herself now. Alone. Her door locked. Knowing all the people working in this little community, from Lieu to Quanh to Tiny Hoi, from highest to lowest, were linked to Khiem. She, Hoan, was connected to him as well. But as part of him now, the same flesh, the same blood.

Chapter Four

THROWING THE STONE

Khiem saw literature disintegrating around him. Many of the novelists he knew were switching to journalism. Gabriel García Márquez had done it, why shouldn't they? A half-page sensationalistic article would sell for a lot more than they'd get for a three-hundred-page novel. Other writers had simply stopped developing their talent, remaining content with the same style, the same plots, deluding themselves that what they were doing was preserving classical forms. A third group would publish one book after another, cleverly plotted or containing provoc-ative material, but devoid of art and imagination and insight into the minds and hearts of human beings. Still others declared that literature must be cheerful, popular, and optimistic, and not disturb anyone. Never mind depressing classics like *The Tale of Kieu* or *The Lament of the Warrior's Wife*. Better to write tales of love affairs between three or four people at the same time—this one sleeping with that one's wife, or boyfriend, or girlfriend—stories that often become the basis for instant-noodle video soap-operas, dashed off and filmed quickly and to order. A little more sex here, a little more love there, finish, and they'd make ten times what they would have doing a collection of short stories. Then there were those who labeled all other writers literary slaves, maintained that the only work that mattered was writing that stripped the so-called beautiful and good down to its true, diseased, skin. They wrote from a sullen, loveless resentment rather than out of sorrow or outrage. Their books, often praised as daring, were usually written as political fables. But they had discarded their art to take on the role of polemicist, without seeing how it would finally debase their talent.

So. In Khiem's view, if God would look down from His heaven at an earth thick with humanity, all five billion human beings—many blessed with the talent to put words on paper—He would see only one, minuscule, group of true writers. They were dreamy and unrealistic. They didn't know how to write a petition to have their salaries raised. They didn't even pay much attention to getting paid for their work, to their royalties. They didn't know how to howl with the wolves. They cared solely about their own work and didn't want to compete with other writers for prizes and fame. They knew literature was not politics and not economics. Not a thirty-ton Komatsu truck, or an ox-cart stacked with ideological cargo, whether sold dear or cheap. Literature was literature. Their concern was to describe humanity. Their talent was as natural as life. It was life. Life was the only force that could control it. They brought people joy or tightened their hearts with pain, or left them stunned and depressed. They were impervious to being disdained, rejected, led, or seduced by society. They could only be invited.

Khiem knew that in the same way every period considered itself the greatest and most important time, writers had never considered themselves ordinary human beings, even though once, in China, they were placed in the ninth rank, below prostitutes. But no writer considered himself or herself second or third best. He, Khiem, was no exception. In his deepest heart, he believed there were only five or six or seven other writers working at his level. They didn't form an organization or club or center or association. They knew writing was an individual act, not something produced on an assembly line. They each swam alone. Yet they all felt close to each other, and sometimes they got together. All were poor. Since among them Khiem had achieved the highest position, sometimes they'd warn him about being co-opted by the bureaucratic mentality. The best, most valuable writing was natural, and the worst was written out of ambition. Khiem remembered a folk poem one of his friends had read to him:

In the full moonlight she thinks it is dark
In this she shows what she has in her life
It is as big as a banyan leaf and as dark as a dog's mouth
What a damned thing it is.

Literature needed to be like that: innocent and imaginative, Khiem's friend had said. Khiem had nodded. He liked the poem, But he felt that along with innocence and imagination, there also had to be discovery and intimacy.

And Vietnamese literature was the karma of writers who saw themselves as the continuation of two thousand years of civilization, whose art grew from the Zen poetry of the Ly and Tran dynasties, and from Nguyen Trai's in the Le dynasty, from the great poets and scholars of their culture. Their work acknowledged and grew from that past, while at the same time put something new into the world. The Creator brought water into existence, and when it was mixed with yeast and rice it became wine. To feel the essence of such patterns, a writer had to truly live life, with all its vicissitudes and contradictions, to live in it and understand it, to use life and nothing but life to illuminate life.

These were all the things Khiem told himself on his way to the meeting that had been called about his book.

Once he'd said to his good friend, the argumentative Dr. Thinh, that Thinh's decision to quit poetry for medicine was an attempt to escape time. But he, Khiem, had to live in time and write from its wounds in his spirit. Kim Lan had said: a writer must polish himself down to write. Exactly. To polish oneself down to the essence of your own life. To drain yourself into words. Until you're as exhausted as a used battery. Until you end.

O.K., he understood the limits of his own freedom. He was part of a school of fish that swam freely in the ocean, but still were moved by the same invisible currents. He was no different from Old Tuy, who always acted independently, but had to obey the rules of the Great Whale, and to act out of respect and admiration for the princess My Chau. Art was free, but swam in a silent partnership with the flux of society. He'd always believed that. In the 14th-century love story, the scholar Nguyen Trai and Nguyen Thi Lo were the perfect Hero and the perfect Lady, and yet they contained all the characteristics of any ordinary couple, of the love between any man and any woman. The scholar, seized by suspicion, wrote "life is as capricious as a woman's heart." And his beautiful lady had replied with an ancient Chinese saying: "One should only guess at the heart of another. This is the strictest rule of Heaven and should not be disobeyed." Even in love there were borders that could not be crossed, and no love could exist that was totally self-indulgent. Art, like love, could not exist completely without boundaries. And yet art, like love, demanded courage, and pride, and immense passion. Nor were these attributes monopolized by love, or by art. They were held by the naval engineer Coc and by Old Tuy, by those who died singing a song for the future they'd never see as they were taken to the guillotine, by the old communists groping in the darkness who had written "Long Live the Revolution!" with their own blood on the walls of their prison cells, before drawing their last breaths.

Nothing changed, nothing progressed, until a person developed in himself the ability to face misunderstanding, slander, injustice, and sacrifice. He had to remember that. In the beginning, truth always appeared in the shape of a maniac. He who would have absolute safety, who would avoid danger, who considered self-advancement and self-preservation as the highest goals of his life, had no reason to dance with that maniac. But nothing changed without the courage to see all limitations as artificial, temporary conventions. Every person stood in front of the yet-unknown. Marx had said: a writer needed to be ready to sacrifice his life to defend the life of one page in his book.

Khiem remembered a time when he had been riding his motorbike back from the office and had to stop to let a huge funeral procession go by: a flood of mourners flowing from Cua Nam Street to Nguyen Khuyen Street. Watching, he overheard the conversation of two cyclo drivers waiting next to him with the others stuck because of the procession:

"Whose funeral is it? Some big-shot leader?"

"No. It's a poet."

"A poet?"

"Of course a poet."

"Why do you say it like that?"

"Writers and poets are always nothing when they're alive, but turn out to be great after they've passed away."

It had been the funeral of Xuan Dieu, the great writer of love poems; one of the innovators of the new form of Vietnamese poetry. Khiem had smiled at the banal exchange between the two cyclo drivers. He'd heard those same sentiments many times before, but it was good for him to remember that great work always outlived and eventually eclipsed its authors. Pushkin and Mayakovsky were considered ordinary people while they were alive, as were Nam Cao and Vu Trong Phung, and so many other writers who were badly treated and suffered. After Nguyen Tuan passed away, someone had written: "He fell like a banyan tree, leaving an empty space in the forest." It was the same with Nguyen Binh, the poet.

It was good for him to remember. Now. *The Haven* was like a flower that had grown from a live tree, naturally and simply. "I write like I'm tossing a stone," he had said; though in his mind now the picture this conjured up was a prehistoric figure killing his game with a deadly throw. *The Haven* used vulgar, ordinary language as a way of proclaiming its connection to the warmth and turmoil of life: he had written it out of love of life and from the freedom of his heart. But where had it come from? How had he written it? It's metamorphosis was a strange one, even to him. It wasn't that the novel described a spontaneous, revealing emotion. It was layered and resonant with metaphor and multiple ideas and meanings. What inside himself had produced it? He had once read a line from the 18th-century German philosopher: "Nothing in life is more mysterious than books. Those who publish and sell them don't understand them. Those who edit, read, or criticize them don't understand them. And, yes, even those of us who write them don't understand them." Was there any mother as astonished at the sight of the child born from her flesh? It wasn't a simple matter of craft. The book was a great leap for him. O.K., he knew he had never truly been a modest man. Lieu was mistaken in calling him that. He had gotten close to Khiem, and sometimes seemed to believe that they were inseparable, that he was truly a brother. In reality the distance between them was infinite. Lieu imitated Khiem's behavior, but they would never be the same kind of person. He knew Lieu would never make a move without calculating its effect on his career. When he had read *The Haven* in manuscript, he'd told Khiem that it had touched him deeply and brought tears to his eyes...and was truly a terrible book. It would contradict the ideas and expectations of most readers, he said, and give General Director Pho, who hated Khiem anyway, an excuse not to release the book and to attack him. Khiem needed to take that into consideration.

In contrast, he remembered, smiling, that when Hoan had read the manuscript, she'd said she felt she was seeing the world for the first time through the eyes of his soul.

He couldn't deny that the novel was a plot of land on which the shadows of his real life moved, fiction framed by autobiography. But it had been sifted through his imagination; its verisimilitude and art didn't come from a recitation of facts, of so-called objective reality, but from the recognition that human beings were a mix of the conscious and the subconscious, of instinct and spirit. *The Haven* was a novel. It was not a political fable. Nor was it a scream nor an insult nor a poem. He had invested all of his passion and all of his pain in it—but none of his hatred. The most brutal details in the book were lightened with humor—the cosmetic of literature that softly covered the harsh lines of cruelty.

His feelings of artistic triumph about the book and the sense of renewal his love for Hoan had given him had helped him rout the illness that had overtaken him at the beach, helped him also to survive the chronic tension between himself and Thoa. He'd even found himself thinking of writing a short story, about the sea and about love: a story which would bring his time with Hoan to life again, along with Old Tuy, and Coc, and the retired director of the dairy farm, all played out on the shore of the magnificent ocean.

What could they accuse him of? On what basis could they hold back the novel? He knew that *The Haven* didn't betray the silent covenant he had made with his society. It didn't camouflage its meaning in an elaborate political allegory. It was written about human beings and for human beings. If it were banned now, it would only be because of a coward's revenge. A revenge taken for no other reason than to demonstrate the power of a petty dictator.

Khiem walked into the room where his fate would be decided.

The white formica conference table stood in the center of the main hall of the General Department like a letter O. Khiem was asked to take a seat. He immediately noticed two strange things. The first was that Quanh, Lieu, Khoai, and Phu all seemed afraid of catching some contagious disease and had seated themselves so there would be three or four chairs between each of them and him. Second, facing him directly, was Pho, with Duc, from Culture and Ideology on one side, and Hien, the managing director, on the other.

He felt isolated, remembered how Hoan had chided him for being too trustful. Looking over at Quanh, he thought how he had tried to consider him as a model for a character in a future novel. Maybe he'd look at the others at the meeting in the same way—as if he were here meeting with a group of characters who would one day go into a novel. He smiled. The mind-game allowed him to feel detached, elevated him to the safe position of observer.

His first character, of course, would be Nguyen Van Pho, sitting directly across from him. The General Director had been born in the Year of the Rat and was now 59 years old. But how would he describe this persona? A flat face and crooked neck create a bizarre appearance that denotes dishonesty and greed, went the old folk saying. Right. That fit Pho's appearance perfectly. His round, flat face was tough and cold, his chin rested on a roll of fat. He was going bald. His nose was large and, under it, his mouth looked like a carp's. There were black rings under his eyes, signs of the kidney problems which forced him to go to the toilet several times during the night, kept him sleepless. But it would be hard to define his personality from his appearance alone. Pho looked at once stupid yet cunning, cold and detached yet crafty. His background, his character, showed little evidence of any real social consciousness. At seventeen, Pho was expelled from school for both poor grades and bad behavior. Soon after, he applied for, and got, a job as a transport worker in a railroad station. Although he was a lazy worker, his cunning soon brought him promotion. Since the other, older, workers were all illiterate, Pho presented himself to the managers not only as someone who could read and write, but also as the son of an old revolutionary. He was soon reassigned as a clerk for the transport team, and then a year later was promoted to be in charge of disbursing salaries. Next, he got himself sent to a trade-union college. Until this point, his rise had been easy: he'd had neither to serve in the army nor to study hard. All he had needed was to be sharp enough to see opportunities and to obey without question anyone in authority.

Obedience, Khiem thought, was the talent of the stupid. Pho was incompetent both in practical work and in theory. He had neither knowledge nor experience, nor a political point of view. As General Department Head, he had coasted, making no particular effort to improve or advance the department, hardly capable of running a meeting or drawing conclusions from one afterwards. His favorite saying was: "I don't need talented people; I need loyal people." It was his weapon against anyone who dared to go against him during a vote or an internal reorganization. In short, he used his power as vindictively as he wished.

The irony was that Pho had been Khiem's student in the sixth and seventh grades in Lao Cai Province, where Pho's father was Deputy Chief of Land Settlement. Pho had been very well known for being a spoiled child and a bad pupil. Khiem remembered one well-known story when Pho's fifth-grade mathematics teacher had made a point that something was as clear as five fingers plus five fingers make ten fingers. Pho had stood up and declared: "Teacher, you're wrong.

When I put both hands into the front pockets of my trousers, that makes eleven." The teacher had blushed. Pho also threatened his classmates, stole their rulers and pens and sold them to the street vendors. At first, he was suspended for a year. When he came back, he was very bad, particularly at language and literature, and had no idea of proper grammar. Once, instead of writing an essay, he had handed in a paper on which he had written: "Mr. Khiem, I hate your literature classes." Khiem hadn't really minded, regarding it as the disturbed behavior of a bad student. He didn't punish Pho until the semester final exams during seventh grade. Pho was caught copying the answers from his textbook by the test proctor and punched the man in the jaw, injuring him. The limit had finally been reached, and Khiem was the one who signed the decision expelling Pho from school.

He was sure it was an act that had been neither forgotten nor forgiven.

There had been more recent frictions between them as well. Khiem had refused to publish a clumsy and graceless speech Pho had written, and had criticized the bad grammar in the General Department Head's New Year letter to the staff.

But what about the others? He had neglected the two men sitting on both sides of Pho.

Unfortunately, they were rather colorless and would make fairly flat characters. Duc, sitting to the left of Pho, was about a hundred and seventy meters tall, and well built. His main peculiarity was concentrated in his thick face: a black birthmark under his nose that made his smile look as naive as a calf's. There was a folk saying that thick-faced people are always stupid, and Duc had never been a thinker, only a doer. One of the first things he'd done was when he'd worked as an assistant accountant for a manganese mine in the north and faked a financial report so he could take a share of the profit. He'd been arrested and was about to be put on trial when Pho first met him. Pho had arranged for his release and a transfer to Hanoi as Pho's assistant. Duc had avoided imprisonment, received a promotion, and was making more money than he ever had before. Pho had bought himself a slave for life.

Hien, who sat on Pho's right, was like a physical contradiction of Duc. Skinny, with a narrow face, hollow eyes, and a protruding chin, he had started as a driver in the Dong Trieu coal mine. Once, on a run, he had fallen asleep at the wheel, crashed, and lost an eye. Afterwards he was reassigned as a Youth Union cadre, but was caught several times peeping at the female workers changing clothes or going to the toilet. He was in disgrace when he met Pho, who was looking for a driver, and someone to run errands and do scutwork for him. Pho arranged to have him sent to a management training course, after which the slate was wiped clean and Hien came back into the world, a new man with a spotless record. He was a manager now, and as with Duc, owed Pho his life.

Hien's and Duc's role in this affair didn't surprise Khiem. The two acted like carbon copies of their master. If Pho was quiet and angry, they were quiet and angry. If Pho turned a cold face to Khiem, they would do the same. Master and servants.

What did surprise him though was the way his own staff was acting. Quanh, Phu, Khoai, and Lieu were all sitting deliberately apart from him, gathering instead around Pho. Watching them, Khiem was reminded of the way people at Thinh Luong beach had subsumed themselves into a mob. There was something similar at work here. But the true force that was melding these individuals of such different backgrounds was the silent acknowledgment that all their fates were sealed now to Nguyen Van Pho's authority. It was stronger than what he'd witnessed at the beach. It was legitimized by power.

When Tiny Hoi came into the room, Khiem saw she too

had adapted quickly to the new order. She was wearing a white blouse and high-heeled shoes, her hair curled in a perm, her face carefully made-up. When Quanh told her to serve tea, she beamed cheerfully and seemed at ease as she tilted the teapot over Pho's cup, saying: "With respect, for you, dear leader." One by one, she went around the table, asking each man in turn if he wanted tea, moving in strict order of rank. First Duc and Hien, and then, turning to the staff of the cultural affairs division, she started with Quanh, then Phu, Khoai, and Lieu, saying each time, "If you please, Big Brother," smiling, and moving the cup in front of each. When she reached Khiem, she poured the tea, but didn't ask him if he wanted any, nor did she move his cup closer.

He was bemused at how quickly she had turned her face from him: there wasn't the smallest bit of nervousness or shame, or even pity, in her face. It was the same with the others. No one had greeted him. No one would make eye contact with him. When he looked at Lieu, his chief editor looked down and busied himself rolling a cigarette, licking the paper, fumbling nervously in his pocket for his lighter. At least he had the grace to seem ashamed. Phu and Khoai on the other hand were speaking easily with Duc and Hien about Zen exercises, the Yalu river hydroelectric project, the falling prices in the market for pet animals. He heard Khoai tell Hien he was looking better and younger, but he would make arrangements for his wife to bring him to their herbal doctor, the famous Dr. Thuoc—he happened to be a relative of Khoai. Thuoc's treatments, Khoai assured Hien, would make his wife feel as young and look as good as her husband. In the meantime, Phu, whose son was in the same class as Duc's, was telling Duc how much his boy praised and admired his classmate.

The superior man never reveals himself; the small man always displays the characteristics that make him small. Quanh had both hands on the table and had fixed his squint-eye on Pho, tightened his lips, and was nodding respectfully, as if to demonstrate how attentively he was listening to the General Director boast about the already well-known story of a gang of drug dealers who had been busted in Son La. Oh, Quanh, Khiem thought. Until now, whenever anyone mentioned Pho, Mr. Squint-Eye would spit out vehement curses like a machine-gun. "I know all about old iron-face," he'd say. "He hired a tutor to teach him French, but after two years all he can say is 'Bonjour!'" Or: "Do you know how ignorant Pho is? Once he was hosting a visiting Italian capitalist, and he kept calling the man 'comrade.'" Or: "That ex-porter is like a goat. When he stayed at the International Hotel as part of his job for the Ministry of Transportation, he refused to pay for his room, and even had an affair with a waitress named Huu Loan. He got her pregnant, but refused to pay her support, until she threatened to inform on him. Now every month he has to shell out a million dong to keep her mouth shut." And: "Do you know how much I despise that guy? I don't understand why an educated person like Khiem doesn't write a criticism of Pho and give it to his superiors, get rid of the guy. The longer that worm is still in his position, the more Duc and Hien and their mothlike natures will ruin this division."

And so on.

Meanwhile, everyone now in this room knew that it was Pho who had demoted Quanh from interpreter to printer. He had been Quanh's enemy.

Pho stretched out his legs, placed his hands on his belly and leaned back, smiling, clearly enjoying Quanh's flattery. Quanh commented on his smile, mentioning how wrong people were when they said Mr. Pho always seemed so serious and forbidding. Khoai and Phu, pretending to pay attention to Duc and Hien, but really with their ears cocked towards Quanh's dialogue with their boss, piped in immediately: "That's true, sir; he's right."

Lieu felt that his own smile was pasted on his face like a mask. He recognized the grotesque, tragicomic nature of the scene. But he immediately bent down, and when he straightened up again his face was blank and empty. Even the fiercest predator in the jungle looks after its own safety. Human nature is the same, he thought, but the difference is that human beings can acknowledge and deal with the truth about themselves. He had studied enough literature by now to understand that. He could recognize the traitorous hypocrisy stamped on the faces of Quanh, Phu, and Khoai. And he had hated Quanh from the day old Squint-Eye had voted against his Party membership. But he understood them. He understood cowardice. The cowardice that comes about because people need to make a living. The cowardice that comes about because people want prestige and power. Because they feel weak and helpless in the face of powerful forces. Because they are afraid of dinosaurs, lightning, thunder, ghosts, genii, and devils. Because they have been taught not to go against the majority. Because they have been taught always to obey authority. Because the democratic system hasn't yet been perfected enough to avoid allowing power to fall into the hands of dogmatic individuals. Because of the force of a leader's personality—a man like Pho, an illiterate, but ruthless and fierce at the first sign of disobedience. Lieu understood all of it. If he had been able to find Khiem in Thinh Luong, he would have warned him about the situation. But now Khiem was in a weak position, and it was difficult for him, Lieu. He didn't want to act as shamelessly as Phu and Khoai. But what could he do?

He leaned over, drew a bent cigarette from his pocket, tapped it straight, and asked Quanh if he would like a 555.

"I thought you rolled your own cigarettes," Quanh said. "How do you happen to have State Express?"

"Just something I kept for you, Big Brother."

The smoke pouring from their mouths and nostrils mingled, wrapped them to each other, the atmosphere of their new alliance. Khiem waved it away and tried to keep from coughing. He was completely alone here. A new order had been fully established now, formed by the pressure of power and the acquiescence to fear, by the need to follow and by the perception of self-benefit. It had enveloped each individual. It had evaporated all resistance with an overwhelming strength. It was the flood and now Khiem was walking against it. He understood that now both the fate of his novel and his own fate would be decided, not through a proper debate of equals, but through this confrontation with ignorance and cowardice.

He felt absolutely defeated, but somehow not depressed. He'd decided the only way to deal with the situation was by keeping his sense of humor. By keeping these people characters in a book. One of the secretaries had told him about the way Nghiem had asked Quanh to explain the word *thiem thu*. Maybe he should use that name for the Quanh-based character. Mr. Thiem Thu. Mr. Thiem Thu clenched his little teeth. Having endured a hard life, Mr. Thiem Thu often worried. Khiem looked at the others, seeing how he would describe them. Khoai, talking as fast as a horse eating crackers. His cunning soul hidden under a handsome face. And Lieu? Lieu was easy. For Phu, he came up with a line Hoan had often read to him from her book of faces: *he who walks bent over with his shoulders shaking is often selfish*. Khiem laughed to himself, remembering suddenly how Hoan had told him she'd gone to get advice from a fortuneteller who said the land under their office was good ground for bad spirits.

Good ground for bad spirits! So the bad spirits had won. So it went. But even if they were the majority, they weren't truly powerful, Khiem told himself. After all, they didn't know what *"thiem thu"* meant. They were good at driving and carrying and counting. Quanh was good at printing. Lieu was a great horse-cart driver. Now they would judge the fate of his book. So it went. History was moving backwards. He recalled his friend Thinh commenting that literature was a kitchen garden that anyone could jump into and start to smash vegetables. Once Confucius had been asked by his student Tu Cong what it meant to be a good person. Always the dialectician, Confucius had answered the question with a question: "Is someone loved by the whole village a good person, and someone hated by the whole village a bad one?" He went on: "The one who is loved by all the good people in the village and hated by all the bad people, might be a good person. The one who is loved by all the bad people and hated by all the good, might be a bad person."

The story brought Khiem's mind to his father, the revolutionary intellectual. "If being an intellectual is defined by the majority," he'd said, "then being an intellectual simply means being the sum of the combined views of the crowd. This is not being a true intellectual." At the time, his father was chairman of a provincial government in the central highlands. He had tried to play the role of Bao Cong, a legendarily fair and just Chinese judge who always found himself in the minority. It didn't matter; he was confident in his judgment and in himself. A majority believing that a lie was true did not make it so. It was difficult enough to find truth through reason or through metaphysics or through the beautiful but imprecise explorations of art. And if the wrong was unacknowledged, how could right ever be known? The characteristic of the mob, the majority, is to listen only to itself, to eliminate the individual ego. How could a mob ever think clearly? Much less a mob controlled by a man like Pho?

We are the true intellectuals of the revolution, his father had said proudly before he was murdered. His words screamed silently in Khiem's head now. He wanted to scream them out loud. His sense of detachment was gone and he felt the anger now. He heard Duc, Pho's spokesman, talking about his book. Talking without saying anything. He saw Pho stand up. Heard him say: "We three, the leadership of the General Department, including myself, Mr. Duc, and Mr. Hien, have voted. The result is unanimously in favor of not allowing Mr. Khiem's book to be distributed."

In spite of having expected it, Khiem was still stunned. Who were these men to judge his work? He started to rise: he would tell Pho that he had no complaints, since he belonged to the group that knew that five fingers plus five fingers make ten fingers. He'd never told that dirty little anecdote to anyone. But before he could move or speak, he saw Quanh stand, looking humble and timid. He wished to respectfully report to the leadership, Khiem heard him say, that he had held a meeting to gather the staff's opinion. The result was that one hundred percent of the staff, nineteen people altogether, with the exception of only Khiem himself, had whole-heartedly agreed to petition the General Department to dismiss Khiem from his position. Solemnly, he began to read the list of signers. He read each name slowly, and after each he reversed the paper so everyone could see the person's signature. The last name was Hoang Thi Hoan. When he said it, Khiem felt a terrible pain in the left side of his chest, and then a steel band tightening around his head and throat, choking him. A black blanket was being pulled over his head, smothering him. As it closed around him, he collapsed onto the table.

Chapter Five

THE MAJORITY

At midnight Hoan woke with a shock. She felt as if something had exploded in her body. Covered with sweat, hugging her pillow to herself, she shivered, felt the blood coursing through her veins and then a wave of nausea. Lying still, her eyes tightly closed, she imagined the transformation occurring in her body, the sense that she was a stranger to herself. She had been back from Thinh Luong for only a little more than a week, but she should have already had her period, and she was usually very regular. She was certain she was pregnant.

Still sleepless at three in the morning, she got up and took a bath. Afterwards she stood naked in front of the mirror, giddily picturing herself in Khiem's embrace. She put her hands under her breasts and lifted them, imagining she felt them heavy with milk. She would be a mother at the age of forty. It was late in life, but so what? Her age meant nothing.

She heard a noise from the apartment below and quickly dressed. Opening the window, she looked out towards the north side of the city. The stars were still out, and in the sky above the building where Khiem's flat was, she could see the seven stars of the Great Bear, the last directly above his roof.

His building listed five degrees to one side, the result of being built during the pre-free-market economy when workers stole cement and bricks from construction jobs. It was modest, compared to many of the old places which were being repaired or renovated by the *nouveaux riches* or other big shots. In her mind she called it the Leaning Tower of Pisa. From her house to the Leaning Tower of Pisa was only one kilometer as the crow flies. It was always in her view, always on her mind. Khiem's proximity was the reason she kept her flat in this commercial district.

The building in which she lived used to be owned by four families, but two of them had moved. Hoan lived in a twenty-square-meter flat upstairs. The ground-floor apartment consisted of a forty-square-meter area, plus an auxiliary attachment thirty meters wide. It belonged to a man of Chinese origin, named Vang, who operated a gold shop.

Vang's father had come from Con Minh, and had married a Vietnamese woman. Vang was a fat man with a piggish face and narrow eyes.

He had tried several times to buy Hoan's apartment, offering her twenty ounces of gold. When she refused, he had bought another apartment elsewhere for his wife and daughter, but stayed here, living in his shop. Hoan knew that he was attracted to her. In her experience, men were like boats floating along the river, willing to drop anchor in any harbor offered them. She sensed that if Vang could do it, he would try to possess her. But, unlike other men, he had never even dared to flirt with her. She wasn't sure if it was because she had always been careful to keep her distance from him, or because of her personality, or because he sensed that she looked down on him.

"Ms. Hoan, I'm not making excuses to you," he'd once said to her, taking her into his confidence. "But everybody has to make a living—whether it's me, or a drug dealer, or a cop: all of us are different sides of the same coin. But what I want to say to you is, this: I only wish for your happiness." Saying this, he was so moved by his own words that he almost choked. Hoan couldn't imagine why he had made the comparison he had in his first statement, but at least he had asked nothing of her, only declared his wish to make her happy. She'd long ago decided not to take offense at his feelings.

She seemed to be the reason for his joy and for the depths of his sorrow. Because of her, one day he might be cheerful, the next depressed. During the days before Thinh Luong when the love she'd been feeling for Khiem had reached its peak, she would come home late at night, toss and turn in her bed. Vang was in the habit of watching her closely, night and day, and he was also a man experienced in the ways and signs of love affairs. Before she'd left for the beach, he'd passed her a note, mumbling, "A stranger asked me to give this to you." The note read: "I know your love is reserved for another. But please allow me to love you in my heart. In your situation, alone in life, with no relative to be beside you, if you need my help, just say the word. I will be there for you." Hoan had burned the note immediately, and then sat motionless for a time. But she'd said nothing. A sixth sense told her that some day she might need Vang.

Early that morning, Hoan came downstairs, taking each step very carefully, holding her belly with her left hand. In the kitchen, she heard snatches of noise and conversation, the scattered barking of the house dogs, Vang's grumbles, and the nervous whispers of several of his friends. From what she could overhear, it seemed they had escaped from some kind of chase, thanks to a lucky accident, two crashed cars that had blocked the road and prevented the police from catching up to them. She wondered if they were trafficking in pet dogs, like Lieu the Flatterer—what they would do if the price dropped? But she didn't think so. She was sure if they sold dogs, it was just a front. Probably the dog kennel, full since she'd noticed their return from the border, made a good place to hide whatever they were smuggling. In her heart she knew what it was, but she didn't want to name it.

She walked to work, suddenly feeling a wave of hatred towards her bicycle. As she climbed the stairs to her office, she felt the gathered weight in her lower belly, the leadenness of her feet. That heaviness cheered her up. She didn't even mind Tiny Hoi's giggling into the telephone at the reception desk as she walked by. The center seemed empty, something strange about it. She closed her door, shut it out. Living in, drunk with, her fantasy, Hoan was not aware of the meeting banning the distribution of *The Haven*, firing Khiem, and promoting Quanh to acting director. Nor did she know of the way her signature had been forged on the petition, or how seeing it had broken Khiem.

***

"For sure I have to obey my new boss. What else can I do, a little worm like me?"

Tiny Hoi was joking on the telephone with her biker. She saw Quanh carrying his briefcase, shuffling up to her in his slippers. She quickly turned to him.

"Good day to you, Director."

Quanh stopped and looked at her, very serious in his flowered shirt, black tie, and sunglasses. "Hoi, have you seen Lieu?"

"Here I am." Lieu stuck his head out of his room before Hoi could answer. At the same moment, Khoai emerged from the office next door, chirping cheerfully.

"Ah, Mr. Quanh—the day before yesterday, at the meeting when you were promoted, Mr. Pho said this year he'd get us some computers and exchange the Rumanian jeep for a new Toyota...and do you remember what else?"

"Two round-trip junkets to Singapore."

"Right—what a good memory you have, boss!"

"Oh, there's more than that. This week, you and I will meet with Mr. Khan from the financial department, and Mr. Luu from administration. I want you to make a proposal to have all our old furniture replaced, and the division re-equipped with an up-to-date telephone system, a television with a VCR, and a table-tennis set also.

Khoai nodded enthusiastically. "Great! Boss, you know how to be a director!"

Tiny Hoi carried the electric water heater into the hall, her high heels clicking on the floor.

"Uncle Quanh, since early this morning there have been many telephone calls for you."

"Were there any messages?"

"Most of the calls were congratulations on your promotion. But two were from journalists."

Quanh licked his lips. "Be careful—don't spread any gossip around." He turned to Khoai and Lieu, who were staring at him, and said seriously, "A lot of noise can only bring us trouble. Reporters hunt for news. Khiem's novel is banned internally, and if they find out, we can have some legal problems. It's ridiculous—none of it has anything to do with the book," he muttered, "that was just the excuse to..."

He trailed off, sensing he had said too much, then changed the subject. "The truth is, I had to respect Mr. Pho, Mr. Duc, and Mr. Hien, and I had to act for the collective good of this division. It was correct to dismiss Mr. Khiem, but without having a strong man at the helm to lead and take responsibility, the people would have no guidance."

Khoai leaned towards him. "It's a good thing you came into power. I hope you'll keep this position, at least until the year 2000."

"To tell you the truth, I've been hesitant. But on balance, I'm as qualified as he was. First, I'm older. Next, on the intellectual side, he graduated from the pedagogical university, but I graduated from real life. Politically, I graduated from a full-time ideological training course at the Nguyen Ai Quoc Institute, while he only finished a part-time course. Morally, I'm clearly much better than he is, since I'm trusted by both the upper echelons and all my colleagues. I have heard some people say I lack will power. That's wrong. I come from Cam Thuy, in Thanh Hoa province, the home of King Le. Coming from those origins, I must have more will power than Khiem. But I know there have been rumors that I plotted a coup d'état against Khiem."

"Oh, no," Khoai said.

"Oh; yes."

"How you should reply, then, is to say frankly: 'I obey the orders of my superiors. Mr. Pho is my boss, and I do what he tells me. Who pays my salary? Mr. Pho. Therefore he is the one I follow.' Right, Lieu?"

Lieu kept his face straight. Khoai was an ex-carpenter, garrulous but simple, and he was often inadvertently funny. But he was also quarrelsome, always ready to pick a fight. Lieu said nothing. Quanh turned to him sharply.

"Why do you look so nervous, Lieu?"

Lieu scratched his chin. "It's nothing. Last night I didn't get any sleep—the puppies ate oyster soup, and they all got diarrhea. It's not my fault the price of dogs dropped—it's all because China has banned their importation. But Thuc keeps screaming at me that I'm as stupid as a dog. She needs money, she screams. Money. Money. She wants me to get a job that earns something, and not starve in publishing."

Quanh knit his brow. "You always manage to bring the conversation back to the problem of your dogs. But I hear you have still kept some ties with Khiem."

"That isn't true—please don't say it."

"Really? What did you say to Ms. Chuong after the dismissal meeting?"

Tiny Hoi overheard Quanh as she was taking a thermos of hot water into Khoai's room. She popped her head out of the door and grinned. "Brother Lieu, since the price of dogs has dropped, I liberate you from the oath you swore some time ago!"

The little shit. Lieu paled and clenched his teeth until his jaw ached. If he didn't control himself, he'd punch her little rat teeth out. He had sworn his loyalty to Khiem when he'd thought no one else was around—how had she found out about it, had she told his wife? And now she was indirectly reminding Quanh of his closeness to Khiem, as much as to tell Quanh he couldn't trust him.

"Ah..." Lieu kept his face blank, pretending not to hear what Tiny Hoi had said. He looked around, trying to bring the conversation back on course. "What I told Ms. Chuong was that when one of the wheels of a bicycle is broken, it has to be replaced immediately. Someone being fired isn't at all unusual—she shouldn't be so disturbed by it."

Quanh tightened his lips, clearly suspicious.

Tiny Hoi realized she'd made a mistake mentioning the oath Lieu had taken to Khiem. She tried now both to extricate Lieu from the awkward situation into which she'd thrust him and to please Quanh at the same time. "Brother Lieu, you told me something very interesting before. Why don't you report it to our new boss?"

"What did I say?" Lieu glared at her. But she kept going. "You know, about what happened at Thinh Luong beach between Ms. Hoan and Mr. Khiem. Remember?"

"Ah." Lieu let out a long sigh, then said quickly, "Yes, I wanted to report to you, Mr. Quanh, that Mr. Khiem and Ms. Hoan took their vacation time at Thinh Luong beach— they stayed together there."

Quanh sucked in his breath sharply and leaned against the wall. At that moment, Khoai, who had been standing next to his door eavesdropping, stepped out and walked over to

Quanh, rolling his eyes, grinning in pleased surprise. Both men were clearly excited at the news. They pressed in closer to Lieu, started to ask him for the details. As they did, someone screamed from the stairwell:

"Are you playing at being Teng Shui Weng, the Chinese king who ordered books burned? Is that it?"

Nghiem had appeared at the top of the stairs, his soldier's hat cocked on his head, his face sunburned, his white shirt flapping loose, his belt cinched hard around his middle. Behind him were Ms. Chuong, Ms. Tam, Ms. Tuyen, and several other women staff. Each was carrying a stack of books and walking slowly and heavily: they were moving the two thousand copies of *The Haven* that had been printed. The title was in dark blue letters against the white cover with its image of the distant bank of a river, designed by the artist Van Sang. At Pho's order, every copy had to be moved into storage. Ms. Chuong, sweat glistening on her oval face, grumbled to Nghiem: "We know nothing. We're just doing what we were told."

Ms. Tam, small and stout, suddenly put her stack down. "You know that this book has committed no sin."

Tuyen, stuck behind them, yelled: "Right in the morning, wrong in the afternoon, and tomorrow right again. And we're in the middle—how can we know what's right or wrong? Let these damned people do whatever they want. If we're told to put the books into storage, what choice do we have? Ruthless people have all the power."

Nghiem turned to them and raised his voice, making sure Quanh, Lieu, and Khoai heard what he said. "The Koran states that words and language are genii, since they are as powerful themselves as genii. Words contain spirits—remember that whoever destroys books will bring ruin on himself."

He's pretending to be mad so he can cause trouble, Quanh thought. We'll have to call in Phu to control him. He

117

turned away and shuffled off in his slippers, motioning for Lieu and Khoai to follow him.

"Get away from there or you're all dead," Phu shrieked suddenly from the stairwell.

"What are you—Mr. Thunder?" Tuyen cried, then burst into laughter. "Like Mr. Thunder who pulled out his wife's belly?"

"Hey, here comes Mr. Policy too," Ms. Tam shouted.

A truck was backing up to the front of the building. It was filled with new furniture, sent down by the General Department.

Mr. Thunder was the new nickname Hoan had created for Phu, though so far only Ms. Tuyen knew it. It fit him remarkably well: his loud mouth and explosive temper. The others, hearing it for the first time, had to stop and look at Phu again. He had a body and face that looked carved from wood, except for the stye marring his left eye. He was toting one end of a huge leather sofa while his driver, Thong, who came from a Muong background and was called Mr. Policy by the women, was on the other side of it, helped by two other young men.

With the end of the sofa on his left shoulder, his right arm hanging down at his side, Phu walked in through the door of a room as straight as a soldier on parade. If the three men behind him hadn't yelled, "Put it down for a minute," they would have smashed their hands against the door jamb.

"It means nothing to me!" Phu lowered the sofa and clapped his thick, heavy palms together, the stye on his left eye twitching. Spotting Quanh, he stuck his face into his office. "Collect anything that belonged to Mr. Khiem and throw it away. That plaque with his name on it as well—toss it out."

Before anyone else could move, Phu rushed into Khiem's office and grabbed the edge of the plaque with a grip like an iron thong. It was fastened to the wall with three-centimeter nails. It loosened and came off with a groan and fell to the floor, the six nails sticking straight up in the air.

"How terrible!" Tiny Hoi shrieked. Holding her nose with one hand, she walked through the cloud of dust and emerged holding a Russian-made electric burner. Khiem had brought it in because he felt sorry for her and would cook lunch for both of them on it so she could save money. Now she brandished the electric ring like evidence. "How dirty and messy that Mr. Khiem was!" she cried out.

Mr. Thunder and Thong came back into the office. All Khiem's old, moth-eaten furniture was thrown on top of a heap made of his curtains, shoes, picture frames, and clothes on hangers, Bam! A pile of books, notebooks, and papers held together by file clips was thrown fiercely on the pile by Phu. The papers scattered and flew everywhere—Khiem's manuscripts and notebooks. Phu walked out of the cloud of dust, holding a broken shoe and a torn woolen scarf. "We'll hold an auction for these," he said loudly.

Tiny Hoi wrinkled her nose. "Terrible. Look at that briefcase. I don't think Mr. Khiem has washed his scarf for a year! What a slob."

Khoai rushed across the hall to join them. "Mr. Quanh—why don't we buy these things and give them to the Museum of Twentieth-Century Writers?"

They laughed nastily. Ms. Chuong walked over, sat down next to the pile of torn manuscripts and notebooks, and quietly began putting them into some kind of order. Tears ran down her cheeks. Poor Khiem. How could human beings be so cruel to each other?

"What are you doing—get out of there! Do you want to get smashed?"

The voice threatening her came from a big leather armchair that was moving inexorably towards her. She stood up and pushed the pile of paper to the side, giving way to Phu who had the armchair on his back like a turtle shell. "What rubbish," he said to her. "You'd cry for a moth, but not your own father's grave." Another large armchair was moving behind him. She saw Lieu's balding head sticking up from its back.

The atmosphere was busy and noisy, the men's faces stamped with arrogance. Revenge! Coup d'état! An earthquake!

A short time later, rubbing his hands together, Phu invited Quanh into the office. "Boss, I'll put the new computer and telephone Mr. Pho's giving us in here. OK?" Before he had time to answer, Phu rolled his eyes and said. "The boss's office has to look decent. You should have been here a long time ago, not Mr. Khiem."

Khoai had come out of his office and was looking at the empty place where Khiem's name plaque had been fastened. He mumbled something about ordering a new one, white words on a dark blue background, then knit his brows and spoke loudly enough for Quanh to hear. "Mr. Khiem hasn't shown up here for days. If he's ill, he should have reported it—everybody has to follow the rules." Meanwhile, Tiny Hoi went quickly into Quanh's former office and carried his briefcase across the hall.

By afternoon, Quanh was fully installed in the director's office, and the door to his old office had been locked.

***

Chuong had gathered up all Khiem's notebooks and manuscripts and brought them to her room. "I can't imagine why they were so mean to Mr. Khiem," she said, tears in her eyes.

Tuyen rushed in, poured a cup of green tea, gulped it down, then wiped some of its spill from her chin. "Go and see Tiny Hoi sitting on the sofa and chatting away with Squint-Eyed Toad and the Flatterer and Mr. Thunder and

Khoai. Poor Mr. Khiem. He always protected her and thought well of all of them, and now they've cut the string of his kite."

Chuong still had tears in her eyes. "He never knew how much they schemed and plotted while he was gone. I saw Khoai taking a case of beer as a gift to the Squint-Eyed Toad. And Thunder went to Quanh's house and fixed his toilet and cleaned out his sewage pipes. As for the Deformed Fetus, she replaced all the locks on the bathroom and keeps going to Quanh's house to help with the cooking. She even took his wife to the tailor to get a blouse made. We kept warning Mr. Khiem that he was looking at an empty glass and seeing it full of wine. The poor man."

"Why have they done it?" Tan moaned.

Tuyen was still furious. "I told them, just like you did— Mr. Khiem is ill; it isn't right to break into his office and clean it out when he can't be here. So Tiny Hoi says, 'when a wheel of the bicycle is broken, people can't wait around until it can be ridden again.' That damn Deformed Fetus, I despise her! And Lieu doesn't say a word—that man who used to boast so much about his relationship to Khiem. 'Oh, you're more precious to me than my own brother,'" she mocked, singsong, "'You've saved my life, and if you tell me to live, I'll live, and if you tell me to die, I'll drop dead immediately.' Right— the price of dogs has fallen, so he just worries about his own tail. As for Quanh, all he says to me is: 'It's Mr. Pho's order.'"

"Did you hear how he boasted in the speech he made when he replaced Mr. Khiem?"

"I wasn't there."

"He said: 'My dear colleagues—I see in your dear eyes your love and hope in me. All of us are now in the same boat, riding the wild waves in the ocean. Therefore, I take this occasion to declare five new principles to guide our work. First: obey absolutely any orders issued by Mr. Nguyen Van Pho, the highest leader of our General Department. Second...'"

She couldn't go on. "It was shameful to see him act that way, a man of his age."

Tuyen rolled up her sleeves and sighed. "Don't worry, there are still more dramas for us to watch. Now we can sit back and watch the three of them compete to become deputy director."

"It's just terrible," Tam cried. "Terrible. I feel like we're watching a newsreel about Pinochet's coup against Allende, or the Red Guards in China during the Cultural Revolution. That fortuneteller who told Hoan the ground we're on is a good place for bad people—was right. All of those guys resemble each other in their arrogance."

"Speaking of Ms. Hoan, have any of you seen her?"

"She's closed her door and is staying inside her office."

"I can't understand why she'd sign the petition against Mr. Khiem."

Tam looked up. "Why did any of us?"

Tuyen waved her hands helplessly. "Khoai lied to me—he told me it was a petition asking Mr. Pho not to punish Mr. Khiem. That's what I thought I was signing. That damn cheat."

Chuong looked puzzled. She crossed her hands on her chest. "But no one gave me anything to sign. Do you think they forged some of our signatures?"

No one could answer. Silence. Each felt it evaporating into a paralyzing sadness. In it, each woman could see clearly that human beings were dark abysses that could never be known fully. That some hide their obscure thirsts until they smell some benefit to themselves, and then will come out in the open, fully exposed and without shame.

As on the previous days, from the time she arrived in the morning, Hoan had kept the door to her office tightly shut, kept herself isolated from all tumultuous events outside.

Alone, she could let her imagination fly to Thinh Luong, glide along the waves, swim to the shore, and search again for Khiem. She could walk with Khiem on the dike, her hair blowing wildly in the salty wind of that dream world.

Proofreading galleys, performing her duties, she was still living in a fairy tale. If anyone could have seen her, she would have looked the way she looked that day in Old Tuy's house, she and Khiem discovering each other, searching passionately for the perfection of their lives, unaware of the storm moving in from the ocean. Unaware that life was going on as it always did, its most sublime, transcendent moments existing simultaneously with its vulgarity, its limitations, its shame.

She knew what was happening outside her office, outside the dream in which she was living. She had heard the voices outside her door arguing about Khiem. She could imagine their expressions and gestures. She understood what they were doing, who they were. How empty they were. Like the puppies Lieu sold: worthless except when people made a fad of them. It was sad when something's value doesn't come from itself. That's what they were, these untalented, immoral people—they were the type of commodity whose worth always depended on something outside themselves.

But she was not angry. No. The act of tearing away all signs and vestiges of Khiem's presence was simply childish and stupid. The people involved were merely tearing off their masks, revealing the depth of their desire for power and titles. In the end, it wouldn't matter. It couldn't disturb her happiness, the sense that she was full of life. That she was twice herself now.

She knew the seed of their love was germinating inside her. Holding her pen in her right hand, she covered the lower part of her belly with the left, imagining she was protecting from an external danger what was precious and growing inside her.

"Over there—her office is one of the last with a door that can close. Pound on it until that woman comes out!"

She was right—the sixth sense that told her something terrible was going to happen was correct. Danger was arriving, and not just in her imagination.

It was three in the afternoon. Hoan heard Tiny Hoi's voice again, sounding strange, abnormal. She put down her pen, stood up, and then took a step backwards as her door swung open. It hadn't been locked, only closed.

A heavy female body appeared in front of Hoan, the odor emanating from its armpits strong and rank. Hoan slowly recognized who it was. Wide shoulders. Big breasts. Large hips. Round face, round nose. Narrow eyes gleaming with a repressed lust. In other words Thoa—Khiem's wife. Feeling bitter but resolved, Hoan acknowledged to herself that there was no chance they would not meet, not once she had set foot on the path she had chosen. They had to face each other. Four tough-looking young men come in behind Thoa. As soon as Hoan looked at them, they shook their fists at her and shrieked: "Let's beat this whore to death."

"Have a seat," she said.

"Congratulations on being so calm." Thoa laughed sickly, drew out a chair, sat down two feet from Hoan. Her chubby thighs bulged in her polyester pants. She held a green bag defensively between them, as if she were hiding something under its cloth. Tilting her head back, she regarded Hoan slowly, with exaggerated curiosity. Her lips tightened in contempt, her small eyes slit into two knife edges.

"Well, you look like a ripe fruit with many seeds inside you," she said. "When were you born? The fifties? That gives you, what? Just forty youthful springs? Yes, you're quite attractive, aren't you? Nice eyes too. Not some teenager, just sprouting new hair and new desires from her parts. Not some middle-aged slut with floppy tits, ready to run after any man who waves his hand at her, isn't that right?"

She repeated the question, harder, as if flinging it into Hoan's face. Hoan felt numb. She didn't know how to deal with the situation. Deep inside herself, she affirmed, clung to, her right to love Khiem. She loved him passionately; she would die for him. But she was not a shameless person. She knew there were limits. She knew there were conventions she'd broken. She knew what she had done would be considered wrong. But those ideas were abstract and general and didn't seem to have anything to do with her and Khiem. Why did freedom always seem to belong to someone else? How miserable and unfair the situation was. From the outside, she would be judged as the culprit. The other woman in the usual melodrama. But the whole old dance of infidelity and jealousy seemed so petty and mundane and irrelevant as a way of framing the love she felt for Khiem.

Now this woman who would judge her stood up. Like a huge and complicated structure rising to its full height. Hoan felt she had no right to condemn her or feel contempt for her, to dismiss her as rude or stupid. Thoa tilted her head to the side, her eyes fixed on Hoan, then said sweetly: "Well, I've come here today to thank you, Hoan. Thank you so much for helping me out. I'm just a person without much education, see; I have to earn my living, so I have to work like hell. The way it is with my business, I have to travel from province to province. So I don't have the time to share my table and my bed with my husband. I haven't been able to be there to stretch out my arms to be his pillows at night, to warm up his body all the time. So here you are, all ready to fill in for me. How lucky for me. But I'll tell you, Hoan— when you find that someone else's husband is nice, you'd better be ready to pay for him."

Hoan rose to her feet as Thoa spoke, as the cruelty in Thoa's face intensified, accentuated by the deep grooves running down from the two sides of her nose, the mocking twist on her lips, the edged, false sweetness of her words. Her feelings of sympathy for Thoa disappeared. As if seeing this, Thoa tightened her jaw; now she spoke through teeth clenched so hard that each word seemed to stab out straight into Hoan's face like a piece of sharp metal: "Well, thank you so much for taking care of my husband for me. For taking care of him even more than I did. Which means..." The last word was drawn out, stretched into a terrible shriek, the woman leaning forward with her whole hot heavy body "...Which means lying down to let my husband fuck you. Which means you're a true whore. Which means you're a bitch. Which means you have seduced my husband. Lieu, my husband's godbrother has told Tiny Hoi everything, and Tiny Hoi has told everything to me. How many times have you slept with my husband? Tell me! In Thinh Luong and where else, you whore! You think you're so smart. You want to have something and not pay for it, don't you? Well, let me teach you something. A person can lend another person food, or clothes, but not her husband's cock!"

Her eyes blazing, she stepped forward, her right hand raised. "You're carrying his baby inside you, aren't you? I can see it in your face. Well, take good care of it. Carry it well, because after it's born, I'm going to come get it and bring it home and raise it. Raise my husband's child. Do you see what you get, you whore!"

The raised hand slashed down. Hoan stepped backwards, covering her belly with one hand, her face with the other. Too late. A cry choked in her throat. Her left cheek felt as if it were on fire. Blood poured out from the cut, splashing onto her chin, her neck. A whistle sounded from the other room. Thoa slipped the razor into her bag and rushed out.

Hoan stood motionless, like a condemned criminal waiting for the next stage of her execution.

From the corridor, she heard the shuffle of slippers, and then Quanh's voice, raised artificially. "Tiny Hoi, why did you let Mrs. Thoa and those men in here? What a coward that Khiem is, taking revenge on poor Ms. Hoan just because she signed the petition to have him dismissed! All of us thought he was a decent man, but look what he's done, look how wrong we were..."

Chapter Six

DELIRIUM

Khiem looks around. He is sitting and drinking rice wine with the old fisherman from Thinh Luong and Dr. Thinh, and sometimes the engineer Coc seems to be there, though he says nothing, and the herbal doctor Moc, Thoa's new boyfriend, sits in their circle also, leering evilly at him. They seem to be in the middle of a conversation about the war.

What I remember most was the hunger and thirst, Old Tuy says. We hardly ever had enough to eat. Never mind rice, we didn't even have grains of cereal. We were constantly hungry. When I re-enlisted and was sent to the battlefield, in the fifth zone, we spent about one third of our time fighting, and the rest farming and transporting rice. It had to be like that— without anything in your stomach, how could you fight? I remember there was a saying: "Commander Rice makes the final decisions." Once, I was sent on a mission to the Delta, and was given a bag of two kilos of rice and was told it would have to be enough to last me a month. I put the bag into my knapsack and started away. Then the commander called me back, made me open the knapsack, and poured in another bowl of rice, his own rice. Holding that bag with that one more bowl of rice in it, I felt tears run down my cheeks. Yes. That was it. We were always hungry. Whenever I saw a snake, I wanted to eat it. I was hungry even when I was asleep, even when I was ill with malaria. My whole body was shaking, but when I smelled some rice, I sat up and could have eaten three bowls. Hunger! How terrible it was to be hungry. And how poorly we remember that. And the thirst? Yes, I still feel the thirst. It was there all the time. We lived with it. Five of us in the middle of the jungle, so thirsty we would drink urine. One day we dug a hole under some dead, rotten leaves, and drew about two handfuls of water from it. Then someone remembered that the Americans had sprayed the area with Agent Orange. We all looked at each other and we recalled how once when we were transporting rice three C130's had swooped down and released a spray of that stinking liquid over us, and we had covered our faces with our scarves. But the others were so thirsty they couldn't help themselves. Each in turn took a drink. I was a fisherman; I was used to going without water, so I was the last. Now all four of my comrades-in-arms are dead from cancer of the liver and bowel, and only I am left alive.

Dr. Thinh shudders, waves his arm, pats his chest, stares at Khiem. The final, truest aim of war should be to diminish cruelty, restore the harmony between society and the universe, Thinh lectures. But seen through more immediate lenses, of course, it seems war is only representative of risk and death. As for me, I was luckier than Old Tuy. I was never hungry during the war. My only fear, my only obsession was the fear of death. I came close several times, and when I remember those times I still feel afraid. Once I was coming through the jungle with two other scouts. We had some loose tobacco but no way to smoke it. Then we came across a small crater full of water, about as big around as a conical hat, and we decided to make it into a kind of earthen water pipe. We dug a small ditch from the near-by stream, cut down a stalk of bamboo to use as a straw, and began to smoke. Excellent! Soon we were all feeling good, but it was almost dark, and we urged each other to return to camp. But Can, one of our comrades, told us to go ahead: he wanted to smoke a little more, and would join us when he was finished.

We had gone about a hundred meters when we heard a huge boom, felt the earth shake beneath our feet, and were thrown into the bushes. When we recovered, we went back, but Can had disappeared. Apparently, the little crater had been made by a time-delayed bomb. We searched the area, and then saw Can's guts, hanging from the branch of a jackfruit tree. It was a terrible sight.

Another time, we were digging a shelter, and before we could finish, we were bombed by American planes. When they'd gone, I crawled out and looked for my fellow soldiers. Then I saw the body of Loc, our company commander, embedded in the side of the hill. I tugged at him, trying to pull him out, and suddenly, whapp! I fell over backwards and his corpse was on top of me, still in my arms, but with his head gone. Embracing him, I wept and felt chilled with fear.

Yet all of that was not as terrible as the time we were given the mission to open Noi Pass. We were on the way there, when suddenly we heard an explosion. We rushed towards the noise, and then stood there stunned. A huge boulder had slid down and crushed three of our friends, but in a strange way: their bodies were under the rock, but their three heads were untouched, their eyes rolled up, their mouths open, their tongues protruding. We cried out, and our hearts ached with pity, but what could we do? The boulder was as big as a house, and we were too close to the enemy's base to explode mines under it, to shift it off the corpses. But at the same time, we knew we had to do something—this was the trail our troops would come down later. Do you understand what we had to do?

Tell us, Old Tuy says.

We had no choice. We had to cut off the three heads and bury...

I could never do that.

Neither could I, Thinh admits. *I told them, even if I were punished, I wouldn't do it. Finally, our commander had to do it himself.* Thinh shakes his head, rubs his arms, trying to calm *himself. I was always frightened, he says. No one can get used to deaths like that. In my eight years in the war, I buried eighty of my comrades-in-arms. Once, after covering a corpse, I raised my K54 and emptied my magazine into the air. Are you afraid of something? my commanding officer asked me, and I told him that yes, I was.*

He swallows, continues. But the most frightening moment for me came from something very simple, but so terrible that even now I tremble when I recall it. That night I had to in-filtrate the perimeter of the Pleiku airfield, just before we were going to attack the place, and verify positions I had scouted out previously. It was very dark. I crawled and slid through all the coils of barbed wire, and was on my belly at the edge of the tarmac. At that moment, I head two Saigon soldiers, whistling, coming towards me. I was well camouflaged and hidden in the tall grass, so I was not afraid of being discovered. But suddenly a frog leapt up over my head, in their direction. Turning on his flashlight, one of the soldiers ran after it and caught it without difficulty—maybe he was a peasant. He unfastened the cord that held his pistol and looped it around the frog's belly. Then, as if he was remembering some kind of fun he used to have when he was a kid, he began twirling the cord around his head. It was pretty long, and the frog's head hit the ground continually. I lay there, shivering, my hair standing on end as the frog whooshed by, close to my face. My God, I still see the wet, muddy skin of that creature. Lying there, those two Saigon soldiers with their weapons ready only a few feet away, I wet my pants. Have you ever been that afraid, Khiem? Khiem, do you know scientific research has shown that if a person sleeps eight hours a day, he or she will dream twenty-five percent of that time? he asks didactically. One twelfth—the equivalent of five years—of the life of a person who lives for sixty years will be spent dreaming. Not including daydreams. Nor fever dreams.

Khiem can feel the wet, slimy skin of the frog on his own face, feel the fear of death.

The herbal doctor meanwhile sits and smokes silently. He is a stout man of fifty, with a square face and a nose so flat it makes him look like a whetstone. From an awareness that exists outside of the dream, Khiem remembers Thoa telling him she was bringing the herbalist home to treat him. He remembers how Moc has a habit of bursting into loud, jarring laughter for no apparent reason.

He does this now. Hahahahahaha.

Then he wipes his mouth and stares at Khiem.

What about you, Mr. Khiem? he says. What was the most memorable event in your time as a fighter against the Americans? The most impressive. Please tell us.

After you, Mr. Moc, Khiem says.

No, please; you first, keep the order. I want to be the last to tell.

The word betrayal for some reason surfaces in Khiem's mind. The betrayal of Jesus at the Last Supper; the Passover Feast of Unleavened Bread. Judas Iscariot, the betrayer of Jesus. He didn't know why that story had always stuck in his mind. He'd first heard it when he was nine years old, from his teacher in a primary school in Son Tay province. After telling the story, the teacher had said, only half-joking: Don't trust those who kiss you.

Once (he tells his strange circle of listeners) three soldiers from my company, Tu, Ngo, and Hi, were sent to reconnoiter an American base near Da Nang. Of the three, Hi was very brave, but Tu and Ngo, both of whom came from Bac Thai, were cowards who had both tried twice before to desert. The two decided that they would take advantage of the mission to defect to the enemy. In order to keep what they were doing secret, they offered Hi a chance to join them. He refused, and having already told him their plans, they'd had no choice but to kill him. The two cowards grabbed Hi and strangled him, then tried to make their escape. But, soon after, a stray artillery shell fell near them, killing Ngo. Tu, terrified that the shell was the curse of destiny, went mad. He crawled back to the unit, tore open his shirt, and cried to me: Please kill me! Since that time he has been confined to a mental hospital.

Another time there was a lieutenant colonel, my superior officer—the deputy commander of the regiment. Dreaming of the life of luxury he'd have if he defected, he gave our attack plans to the enemy. Our advance failed, and our battalion lost half its soldiers. The deputy commander was given a luxury villa by the enemy, as his reward, though he had to crawl around it on his hands and knees—they slashed his Achilles tendons to keep him from running away. Even the enemy refused to trust a man who had already betrayed his country and his comrades-in-arms.

The third time I was betrayed was after I became deputy commander of the battalion. I was slated for promotion to staff rank, was sent to numerous training courses, and was in line to be sent to the Soviet Union for further training. But all of that made my C.O. jealous. He ordered me to lead an attack down a heavily fortified road; then, when we started, deliberately broke radio silence, allowing the enemy to locate our position. Under a rain of shells, we broke through, but the road we opened was covered with the corpses of our comrades-in-arms. Out of the whole battalion, only I and three others survived. I was wounded, and the other three had nervous breakdowns and never regained their sanity. Meanwhile, our commanding officer went on to be promoted to higher rank.

I only kept myself sane by my desire to expose that man some day. His betrayal. I'm sick of betrayers. The act of betrayal is unforgivable. Yes. Anything else can be forgiven. Greed, ego, profit, personality, pride, arrogance, cowardice, laziness, dishonesty, hunger for power, enjoyment of flattery, lust, everything, every lousy thing in life can be forgiven. But not betrayal. Forgive. Yes, yes, let's forgive everything. Doesn't kind-

ness include mercy? How can we live without the moral generosity to forgive human error? But betrayal isn't human. It turns back to front. Judas got his thirty pieces of silver. Traitors get silver, promotions, easy lives. Sometimes even a crown. Judas knew the way to the Garden of Gethsemane in the valley of Kidron where his teacher Jesus Christ was hiding. Betrayers allied themselves with the foreign enemy during the Tran and Le dynasties. Betrayers led the French secret police to their comrades' hiding places during the 1931 uprising. Traitors. The cruelest thugs in the Saigon regime's prisons and reeducation camps in Polo Condor had once been cadres, party members— they were worse than the other guards and officials. Maybe I'm stupid. Maybe I trust people too easily. I always agree with them. Maybe it's easy to cheat me. But isn't it better to be cheated than to live always suspecting your friends? What kind of life is that? Lenin said gullibility in a revolutionary is a sign of love for humanity, didn't he?

The herbal doctor looks at Khiem's innocent, dreamy face and laughs. Your memories about the American war are very impressive and educational. As for me, mine are very shallow.

Are you being modest? Old Tuy asks.

The herbal doctor shakes his head and laughs. Permit me to tell you, he says.

Go right ahead.

If you don't mind...the incident that left the greatest impression on my mind during the American war, my most unforgettable memory...was when I played the role of midwife to a Youth Volunteer girl.

He brayed out an exaggerated and silly laugh, then hiccupped.

The truth is, I was seventeen years old then, and it was the first time I had seen that pretty butterfly-shaped thing. Hahahaha...impressive. Unforgettable! It was on the Paten pass...this young woman had had sex with soldiers passing through, going down the Trail to the South. She'd gotten pregnant and had started to go into labor while she was clearing the road. Her fellow volunteers didn't know what to do. As for my squad, our job was to link up the communication lines. I was the only one with nurse's training, so I chased everyone else away; I was all alone with her. I did whatever I wanted, and she didn't know any better...it was great...

***

"Daddy! Daddy!"

Khiem tried to raise his heated eyebrows and open his dry, cracked lips. He wondered hazily why he was still lying on Thinh Luong beach. Then the haze cleared and he recognized Hong Ha, his daughter, with her short hair and round face, like a copy of his own, bending over him.

"Oh, Ha, my daughter," he managed to croak.

"Your temperature is very high—your skin is so hot. Daddy, you've been unconscious for a long time, but I have to tell you: yesterday, Auntie Nguyen called from Phu Tho and said Grandma is seriously ill."

A faint blue spark of light entered Khiem's dark and tumultuous mind. Then faded. His mother was seriously ill. He tried to sit up.

Something pushes him down. A huge black rock sits on top of him, suffocating him, the same rock that crushed Thinh's three fellow soldiers but left their heads untouched. It is he, Khiem, who has to cut off the three heads. Not Thinh, and not his regimental commander. His regimental commander is trying to use the enemy artillery to kill him. Now again he calls him back and says, I, as Party secretary, assign this duty to you, comrade. He feels sorry for those soldiers. Trembling, he knows he has to cut off their heads. He sees the headless bodies flying. He sees the bodiless heads. Thinh's comrades-in-arms float towards him, their eyes rolling, blinking, as if they want to thank him but at the same time as if questioning: where are our bodies? Oh my friends, your bodies have become stone, and that great and painful time of our lives has been turned into stone also.

The pain, the visions of the tumbling heads, the nightmares tortured him. His body felt as if it were burning up from the inside. He felt his heart beating so hard he thought it would burst out of his chest. He'd never been this sick. During his five years in combat, he'd never once passed out or collapsed. But what he'd been through apparently hadn't forgotten him. Hunger, exhaustion, tension, and trauma had all burrowed inside him somewhere, waiting for the right chance to emerge, erupt, strike him down. He felt as if he were dying now.

Thinh's corpses. Old Tuy's crater, plugged with a mass of rotting, toxic leaves. A terrible thirst. He bends over the crater and sees a woman's eyes staring at him. Not Thoa's. These eyes are limpid and shine with love. Hoan sobs: Khiem, forgive me. He embraces her and shakes her shoulders and pulls her to him. Hoan, there can be no real betrayal in true love, he tells her. Someone screams: Comrades, no one is allowed to sleep in this cave! Khiem releases Hoan quickly, rushes out of the shadows of the mountain and above him is an OV10, the noise of its engine echoing around him like the buzz of a huge fly. He is in North Laos where one range of mountains links continuously to another, and caves are as numerous as crab holes in a rice paddy. But they aren't allowed to sleep in the caves. Sleeping in caves makes you weak and shows cowardice. He is a fighter. He knows that only if one can openly face bombs and bullets and live closely with death, only if one can show courage in the face of betrayal can one be saved and come back to life.

He opened his burning eyes again. Looking around, he dimly recognized the cupboard inlaid with mother-of-pearl facing his bed. In the corner was an elegant antique flower pot. Where had he seen that before, why did it remind him of something now? Yes—a conversation between Thoa and one of her business partners he'd overheard; she hadn't known he was home. They were sitting together on the brand-new sofa, and Thoa had wondered aloud, sarcastically, how her man could afford this beautiful flower pot, a precious antique from Guangzhou.

Hong Ha put a glass of lemon juice on his nightstand. "Daddy, Mom's gone to Hue on business. She told me to put you in a cyclo and take you to the hospital.

Tears sprang to his eyes at their fifteen year old daughter trying to effect a reconciliation between his wife and himself. She was a witness to the tragedy of this family, living for over ten years in the midst of the battle between himself and Thoa. To be fair, it was not totally Thoa's fault, or his own. War and separation had played their parts. But he knew many couples who had been separated for decades yet still remained faithful to each other, even though they had to suppress their natural desires. Desire and instinct were common to all people, but not everyone gave in to them. During the war, husbands and wives were expected to remain true to each other. But he and Thoa were two very different people. Thoa's needs were simple and physical and seemed limitless. Shortly after their marriage, he had become aware that she was having an affair with the manager of the factory canteen. After him came a photographer who drove an MZ 150cc motorcycle, the first motorbike of that size in that mountainous province. A heavy set man, big as a porter, his mouth always sneering, he would roar down the province's narrow roads, stopping by Khiem's at night whenever he saw that Thoa was at home. Thoa would nervously pat her hair and avoid Khiem's eyes. Once she disappeared for a day and a night and came back with two big carp, telling Khiem she'd gone to Coc San lake because the fish were so cheap there. When Khiem said nothing, she took the fish straight to the kitchen, cleaned them, and put them in a pot on the stove.

Then, exhausted, she slept from early morning to late afternoon and the fish burned to a crisp. Finally, there was a day
when the police came to inform Khiem that they had caught
Thoa and the photographer in the act under the Coc Ly
bridge. They would only release her if he agreed. The war
came, Khiem enlisted, and Thoa went wild. She was shameless about her affairs during the five years he was away. She
had to have three abortions. Khiem couldn't pretend he
didn't know, nor could he pretend to forgive her. In bed,
pictures of the other men she'd been with tormented his
mind. Neither could satisfy the other any more; as a result,
Thoa became angrier and more frustrated. She needed, she
often said, a healthy man, a money-making man.

Khiem had moved his family to the city, hoping the
change of environment would change Thoa's behavior. It was
a mistake. The city's atmosphere stimulated her appetite for
things and for amusement. Once more, she had to ask him
to sign a permission form so she could have an abortion.
They hadn't slept together for ages.

Thoa didn't need him anymore. Their marriage had
gone wrong at the moment they chose each other. It was that
simple. That was the root of the tragedy. He wondered if his
daughter could ever acknowledge it.

"Hong Ha," he whispered. "My daughter." Her hand was
lightly caressing his forehead. He covered it with his own
hand. Her skin was cool and was trembling like a new leaf.
Hong Ha bent over him, trying to hold back her sobs.

"Dad, let's go to the hospital."

***

The hospital. No, he won't go to the hospital. Not again.
An image surfaced in his mind that epitomized the place to
him: the tattered medical records piled high in the reception
area. When he had been there two weeks ago, he'd asked

himself: "Have I become one of these poor victims now?"
The benches along the wall were lined with gloomy, emac-
iated, fading people. Others had nowhere to sit and their
relatives held them up as they leaned against the wall. He
was overwhelmed by their misery. It was delusional, utopian,
to think of helping anyone. There were too many people for
his pity to encompass. Khiem had waited from early
morning until noon before his name was called. Having
finally reached the examining room, he'd allowed himself to
relax, not knowing he was stepping into a worse situation. A
doctor with a mustache was chatting with a curly-haired
woman who was resting her huge breasts on his desk, her big
bottom pointed towards Khiem. "Damn their ancestors," she
said sulkily, "that woman held the doctor's dick for him when
he pissed, so he signed off on her request to go to Angola
with him as a specialist—I know that's the way it happened.
Hell, I'd press my thing on him too, if he'd let me—I don't
care: I want to go abroad."

The man with the mustache chuckled. "You can press
whatever you want into him, it wouldn't matter. He doesn't
want you, dear. Be content to stay here and help pick up the
pieces from all the love-affair casualties we're getting; you'll
make more money."

What did it mean? How could this woman be a specialist
in Angola? Who was this man—a doctor or a gangster? From
somewhere a voice screamed: "This hospital is a market, and
the doctors are peddling death, oh, my fellow countrymen!"
Khiem had covered his face with both hands. What had
happened? Everything was strange. Everywhere that had
been sacred, everything he'd fought for, was being twisted
and betrayed for profit. Traitors were everywhere.

"You, over there, come on!" the mustached man called
to him, taking a break from the stream of filthy words he'd
been pouring into the woman's ear. He picked up Khiem's
medical records. "What's your name?" Khiem watched him

glance down at the sheet. So much for literary fame, Khiem thought. The man lifted his eyes off the sheet, continued to look blankly at Khiem's face. "You have chest pains?" the man asked. Without waiting for a reply, without touching the stethoscope he wore to Khiem's chest or making any other pretense at examination, he wrote down a prescription for some dozen vitamin B1, vitamin C, and sleeping tablets, none of them with any possible connection to his illness. "Do you do morning exercises?" the guy asked. "You should do them regularly." What great advice, Khiem thought bitterly. He stared at him, wanting to say something, call him a betraying son of a bitch, another betraying son of a bitch. But he was sweating all over and too weak even to open his mouth. He had gotten himself out of the room, leaning against the wall every few minutes.

That had been two weeks ago. There was no way he would go back, have to see that mustached face again. Even though his sickness was torturing him now.

Over the next days, the fever struck him hardest in the late afternoon, and the ache in his chest grew deeper, harder. Now and then he would slip again into delirium. Now his own body betrayed him as well. And he needed his health more than ever now. For revenge. To prove he'd been right. For his self-confidence. His sickness had become the ally of those who wanted to knock him down, rub him into a zero.

One afternoon, slipping in and out of delirium, he heard the noise of a crowd of people entering the house. Then the shriek of Thoa's voice. "Look at him, lying there, defeated by a woman he looked at as if she was an envelope with money inside."

"You're right," someone else laughed.

"All fucking men are alike. They chase after strange women and avoid the one they know. When they see that thing, all their willpower drains away. It's the same from the big shot to the cyclo driver."

Khiem heard their approving laughter roaring all around him. Echoing strangely in his ears. Then after a time, silence. They were gone. Suddenly Khiem felt the heat of his wife's body bearing down on him.

"Still sick, eh? Well, going out with them helps me forget this sad house. Come on, let me have a look."

She pressed into him. He smelled the familiar odor of her armpits, felt the heat of her body, her coconut round breasts squashing against him. Her appearance, every act, dripped with vulgarity. A counter-image of Hoan's natural serenity came to him.

"What's wrong with you?" his wife said. "Too much rolling around on the beach and in the bushes with that whore, is that it?"

She was wearing a short skirt with nothing underneath. She squatted on the bed above Khiem, tormenting him. If he were a truck driver instead of a pansy writer, she whispered into his ear, he'd push her down and come into her and they'd scream when they came and shake the bed. Then she could tell him they were even, they'd both betrayed each other, and she would have never....Sex would reconcile them, right? That's what couples did.

Khiem felt nothing. Even when she rubbed him, nothing happened. There was a vague rise of desire, but it quickly faded. He lay there, Thoa mashing her huge breasts against his mouth. Khiem closed his eyes and shook his head. "You're like a dying chicken," she said, and pushed him back on the bed. She raised her voice: "Hong Ha, go find Mr. Moc and bring him here. Your father felt sorry for his girlfriend and it made him sick. Now he's dying alone because no one cares for him. Who would bother to come visit a fired boss?"

Khiem felt he would like to be a headless corpse.

***

These were the unhappiest days of his life. It was hard enough to be sick, but he was also to be the object of Thoa's curses, her torments, her cruel mockery. He was too weak to move, to do anything.

Moc made it worse. The so-called herbal doctor who considered a naked woman to be his most impressive memory of the war, a story so foul it had even crept into and contaminated Khiem's dreams. He was a gangster disguised as a healer. A wide man, but short, shorter than Thoa, flat-faced. His mouth resembled Pho's, but it was larger and harder to look at. To Khiem, his body looked like a block of flesh. A rank, intrusive reek of sex exuded from it. Moc's every gesture and attitude and word towards Thoa were freighted with sexual references, even in front of Khiem and Hong Ha. "Bring me that lighter, will you, Thoa? How come you look so tired—what were you doing last night, eh?" he asked, leering and winking.

Khiem knew the habit of herbal doctors to make huge claims for their cures: after three days of my medicine, your father will walk normally again, and so on. But he'd never heard boasting as shameless as Moc's. The man's tongue wiggled in his mouth, flexible as a snake. His ancestor, a thousand years before, had cured an Indian Prince's sterility. Moc was the best herbalist in the military, but had asked to be discharged after a dispute with a general because he wouldn't compromise. He had studied in many different schools of traditional medicine. He knew many theories. He'd even had the Central Health Protection Service come to him and ask him to take care of certain members of the Politburo. Mr. This and Madame That, and Minister the Other had all been cured by him. He'd been invited to go to Macao, to Taiwan, but he'd refused, he only wanted to stay and help people as he could. Even when the ambassador of a rich Scandinavian country had tried to give him a diamond, he'd refused, asking only for two rhinoceros horns instead, so he could cure people of their problems. Using acupuncture, he'd even melted the fat from the belly of a Swedish man.

Apparently there was nothing he couldn't cure. And nobody to contradict his boasts.

While Thoa was making juice for him, he came and sat near Khiem's bed.

"Your destiny is twisted. Where your nature should be male, it's female. You look for one, but you get two. You come from a sacred source of a family. But you have ruined your career because of pride. Your disease appeared in your nose. Once, when a patient was brought to my house, I saw he had a big, yellowish nose, and I said to his family: lucky you brought him to me; otherwise, he'd have been dead in ten days. You're the same way; you're lucky I'm here. You must thank Heaven—if I weren't here, your soul would soon have flown from your body."

Thoa handed Moc the lemon juice. He put his arm around her waist and drew her to him. Thoa accepted his embrace as if the action were natural. She only pushed him away when he leaned over and whispered something into her ear. "Enough. That's the only thing you're good at."

Khiem was being tortured. The two of them didn't care what they did in front of him. They continued to touch and caress each other, to rub against each other. He turned his head away, but Moc's voice kept on, continuing to brag about his medical knowledge and talent. Khiem's disease, he affirmed, came from his circulatory system. Twenty years ago, he was sure, Khiem had almost died from a cold, right? Yes, yes, Khiem said, hoping the answer would stop Moc from talking more. It didn't. "At that time," Moc grinned, "I bet you felt something like a grinding in your head, right? Our traditional medicine calls that rheumatism. Its symptoms are the same as when you have an allergic reaction from eating seafood. It starts when your two birds' eggs get swollen—birds' eggs, hahaha, know what I mean?" He winked again, kept talking. "So besides acupuncture, acupressure, and applying cupping glasses, I'd give you two other kinds of medicine: you take one on one day for your disease, the other on the next day as a tonic. After a month, believe me, you'll be so vigorous your wife will be screaming: please, please, enough, yes, hahahaha!"

How vile the man was. Khiem was so weak he couldn't speak or move a finger. He struggled to open his eyes and look at this fool of a so-called doctor with his so-called medication, wondering if this game would continue until he was dead.

Moc kept the medical instruments he claimed were for a hundred kinds of diseases in an American claymore mine casing, very old, with several holes rusted through the sides, caked with hardened crud. He drew out something that looked like a drumstick, some eight inches long, then six cupping glasses, a small bottle of alcohol, and six iron acupuncture needles. The last object he took out was a bottle filled with black pills, each as big as a fingertip.

Without another word, Moc jumped up and squatted on Khiem's bed, planting his thick dirty feet on each side of Khiem. He placed his hand on Khiem's rib-cage and rolled him over like a log. Khiem, face down in the pillow, felt his shirt being yanked up over his head, two big knees pressing in on both sides of his body. Was he this man's enemy, held down to be tortured? Moc began striking his body with his fists. Each blow was more painful than the last, until finally he began pinching the flesh and pulling up the folds of skin until Khiem couldn't bear it any longer and cried out.

"Lie still!" Moc yelled. He pushed Khiem down and placed the six cupping glasses along his spine. Khiem felt the air being gradually drawn out. It was as if the very roots of his hair there were swelling. His skin felt as if it were on fire, as if six nails were pinning his body to the bed.

"Now don't move," Moc admonished him. He jumped off the bed, rubbed his hands together and walked to the living room, where Thoa was waiting for him with tea, cake, and fruit.

***

When they think of Western medicine, people often think of surgery or tremendous dosages of drugs with strange or terrible side effects...once you put yourself in a Western doctor's hands, they believe, that is what you will have to suffer. Eastern practices, on the contrary, are seen as involving only natural and gentle homeopathic herbs and sweet massages. It was a lie, Khiem thought. He lay helpless in his bed for three days. When Hong Ha lifted his shirt, she'd cried out, "Daddy, why have the spots turned purple?" After the three days, he was further tortured when Moc pressed the drumstick-shaped sticks into his flesh again. The short, stout man pushed with all his strength. Khiem, horrified and helpless, was afraid he would puncture his skin, leave six holes.

He raged inside at Moc. "I'll remember this and your ill-bred face, Moc, you foul bastard," he cursed the man. But he was still glued with weakness to his bed, falling in and out of sleep. As he lay helpless, as if pinned down by the acupuncture needles, Thoa and Moc's voices echoed in his head. They no longer cared what they said in front of him. "This tea is so strong it'll help you do it all night, huh?" "Sure. That husband of yours is like a dying tiger—didn't it bother you to sleep alone?" "Not a bit—I stopped feeling any desire years ago." "You liar. You're just like my wife—if I don't make it with her at least twice a week, she gets mad at me."

He heard them whisper something. Feed each other

fruit. Kissing, the furniture moving, glasses falling to the floor. The woman moaned. The man said nothing. The sound of his slippers shuffling across the floor. They were in the corner. The man whispered something again. "Not now," the woman said. "Then tonight, in my house—my old lady is away in Quang Ninh province. No, you're too fucking beautiful, Thoa; I can't bear to wait." Noises. "Hey, don't be quick as a frog—you won't last more than thirty seconds." The woman's voice rising in a scream of passion. Cut off when the door bell rang.

Thoa pushed Moc away. "Are you back from school already, Hong Ha? Wait a minute."

***

He had always revered doctors. He'd seen death and knew nothing was more precious than life. Nirvana and paradise were consoling illusions. Death ended everything, and man on earth could only create property. But property could never create man. Only doctors could preserve him. Watching Moc's shamelessness, he felt sickened. All the man cared about was what he could get, including the use of Thoa's body. Each day, forced to look at Moc's face, Khiem felt himself declining, sinking into a bottomless well of sadness and exhaustion. But when he looked at Hong Ha, tears welled in his eyes, and he tried to gather his strength. He still had too many things to do in this life. He had to survive. He only wished he could finish what he needed to do and die quickly.

***

After a month of Moc's treatment, Khiem looked like a skeleton. Sometimes he couldn't tell if he were still breathing. If Hong Ha didn't move him, his skin would be rotten with bed sores. He hurt all over. He was still burning with fever. He couldn't sleep, couldn't eat, only swallow a few spoons of rice water. He lay and counted the days, too exhausted to do anything. Moc and Thoa kept having each other a few feet away from him. Moc kept giving him useless medicine he couldn't refuse. One day, he said to Khiem: "I think there's a woman buried under your floor, and that person's ghost keeps hanging around you so you can't be cured."

Khiem was in a labyrinth. Half the time unconscious and delirious. One day he opened his eyes and saw a stranger, another stout man, touching him and exclaiming: "You have an acute sore throat and a weakened lung. And something is wrong with your stomach. And your kidney doesn't work." With every part or organ he named, he pressed an ointment on Khiem's body. It felt hot and sticky as asphalt. When he was finished, he ate a bowl of soup Hong Ha brought him, took twenty thousand dong, and declared that Khiem would be cured in a week. Then he disappeared.

Moc came back after a week, boasting that he'd had to fly to Saigon to cure a big shot who'd had a stroke. The man's mouth had twisted and he couldn't sleep for two months, and he had to go to the United States for a conference. Thirty minutes after Moc arrived, he assured Khiem, that man was completely back to normal. He'd offered Moc one of his villas, in gratitude, but Moc had refused.

He decided he would use only acupuncture on Khiem. Again, he told Khiem to lie absolutely motionless. Again Khiem fell into his half-sleep. Again he heard Moc and Thoa describing filthy acts to each other, asking each other about the other men and women they'd had, making their noises, crying out in their orgasms. Sometimes Khiem came fully awake and heard it all, the sounds and words and cries filling the air in his room. They had between them a private and filthy language that Khiem came to know. If he described what they said in a novel, would readers think he was exaggerating? Would they say that such things really didn't happen in life? That people weren't like that? But they were truly like animals, these two, and even sometimes pretended to be animals during sex, and would scream filth at each other, as if it increased their pleasure.

Once, he heard Moc say: "I haven't enjoyed doing it like this since the first time, when I was in the army, at Paten pass."

Once, he heard Thoa say: "Be careful. I've already had to get Khiem's signature several times for permission to get an abortion."

Hearing his name coming from her mouth, Khiem shivered. He felt as if all the points on his body pierced by the acupuncture needles were bleeding.

***

"Who is it? Who is in the mirror?" Dr. Thinh's voice insisted.

Inside the rusty frame of the mirror was the face of a man with salt and pepper hair, two weary eyes under drooping lids, dry, cracked lips which hardly covered yellowish teeth and the exposed white tip of a tongue, hollowed cheeks. Only the high-bridged nose he'd once liked to think of as intellectual-looking was still recognizable to Khiem. He couldn't imagine himself so eroded. He no longer looked like the man he liked to think of as himself, the man Hoan had described as handsome, not in a superficial way, but because he looked as if he were in harmony with his spirit. She had said that when they were at Thinh Luong beach. A pity he hadn't taken that photo together with her then.

That sudden memory of the beach made his eyes sparkle. Seeing this, Thinh took the mirror from Khiem's hands and placed it back on the wall. When he turned around, his face was angry, his fists clenched.

"Now I can truly acknowledge that stupidity can be found everywhere. How could you trust your so-called wife and her so-called doctor lover? No one can understand you."

Thinh, his closest friend. The failed poet, the brave soldier who had witnessed so much horrible death during the war. A self-confident, honest, healthy man. Tall, with broad shoulders and a broad face, Thinh had always looked to him like the embodiment of the elegant intellectual. They'd met when he was a headmaster in the mountains, and Thinh had directed the small hospital nearby. "I'm the director, but I'm not a Party member," was the first thing he'd said to Khiem. "I'm the son of a former bourgeois, and I finished the Albert Saraut Lycée, and I don't like to pretend to be anything I'm not." Later, when the population of the province had grown, Thinh was demoted to section head, and then just to staff physician. He'd laughed as usual when they met afterwards; he didn't care. Every time Khiem had gone to the hospital, Thinh would give him prescriptions for extra vitamin B and C, plus an order for three *hao* over ten days. During the sixties, that meant you were given a kilogram of pork for your family. A bond of mutual understanding and compassion grew between the two men, though Thinh was never a flatterer. The most praise he would give when he'd read one of Khiem's short stories was, "It's so-so. Readable." Khiem would get angry. "You pronounce that like you're a great critic. Why don't you try to write yourself?" Thinh would just laugh at him. "Remember, I learned French at the same time I learned Vietnamese— I've read Sartre and Camus in their original language." But when he read *The Haven*, he said, "To tell you the truth, now you've reached the Palace of Literature."

How lucky they'd both been to have survived the war, to continue to be in each other's lives. Thinh was the reader

Khiem always tried to keep in his mind when he wrote, the invisible presence that demanded, would only accept his best craft.

***

"I was going for a walk," Thinh explained. "I've just completed my training course in Portuguese, finished up the paperwork I need for my work in Angola. It all took a long time—there was a lot of competition, everybody trying to push everybody else out, right until the last minute. I was the final choice, not because I'm the most talented, but because I knew the difference between a villa and a village. Anyway, when I was finished, I came to the office to look for you—I wanted to invite you out so we could try that new dish everybody in Hanoi is talking about, the barbecued chicken feet from Guangzhou. Then I found out you'd been dismissed and had gotten ill. Why didn't you call me? What kind of friend are you?"

He examined Khiem and took his blood pressure.

"Too high," he clucked. "Anyway, when I walked upstairs to your office, I called out your name, the way I always do. Usually, Tiny Hoi or your precious brother Lieu would poke their heads out at that point and demand to know who was uttering their boss's great name. Instead, there was only silence. I felt something was strange. Then when I looked into your office, I saw something like a guinea pig sitting there. On closer examination, it turned out to be Tiny Hoi, stuffed into a white blouse, her breasts and her nose tilted up proudly to the sky. She didn't utter a word to me. Seems she'd just completed a ten-day secretarial training course and is now the Squint-Eyed Toad's private secretary."

Looking at Thinh, Khiem felt the blood stirring in his veins, a surge of vitality running through him. Maybe Moc's female ghost had been chased away by his friend's presence. Thinh truly was a tonic for him. He'd been alone and friendless so long, and he realized now how much that had weakened him. He watched Thinh out of the corner of his eye, smiling at the sight of his friend waving his arms, talking vehemently.

As Thinh had been about to leave, three of the women— Ms. Tam, Ms. Chuong, and Ms. Tuyen— had drawn him into their office and told him what had happened. That stupid animal Pho had been supported by all the opportunists in the division, and so his immoral actions had been successful. Now all of the rest of them were scrambling around trying to prove they'd been correct to denounce Khiem. The division had been given computers, a new telephone system, new furniture, everything to make it seem Khiem's dismissal was a good thing, all of them chorusing their praise of Quanh, giving him credit for reforming and renovating operations. But the only thing truly re-formed was the new board, and how could they renovate their own ignorance? All they could do was just keep repeating that Khiem was undisciplined and paternal. Khoai had been promoted to chairman of the office trade union, and Phu had become Party secretary. The Squint-Eyed Toad, as acting director, held meetings at least two or three times a week, and had started publishing his own poetry in the house newspaper. It stunk up the pages, the women said, just a combination of nonsensical words. But the one who had surprised them the most was Lieu. Ms. Hoan was right to name him the Flatterer. He was a little better than the others, seemed a little ashamed, didn't quite hold the pot for Quanh to pee into like the others. He often told them that he still respected Khiem, but since his "big brother" was so tough with Mr. Pho, his "two brothers" had to be separated from each other. Now Mr. Pho was in power, and he got his salary from Pho, so he had no choice but to obey him. He acknowledged that Pho, Duc, and Hien had limited intelligence, that compared to his "big brother" they were like slow-moving carts while Khiem was a race horse, and that's what made them angry, made them take their revenge on him. What an excuse! Meanwhile, the position of deputy director was still open and was like a piece of fat sitting in front of three cats: Khoai, Lieu, and Phu.

Pulling his chair closer to Khiem's bed, Thinh raised his voice. "Khiem, the tragicomedy continues. In life, baseness is normal and unlimited. You should have taken more care in reading their appearances and in being aware of their family backgrounds. This world is a pyramid. Truly noble people are rare, the peak, but shameless, greedy hypocrites, ready to turn white into black and to stab anyone in the back for gain, are everywhere. The French artist Alain DeLong said, "Only the base are happy." But Khiem, consider, if not for those people, where would you find characters for your novels? Wasn't I right when I told you literature is like a kitchen garden—even a district ideologist can jump into it. No, I'm just joking. In reality, I believe writers can be happier than most people, since you get the chance to bring out the truth finally. Get well, Khiem, so you can toss the stone from your hand."

He laughed, trying to cheer his friend up. "Don't be sad, Khiem. Just enjoy yourself analyzing those characters playing out their roles in your office, like you told me you did. You won't be upset any more. They throw their gratitude off their shoulders like a burden instead of keeping it in their minds. You were too good to them. You should take this illness as a valuable chance to reassess your life. It may help you reach a turning point in your talent. And remember, you still have many people who love you and need you. First of all, there's your daughter; she's the one who worries about you the most. She knows her mother's characteristics too well—she told me how she urged you not to take the medicines her mother and that guy gave you. As for your wife—well, surely that's over. But there's also your wonderful sister, Nguyen— when I think about her, Khiem, I'm sorry I missed the opportunity to be your brother-in-law. And your fellow writers: many of them have been telephoning your office, the women told me, and they've petitioned the government about Pho having your book banned. I take back everything I ever said about writers!"

Thinh rose, flung open the window and cried, "Look, Khiem, autumn in Hanoi is beautiful! I'll stay until it ends, and then I'm off to Angola. Right now, I'm going to telephone for a cyclo and get you to the hospital. I have a good friend there; he'll take care of you, get you better. Cheer up! 'Love whatever you won't see again in your life!' Who was it said that? Alfred de Vigny? This time, Khiem, you're not going to toss a stone from your hand, but push away a boulder!"

* * *

There remained two things that Thinh didn't tell Khiem. His mother had passed away in Phu Tho. An urgent telegram had been sent by his relatives, but Tiny Hoi had put it aside for half a month now. And Hoan had disappeared as well. Ms. Tam, Ms. Chuong, and Ms. Tuyen had all looked for her. They told Thinh: "After Thoa slashed her face, she didn't come back to the office. We went to her neighbor, Mr. Vang, but he didn't know where she was either. He said he hadn't seen her for a month."

Chapter Seven

AGAINST THE FLOOD

"It's strange—you never had high blood pressure before. You're reading 160 over 90. 90 is nothing to worry about, but 160 is rather high."

Thinh knit his brows. It was the third time he'd examined Khiem, and the result was the same. Also, Khiem was still having chest pains. Thinh feared there was some problem with his heart or lungs, but his ancient stethoscope didn't pick up anything very irregular. The heartbeat was regular and strong, perhaps just a little fast. "I have a good ear," Thinh told Khiem, "as good as an X-ray. But I don't understand why you have that pain, and the low-grade fever." Khiem didn't know what to say. Had his rheumatism returned? "Is your throat sore also?" Thinh asked. No, it wasn't. "OK, once again. Take a deep breath. Cough again."

The results still weren't clear.

Thinh took a deep breath. "I think it's time we went to a cardiac specialist."

The cardiologist looked old for his fifty years: his hair had gone white and half his teeth were false, like those of many people born and raised in the limestone-rich areas of the country. He seemed very patient and perceptive.

"When you walk upstairs, how many times do you stop to rest?"

"Usually, I go straight up without stopping. During the summer, when we had a drought, I sometimes carried up two full buckets, about twenty kilos each, from the first floor to the fourth, where our flat is."

The doctor frowned. He could see nothing wrong with Khiem's heart during his external examination. He sent him for a cardiogram, and to make sure, had it repeated. Both doctors, looking at the results, diagnosed a slight thickening of the left ventricle. But there was also the possibility that they were seeing some damage caused by long-term hypertension. They sent Khiem to be X-rayed, and then to get an ultrasound test.

Khiem was disturbed at this evidence that his body had reached a turning point. But he also felt he was moving back out of the embrace of those who had betrayed him and into the arms of friends.

The doctor gave him a series of exercises to do, and after a week he started to feel better. "You're in your early fifties," Thinh said. "Everybody is the same at that age. Don't worry —you'll live to be 84 and throw out ten more novels and a dozen short story collections and win a National Award. As Tolstoy said: 'Only write, write, and you'll discover all human beings are the same.' As for me, I'm going to die in Africa at 53, far away from home, having achieved nothing." Thinh laughed loudly and recited in a childish voice:

> The two sisters Trung were born in Africa
> Now doctors and professors are searching for their traces
> And asking how they can earn some dollars
> To bring back home to save their country
> and by the way, their families and themselves

He would work for two years as a medical expert in Angola, to earn some foreign currency. He had two old parents, always ill, he said apologetically to Khiem. And a wife who taught kindergarten and two children he had to take care of.

***

Khiem felt renewed. The hospital Thinh had brought him to was located on the outskirts of the city. It was autumn now, and every morning he watched the dew evaporating into a white mist above the marshy land. The fragrance of newly tilled earth, mixed with the sharp smell of rotting leaves, drifted to him. A lonely egret walked on the straw covering the rice fields, wild flowers blossomed along the pathways, and the thatched houses of the peasants were reflected in the fishponds. In the afternoon, he watched geese flying across the sky, leaving behind them a deep sense of serenity in his heart.

But autumn doesn't last long in Vietnam. Soon the rains started. Watching them fall, he let his mind retreat to the sunshine of Thinh Luong. He had found out what had happened to Hoan, but had no idea how to find her and until now had been too weak to look. He'd only just become healthy enough now, in Thinh's view, to receive the news of his mother's death. When he did, he wept in the rain, with the rain, his mind returning to the midlands, where he had been born and raised. When Thinh told him he had to go into town to get his airline tickets for Angola, Khiem decided to leave the hospital.

They walked into the city together. The Red River had flooded over the entire cultivated area, and its water lapped against the base of the dike under their feet. Once he had sat on this dike with Hoan, watching the children play with boomerangs as they kept an eye on the cattle. Hoan had wondered how that game had become so popular so fast in Vietnam.

In town the streets surrounding the main railroad

station were flooded as well. The loudspeaker announced that the train to Phu Tho would only go as far as Viet Tri; the tracks had been washed out. Thinh gave Khiem all the money he had in his pockets, enough for Khiem to get a ticket and live for a few days. He was penniless now.

"When shall we meet again?" Thinh asked, embracing Khiem. Khiem shivered at the words, feeling a sense of premonition so strong he couldn't speak. Thinh boarded the bus back. With an hour before the train left, Khiem walked alone down Cao Ba Quat Street until he realized with a shock that his feet were carrying him to his office, where he no longer belonged, where Hoan's image remained clear in his mind.

He turned and walked quickly back to the station. In the waiting room, he bought a few sheets of paper and wrote a long letter to Hong Ha, telling her he had to go back to his native province to pay his respects to her grandmother. In his mind now, tightened to his heart, were the images of three people: his mother, his daughter, and Hoan.

***

The train came to a halt before the Viet Tri bridge, at the confluence of the three big rivers, all of which had over-flowed their banks. The bridge was washed out and the rice fields were completely inundated.

Most of the other passengers bought tickets back to Hanoi. Khiem and about a dozen others decided to hire a sampan to cross the river. They splashed through ankle deep water for a few kilometers until they came to the road, built on a berm that stood out of the water and was overgrown with wild grass At about three in the afternoon, they spotted a boat moving upstream and bargained with the owner. Finally they agreed on ten thousand dong apiece, a reasonable price.

The boat was made of cement. It was two meters wide and twenty in length, propelled by poles, oars, and a sail, as needed. Such craft, made in a factory in Nam Ha province, once were famous. The cement made the boats look heavy, but created a sense of stability for the passengers. The one Khiem boarded now belonged to the Meteorological Service, and measuring equipment was clustered in one place on deck, so there was plenty of room.

It was almost dark when they boarded. There were five people in the crew: the captain, a man with betel-leaf-stained teeth; and four younger, muscular men, just finishing up their supper. Near the stern, a few passengers were sitting under a battery-run, six-volt light bulb, playing cards and chatting. Khiem and the four newcomers from the train found places for themselves on the other side. They were exhausted and soon fell asleep, their snoring echoing against the inner hull of the boat.

The crew cast off, two of the sailors with coils of rope jumping onto the bank, while the other two stood across from each other in the bow and pushed iron-tipped poles into the river bed. Then they walked slowly to the stern, the men on the bank bent nearly double, their ropes taut, all four pushing and pulling in harmony, until the boat slowly got underway. For a time it moved through the darkness of dusk and then a full moon rose behind the silhouettes of trees along the spines of the hills. The moonlight made everything it bathed seem enlarged. The river seemed strangely limitless, its surface seething with waves. The banks disappeared and a dewy mist surrounded them. The captain proceeded cautiously through the floating debris, sometimes halting near the bank when the waves grew too rough.

Listening to the water smacking against the bow and the sides of the boat, the footsteps of the crew running back and forth on the deck, Khiem felt he was falling back into his delirious dreams. It frightened him. All the memories he'd thought put to rest were returning to him, vividly.

Nothing disappeared. His father still existed. Khiem could see him: a real man, a father who loved his children. When Khiem was nine and he and his mother were evacuated to her native province to escape from the French at Son Tay, his father had gone with them, up this same river. He had been born in Hanoi, but Son Tay was where he had met Khiem's mother and the revolution.

On the particular morning that came back to him now, he and his father were resting and eating sticky rice in a small hut on the bank of the river. Suddenly a loud explosion shook the earth and they saw a span of the Viet Tri bridge fall into the river, sending up a plume of water mixed with smoke and dirt. The resistance was destroying fortifications and strategic points all over the country, sacrificing everything in the fight for national independence. That falling bridge left a glowing, glorious warmth in Khiem's young heart. Nearby had been a boat being pushed and pulled at the same time, moving upstream against a flood, as the boat he was in now was also, still, doing. The motion of the boat, the labor of pushing and pulling were still the same. The bass notes of the pole hitting rocks on the bottom. The footsteps moving back and forth. The sounds of a hardworking, brave life. And the patience of the lonely boat struggling against the fierce current, pushing ahead upstream, overcoming the waves that were trying to sink it.

His father had been chief comptroller of the province. He had always tried to be fair and honest, certain that was the way to live. But he couldn't win against corruption. He died one night while checking the dike in a storm, investigating the selling of substandard material by some of the province's big shots. The cause of his death was a mystery: his body was found in the opening of a sewage culvert at the mouth of the river. Khiem had been thirteen and his sister Nguyen four. With their mother, schoolteacher Hue, they rushed to the place. His father's body had been covered with a mat, only his two feet sticking out. For the rest of his life, Khiem remembered those ten battered, broken toes, the second on each foot elongated—a genetic trait in his clan. The province's bosses made sure there was no memorial service for his father, without giving a reason, though there were many rumors. It wasn't until he had graduated from teachers' college that Khiem understood. The war, the string of betrayals he had witnessed in his life, had brought him a deep empathy with his father. An eagle flew against the wind, a tiger ran alone, a whale forged against the current. Real men did what was right, and did it in loneliness. The great writers—Nguyen Du, Nguyen Trai, Cao Ba Quat—were all lonely people. His father had been all alone also, in the last minutes of his life.

***

Khiem's fellow passengers were a mixed group, and the long journey and close quarters created a kind of festive atmosphere.

Near the bow, the card players, both male and female, chattered noisily like black martins in a banyan tree. They criticized each other's moves, all the while gossiping about a trial going on in the district. The provincial court was right, some said. No, the judge was wrong, a man said, if the woman had taken off her clothes, how could the man be convicted of rape? The women yelled at him in protest, laughing. Then the battery powering the light bulb failed and the light flickered out.

"OK, let's put the cards away and tell some stories to keep from sleeping." a man with a thick country accent said. The women stirred and one called, "You go first, Mr. Diep. You're a poet—you used to be the district cultural cadre. Tell us some stories."

Mr. Diep was the man who had suggested stories in the first place, but now seemed reluctant. He clucked his tongue against the roof of his mouth. "Oh, I have many stories. But there may be some here more talented, so I have to ask them to speak first."

"Don't be so modest."

"Me? I'm not modest. Nor am I a poet or a cultural cadre. I just know a few funny old folk poems. Enough. I'll start by giving you a riddle, OK?"

"Sure, go ahead."

"Here it is: 'It is covered by grass. If you want to reach it, you have to kneel on one knee. When you put it in, it moves around. When you take it out, you yell, 'Damn it!'"

"Hey—that's dirty!"

"You're making fun of us!"

Mr. Diep waved his hands, as if chasing away the voices yelling at him from all sides of the boat. He smiled and shook his head. "No, it's not dirty at all, and I'm not making fun of you. Listen!"

"It is dirty!"

"Listen! The grass covers it, means the entrance to the crab hole in the rice field. When you catch the crab, you have to kneel down on one knee. When you put your hand in, you have to move it around. And when the crab pinches you, don't you yell 'damn it!'? Or do you say, 'Thank you, crab'?"

He laughed uproariously. The other passengers were all awake now, smiling and asking him to tell them more stories.

"Tell the one about the provincial beauty contest, Mr. Diep!"

"No, the one about putting in the IUD is better."

"Mr. Diep, I haven't heard the 'Let the Bird Drink Water' one yet."

Mr. Diep shook his head. He never made up stories, he

said, smiling, they were all true. His voice booming like a loudspeaker, his tone half-joking, half-sweet, he continued:

"One time when I was in charge of the ambulance service, I was in a story-telling competition. In short, I told this story: once during the season of floods, my sister came in from one of the outer hamlets, crying and pounding on my door. 'Oh, brother,' she said, 'how can I go on living? The flood has washed away everything I owned. Oh, poor me, my brother.' I was very worried about her, but I gave her some tea and tried to calm her down. 'What about the clock with the pendulum you had to give a whole water buffalo to buy last year? Did the water get that?' I asked. She rolled her eyes for a while, then clapped her hands. 'Oh, no, I asked Mr. Le to keep that for me.' 'Well, what about the new sofa?' 'No,' she said, 'I tied that to the roof.' 'And the cupboard?' I continued. She told me she had had enough time to put it on a pile of bricks, so it hadn't gotten wet. On and on it went like that. The last question I asked was about her chickens. She said cheerfully that they were very wise and had jumped up into the jackfruit tree and saved themselves. 'So you lost nothing,' I concluded. She looked stunned for a moment, and then agreed. 'Yes, you're right! Why did I think I lost everything?'"

The people laughed. "How funny," someone said.

"Yes, it was. But the funniest part is what happened after the contest. A cultural and ideological cadre had come to it, and afterwards he called me in for an inquiry. 'What was your intention in telling that story?' he asked me. I answered: 'My intention was to cheer people up. My job is to bring joy to people, or would you rather I bring sadness instead, and sell it to the stupid?' Hi, hi, hi...he got very angry with me. You know the one...he used to sell dogmeat in the district market. Then he pointed his finger at my face and yelled, 'You'd better take care! The chain on my dog is only a meter and a half long. Stay away from it!'"

"How did you answer him?"

"Let him have a sip of water first, come on!"

"Don't rush me," Mr. Diep said. "We still have a long night ahead of us. What did I answer? Yes, I told him: 'Dear Sir, I would like to stand inside the reach of that chain.'"

"Interesting!"

Khiem listened to Mr. Diep tell one story after another, from an endless store of jokes and anecdotes. He might very well have heard or read the anecdotes somewhere, Khiem suspected. But the way he told them made them come alive. In between, he improvised poems on the spot.

"Hey, tell us the one about the guy who was wrongly accused," a female voice interrupted him. Mr. Diep slapped his thigh. "That man was my neighbor, you know. He was a kindly man. But his assistant was jealous of him and kept trying—and failing—to get rid of him. One night, during the full moon, his wife invited my neighbor to come to their house. He agreed, but when he arrived, he saw that the husband was not there, and the door to their bedroom was wide open. He began to get suspicious. Then the woman told him: 'You know how unfortunate I am, since my husband and I have never been able to have a child. When both of us look at your family, with your beautiful sons, we really want to have a child of our own. So my husband told me to ask you here so you can give us one. It would make us both very happy.' My neighbor said, 'Do you mean you want me to give you one of our sons for adoption?' 'No,' she said, 'that's not what I meant.' And before my neighbor could react, she grabbed his arms. 'I mean I want to have a child myself. I mean I want you to put it right here, in my belly.' Right at that moment, her husband and his friends barged into the house, trapping my neighbor right where they wanted him.'

"How filthy!"

The old captain's voice rose above the uproar that

followed the story. Until now he hadn't said a word. He asked Mr. Diep who he was and where he was from.

"My name is Diep. Le Van Diep. It means the plow holder. My mother gave birth to me when she was plowing the rice paddy, and I was born right next to its blade. Now I live in Co hamlet, Thanh Hoa commune, in the district next to the river. If you come there, ask for the man in the house which no one can buy and no one can keep away from. Ask for the man whom no one can look down on and who is always invited. Then you'll find me."

Khiem looked off into the darkness. His family lived in the same hamlet.

It was dawn. They anchored by a white sycamore. He could hear the sound of a helicopter somewhere above the white clouds. The ropes used to pull the barge had been coiled, the poles stowed, and now the four sailors rowed the boat forward. The old captain smoked a waterpipe, peering at the bank as if trying to assess the situation. Khiem followed his gaze nervously. His haven was on the other side of this river.

The nature of the river had changed since the night before. He could hear the roar of the water, as if it were pouring down off the roof of a high building. The force of it sounded huge, mythical. Khiem felt the same sense of awe and immensity he'd experienced watching the sun rise from the ocean. The river was demonstrating its power now, challenging a man to have the bravery and skill to dominate it.

The tide was rising and the waves were growing larger, more agitated. In the middle of the current they leapt and twisted, slapped against each other, then fell. The people on the boat could all see that the water was rising, flowing madly, carrying debris swiftly down the river. A huge timber raft. Tangled banyan trees with thick canopies and hairy roots. Small and large houses. Broken bamboo. All manner of garbage, bounded wildly past the boat. Under the roar of the water, the passengers could hear the faint cry of people calling for help somewhere, a sound that made their hair stand on end. The waves beat against the bank, made crashing, booming sounds that startled everybody. A part of the bank, lined with trees, dropped suddenly into the river. To the right, a visible current split in two and changed directions abruptly, speeding obliquely towards the far bank like a flung lance. Then suddenly a whirlpool, as big across as a paddy drying-tray, its center a deep hole like a monster's mouth, opened and swallowed a tree trunk. With a huge waaanging sound, a tremendous wave leapt up and broke.

Everything looked strange. Khiem nervously watched the old captain and his four young crewmen preparing to cross the river. He remembered what Old Tuy had said: the riskiest travel is on horseback and by boat.

"Everybody sit still!" the captain yelled. "Well!" With that simple order, one of the crew began by pushing his pole down into the water, moving the boat towards the current. It moved away from the bank and was picked up immediately by the rushing flow. The other two rowed madly, while the old man, standing braced with his legs spread, one leg forward, the other planted behind, struggled with the tiller. The veins corded out on his muscles as he strained to keep the bow pointed straight ahead.

They pulled away from the safety of the bank. The job now was to fight the current and move across the river to the opposite shore.

Wooo-eet, wooo-eet, the rowers in front pulled with all the strength of eight young arms. Their oars cleaved the waves. Khiem could feel the effort of the boat to keep itself from being swamped, swallowed by the waves dashing over it.

The real challenge had begun. Khiem was flung sideways. He and the other passengers, shocked at being thrown suddenly into this chaos, grasped the sides of the boat and hung on. Another wave hit the bow, stopped the boat dead, began pushing it backwards. The old man screamed orders to the crew. They bent to their oars, and the boat rose, balancing shakily on the crest of a wave, then slipping backwards, unable to dominate it. Another wave smashed the bow, and smaller ones continuously hit the starboard side of the hull. The water was boiling up into a thick curtain of white foam. The boat lurched out of control, shook, and began sliding sideways, tilting dangerously. All the people on that side screamed as they were hurled into the railing. "Row harder!" the old man yelled, and, clenching his teeth, he struggled with the tiller, trying to keep the boat from tipping over. Luckily, at that moment, an underwater current must have hit it from the left, counterbalancing, and it slapped back down on the water. But it was out of control now. The huge block of cement with its iron frame was being carried along like a peanut shell. Seeing a huge tree trunk rushing towards them on a collision course, the captain yelled for the crew to backwater, then row with all their might on one side. Once more the boat was plunging sideways down the river, but the young crewmen got it turned just in time, and the trunk just scraped along its side. Their skill and bravery had saved the boat, but it was as if it were cursed; suddenly it was grabbed by a whirlpool and spun madly. When they emerged, they found themselves where they had started.

"Back to this place, eh?" the old man said, rubbing his face. He immediately ordered them out again. Using the experience he'd gained from the first try, he moved further along the bank this time, avoiding the current, and then plunged diagonally into the river, sideways; apparently he wanted to catch the crosscurrent, use it to ride across to the other bank. But once more they failed. It wasn't an even competition. The boat whirled around its own axis, pinwheeling in the center of the river as if they were being mocked by a water djinn. The passengers sat stunned, motionless and breathless, their eyes shut tightly, their fates completely dependent on the craft and the crew.

By the third time they were pushed back, everyone could see that the crewmen were exhausted. Before trying again, they decided to rest and eat for an hour, then try again before dusk.

When they were ready, Khiem and Mr. Diep went forward and asked if they could help. But the crewmen waved them back, assuring them that this next time they'd make it. At first, they followed the same route, sticking close to the bank, but going further, as far as the submerged banana grove they'd noticed before. On the other side of the river they could dimly see a row of bamboo stalks that they would use as a target point. They turned and started across, aiming directly at the line of whirlpools that seemed to have become a kind of sentry in the middle of the crazily boiling waves. They hit the first straight on, the old captain skillfully working the tiller back and forth, the stern twisting and threatening to whip around, and then the boat tipping, straightening, and sliding through. "Row faster, faster!" the old man shouted, and the four young men bent their backs into it. The waves beat fiercely against the bow, washing over onto the deck.

Upstream! The boat seemed to surge forward as if suddenly filled with joy in its freedom, with the fierce spirit of its challenge to the river. Upstream! Khiem's heart swelled with the rush forward into danger, with the answers it gave him. Upstream! Upstream! As it should be! Clench your teeth, let the blood run out of your eyes, swallow unbearable pain and suffering of the heart, keep every bit of your humanity, believe in the truth, and overcome the deluge!

They were on the other side of the current. The oars beat the water continuously, harmoniously, and the boat shot forward. It was out of the main current now and moving along the opposite bank, a few small whirlpools in its path. There was only one more serious obstacle: a confluence with the mouth of another river, which held them with a ghostly force for a time, until they struggled forward and escaped it.

As he got ready to disembark, Khiem grasped the captain's hand and mumbled a thank you, to indicate his gratitude and respect. The boat had reached its destination and the familiar scenes of his home province, the heartland of the country, spread before him. The old man just shook his head. "That was nothing. During the war against the Americans, I carried weapons across this river during the night, without any lights. And I never failed."

Chapter Eight

THE MIDLANDS

Although he was overwhelmed with sadness, with every step Khiem took, he heard breezes whispering in his ears: "Stop and look, my friend." Scattered clusters of palm trees flourished everywhere on the dry, hilly land, and looking at them made Khiem think of the sweet young girls of the midlands region. In the old days thousands of them would gather in the open-air theater near here and dance, their accompanying music the soft flutterings and clickings of their ivory fans.

The beauty of this place was natural and consoling to him, even now, on his way to pay his respects at his mother's tomb.

The low, palm-studded foothills and the forested mountains beyond caressed his eyes. The nervous beat of his heart, the plop of water buffaloes' hooves in the narrow, muddy rice paddies, the caw of crows in the palm fronds, the jungle myna's cry, the drip of water in the deep limestone wells, all were absorbed into the vast blue peace of the sky.

He felt recovered from the journey, the countryside soothing and strengthening his spirit. Let people keep cheating, lying, betraying. Let them keep slandering; let them be cruel and base. Let them focus their lives on revenge. It had nothing to do with him; he couldn't be touched.

Tendrils of smoke from the incense sticks next to his

mother's tomb twisted in the slight breeze. Kneeling in the young grass just sprouting by the new earthen tomb built next to his father's, Khiem let his tears fall. He turned to Nguyen, his sister. "My sickness lasted too long, Nguyen," he said in a voice barely above a whisper. "I was only given the news of mother's death after I'd recovered."

"I guessed it was something like that," Nguyen answered, her handkerchief wet with her own tears, her voice choking. "Mom was in the hospital for a week, but kept insisting on being brought back home. Finally our neighbor Mr. Diep and my Khuong carried her back in a hammock. She told them to stop at the village gate and asked if they could smell the perfume of the hyacinths in Mr. Tue's garden. She told Diep and my husband how once our dad had grown a hyacinth bush in our garden, but it withered after his death. After she got home, she remained very alert. Whenever she heard the train whistle at En station, she told my daughter: 'Prepare the rice, Hien: your Uncle Khiem is coming home." Then after a few days, she stopped mentioning your name. Maybe she sensed something had happened to you. Finally, one day she told Hien: 'When your Uncle Khiem returns, tell him he must keep being patient.' The whole family burst into tears."

Dusk was falling on the meadow, fading the grass to gold. A cool breeze rustled and rattled the palm fronds. It was after the harvest, and the rice fields were stubbled with dried stalks. Beyond the terraced fields, the mountains towered against the sky. Khiem knew that his family had chosen this land carefully, according to *feng shui* principles, and that his parents were well loved, and well mourned in this place. His mother had been a kind and devoted teacher, and all the people in the surrounding area had been her students when they were children. Her image would continue to exist here as a symbol of kindness and elegance.

"Mom! Now my brother has come to be with you—can

you see him?" Nguyen cried. Khiem couldn't hold back his own tears; they burst from him. Nguyen's words and posture made him think of his mother when she had wept in front of his father's grave. Nguyen was like a copy of his mother. She also taught at the secondary school, and was kind, elegant, and beautiful. Her face was gentle as a leaf, in harmony with her two liquid, shy eyes, and small mouth. On her left cheek was a small, charming beauty mark. She had a quiet, simple manner that reflected a clear mind and generous spirit. "Mom, where are you?" she wept. "You are no longer here to tell me how to educate your grandchildren, to remind me not to scold them loudly and frighten their spirits, oh, my kind mother..."

Khiem heard a rustling sound in the grass behind them. Someone was walking up towards them from the rice fields. Nguyen wiped her eyes and they both stood. "Ah, Mr. Diep. Have you finished in the rice field?" Nguyen said.

Diep lowered his hoe, unrolled the bottoms of his trousers, and looked at Khiem and Nguyen. The storyteller Khiem had met on the boat was a small man with a large head, big eyes, and big ears, but a sharp chin. "Good evening, Ms. Nguyen. And are you Mr. Khiem? I was on my way home, but seeing someone up here, I came to say hello. Ms. Nguyen, you really should build a fence here to keep out the water buffaloes."

Khiem had known instantly who he was from his voice. As for Diep, it took him a moment; then he rushed to Khiem and gripped his hand tightly and shook it energetically. "I'm really getting old," he said, "my mind is going—you have to excuse me!"

***

Mr. Diep had been born in the year of the Horse, the month of the Rat, and the hour of the Dragon. His mother had gone into labor while she was plowing a rice field. Diep, "Plow-holder," was the name his father, who knew a little of the ancient Chinese, gave him. He also inherited his love for literature and poetry from his father, and became a rural folklorist, even though he had never been formally educated.

Diep fought against the French and, later, the Americans, and was wounded severely by the pressure from bombs being dropped during the defense of the Quang Tri citadel. Afterwards, he was demobilized with the rank of captain, and assigned to work with the People's Committee in charge of cultural activities for the masses. But he had had to deal with too much stupidity, too many people telling him what he could and could not do. He felt as if he were playing a role in a Chinese lantern show. It wasn't something he cared to do, so he quit and worked quarrying limestone, digging wells for people, farming. He was devoted to his country, and for him there was no shame in any work he could do for his fellow villagers. Still, his talent was well known, and some of his poems won province-level prizes. Those prizes, along with his background as a veteran, caused him to be appointed district head of culture. He continued to write critical poems, using "The Plow" as his pen name, digging up and exposing whatever evil he found. His reputation increased.

Finally, Mr. Hung Manh, the chief of the district's cultural and ideological department, and the owner of the Seven-Dish Dogmeat Restaurant, called Mr. Le Van Diep onto the carpet. Said Mr. Seven-Dish Dogmeat to Mr. Plow: "So, there are no more good people or good deeds in this district—is that it, Mr. Diep?"

Mr. Diep wrung his hands and pretended to humble himself. At first he spoke sweetly, but, as he continued, his voice rose: "I must report to you that the earth is five billion years old, and that some microbes have been on it for 3.5 billion years. Compared to them, human beings have only made their appearance recently. Microbes are older than human beings—it's as simple as that. So it is with our karma. My name is Diep, so I have to plow. Plowing doesn't mean rejecting or slandering. 'Honey kills flies/honesty is bitter,' we say. We also say, 'A hundred blows from your mother aren't equal to a threat from your father.' So here I am being threatened. I don't really want to talk to you about what I do. But since you, Mr. District, have asked, I have to report. So. Since Mr. Kien, the head comptroller, died, there hasn't been a decent official in our province. All of them are like ants rushing to a honey pot! Money comes first, good judgment last. People want to walk in high places and water runs downhill."

He took a breath and continued: "Mr. District, let's not close our eyes. What does it mean if the four tall legs don't belong to the cows and the four fat thighs don't belong to the pigs? Two words, 'Money' and 'Lust,' blind people's eyes. 'No matter how intelligent you are, the sight of a vagina leaves you only three of your seven spirits.' That was something our ancestors taught us. And: 'I enjoy her waist and her breasts/what do I care what rumors fly?' And you remember the story of the big shot in our district who pretended to divorce his wife so she would be given a new plot of land, and then they sold it for a hundred ounces of gold?

> Divorce can get you
> Both land and gold
> and jobs for the lawyers as well
> At night he still beats the wooden fish
> and waits for its echoes as of old.

That's it. Another Party comrade doesn't care if he has to pay a million dong for a kilogram of turtle blood, so he can put it in his wine and drink with the girls. Meanwhile, people have to pay ninety thousand dong a day to stay in the hospital, so poor people go home to die.

> *Who will save me?*
> *Poverty buries me alive*
> *The people are in pain*

That's reality! That's what I compose my poems from!"

Mr. Seven-Dish Dogmeat hadn't the time to open his mouth. Mr. Plow continued:

"So, Mr. District, do you know that each district Party leader gets a brand new Toyota costing five hundred million dong, while a water buffalo only costs a million? That means each district Party leader is riding on five hundred buffaloes—all of the buffaloes in our district. And no one punishes them for that, but when Mr. Tue disguised himself as a beggar and went to investigate how people really lived, and found out how the cooperative leaders were cheating the farmers—he was punished!"

Mr. Hung Manh was furious already, and hearing Tue's name infuriated him more. He pounded on the table and glared at Mr. Plow. "That's the business of the upper echelons, and I advise you not to cross that line. Remember, my dog's chain is a meter and a half long, and you should keep a meter and sixty centimeters away from him!"

"Thank you so much, Mr. District, for sharing your experience and giving me that lesson. But please allow me not to learn from it. Let me give you another example. So far, nobody here has ever grown tomatoes before the new year. But Mr. Tue imported seeds from Bulgaria, and now he has cultivated 120 hectares, each producing sixty tons of good quality..."

"Are you writing a story, Mr. Diep?"

"Sir, literature and poetry are Heaven's karma. One can't refuse karma. But dear Mr. District, if Mr. Tue took your lesson to heart and stood outside the length of the dog's chain, would that be useful to people? I would follow Mr. Tue instead, and stand within the dog's reach."

"What?"

"The narrow-minded ones who punished Mr. Tue are thieves, traitors, and cheaters who take credit for other people's efforts. Mr. Tue was the one who dug a well for the soldiers, donated tents for the displaced children, and food and clothing for the old people. Instead of praising him, they smashed his feet. I am against the ones who did that, and I will expose their faces so everybody will know them."

"Well," Hung Manh said.

"What is your opinion?"

"My opinion is that you have now revealed your dark heart!"

"My dark heart—or yours?"

"Yours, Mr. Diep."

"Who is it who considers the law to be a fierce dog?"

"You take care, you dark-heart."

The poet smiled and stretched out his arms. "That is your way of thinking. As for me, I'm poor, but I'm not a coward. I'm not afraid of threats, I don't waste my time, and I'm not easily swayed. A poet fulfills a poet's duty. Every word written by me is a brick, a vote. Only an honest person can struggle against cruelty and evil. In short, that is my way of loving life. It's a cat's love. Do you know about a cat's love for its kitten? Listen. Once a cat was nursing its kitten. Suddenly a cruel sewer rat leapt at her, trying to snatch the kitten. Since the cat knew it wasn't strong enough to defend its child, it immediately swallowed it."

It was a simple story, but it had depths that he knew Mr. Seven-Dish Dogmeat would not understand. Their dialogue ended at that point. But Mr. Diep was the mother cat. He had hidden all his poems and stories away, avoiding the sewer rats. But at last, what was begun had to be ended.

When he was forty-nine—the age Asians consider the first turning point in a person's life—Diep had started composing verses under several pen names. He'd finally been called up by Hung Manh when someone read between the lines of his last poem, analyzed it as an exposé of the affair between the district chairman and the deputy chair of the women's union.

Soon after his meeting with Dogmeat, someone threw a stick into the spokes of his cartwheel, and Mr. Plow was thrown into the rice paddy. The next day, he was splitting bamboo in front of his house, when a huge rock smacked him in the forehead. He began to get anonymous threatening letters stating that someone was growing enough bamboo to have many sticks with which to beat him until he was crippled. Mr. Tue read his fortune and it told him there were devils in the words of those letters, and his karma couldn't be avoided: a great man had to expect to face vicissitudes. Diep decided then to quit the arena for a time, telling himself that mandarins were always temporary, but the people went on forever.

***

Mr. Diep sat across from Khiem on his wooden bed, assuming a meditation posture. He had just been chewing betel nut leaf, and his eyes were sparkling, his complexion slightly reddened.

"Khiem," he said, "I know you're a well-known writer, but forgive me if I quote you some advice from a book I read. 'One can create friends. One can create enemies. But neighbors are given us by God.' It's true, and I have to thank God for putting me next to your parents, and Ms. Nguyen's, and Mr. Tue. Your father was a man of strong morals, and no one forgets him. As for Miss Teacher, your mother, I was always grateful to her. When I was having my difficulties and felt upset, she came to me and said, 'Mr. Diep, you're an honest man at heart and you act like a writer should. If everything begins beautifully, it means you are already half-successful. You're wrong to be so sad."

Shaking his head, Mr. Diep laughed and pulled up a card with the word "Happiness" printed on it in red. He lowered his voice.

"Now I have some family matters I'd like to talk to you about. I'm very lucky you've come back to this village. In the middle of the month, we're going to organize my youngest daughter's wedding party. She's been engaged for a while, and the groom's parents have already brought offerings to us. All the other ceremonies have been completed. So now the fruit is ripe, and I'll let her go live with her in-laws. I told the groom's parents that if my daughter were smart enough, they wouldn't have much to teach her, and if not, that will take up most of their time. Am I right, Khiem?"

Good people are often easily moved and talkative when they're cheerful. The folklore poet seemed to want to prove his happiness. But when he continued, he seemed suddenly gloomy.

"As a father yourself, you probably understand me well. My daughter wasn't lucky at first. Her mother was working in the limestone pits when she was pregnant with her, and when she was born, she was like a weak bud. By the time she was sixteen, she was still as skinny as a ten-year-old. My wife and I both wondered if we'd committed some sin and were being punished by the Creator. But it wasn't that bad. When she turned eighteen, she suddenly blossomed into a beautiful young woman. I always thought it wasn't because of our rice, but thanks to the beneficence of the Creator and the Buddha. The young couple have known each other for over a year, ever since he came back home for the Tet holidays." He blinked. "He's from a good family: the parents came from Nam Ha province, moved to Tan Lap, and lived for a while with the Dzao minority. He's in an armored unit based in Dong Nai province."

"That's not so far—only two days and a night by train," said Khiem's brother-in-law Khuong, from the kitchen. He was lighting the fire, a disabled veteran, thin, the left sleeve of his shirt empty.

Mr. Diep turned cheerfully to the kitchen. "Where have you been? Don't bother making tea, come in and sit with us!" He drew a sheet of paper out of his pocket, and showed them the poem he'd written to present to his daughter at her wedding:

> *Now you go to live over there*
> *Be cheerful and love the one who loves you*
> *Leave all sadness behind, my dear one*
> *Bring to your new life only pleasure and joy*
> *Farewell my precious jade*
> *You will be a precious jewel for your new family*
> *and always my innocent angel*
> *I worry when I think of your duties as wife,*
> *as daughter-in-law*
> *Your mother and I don't want you to leave*
> *Your new family wait to welcome you*
> *While they sit in hope*
> *Here we sit in sorrow*
> *Though our tears will fall in farewell*
> *Please smile when you arrive*
> *In your new place of love.*

"Hey, Nguyen," Khuong called, standing up. Nguyen had just returned from school and was standing still, listening to Diep's poem, her eyes wet. But she was smiling. "I'm happy for her good news, Mr. Diep. Remember the day we had to take her to the hospital for emergency treatment? My husband rode his bicycle with me carrying her on the back, and mom and your wife running after us. It was raining so hard...and when we got to the hospital, my mother burst into tears, thinking we were too late."

"Dear Madame Teacher," Mr. Diep whispered, standing and lighting incense sticks on the altar of Khiem's mother, "Please bless my daughter. You took care of her when you were alive as if she were your own daughter—now come back and bless her."

Khiem looked out of the door. The mountains and hills were motionless, but as strong and immortal as the love human beings have for each other, the love which joins them to the universe.

***

Similar people tend to find and befriend each other. Khiem was now fifty years old, Diep sixty-two, and Mr. Tue, the best-known person in Co hamlet, was seventy-four. In Asian terms, each was born in the year of the same Zodiac animal, and in spite of the differences in their ages, the three quickly grew close to each other. Khiem looked at the others in the way his mother had taught him, and in these two men he saw harmonious qualities and only slight differences.

Mr. Diep's internal honesty shone through his inelegant exterior: he'd lived in the midlands countryside since he was a young child and looked rough outside. Khiem, on the other hand, living in the literary world for so long, looked the way people thought a writer should, and carried himself with a certain natural grace as well. Mr. Tue, the defeated professional revolutionary, fell somewhere between the other two in looks. Khiem had met him shortly after meeting Diep, who asked him to come with him to invite Mr. Tue to his daughter's wedding. The three of them had talked long into the afternoon. That night, Khiem wrote about the encounter in his notebook:

When I first saw Mr. Tue, he was talking to the trees and plants in his garden. The garden is a real botanic collection, filled with strange and abundant plants that seem to have taken on a spiritual life. The garden seems the embodiment of Mr. Tue. If each area of the country, according to psychological and natural laws, gives birth to a person representing a certain mystical level, then in this central region, that person is Mr. Tue. That's my slightly idealistic theory anyway.

He is one meter, seventy-two centimeters tall, and his appearance is marked by five characteristics (as my mother taught me to look): a large face, a short neck, big teeth, big ears, and a wide mouth. He is robust but not vulgar, and his voice booms when he speaks. People say that the Creator hasn't stopped caring for the earth, and therefore talented people can still be found in the most remote regions. As Mr. Diep commented: "If there were no one like Le Tue, my nights here would be endless. Once we met again, I recalled the wonderful memories I have of him when I was a child. He used to dig wells eighteen meters deep. Once, he let me eat some of the jackfruit in his garden. And he often had nice stories to tell.

Tue has been an active Party member since he was twenty. He established revolutionary bases in areas where the enemy dominated, and led the masses in their armed uprising to liberate Lao Cai province. Later, he was promoted to political commissar of a special military unit operating on the western front. All glorious pages in the history of his life, more than enough to enshrine his reputation. But all of that was nothing compared to what he did for the people of this province during the seventies. I've heard people say a bronze statue, with his name inscribed on it, should be erected to him for his actions then.

He was the originator of the contract system, a great leap forward for the millions of peasants who were suffering famine and poverty because of the collective system. He was also a victim of that great innovation, but he is still adored by millions of people. Although he is also the product of a traumatic historical period, he is as unlike Lieu's brother as one can imagine.

Mr. Tue was forced to retire about twenty years ago, but he has never stopped working. He stays busy all day, receiving guests at his farm, or reading, or hunting. He eats three bowls of rice at every meal, and drinks pure green tea. He was educated during the French time, and started his life as a teacher. During the revolutionary period, he traveled throughout Cambodia and Laos, working for the revolution. He is a person worthy of his ancestors.

Mr. Tue and Mr. Diep are both characters I'd include in my big novel. But how would I start? Building a novel is not like telling a story: the writer has to create descriptions so the readers can see what they can't see when they look at human beings.

When Tue met me again, he whispered: "Great people are rare, and jealousy is the karma of writers. It isn't only peasants who are unlucky, but intellectuals and artists as well. Do you know what the Chinese poet Tu Fu said? 'Literature doesn't like those who are lucky'!"

Then he asked me to go boar hunting with him in Tan Lap, where the Dzao ethnic minority live. "Hey, writer," he said, "If you know how to read, then you'll find out that mountains, water, birds, and animals are also books. Have you ever been hunting?"

"I'm a very bad shot," I answered.

"After you've finished a book, if it's really good, do you know it?"

"I do," I answered. He laughed.

"Shooting at a bird is the same. As soon as the bullet leaves the barrel, you know immediately if it will hit the target or not; you don't have to wait until you see the bird fall down or fly away."

Oh, Mr. Tue—a person of clear reasoning and magnificent sense. I'd like to understand him better.

***

The three men walked single file through the forest. Mr. Diep wore a canvas raincoat, light trousers, boots, and a dark blue hat with a fake feather sticking out from it, and he held a Czechoslovak rifle over his shoulder. Mr. Tue, the tallest in the line, was in rubber boots and a gray Russian overcoat with brass buttons, and he walked as easily as if he were strolling down a street, his German-made shotgun slung obliquely across his back. Bringing up the rear, Khiem was dressed simply in a jacket and cap, and carried a canvas sack. He held a bamboo cane, just to have something in his hands. They were walking down a dirt path that began along the edge of the newly tilled plots of land, all ready for the winter crops, and then wound through hills covered with artemisia, myrtle trees, and wild foliage. The path widened and then narrowed, became overgrown with wild grass that signed winter in its thin and fading blades. The light was dim, the sun blocked by the weave of the forest canopy.

Khiem was perennially the slowest, partly because Diep and Tue were more familiar with the forest, and partly because sometimes he found himself wondering where he was and what he was doing there, and would stumble and stop. He would try to calm himself down, reorient, but had to admit that no matter how deep-rooted his love of life, he was still tormented by worry, melancholy, bitterness. There remained plans he still needed to carry out, many debts he still needed to pay off.

"How come the younger man is slower than the old ones, eh Khiem?" Mr. Tue laughed, his teeth shining. He had turned to wait for Khiem.

"I'm not a young man anymore, Mr. Tue."

"That's something you can control. I always order myself not to hear the word 'old.'"

He turned and continued walking, with his long, quick, natural stride. Khiem almost had to run to keep up. As he did, he thought: the character in my novel has to have this characteristic—even in a besieged position he still would keep his pure, natural power. He's a man who would dare to spread his wings against the wind, a unique man who doesn't become drunk with pride when he wins a victory or humiliate himself with shame if he fails. Excited, Khiem almost forgot to keep walking, then had to rush to catch up again. Certainly the character must be like that—the novel's hero would surely be a Mr. Tue, beautiful in his pride, while everybody around considers him defeated. Losing his position, he just spits on his palms, grabs a hoe or an axe, and goes about having a full life, planting his trees, digging wells, building houses, listening to music, reading, visiting friends, the same as before. Keeps himself in good shape, internally and externally, according to his own style. Even keeps hunting, as he did when he was District Party secretary and executive member of the Party Committee—although then, someone else would prepare his vehicles, guns, and even the part of the forest where he would hunt. Now he walked alone, a true hunter, seeing everything with his own eyes, touching everything with his own hands.

Mr. Tue stopped to wait for Khiem again. At the same time, the three men heard a burst of gunfire from their left, followed by the frantic barking of hunting dogs, the shrieking cries of the birds exploding up from the wild reeds and flying off in all directions.

A cool, clean rush went through Khiem. He could see the marsh in front of them now with its mirroring water, the wild birds circling above their heads as if performing a dance ceremony. The surface of the water was ablaze with lotuses and water lilies which, blooming out of season, Khiem imagined had attracted the birds to the marsh.

It was impossible to tell which call burst from the throat of which bird, but the area suddenly sounded like a natural choir: the songs of two birds and the songs of hundreds of others rising and blending in chorus. The three men crouched behind a clump of marsh grass. "There," Mr. Tue called, pointing. Khiem followed his finger, and saw at a distance a flock of wild ducks getting closer, at first just small points in the sky and then, suddenly, shockingly, Khiem could see a front rank that must have had at least seven hundred water fowl in it. The flock suddenly, in unison, shot upwards, climbing in a straight line directly above the heads of the three men, then wheeled down towards the marsh in a sweeping curve. Apparently sensing some threat to them, Mr. Tue suddenly straightened up, spread his legs, turned sideways and raised his gun to the sky: *Bam! Bam!*

The shells exploded in the path of the flock, warning them away from the danger. Khiem stood and Mr. Diep joined him, jumping up and down and yelling to chase the precious birds away. In a moment, they were gone, as if they had never been there, and the marsh was quiet and sad. They could hear the barking of the hunting dogs coming closer.

***

"Hey, Party Secretary, this morning the fire danced in my kitchen and the magpie sang on the roof of my house, so I knew immediately there would be some precious guests coming. Even though we've been separated, the sympathy between us remains, right, Party Secretary?" The speaker was Old Thoan, the Dzao village chief. He was a small man with fish-shaped eyes, a bird beak of a nose, and not a tooth in his mouth. Mr. Tue didn't correct his use of his former title.

This group of Dzao lived at the base of a huge mountain,

their houses scattered widely, each on its own small hillock. In spite of that, all the houses were divided in the same basic way. The bottom level with its earthen floor contained the altar of the ancestors, a cooking area, and storage for farm tools. The upper part was built on stilts and floored with aged bamboo; it served as the family bedroom and was a place to sit with guests.

Old Thoan's house was longer than a stable and had two large hearths: one to keep the sitting room warm and the other for cooking. The visitors had just sat down, and Old Thoan's daughter-in-law carried in a tray of food. Old Thoan put on his indigo coat, the Heaven's Seal design embroidered on the back. "I don't know how to say nice words, and formality ruins the relationship between human beings," he said, with cheerful dignity, "but I consider your visit to my village an honor, Mr. Party Secretary."

Mr. Tue waved the words away, and introduced Khiem. He was about to say something about Mr. Diep, when Old Thoan raised a wine cup to the poet.

"Sweet words rest in your bones. I remember well how Mr. Diep came to explain the new production policy and how it would help build a new life for us. Please, this first cup is for you."

Mr. Diep shook his head. "My dear Mr. Village Chief— wine makes me sleepy. I wish to be awake, and hear my brother, Mr. Tue's, words."

"No—the first cup will make you rise up as beautiful as a dancing peacock," Old Thoan insisted, then lowered his voice. "Last night, a boar destroyed some of the cassavas in my field, close to here. After the meal, you'll have a nap and I'll lead you there. Please—bottoms up!" He drank, then picked up a chicken wing and offered it cheerfully to Mr. Tue. "Use your fingers please, Mr. Party Secretary."

Mr. Diep smiled widely: "'Chicken, sticky rice, and women, these three must be enjoyed by hand,'" he quoted.

The men laughed and drank. As he raised his cup again, Old Thoan remembered something. "A group of hunters led by the district chairman just arrived from Tan Thien village. The party has vehicles and beaters with it."

"Is the chairman a big man, used to own a dogmeat restaurant in the district capital?"

"I don't know him. But he speaks very rudely. 'Show me where the wild ducks come,' he said. I told him we'd stopped killing wild ducks a long time ago, since they carry good news to us. That didn't please him, and he left without saying goodbye. Never mind, now I'm drinking with Party Secretary Tue." He and Tue toasted each other, draining their cups. Tue laughed mischievously.

"Old Thoan, you shouldn't call me that anymore— otherwise the people will stop loving me."

"People here are still grateful to you, Mr. Tue."

"I worked for the people. It was as it should have been, Old Thoan—I don't deserve special praise."

Old Thoan stopped pouring the wine into his cup. "I don't agree with you...Mr. Party Secretary. You were the only one with the courage to step every day into the rice paddies to understand the way rice is grown. You were the only one who dared to look into people's daily lives. It was hard for anyone else to do that. Ruling a country is like barbecuing a fish: the smaller it is, the more dexterity it demands."

"He's right," Mr. Diep nodded approvingly.

Mr. Tue nodded. "In reality, when a person becomes a mandarin, he is apart from ordinary people. He forgets that learning to love other human beings is the most important part of his education. He also doesn't think carefully, or stop to reconsider his actions. The morals of society, from ancient times until now, have demanded that first of all people should never suffer from hunger. It's natural that people think first of all of feeding themselves, and nature follows its own religion and its own rules, like it or not. You can't eliminate winter because you are afraid of the cold. That was why even though I didn't have the approval of the Party, I was still determined to let people use the contract system."

Old Thoan clapped his hands together. "Long live our Party Secretary's religion! What a nice one it is!"

"Ha!" Mr. Diep called, "'The mandarin's road is wide and long, and there you can fly if you have talent, and there you can run, if you're strong.'"

"Bottoms up!"

"Old Thoan, let's drink to this great writer, Mr. Khiem!"

Khiem raised his cup, his face reddening, though he was not at all drunk. Old Thoan, after hearing his story, clucked his tongue. "The circle always comes around. Don't worry: a tiger will forever give birth to a tiger, Mr. Khiem." They drank merrily. But by the end, Old Thoan couldn't keep up with the poet, and begged off, saying he was too old.

"Tell Mr. Khiem what the Dzao say about age, please," Mr. Diep told him.

"Yes. When you are ten years old, you can bathe without feeling cold. When you are twenty, you can love without getting tired. When you are thirty, you can shoot down a bird without a bow. When you are forty, you can do business. When you are fifty, your neck becomes wattled. When you are sixty, you start going deaf. When you are seventy, you see your wife, and can't make love any more..."

They burst into laughter again, though Khiem held back, feeling somewhat outside their circle. He wasn't playing at being the writer as observer. But he understood more clearly now that one can only describe life when one really lives in it, and forgets what his prescribed role is supposed to be. He remained sunk in thought until he heard Mr. Tue ask Mr. Diep about a line he'd just recited: "thinking of the political arena frightens you all the more..."

Mr. Diep clucked his tongue. "It was Vo Van Truc's poem.

He meant that magnificence is born from true art. But politics only gives birth to deformed offspring."

"A person who looks for his happiness in the political arena is someone who enjoys dominating others, right, Mr. Diep? Please, recite the whole poem."

"'All our other friends have dispersed
only we few sit together
We who have come to understand life's depths and shallows
who don't finish the cup of joy
before the cup of pain is refilled
I say one word when I'm not quite awake
Another when I'm drunk
Friendship's warmth drives away the bitterness of the times
Would it be better if one only cared for, and pitied oneself?
Throw away your high position and come back home
Thinking of the political arena frightens you all the more
Your tongue becomes numb with bitterness, and numb
your hand gripping the cup
We look at each other and our cheeks are wet with tears
Some fall in our cups of joy and some wound our hearts.'"

"How interesting!" Mr. Tue slapped his thigh and looked over at Khiem, as if he wanted to ask him something. "But the sentence, 'we look at each other and our cheeks are wet with tears,' is a little too melancholy. It is melancholy! Is everyone in such pain? But I suppose so. For myself, I had to clench my teeth and bear it. They knocked me down even though the people in this area loved me. They rushed to my house and bound me and then held a meeting and used their majority to make their resolution condemning me. I was alone, ostracized, my words silenced. But still, a poem shouldn't be too sentimental, I think." Suddenly Mr. Tue stopped, apparently feeling he was talking too much. Khiem remained silent also, but in complete empathy with him. He supposed that Mr. Tue had wanted to say that the side effect of bitterness can be sweetness: the more you suffer, the more you feel the sweetness afterwards. Human beings, they both knew, had a huge capacity to bear suffering, to accept everything, including betrayal and revenge.

Mr. Diep began speaking to Old Thoan, inviting him to his daughter's wedding. As he did, Mr. Tue turned to Khiem, and lowered his voice. "Khiem, your father was senior to me. Once he asked me if it was true Buddha said the compassion in people was as thin as the layer of dirt on one finger. It was the day before he was murdered. That case is still on the record, and I believe that one day the truth about it will be made known. Khiem, if Heaven always took the side of evil people, then the world would belong to them already. Nguyen and Khuong told me about your case, how those base, cruel colleagues of yours have blocked distribution of your book. Khiem, I think you understand quite well that intellectuals will always be defeated by thugs. Don't be embarrassed."

Khiem felt a chill run down his spine, then shivers through his entire body. A strange sensation, as if everything inside him was being refined to some diamond-hard essence. Then he heard the sound of the linked wooden fish rustling in the garden, disturbed by something touching them, sounding their warning. The boar was coming; it was time for them to take up their guns.

***

"Brother, after we've finished the forty-nine days commemorating mom's death, I'd like to bring her spirit to the pagoda," Nguyen said, glancing shyly at Khiem. "The head Venerable there respected mom a great deal. At the same time, we can bring dad's spirit as well." She stopped for a moment, too moved to speak, then continued: "I've dreamt of her every night since her death. I try to talk to her, but she says nothing, only I see her eyes getting wet. I'm nervous, afraid something bad will happen to us."

Nguyen couldn't hold back her tears, and Khiem felt on the verge of crying himself. His sister looked like the image of their mother now. Nguyen had been the one who had supported their mother through all her troubles and illness. She was neither a rich nor a healthy person, yet always tried to sustain the other members of the family. He didn't know where she got the strength. She taught school, farmed, sold in the market. She was responsible to everybody, as a teacher, as a daughter, as a mother, as the wife of a wounded veteran early-retired with asthma from a forestry farm, a burden for the rest of her life. And now she had to worry about him, Khiem, as well.

He knew that his sister understood his situation fully. She was like a hen, widening the spread of her wings to encompass her brother, as if she had truly taken the place of their mother. He thought of what Mr. Tue had said. He still didn't feel calm; his emotions were still confused. Looking at Nguyen standing in front of their mother's altar, surrounded by smoke from the burning incense sticks, he understood that she was praying for him.

"At the wedding of Mr. Diep's daughter, I was seated at the same table as some people from the District People's Committee. They really enjoyed telling each other about how Mr. Tue had chased the wild ducks away and saved them from the chairman. Hearing that, I told them you're a veteran, and have come back to recover from your illness, and registered your stay here with them." Licking her dried lips, Nguyen continued. "Brother, we no longer have our parents. It is only me and you in the world. I hope you can calm yourself, and not be so upset. Let your wife be—Thoa has chosen the way she wants to live. I'm only sorry for, and worry about, my niece Hong Ha. You have to stop brooding about your former colleagues also. It's difficult to behave correctly with good people, but it's easy to deal with bad ones."

Khuong, who was cleaning rice in the backyard, interrupted. "The river always reaches its turning point, and each human being has his time. The people who have hurt you are cowards, and if you destroy yourself because of them, it would please them. Forget them. Next month, I'm scheduled to go to Hanoi to have my wound re-examined. I'm going to go to the General Department and ask them directly what they want, and ask them also if they know they have violated the law in your case. I'm also planning to go to the Lawyer's Association. It isn't that easy to harm someone this way, brother."

"Don't worry about living here," Nguyen continued. "We're not so poor, and anyway, one can live on what one has. If you want to work, I can ask the headmaster to invite you to teach literature at my school. He studied in your Teachers College, some time after you were there."

"The students would love to learn from you," Khuong said, smoothing back his salt and pepper hair. Khiem, looking at him, noticed for the first time what a determined, intelligent person his brother-in-law was. Khuong and Nguyen complemented each other exquisitely.

But he remained silent. How could they understand his feelings now? He had overcome the initial shock, but had fallen into a bleak depression. It wasn't even what had happened to *The Haven* that had brought him to this state. He was more and more plagued by the question of what human beings were, what drove them. And Hoan! The memory of her was strong and vital and deep. There was an immense distance between them now, and he kept asking himself if he had done anything to hurt her. He had never believed she'd signed the petition to dismiss him. There could be no suspicion with real love. And Thoa's barbarous action came from Thoa's barbarous nature. He felt that through their sufferings, he and Hoan had come to belong to each other. But how could he tell her what he felt? They were far away from each other, and she hadn't left a trace behind. But what was between them had just started, and he felt driven to complete it.

That night he dreamt a beautiful dream. Everything that had happened in Thinh Luong came back to him again, but transformed and mythical, so it was like watching a ceremony bright with festive colors. When he woke up, he began writing.

The words that had seemed hidden somewhere for so long now poured out onto the paper. He was drunk with writing, with the joy of explaining, as his friend Thinh had said. As if he were tossing a stone from his hand. As Thinh said, and as Mr. Tue said: he could feel each word the way he could feel a bullet would reach its target as it left the gun. He wrote from the crises of his tortured heart, and he wrote against the oppression of time. After finishing each story, he inscribed clearly on its first page the date, and his address: Co Hamlet, Thanh Hoa commune, Song Thao district, P. Province. To prevent Pho, Duc, and Hien from blocking his publication in the newspapers, he signed a pen name: Thinh Luong.

Thinh Luong, Thinh Luong. The memories of the passionate, loving days he had spent there with Hoan floated around him, knit with the words and music of the festival song:

> *Goosefeathers spread on the wild meadow*
> *Cau River stretches between two sandy banks*
> *Floating in the dying dusk*
> *Oh for whom is this bracelet of pearl?*

Chapter Nine

THE BLOW

Mr. Quanh, the Squint-Eyed Toad, acting director of the Cultural Affairs Division, and sometimes known as Thiem Thu, called a four-man meeting.

"We know that Mr. Khiem has gone home," he said. "The question is, where is Ms. Hoan?"

His stare slashed like a razor through Lieu, Phu, Khoai, and the driver Thong. The Muong lifted his chin and plucked a hair out of his beard. He understood Quanh completely: one had to smash the snake's head before picking it up. The other men sat confused. Lieu had been particularly gloomy lately. For one thing, he had overheard people comparing him to his stepbrother, saying he had betrayed Khiem in the same way, shared the same traitorous nature. Also the price of dog had dropped even more. Only Khoai was cheerful and garrulous. "Hey, did you hear the one about the teacher who asked her students about the characteristics of the heart?" he asked the group. "One stood up and said, teacher I think the heart has legs, since one night I heard my dad tell my mom: 'oh, my heart, spread your legs, please.' When nobody responded, he started: "Hey, how many heads does a man have?" and then saw everybody look down and understood his behavior wasn't appropriate for a meeting. He immediately assumed a solemn air and took his pen from his ear, a habit he had kept from his time as a carpenter. He began to write in his notebook, muttering, "I think that...yes, yes, I think that..."

But he had no time to finish whatever it was he thought before Tiny Hoi's shrill shriek penetrated the room. "Oh Heaven! If he gave me one, he took away ten! If he was so good, why would the General Department dismiss him? You think he was so good, why don't you go lick his ass?"

Thong, recognizing the language of a cart-drivers' quarrel when he heard it, rushed out of Quanh's office to see what was going on, his small eyes taking in everything. He saw Ms. Tam, Ms. Chuong, and Ms. Tuyen walking out of the lounge, looking angry. Seeing Thong, Ms. Chuong raised her voice. "Mr. Thong, dogs go crazy in summer, but human beings are crazy the year round. This one invents stories, and since we are older, we felt we had to give her advice."

Thong nodded silently.

"Damn her!" Ms. Tuyen shouted suddenly, stamping on the floor. "She eats the soup, then pisses into the bowl! She's a complete ingrate! We have to teach her a lesson, do you understand?"

Ms. Tam bobbed her head in agreement. "How can she twist her mouth around so quickly? That girl needs to be taught how to act like a human being," she said bitterly. At that moment, as if to prove Ms. Tam's words, the Deformed Fetus rushed out of her room transformed into a screeching cat. And then shrieked like a mating one: "I tell you, Khiem cheated and exploited me! He is a fake, a phony—why are you praising him?"

The three woman jumped on her, their voices rising, mingling. Tiny Hoi! She'd even been given her name out of Khiem's compassion. If not for Khiem, she would already have been kicked out of this office.

Tiny Hoi looked deranged. Her eyes narrowed cruelly. Her face was wet with sweat and tears running into the thick paste of her face powder and lipstick. She jumped up and down madly, as if her small flat body were possessed by a devil. Ms. Tuyen grabbed her shoulders and pressed her down, saying, "Aren't you afraid of being punished by Heaven, damn you, girl?"

Tiny Hoi had never been so strong. She didn't seem like the same person who could hardly walk up the stairs without breathing like a buffalo. She spun, she kicked, she punched, fighting off the three women. They crowded in, trying to hold her, calm her down. When they were holding her, she began using her teeth, and they released her and backed off, muttering, "She's like a dog."

Snarling, she rushed into the acting director's office. "Have mercy—only I know what a depraved sex-maniac Khiem was," she screamed to Quanh. "He was always after me. I even noted down how many times he touched my breasts!"

"Damn you—Heaven will strike you!" Ms. Tuyen screamed at her. Ms. Tam almost burst into tears. "Ah, poor Khiem," she whispered.

Tiny Hoi looked triumphant. She turned to Quanh. "Since the day leader Quanh came to power, I have had the right to speak and act correctly. I hate Khiem. I condemn him. You cannot shut my mouth. He has done many wrong things. He was always bad-mouthing Brother Quanh. He said that Brother Quanh hadn't finished seventh grade! He said that Brother Quanh is ugly, squint-eyed, an old toad! He called Brother Quanh's poem a toad's poem. He said that Brother Quanh was the bastard child of Mr. Pho. He said that Brother Quanh is a traitor and didn't have any fucking talent! He said Mr. Pho's face looks like a woman's organ!"

"Surely there is a ghost haunting this building," Ms. Chuong wailed. "We're in chaos here!"

"Chaos? True, but if the upper level is indecent, then the lower has to be messy, so don't worry, there's absolutely nothing I can do about it," said Nghiem, strolling into the argument blithely.

The other men looked at him furiously.

"Thong, do you know the Muong saying 'good dishes treat people?'" Nghiem asked.

Thong blinked, and laughed uneasily. "Yes."

"How about, 'the tongue is boneless, so it can be twisted.'"

"Yes, I know it."

"And, 'the upper beam is curved, the lower one is bent?'"

"No, that's new to me."

"And the saying: 'similar sounds sound alike. Similar air breathes alike. Different air turns friend into foe?'"

"Interesting."

"And this one: 'Avoid looking at a squint-eyed person; avoid visiting a short person?'"

"Very nice."

The other men in Quanh's office had remained silent. Suddenly, as if he'd received a signal, Phu stood up, his hands fisted, big as iron hammers, and walked over to Tiny Hoi. "Don't worry, everything will be all right. We'll deal with these people—stop crying, my dear."

Then he stepped back and glared at the three women. "Remember, if anyone should dare to threaten a weaker person, I'll smash that one into mud—I don't care."

"Ah...Mr. Thunder, ha ha," Nghiem laughed and clapped, as if he were watching a performance. He walked towards Phu, who held his fists clenched at his sides, gritted his teeth, and stared at him.

"Oh, Mr. Thunder, last night I dreamt somebody spat in my face. I understood why—they believed I was base. You don't know the meaning of *thiem thu*, but do you know what 'wild plants cover a fallen fence' means? Ah well, everything gets mixed in the market. But I warn you: if you burn a book with one hand, the other hand will be singed."

Phu began to growl deep in his throat. Startled, Nhgiem took a step backwards, but continued speaking. "You can take your seat at the table, but you can't grab knowledge, do you understand, Mr. Thunder?"

"I want to ask you one thing," Phu said, his stye-eye blinking rapidly. "Do you know where that woman is?"

"Which woman?"

"Ms. Hoan. Have you forgotten her? Where is she?"

"Where is she? I don't have to report to you..."

Before he could finish the sentence, Phu punched him in the stomach. Nghiem's mouth gaped open, his eyes rolled and he fell backwards into the wall. "You dare..." he mumbled, trying to catch his breath. Phu didn't let him finish. He punched him in the lower part of his belly. The skeletal Mr. Nghiem groaned, clutched himself, and collapsed. Thong rushed over and caught him.

"He must have a cold," Phu said icily. "Take him into his office and rub some tiger balm on his temples, Thong."

Listening to Phu from Quanh's office, Lieu quickly assessed the situation. After Tiny Hoi, Phu had now shown himself to be most faithful to Quanh. From now on, Phu would have the acting director's trust, and ear.

Quanh squinted around the room, looking at all of them, licking his lips. "Let Mr. Phu deal with the situation," he said, sending a shudder through Lieu. "We must have order, or everything will fall apart. Now let's get back to our meeting."

Lieu's sharp little eyes moved over Quanh's face. He leaned towards him and muttered: "From what I saw at Thinh Luong, I think that wherever Khiem is, that's where Hoan is."

Khoai didn't really care what Lieu said, but he waited for him to finish before he added, slowly: "We need to watch Ms. Hoan in order to prevent any possible problems later, right? So let me deal with her. My brother is a tax collector in the Luong Nhan district. He has helped me before, and he can be helpful to us now—he told me that he has spotted our Ms. Hoan."

Chapter Ten

SIMPLICITY

After being slashed by Thoa, Hoan had pressed her hand to her bleeding face and had run from the office. Quanh's wheedling, insinuating voice echoed in her head. Did he think she was that stupid? She knew Khiem would never believe she'd signed the petition; more, she knew he would never use his wife to take revenge against her. She'd flagged down a cyclo and gone to hospital P where a close friend of hers was a doctor. The wound took eight stitches to close. But there had been no infection, and after her release from the hospital, still bandaged, she took a train to Dong Giao. She had another friend in that place, a woman with whom she had worked on the same volunteer canal-digging project when she was in high school. She had visited her on her way back from Thinh Luong, had thought of her now because they'd both suffered similar fates: her friend's face had also been slashed by a jealous wife. Their conditions were only different in two ways—one permanent and the other temporary. Hoan had been cut on her left cheek, her friend on her right. And her friend already had given birth to her child.

When she saw Hoan, she took her in immediately. "Stay with me here. I've contracted with the state farm to harvest ten hectares of pineapples, and I've been given some twenty square meters of land right on Highway One, to build a shop. Your being here will cheer up both me and my son." It was just right, Hoan thought. She also would soon have a son or daughter, Khiem's child. She wanted nothing more. She would let herself heal until she could remove the bandage and then work with her friend. The idea of laboring with her hands didn't bother her.

But the next day, when her friend came back from the pineapple grove, she saw Hoan lying motionless in bed, tears streaming down her face. It had all been too much. She'd lost the baby.

"Heaven presents you with another challenge before it will grant you happiness," her friend tried to console her.

Hoan worked with her for the next two months. During that time, she caught the eye of the state farm director, a widower. He began to visit her, bringing along all his medals and certificates, which he displayed for her proudly. His children had all studied and worked abroad, and had sent back a great deal of money that he'd used to build a large house near the highway, now rented out as a restaurant. His life, he told Hoan, was nearly perfect. He had money, land; he traveled abroad regularly. All he needed to complete the picture was her. Hoan wasn't unflattered. He was an elegant man of fifty-five, his love sincere and charming. "Plenty of young women on the state farm have been dreaming of becoming his wife," her friend said. "What are you waiting for?" But Hoan just smiled sadly and missed Khiem the more.

Her rejection intensified the director's passion. He became as agitated as a young man experiencing his first love. He cried, tried to give her gifts of expensive jewelry; finally he showed her a gun. If she continued to refuse him, he said, he'd kill himself like Hemingway, put the gun under his chin and pull the trigger.

At his age, Hoan thought. But she didn't want to be responsible for this man committing suicide. She asked her friend to go to Hanoi and see what she could find out about Khiem. When she learned that he had been hospitalized, recovered, and had also left Hanoi, she decided to leave the state farm. Wearing her laborer's clothes, carrying nothing but an old knapsack, she took the train back to Hanoi, and then caught another to the northwest.

She disembarked at the small railroad station and walked the seven kilometers that brought her back to the place where she'd been born, the place that held her parents' tombs, the place she had left so many years ago to begin her adult life. Her mother's sister still lived here. And here the Kieu river still mirrored the clouds like an ancient poem.

Other than that, everything had changed. The roads had been widened, and everywhere old houses had been torn down, dozens of new hotels, guest houses, and restaurants were jammed in next to each other, all of them pushing her recollections of an idyllic village life into the realm of legend. She could hardly find a trace of the place she remembered from her childhood. Her former friends had all left. Billboards and signs with English words on them advertised bars, restaurants, karaoke night clubs, soaps, detergents, cosmetics, underwear. "They call it development and progress," her aunt told her bitterly. But kids in the schools were shooting heroin now, and there were prostitutes everywhere. When the big spenders had their parties at the night clubs, the girls were always served up to them afterwards; they were called "fresh things."

The reservoir with its canal system she and her friend had helped to dig during the time when high schools had socialist labor days was now a lake bordered by an entertainment district. In it was a hotel called Fairy Scene. Her aunt told Hoan she could get a job there. She agreed immediately. She didn't want to be a parasite.

The hotel's owner was a twenty-five-year-old Amerasian,

a tall man with a long face. His mother had been Vietnamese, but he couldn't speak Vietnamese fluently yet. "I just open this hotel," he told her. "I hire thirty staff, male and female. But if you work here, I will be a tiger with more teeth, my darling." What nonsense, Hoan thought. She was old enough to be his mother—how dare he call her darling? But she kept her mouth shut. She needed the money to survive.

The Amerasian was planning to build a ten-story casino. He paid his workers $100 a month, but everyone had to work ten to twelve hours, night or day, as well as take his abuse and insults. Hoan was made a receptionist, not a very demanding job. She remained silent and saved her money, considering her time here just a temporary way-station. Though she didn't, in the end, know where she would finally go, what she would do.

Often her conversations with Khiem came back to her; they helped her feel she was not wasting her life. They had spoken about trying to experience each day, good or bad, as if it were a new page in a great novel, and she cultivated that feeling now. Each day brought her some new knowledge. Each day, living and working as a cog in the naked operation of this mechanism, she was learning what human beings were like. Selfish. Animalistic. Their one priority and goal, to satisfy their sexual desire. No question of love or morality. Waitresses sat on the customers' laps, kissed them, let them touch anywhere they wanted. No one cared if someone were a pervert or ill-bred. As soon as the men parked their cars and came to the door, they'd ask the guard, "Can we get some 'fresh things' here?" The guard, accepting their tips, would say politely: "Dear sir, please call this number." Rich men, directors of state-owned enterprises, even big wheels from the government, men whose faces she recognized, would openly ask the prices of the waitresses they wanted. They'd come to an agreement for an hour or for all night, the couple would immediately go to a room, take off their clothes, and jump into bed. Money ruled and women were goods. She still remembered her Marx: "The capitalists aren't satisfied with owning their own wives, the daughters of the proletariat, and open prostitution, but also switch their own spouses for entertainment."

A hundred years had gone by since that statement was made, but sex as a commodity still existed. Whenever important guests came to the hotel, the hotel owner would take them to an island and bring them a dozen girls, just out of high school. He'd even give them discount rates if they were the ones who had the power to decide on new hotel permits.

One night, nearly naked, he padded over to Hoan's reception area. Leaning his hairy chest over the counter, he narrowed his eyes and declared: "Hoan, I want you. I love you. I need you. Make love with me." He put his hands on her breasts. "How about a hundred dollars for an hour?" Hoan picked up the glass of water she had next to her, dashed it into his face, then tried to run. Spluttering, he caught her, spun her around, pressed her up against a wall. She bit his hand and managed to get away. What did I learn today, Khiem? That prostitution isn't an act of mutual consent. That it is a way for the poor to be raped by the rich and powerful.

***

After that, she left the hotel. Another friend found her work on a construction site, helping to build a sea dike. She had hoped the hard manual labor would help her forget. But it didn't. Even though it was winter, the dike, the sea, constantly reminded her of the days they had been together. She often remembered a poem she liked by Huu Thinh: *The Ballad of the Sea:*

Mother, the moment I realized cruelty is infinite
Was the moment I recognized the limits of compassion
The plank I float on is the last act of compassion
in this life full of troubles
....death is not as shameful, Mother
as a badly lived life
In the face of all dangers
I'm willing to start over again
with an innocent lullaby
If you run into a mountain,
believe you'll find a pass,
I again rush to the sea
Float like a buoy, swim desperately...

Thinking of Khiem, she again mourned the miscarriage, couldn't bear looking at the sea any more. She had only about thirty thousand dong left.

She returned to Hanoi.

She knocked at Vang's door at nine in the evening. He was dressed in his padded cotton Chinese-style singlet. His mouth dropped open and a look of happy surprise crossed his face. "It's you, Hoan. I went to a fortuneteller to ask about you, and I knew you'd be back. Can I get you something to eat?"

Hoan pulled her scarf more tightly over her scar. "Mr. Vang, I don't want to stay here long. There's something I have to ask you: I need money, but all I have to sell is my apartment."

"Don't be in such a hurry. I'll make an offer for whatever you need." Vang was trembling. "Please sit down, get warm; it's too cold these days. I have to tell you, I've been very worried about you and missed you very much. When I asked the fortuneteller, he said you were in trouble but had a lucky star and would escape danger."

"You're kind, Vang, and I'm very grateful."

"Please don't be so formal." Vang walked to another room and came back with a box. When he opened it, Hoan saw it was filled with gold. Vang remained silent, as if deliberating about what to say next.

"Mr. Vang, I know..." Hoan began.

"Do you, Hoan? Do you know I love you very much?"

He went down on his knees dramatically, his face flushed with hope and excitement. Hoan trying to defuse the tension, joked with him, said her love star was a very bad one. She wanted to be clear about the purchase of her apartment. Vang placed twenty ounces of gold on the table, and then he asked her what she planned to do. When she remained silent, he asked if she remembered what he had said before about people just doing what they needed to do in order to survive in the world. "Do you understand me?" he asked suddenly, and gripped her hand. She could feel the heat of his skin, his veins pulsing against her palm.

"Hoan," he said. "I'm not uneducated or stupid. I graduated from Co Minh University in Yunan before I was forced to immigrate to Vietnam. Like so many others, I've had to make my living any dirty way I could. And after a while, it becomes unclear—what is dirty and what is not? What I want to tell you, is the way to make money..."

For the next half hour he talked about the business of trafficking in opium, the size of the "network" for whom he worked. He wanted her to think seriously about what he had to offer. Hoan let herself listen. She asked him to keep the gold in a safe place; she would come back later to claim it.

***

Two bluestone dogs, one with a broken left ear. A red door with an iron ring hung from a breast-shaped hinge, in the old Chinese style. An ancient tiled roof. The house had all the characteristics she'd been told to look for. Hoan breathed a sigh of relief and felt a little less nervous.

It hadn't been far from Hanoi, only five bus stops. On the outskirts of the city really. The road was lined with lakes, ponds, and marshes. Finally she had come to this small street running parallel to the river. Far out on the water she could see square bamboo rafts that looked from this distance like pieces of cake. The slope of the dike was lined with split bamboo cane, gleaming white in the sun. She walked past an old water tap, placed there by the French in 1947. A wandering mat vendor loudly hawked his products. Under the canopy of a banyan tree was a shrine to the White Tiger Genie. Past the edge of the houses, far away, she could see green rice paddies, white storks flying over them.

The door opened slowly, revealing a neat garden, planted with various types of flowers and bonsai trees. It was more elegant and peaceful than she had imagined it would be.

"Who is it?"

"I am a relative of Mr. Vang. I'm looking for Mr. U."

Exactly twelve words, as instructed. The man put down the book he'd been reading, still open, on the arm of his chair, and stood up. He was tall and wore a dark blue warm-up suit with white trim. He had a handsome oval face, and his high nose, shining eyes, and small mouth gave him a refined air. His Vietnamese was correct in both grammar and intonation:

"I am U. But I was getting ready to leave; I have to catch a flight to Vientiane. I can give you only fifteen minutes."

"Then permit me to disturb you for those fifteen minutes, sir."

"I'm glad to see you."

The first set of passwords was correct. Hoan reached into her handbag and withdrew a thick envelope and a piece of broken mirror. U went inside and returned with a lacquered box. He took another shard of mirror from it, and matched its edge to Hoan's piece. Hoan's face felt numb, and sparkles of light danced in front of her eyes. The yin and yang shapes of the two broken pieces blended into one form. For an instant, it felt as if the two spans of a bridge had been joined and she was peacefully walking across it into another life. What simplicity! How easy everything was! She had always imagined the world of drug smuggling to be nightmarish and terrible, but when seen closely it was really quite ordinary. A garden in winter, and the head of the traffickers an urbane, gentle-mannered man, not a deformity like Quanh, a thug like Phu, or a scheming leech like Lieu.

U took the handbag from her and carried it inside, then came out with a tray of tea. They sat in bamboo chairs under a trellis framed with purple flowers. The perfume-scent of the tea evaporated sweetly in the air between them and helped calm her. She began to notice and differentiate between the fragrances of the different winter flowers. In the hall, through the open door, she glimpsed a bookcase and noticed it held a collection of the works of the famous woman writer Quynh Giao, long adored by the middle class in Vietnam. She had discussed that writer's work with Khiem, who had read most of her novels. "At any rate," he'd said, "she allows us to see a class of people who have confidence that the simple things of life will satisfy them." She felt suddenly breathless: it seemed that wherever she went, there was something that reminded her of Khiem. He was the constant element in her life, her vital strength.

"Do you like Chinese literature?" U asked.

"Yes, very much. I've read almost all the books that have been translated, from classical works to modern novels."

"What about the ones by Kim Dung?"

"You mean the kung fu novels? No, I think they only appeal to adolescents."

She regarded them as strictly escapist entertainment. Yet, she remembered, Khiem had read those books also and when she'd asked him why, he'd said that there were useful things in them. "Kim Dung's message is that beyond the sky there is a sky," he had said. "He is a link between the intellectual, the delicate, and the popular spirit. His work stresses the idea that real art shouldn't be life but a hallucination of life."

U leaned back in his chair. "I have read Kim Dung only recently. On the Chinese mainland, he is ranked as one of the nine great writers of this century, after Lu Tsun. Both have contributed to the modern Chinese language and have deep insights into humanity. Their writing always contains the suggestion of metamorphosis, the power of the word to transcend and transform reality. Kim Dung creates his own world in his books—a great feat, don't you think?"

He was looking at her, smiling. She didn't fully grasp his idea, but talking about literature eased her, made her feel clean. Her mind drifted. Without literature, human beings couldn't develop in harmony with their own natures, Khiem had said. "'Without flowers, one can hardly be honest,'" he'd quoted from the poet Thi Hoang. Sitting in the drug dealer's chair, she remembered how she and Khiem had discussed fiction and poetry. She had been passionate about poetry and used to write it, even though Khiem chided her that her poems always tried to rhyme like songs and weren't real poetry. She didn't care, and she could see he loved her love of literature. In fact, she read everything—foreign and Vietnamese—that she could get her hands on. It wasn't simply diversion. In what she had once thought of as her complicated life, she had searched for meaning and pattern. At first she had gone to poetry. But often she had trouble understanding what made a classic poem good or bad, and had come to prefer novels. She devoured them, often reading a five-hundred-page book in one night. Anything. Even books written by critics, she'd said wryly to Khiem. Every book in the library. Even *How to Plant Azaleas*, she'd said. She used to comment to Khiem about every writer she read. "What about me?" he asked. She'd given him a thumbs-up and smiled. He grinned back. "Whoever praises you once, you should praise twice. Whoever criticizes you once, you should criticize back a hundred times." Hoan had shaken her head. "But you writers never read each other's books. And none of you believe you're in the second rank." Khiem had cried out: "How did you know that?" "Because I know you," she'd said. He'd laughed. "Through you I can see that we writers have some use in life. If every reader were like you, we'd be ashamed not to write masterpieces each time."

But he had helped her create herself, Hoan thought, sitting in the drug trafficker's garden. Since the day she had started to fall in love with Khiem, she had fallen more deeply in love with literature. She couldn't imagine her life without it. After she had read a great book, she believed her internal suffering had been purged.

Half an hour after leaving U's house, Hoan was still walking serenely down the street, feeling free, cool, enjoying the feeling. There was no sign she was being watched by the police, and she was carrying half an ounce of gold in her bag, payment for what she had done. And she had learned a new truth about life today: drug traffickers always paid in gold.

***

Parallel to the visible stream of life is a skein of unseen canals and ditches where traffic runs silently but not less busily. The people who do their business along those pathways are organized according to their own mysterious laws, and their network is very strong and very complex and exists everywhere. Vang was only one of the distribution points for the product that came from the mountains to Hanoi. How many points there were, no one could know. The product came to Vang, and then to U. But Hoan had no idea how many other couriers like herself were transporting it. Nor did she know where it went from U and what happened to it afterwards. The world she'd come into now was a closed circle, its methods and customs determined by hundreds of years of tradition.

It all made Vang very excited. Every fifth day for a month, Hoan brought his "goods" to U. One day, when she checked her bag on the way home, Hoan discovered that she'd been paid twice the amount she'd received before, a whole ounce of gold. When she asked Vang about it, he explained that for the first time she had transported the real product. A chill went through her. Then she felt something warm and tough licking her hand. She looked down and saw Vang kneeling, pressing his thick lips on her hand. "Hoan," he whispered, "Once someone is trusted and accepted into the organization, we live and die together. We're closer than blood relatives or husband and wife." Hoan shivered, as if a toad had touched her skin, and drew her hand away. She had gone deeply now into the country on the other side of the bridge.

By spring, Vang had her going to different areas, performing different duties. She traveled by train to the northwest, jammed into compartments packed with other couriers and smugglers, some hiding velvet cloth around their bellies, some with flashlights and other goods, all trying to avoid tax and custom duties. Whenever the train stopped, they'd scramble up to the roof of the compartment and then leap off and hide in the bushes near the station. When the train started again, they'd rush back and jump aboard, avoiding the ticket sellers, though they'd already made arrangements for the conductors to ignore their presence. Sometimes they'd trip, or miss their jump and fall, smashing their heads or fracturing ribs. Watching them, Hoan was surprised to find that she could keep herself feeling cool and detached. She wondered if she had come to accept cruelty and pain as a necessity for her own survival.

Yet she was not completely indifferent. Not when she smelled the fragrance of the anise flowers blossoming in Lang Son. The smell made her giddy; it brought a flush of warmth to her that evoked Khiem. She began to look for the other places he had described to her, from the time he'd been in the army here. Once he'd told her how after the fighting in Ma Chai San, he and three of his fellow soldiers, all wounded, had been left temporarily under a big kapok tree. All of them were unconscious, but Khiem had awakened to the sound of a guitar playing Van Cao's *The Dreamy Spring*, a song considered too romantic, and banned during those times. But he'd heard it and recovered from his wounds. So today she'd learned that dreaming was also a necessity of life. Although now the hanging bridge he'd told her he had guarded against attempts to mine it had been replaced by a five-span cement one.

She took some time also to search for the teak tree which, according to Khiem, had been planted by the teacher-writer Nguyen Cong Hoan while he was exiled here by the French. She looked for number 54 T Street, where horses had been stabled, waiting to be used by the army for transportation. When he had stayed there in the early sixties, Khiem had started writing his first short stories, all peopled with characters that reflected the warmth and kindness of these small towns. All of them had been destroyed by Chinese artillery during the border war in 1979; there wasn't a trace. But she knew where they had been, and Khiem's stories allowed them to exist in her mind.

Similarly, when she went by bus to Buon Me Thuot in the Central Highlands, the deep reds and blues of dusk at sunset were exactly as Khiem had described. Alone in a garden near Da Lat, she saw a rose and was stunned, imagined it the one rendered by her lover in a short story of his she'd read. It opened a deep and lonely pit in her heart, that flower. As a flower was a leap in the evolution of plants, Khiem had written, beauty was similar to loneliness. His ideas flooded back to her. Violet dew, light sunshine, the curve of a hill, the mouth of a river, a calf lowing for its mother, the whistle of the train; it all took her to Khiem.

She traveled a great deal but she always hurried back to Hanoi. It was still her center, the nexus where her life had been gathered and been defined, from which it had moved in the direction it was going now. She only came at night, and with her face covered. But once in her apartment, she would feel lost, even when she opened her window and looked towards her leaning tower of Pisa, trying to orient herself. She couldn't. Khiem wasn't there anymore. She wrote to her friend at the Dong Giao state farm: "I feel as if I'm in an empty, rudderless boat in the middle of a stormy night." Her friend replied: "Hoan, you're an educated woman, and you have determination, energy, beauty, and talent, but still I worry about you." Hoan knew her friend was concerned about her wandering life. It was true; there were no safe havens for her. And she was in a to-hell-with-it mood. But she still kept Khiem in her thoughts and had to believe he still had her in his heart.

One night, when she'd returned from Haiphong, Vang told her: "Mr. U wants to invite you to go to Hong Kong with him for a few days." Seeing her lack of enthusiasm, he pressed on: "I know you don't want to be tied down. Mr. U and I, we want to let you know that we understand you, and we fully respect your wishes."

"Please say clearly what you mean."

Vang looked down. They knew she was tough and determined and ambitious—they knew she couldn't remain content as a simple courier. Because of that she was an unknown factor for them, a mystery. "What I mean, Hoan," he blurted out, "is that if you ever want to start working independently, we wouldn't stand in your way."

"Thank you." Looking at him, she saw he seemed to be sorry for what he'd just said. Before he could modify it, she said: "In that case, I'd like to do it right now."

That night, she drew up the papers to sell her apartment to Vang for the equivalent of twenty ounces of gold. Vang was still somewhat stunned. After only six months as a trafficker, Hoan had matured enough to be able to operate alone.

***

The next afternoon, she went to the post office and sent all the money to her Uncle Tuy in Thinh Luong. Afterwards, she wandered around the city alone.

Hanoi was large, but every corner of it held some trace of her life. She walked towards the railroad station: from its south portal, she would leave Hanoi forever. As if for the first time, she was acutely aware of the life of the capital boiling all around her, its thick, indifferent crowds. This city had allowed the passionate love between herself and Khiem to develop, had given them a place to be. He always quoted Nguyen Huy Tuong's line to her: "Hanoi is a capital of alleys." It was true. They would wander those alleys together, buy sesame, red beans, and corn, sweet soups and cakes, all of it cheap, from tiny places clustered on narrow streets with no names. Canh Nong Park, where they had first kissed. The tilted stone bench in front of the post office by the Lake of the Sword, where they had sat and complained about the litter. The State Bank Park on a late afternoon in autumn, the drizzle rustling the dried leaves all around them, and Khiem saying, "Where has humankind disappeared to, leaving only the two of us in this place?" West Lake, where they would come after work and try to float away all their sadness. Once, Khiem had turned to her and looked into her eyes as if for the first time, and she could see he felt what she was whispering in her own heart: "Don't be sad, my darling." The row of banyan trees near the army museum that Khiem had never noticed until one day she'd told him to pick the banyan buds, to make a herbal medicine for Hong Ha's sinusitis.

She stopped and rested for a moment in front of 18 Trang Thi Street. Caught in a sudden rainstorm after leaving a movie theatre one night, they had sheltered in this doorway, trying to cover themselves with a tiny piece of plastic. It was pouring. Now and then the headlight beams from a car turning the corner from Ba Trieu Street would illuminate the sheet of water cascading down the front of the building across from them, the reflection dancing on their faces with sparkling colors. They pressed against each other, feeling a harmonious excitement. It was the longest rain shower of her life, and she hadn't wanted it to ever end. "Let it rain until dawn," she told Khiem. "If I came home now, Vang would just grumble at me when he had to answer the door." Then, like two kids, they held on to each other and ran down the street, looking for a drier, warmer place. By dawn, they were hiding under a frame displaying paper flowers, listening to the raindrops falling on the plastic sheeting, wondering why the night was so short. "You just finishing the third shift?" the proprietor of the soup restaurant had asked them when they stopped in for breakfast, and Hoan had laughed and said yes, their salaries were low and they had many children and had to work overtime. They'd had tea then and gone into a bookstore, and it was as if the day would be a miracle also, for there was Khiem's new novel, auspiciously called *Autumn Rain*, just going on display. "I'll take ten copies," Hoan had said, "we'll bring good luck to your store." The owner had smiled and said, "This one's a bestseller. You're buying them to sell them back to your students, right?" And she remembered how a month later, when all 12,000 copies of the book had sold out, Khiem had told her that he found the book to be just "so-so." "The reason it sold so fast was that someone wrote a critical article condemning me for letting the positive character die in the middle of the story. That made readers curious, so they rushed out to buy it. In Vietnam, when a book is a bestseller, it doesn't necessarily mean it's a good book."

The memories overlapped, merged. She walked all night, not realizing dawn had come until she heard the morning exercise commands being barked at the soldiers in Hoang Dieu Citadel. Only then did she let herself acknowledge that the night was over, her last night in this city, with all of its sweet and bitter memories. She had suffered, and she wanted revenge. And, yes, she wanted to be rich, very rich and famous, but, first of all, rich.

She stopped, intending to cross Nguyen Thai Hoc street to the railroad station. Then, quickly, she covered her face. Crossing right in front of her was Lieu. He was jogging, his muscular arms swinging, one still bearing the faded tattoo of a dragon, his face gloomy. She could hear him murmuring to himself as he ran, as if he were still scheming, even when he was by himself.

***

"Why am I doing this?" Lieu was muttering to himself.

The life of the city was marked by fads. A fad would begin, draw enthusiasts to it, and give birth to a different fad. During the last two years, there had been the quail-rearing trend, then the catfish rage, then the Hong Kong parrot furor, and now the craze for pet dogs. The last had gone on for the longest time, and several people had been able to move out of poverty thanks to the profits they made selling dogs. But, as with all the other fads, this one was fading as well. Lieu had brought all his newborn puppies to give away to Quanh, Phu, and Khoai, calculating it was better to have their good will than the tiny profit he would make selling the puppies. He needed sympathy. He needed their support. Now he was training himself to run alone. And this was no trend he was following, like the vogues for drinking pure water for breakfast, various diets, Zen exercises for health, and so on. He had started training himself the day after Phu had beaten up Nghiem in defense of Quanh's prestige. Afterwards, the rumor had started spreading quickly that Phu would be appointed Quanh's deputy. He'd also heard gossip that Quanh considered him a two-faced person without principles. Meanwhile, Khoai had seemed to catch fire with enthusiasm, rushing in and out of Quanh's office all day, scheming and plotting, whispering with him as if they were counterfeiters, and continuously calling staff meetings. They'd begin by exhorting people to start improving the quality of editing, and then scream at them to purify their ideology. Finally, they revealed what they really wanted, and openly declared that whoever knew where Hoan was had to inform the police immediately; she had dirtied the reputation of their division and must be returned so she could be officially fired. She had no right to quit on her own the way she had. And, by the way, the deputy director chair was still open.

Lieu had been training regularly, each day increasing the distance he ran. Sometimes, though, he felt haunted. He would stop in the middle of the road and wonder: why am I running? Why have I set thirty kilometers as my goal? What's the point? But he continued to jog. As he did it now, a memory came to him. He was fifteen years old and had to wake up early in order to fetch water for his family. He was running, carrying two full buckets of water, when he saw his brother Chuong Kien standing in his underwear, scratching his armpit. He looked at Lieu's muscles with admiration. "Running is the best exercise," he had said, nodding. "But don't run until you're exhausted. You need to increase your speed gradually, and breathe in harmony with the rhythm of your run...remember that."

Kien was on his mind all the time now.

Chapter Eleven

LONGEVITY PEACHES

Carrying one red basket and one blue basket, both filled with peaches, Hoan boarded the bus. She glanced down the aisle, saw that seat number four was free, and sat down quickly, putting the baskets in the aisle. The rearview mirror was located just in front of seat one, and in it she could keep an eye on who was boarding from the rear of the bus.

It was late spring now, and warm breezes wafted over the filthy bus station, crusted with garbage and litter. Hoan felt easy, as relaxed as a person returning from a visit to a pagoda. She looked through the window, saying a silent farewell. She didn't intend to return to this place, a small town next to a wide river, in the western cordillera. It had a dam and a hydroelectric plant, and electricity lit its houses. But the tiny glows of human accomplishments seemed puny against the backdrop of the immense valley walled by the mountain ranges running east and west like the ribs of the earth. The eye couldn't encompass the vastness of the countryside, scattered with gardens, orchards, and rice paddies, and pegged by ancient shrines to the spirits of the mountains: the Five Tigers, the White Dragon, the Jungle Goddess, the Earth Mother, and more, all of them perpetually shrouded in white incense smoke.

Like the rest of the women who'd come to this place to

pray for the blessings of those spirits, Hoan had wandered around for nearly a week. She visited and burned incense at each of the shrines, performed the expected rituals with respect and care. Then, after buying her return bus ticket, she had bought the two baskets of peaches. "These are longevity peaches," the young vendor told her. "For you, I'll sell them cheap—only seven thousand dong for a basket." Hoan had laughed. "But these are just Meo peaches," she'd said, carelessly. "How can you call them longevity peaches? What if they give me only a short life?" Then realizing that the words might bring bad luck, she'd smiled at the boy: "You must be speaking about this symbol of longevity on the fruit—straight from the orchard of the Western Queen Fairy, right? OK, I'll buy them all, so I can live forever." Then she gave the vendor fifteen thousand instead of fourteen. In the station, she'd sat among the waiting passengers, taken the peaches from the two bamboo baskets she'd gotten from the vendor, and reloaded them into her own plastic baskets.

She'd been coming through that station for four months, and its appearance had grown very familiar to her: its rusty iron balustrades, the short ticket-seller, rude to everyone except her. Maybe he saw something in her face, or on it: maybe the makeup and lipstick she wore, the same kind she used to give to Tiny Hoi; maybe some vestiges of the soft-heartedness that used to be her main trait, the need to understand and be fair that she'd once extended even to Khiem's jealous wife.

It had all grown familiar to her, that station. Even its dirt and dust and the blind street singer with the beautiful baritone and the song he'd sung:

> *Like the green trees facing the cold winter wind*
> *Without you today my dream is shattered*
> *Encompassed by your warm arms I was in Paradise*
> *Now only pain and bitterness remain...*

He had been there just before she left, with his signature song. She had given the little girl who guided him five thousand dong and tried to hold back her tears. But she couldn't cry there. She couldn't let herself be noticed. She had to keep the now-faint scar on her cheek covered. She had to blend in with the others, act like them. Act normal in the presence of the man who had come in and sat down next to her, throwing his sack of dirty cassava onto the floor, taking off his hat and fanning himself, cursing the heat of this devilish place.

* * *

Hoan was aware of her dual nature. She could be kind and too mild, but she could also be sharp. She could be intuitive about what might happen, but she always tried to avoid confrontation. She believed fatalistically in the destiny foretold in her horoscope, but at the same time believed she could control her fate through her own efforts. She believed she could read people's future and character in their faces and hands, but also believed people created their own happiness and unhappiness. She was tough and she was weak. Experienced and innocent. Generous and selfish. A believer in the sacredness of pure chaste love, and in the enjoyment of her passion and sexuality. She had lived fully.

The day she returned from Thinh Luong beach, she had dropped by her friend's house at the Dong Giao state farm. Her friend had taken her to a fortuneteller who told her she would meet a great misfortune. It had come true when Thoa slashed her face. The next time she had taken sanctuary in Dong Giao, the same fortuneteller had said her karma was still full of bad omens. But she didn't fully believe in the supernatural anyway. "All people can count on is that they will have both lucky and unlucky things happen to them," Khiem had said, and whenever another misfortune occurred she thought of that and somehow it made her feel closer to him. He was the luck she could count on; the one faith she kept was in his love, her belief that he would never betray her. It was why she was always so moved by the story of the princess My Chau and the prince Trong Thuy. Not by its bitterness, but by the way tears had finally been turned into pearls.

Once Khiem had lent her Ngo Van Phu's translation of the Maxwell Arnet story "The Wolf." It was a version of the Little Red Riding Hood fairy tale. In it, the wolf was presented as a reformed, kindly creature who felt terrible about its former habit of eating sheep. But the two children talking to it said: "You can never really be kind, because you've eaten so many baby sheep." And the wolf had answered: "You enjoy eating sheep as well," and the children had to admit it was right.

The story had reminded Hoan of what Vang had said a long time ago: in certain ways both smugglers and policemen were the same. Both were compelled by their natures, both needed to live. When she'd told that to Khiem, she said she felt the same way about the love between them, not accepted by law or custom, but not a sin. Khiem had smiled and said, "Both the wolf and Vang are masters of sophistry. They're as smart as you are, Hoan."

She knew she was relying on the sophistry of the wolf and Vang to justify the life she had chosen now. But she didn't think she was a bad person. Her behavior was her way of taking action against bad people. She would show them how tough she could be. She was stubborn and she knew how to hate and she wanted revenge. She wanted to commit herself completely to it and she wanted her effort to be prodigious. She wanted to appear before them again as rich and powerful as a queen. She and Khiem had been the victims of cowards who acted in cowardly ways, both of them sheltered, naive aesthetes, easy to smash. But she had refused to accept it passively. She knew the risks of the illegal trade she'd entered. She knew she had been forced into it by these circumstances, forced to go into darkness in order to move towards brightness. It was a brightness she could see, she could hold in her hand, if the business she was involved in now went through all right. This trip would be the last adventure of a person who understood who she was.

***

"If you don't have a ticket, please buy one now," the conductor called. He had his collection bag under his left armpit and was standing right in front of her, interrupting her thoughts, shouting loudly to be heard over the noisy passengers searching for seats. Trying to duck out of the way of a man carrying a big box, Hoan turned and, as quickly, jerked her head back. She glanced into the rearview mirror and bit her lips, then pretended to be staring casually through the window.

She had been living in a constant state of vigilance for nearly a year, and her senses had been sharpened. She admitted to herself that the man she'd seen had been observing her. Even before becoming a drug runner, her sixth sense had always been impressive, and when she'd worked in the hotel, she'd helped some of the waitresses make a lot of money by advising them about which lottery numbers to play.

But now she hoped she was wrong. Perhaps she was; there was no one watching her. It was a coincidence. Or maybe she was just too nervous. She truly hoped the guy was just an ordinary passenger, some peasant from Thai Binh or Nam Dinh, or a land developer from Son La, or someone who'd come to visit his relatives in Hoa Binh and had been given that bag of dried cassavas to take home. When he'd sat next to her in the station, his appearance and accent had made him seem country. When she'd given the little girl who led the blind singer five thousand dong, he'd taken a torn five-hundred-dong note, thrown it into the old can she held, and asked her to tell her father to sing "Lan and Diep" and he would give her more. He'd split some sugar cane with his teeth, bitten into it, and chewed, and when the saliva had dribbled out of the corners of his mouth, he'd wiped it with the back of his hand. In other words, he was like everyone else in this crowd: nothing to worry about.

Trying to keep calm, Hoan rested the back of her head against the seat. After a while the steady vibration of the floor lulled her to sleep.

She awoke about twenty minutes later. Except for the noise of the motor, the bus was quiet; all of the other passengers were asleep. Feeling more relaxed after her short rest, she thought perhaps her fatigue had made her over-suspicious. There was nothing about her to draw that man's attention. She was returning from visiting a pagoda, like all of the others. The baskets of peaches she was carrying were the same kind of local produce everyone else had bought: the dried bamboo, earwood, perfumed mushrooms, and other fruits. She was only one more face in this crowd.

***

Through the front window of the bus she could see the macadamized road stretching before them, running along the bank of a river. It was before the monsoon, and the river was drying in its bed and looked no deeper than puddles of rain water. She remembered the river that ran through her native province:

From now, oh Kieu river, I say farewell to you
But away from you my heart is so confused
The lonely boat troubles the cloud's reflection
on the water

Troubles me,
the passenger on Kieu river

She had written that poem just before she left her
province, when she'd finished high school. She had been
sixteen and she knew that her beauty had made her stand
out from the other female students. Men of all ages had been
smitten by her, and each of her male teachers and every
young man in her district had dreamt of being the one she
would choose to take care of her. She had always tried to
keep her distance from them and concentrate fully on her
studies. The principal of the school had been a man of over
fifty, but when she came to say goodbye to him, he had
shown her a collection of love poems called "Offerings to
H," and numbered from 1 to 10. Because of her, her math
teacher who had been born in Nghe An province had
stopped wearing his rough, hand-sewn, brown-dyed Nghe
An clothes and instead bought a yellow polyester shirt. In its
pocket he always kept a perfumed handkerchief. But he
couldn't change his Nghe An accent, and Hoan had made
her schoolmates burst into laughter when she pretended to
ask him to explain something. Then there was the teacher of
literature from Hanoi who told her he dreamt of her every
night. He waited for her after school to give her rides home
on his bicycle. The two teachers had finally confronted each
other, pounded their fists on the table between them, called
each other vile dogs. Her male classmates had openly hated
the literature teacher, considering him an outsider, come to
steal their school beauty. He sent her a letter each week in
which he addressed her as "Kieu River," and signed off with
the initials ILY: I Love You. When that code was discovered,
he changed it to WFM: Wait For Me. Wait until she finished
school, and he would take her back to Hanoi and she would
enter the university, etc.... Wait for me, because people here
were so provincial and backward they would never accept

the love of a teacher for his student. And he would try his best to join the Party, for her. He had a good family background. His father was an executive member of the province's Party Committee. His mother was chairwoman of the Women's Union there. He could do it. Listening to him, Hoan had felt somewhat tempted and moved. But then, suddenly, it was declared that her family had a reactionary background: her late grandfather and her father, who was then district chairman, had been members of the Kuomintang during the time the patriot Nguyen Thai Hoc had led his revolt and had been captured and executed in Yen Bai. Without considering how long ago it had been, not to mention logic, her father had been thrown into prison. Immediately, her literature teacher had written her a letter saying he had been made a member of the Communist Party and was about to be promoted to principal. The letter was cold and formal and asked her to excuse him, but under the circumstances, etc. She called and asked him to meet her one dark night, near the river. When he emerged from a canebrake, as his mouth started to open to say something, she'd slapped him in the face and called him a coward.

Fortunately, she had already finished high school. But after her father committed suicide in prison, her mother had grown withdrawn and distant and wanted to stay away from everyone. Hoan knew she had to leave her native province and go to the capital; in that jungle of human beings, no one would know her, and she could build a new life.

In Hanoi, she lived with a relative and studied at the University of Culture. Thirty years of war had ended then and people were trying to rebuild normal lives. After Hoan's graduation from the university, she was assigned to work for a district radio station in the delta. The station manager was an ex-peasant who had been promoted after the land reform campaign. He too became obsessed with Hoan. At night, making love to his wife, he would call Hoan's name in the heat of passion. The wife threatened to stone Hoan and leave her with a broken face. Hoan arranged a meeting with her at which she told her directly: "Madame, in my eyes your husband is a rock or a bush or a weed growing out of a crack in the pavement. To say it more clearly: he is nothing to me." When she'd slapped her former literature teacher, Hoan had demonstrated for the first time how tough she was. Before, she had been only beautiful. Now, after being hurt, she was like a porcupine: she knew how to bristle up her spikes to defend herself. She was twenty-two years old.

Twenty-two and beautiful, talented, charming when she told stories, skillful in organizing festivals and conferences, a lover of books—Hoan caught the attention of the district leadership. After the trouble at the radio station, she was assigned as assistant cultural cadre of the district People's Committee. But her beauty continued to bring her trouble. She excited men, drew them fluttering to her like butterflies to a flower. The leadership, men who had all gotten their positions during the land reform upheavals, were in the habit of putting both legs up on the sofa, rolling up their trousers, yawning, and speaking in flowery terms. Looking at Hoan, they became as weak as water and understood for the first time the power of a dream. One brought her gifts. Another gave her a card so she could buy a subsidized bicycle or a radio. A director promoted her. He sent her notes declaring his passion, asked to meet her, in the park, at the pagoda, or the district guest house. If she refused, he would turn on her: "Be careful—your future is in my hands." Her damned beauty! It was nothing but trouble to her, creating around her a silent, boiling sea of contention. Hard to imagine that these men molded and forged in war and the class struggle, indomitable, could become selfish, hate each other, undercut each other, all over a woman. The internal solidarity of the Party was so threatened that the higher levels had to send an executive member of the Party from the provincial level to take charge of the district.

Finally, partly because the police had discovered Hoan's tainted family background, the head of the district personnel department decided he had to send her to work on a volunteer labor team. As he handed her the decision, he whispered in her ear: "Hoan, I love you desperately. Believe me—this wasn't my idea. Go there for a month, and I'll get the provincial level leadership to send you back. I want you to belong to me alone."

But he died in an automobile accident a few days after she left, so Hoan never got to experience the great honor of being his alone. To her great relief she only had to be with other women who, for various reasons and from various places, had been sent like her to dig canals and build dams, sluice gates, and drainage systems. She was cheerful, worked hard, and got along with everyone. It was a relief to be away from men.

It didn't last long. The foreman was a notorious womanizer in his forties, even though he had an ugly, pockmarked face. He designated Hoan as a cultural worker and put her in charge of the loudspeaker. She had to sit next to him in his car, go with him to all the parties. He whispered the familiar saccharine phrases into her ear: "You're my queen; I'll be your slave for life," and so on. But he was more dangerous than her other suitors.

One New Year's Eve, he asked her to stay in the office to perform some special duties. He gave her an orange juice. As soon as she drank it, Hoan felt faint and her vision grew blurry. She felt herself, as if from a distance, being pushed down onto the table, felt her clothing stripped away, goose bumps running up and down her legs. The only thing that saved her was the foreman's impotence, brought on by a bout with venereal disease. She managed to clear her head, push him away, clean herself, and run back to the team. Afraid that she would report him, he agreed to send her back to digging canals.

***

The bus rounded a curve, and the driver relaxed his grip on the steering wheel as he came out of the mountains and onto the flatlands. Behind him, people came awake and immediately began laughing and chatting. Looking out of the window, Hoan saw white clouds drifting across her field of vision, the same kind of clouds she had seen last summer in Thinh Luong.

Nearly a year had passed, but closing her eyes, she could see it all again, was flooded with the images and sounds and emotions of those days. Her throat swelled. Oh my love, she thought. Oh my love.

She had felt inexplicably drawn to Khiem the first time she had seen him. The same emotion had overwhelmed her again when she'd swum to him at Thinh Luong.

One day while she had been dredging a canal with her team, she'd heard her name called from the bank and looked up to see a tall, slim, pale young man wearing glasses. He was standing next to a blue Niva and waving to her. "Hello, Uncle!" she'd called, recognizing her mother's younger brother. He was a high-ranking official in General Department T. Smiling, he told her he'd been searching for her for a long time. Both her grandfather and her father had been posthumously rehabilitated. "Don't be bitter or blame people," he'd advised her. "There were errors made, and people suffered, just as you have. But it's finished now, and there's no reason for you to work here any longer."

So there was fate. She had let him arrange everything, had come to the Division of Cultural Affairs, and had begun her work as a proofreader. Her salary was low, far less than Lieu or Phu or Quanh's, but she had felt safe there, as if she had finally reached a destination. She began working there two years before Khiem's arrival, and for the first time since becoming a woman, she had no problems with lovelorn men.

When she met Khiem for the first time, she felt she had returned to herself, regained her trust and sense of innocence. She was intact.

Khiem had been discharged from the army and returned to his teaching position in the mountains. Then he'd moved to Hanoi, searching for an environment in which he could develop his literary talent, and where he and Thoa could start afresh, work on easing the tension in their marriage. The reconciliation had failed. But Hanoi, with its thousand years of civilization could still give a talented person the opportunity to use his gift.

She still wore her hair long then, and the day Khiem came to the office she had been wearing a dark brown blouse with a heart-shaped collar. When Khiem entered the office that morning, she had felt that inexplicable sense of recognition. She brought him to Mr. Dang, who was then director. "I've read your novels," Dang said, "and I'm glad you've transferred here. Unfortunately, this division is very small, and our main duty is to publish pamphlets and policy and regulation documents. But as my deputy, I'll make sure you have time to write."

By chance, his cubicle was next to Hoan's, separated only by a board partition. She would hear his pen scratching away and ask him what he was writing. "Just correcting an old manuscript," he'd say. At that time, Quanh had been angry at not being promoted—he'd been accused of taking bribes— and was always looking for excuses to criticize Khiem, resenting that he'd been brought in as Dang's deputy director. When Khiem's major novel, *Border Areas,* had been published by New Life Publishing House, Quanh had thrown it down on the table, exclaiming: "Yes, the man has talent, but he has no political consciousness."

Khiem wasn't bothered by him. But one day Hoan passed over to him a sheet she'd torn off a calendar and written on: "Wherever stupidity is a model, intelligence becomes insanity." Khiem had understood that she had been referring to Quanh's shameful comment. He had carefully put her note away in his journal and replied, also on a page torn from a calendar: "Man is higher than everything: against him all is measured." It wasn't until much later that Hoan understood him, and in the meantime the days of their calendars became a bridge between them over which they sent lines or stanzas of poems that they found beautiful, new ideas, a nicely worded sentence, a saying they found wise, a funny remark. The more Khiem came to know her, the more he discovered in her the feminine kindness he'd been missing; the more Hoan read his books, the more she adored him. She wrote: "After reading you, I can't read anyone else." He didn't reply. Perhaps he'd been shocked by her forwardness, she'd thought. When she passed him her own poems, he'd written back: "Put all those cheap, easy rhymes, those popular phrases into the garbage." Then the next day: "I was wrong to write what I did—I understand you only want to express yourself, not to be a poet. Please forgive me." Reading that, Hoan had found herself sobbing. Only the most intimate of friends could speak to each other in that way.

They became closer and closer, until sometimes they seemed to be sharing the same personality, identical perceptions. They'd read the same book, find themselves uttering the same comments about a particular poem or issue. Mr. Dang retired, and Khiem was appointed to take his place as director. Quanh said nothing. But Hoan recognized what he was then: a silent, sullen, Squint-Eyed Toad.

Khiem was faced with many obstacles as director. He was the center of everything, and all around him was a great nest of sycophants. He had to keep himself aloof, and because of that remained isolated and lonely. His private life didn't improve either. Thoa hadn't changed her ways since moving to Hanoi; instead she began an affair with a crooked-mouthed photographer who owned a photo shop on Giang Vo Road. The situation became even worse when she announced her resignation from her office and began doing business from province to province. Hong Ha was often sent off to her grandparents, and after work Khiem would wander to the city parks or lakes to gather a few peaceful moments for himself. One late autumn afternoon, the sky a dismal gray, he was sitting in the agricultural park near Hoang Dieu Road. Thoa was on her way to Saigon with her latest boyfriend to have yet another abortion. The situation had become unbearable to Khiem, and he was finally ready for a divorce. But her new lover, like all the others, had told Thoa that his wife wouldn't set him free. To make things worse, the newly promoted head of General Department T, displacing Hoan's uncle, was Pho, Khiem's former student, who had previously been a railway trade unionist. Pho had been shocked to find that his ex-teacher was now in his power, and Quanh, after finding out about their former connection, had started to build up a relationship with Pho while at the same time disparaging Khiem.

Khiem (he'd told her later) had felt at an impasse that day. The park was empty around him, the leaves turning brown and the grass yellow and dry. In his loneliness, he realized he was longing for something, and at the moment he thought that, he muttered the name that encompassed the feeling: "Hoan." He had turned, and she was sitting on the end of the bench. He felt he was in a dream, and he never understood then or later why at the very moment he'd most needed rescue, she had been there, as she would be there later, as they would find each other at Thinh Luong beach. They leaned their foreheads against each other, naturally, as if they were finally surrendering to whatever spirit had drawn them together. Hoan had sobbed, suddenly afraid of the happiness she'd been dreaming of. They kissed each other for the first time under the shadow of the canopy over the street light, and Hoan leaned against his shoulder and then raised her face to him again. "Khiem, I miss you all the time. Please protect me, darling." Khiem held her in his arms and they kissed again, fiercely this time, and Khiem's lips went to her neck, to her breasts, and she held him tightly and whispered she wanted to devour him, take him into herself so she could possess him totally.

The barrier was lifted. They became lovers, though they had to avoid speaking to each other in the office, and delayed the final consummation of their love until Thinh Luong. The city, with its many places to hide away, became their ally.

***

Hoan was drowning in her memories, choking on them, pounded by them as if by waves. She wished she could relive the moment at Thinh Luong when her bare feet had pressed the sand underwater and the cool breeze had brushed over her wet shoulders, and, when she'd opened her eyes, Khiem had stood in the midst of the tumultuous crowd, waiting for her.

Their meeting, their love, was an idea in the mind of Heaven, just as Khiem had once told her that sometimes the words and ideas came out of his pen as if from an uncontrolled, sacred urging.

She felt seized by the idea: it was necessary to find Khiem immediately, tell him, share her happiness with him, clarify everything, name their love. Their love was alive in her now, its images burned into her mind's eye. Her nervousness amid the smell of fish sauce and the storm from the ocean. How she had been both shy and full of joy at being naked in front of him, and how moved Khiem had been seeing her, the first man she had ever let look at her body in that way. How she had been full of desire and when their orgasms had come they had both closed their eyes and felt themselves melding together and at the very peak of it she had opened her eyes and it was as if there was light emanating from his body and she felt so small and yet so perfected. It had all been natural with him, and there was no sense of shame when he had undressed her, when he had lain behind her and caressed her breasts. All of it an affirmation that they belonged to each other, physically and spiritually.

Trembling, Hoan felt her breasts and thighs swelling with desire, and had to close her legs tightly, clasp the seat in front of her to steady herself. Tears ran down her face. Had she lost everything when she'd had the miscarriage?

***

The bus stopped near a small brick house that belonged to the district tax collection unit. Across the road was an outdoor market. Bamboo cages crammed with chickens and piglets, stacks of pumpkins, purple sugarcane were spread out for sale. Boiled cassava bound in bamboo segments was displayed on bamboo trays, next to peanut candies molded into round cakes, and plastic bags filled with rice cakes. Old women hawked barbecued ears of corn. A middle-aged vendor in a French-style beret and the canvas boots a geologist might wear offered newspapers and magazines. He pushed an old Chinese bicycle rigged with a battery-operated loudspeaker through which he barked out headlines and summaries of articles: "Dear comrades and friends, buy the *Daily News* and learn about the prosecution of the corrupting influences in the But Son district bank! Twenty billion dong are assumed embezzled! Read about the wedding party that turned out to be a funeral! Read all about the case of a wife murdered by her husband in Lao Cai! 'Are Human Beings Eating Each Other?' Find out all about the sex tours selling prostitutes to Taiwan and Hong Kong! Who really killed Kennedy? Is Hitler really dead? Get the first news about the corruption scandal in General Department T! Read about the inhuman abortion clinic that has killed a patient! Amuse yourself with new stories by well-known Vietnamese writers and some humorous pieces by the Chinese author Giaping Ao, in *Real Life and Times.*"

Her previous reminiscences had left Hoan exhausted, and she leaned back against her seat now, her throat dry. She recalled the peaches she'd bought, and picked one out of the red plastic basket. The Meo peach was as big as a cup, tinged with delicate violet and rose shades. "Longevity peach," Hoan thought, smiling to herself. She took out a small knife and was about to cut into it, when the news vendor began strolling under the bus windows. She leaned out and bought some newspapers and magazines.

She was unaware now that all of her movements were being watched by the man who sat five rows behind her, and who had first caught her attention and made her worry. She had managed to soothe her suspicions. She still vaguely sensed that something was wrong, but had stopped thinking about it.

The man watching her, pretending to be a farmer carrying a bag of dried cassava, was named Quan, and he was a tax agent for the Luong Nham district. He was also Khoai's brother. Nicknamed "The Dwarf," he was a very short skinny man with a big head, thick hair, pale eyes, blackish lips, and a reputation for slyness and dishonesty. His brother had paid him and given him Hoan's photo, and he'd spotted her traveling back and forth on this road two weeks before. Now he glanced quickly at her two baskets again, then disembarked from the bus and went straight to the tax-collecting office, saying something to the bald, heavily bearded man standing in the doorway. He passed him quickly, then went inside and made a telephone call. "Tell them to arrest the one I'll ask for the price of peaches," he said into the phone.

But Hoan was oblivious to whatever and whoever was around her now. Her eyes had fallen on the name of the author of two short stories published in *Real Life and Times*. She immediately became engrossed in her reading:

The first was called "The Love of Lit, the Mother Cat:"

The mother cat had yellow stripes, a round face, and a beautiful, graceful body. She had been named Lit by her master, Mr. Diep. Lit gave birth to a single kitten. He had his mother's yellow-striped fur, and their master, a folk poet, had named him Nhit. Lit and Nhit, a folk poet's way of naming beloved things. Nhit had been born in an old basket filled with straw. After a week, he opened his eyes and staggered out of his straw bed. He was still so weak that he could only crawl a few feet before trembling and collapsing. His mother ran to him and meowed: "Why are you so bold? Be careful and don't go too far—there are cruel people in the world who want to eat you up." She grasped Nhit by the nape of his neck with her teeth and carried him back to the basket. Then, seemingly without any reason, she seized Nhit's neck fur in her teeth again, clamping down so tightly that Nhit's little legs drew up and his tail curled between his legs. She padded across the floor for a few steps, carrying him, then suddenly jumped onto the oven and then up onto what had once been a crate for 37MM artillery shells, but that Mr. Diep now used to store the manuscripts of his satiric poems. Mr. Diep, enjoying the sight of the two cats on his box, improvised:

Mother Lit, where are you carrying Nhit to?

If you like poems so much, I'll write one for you.

Lit meowed, released the kitten, and began to lick its fur. She loved to lick and clean Nhit, and that helped him grow healthy. Two months later, Nhit was already eating rice, and could climb up to the box, leap to the brick oven, and then down to the floor. On his first try, he fell. By the second, he didn't, though he did find coming down much easier than going up and didn't hesitate to meow if he thought he needed help getting up again.

That was what he was doing now, sitting on the floor, looking up at Lit still up on the stove, meowing at his mother. But Lit didn't jump down to help. She told Nhit, "Crouch on you rear legs, then shoot your front paws out and jump. I'll help you once you get up here," Nhit tried, but this time failed, and Lit leapt down to help her kitten.

Suddenly a foul stench permeated the air. From out of the drain crawled a sewer rat. It was old, and much of its hair had fallen off; its huge canines curled down over its lower lip, and it was hungry. It was as big as Lit, but much stronger and very arrogant. Often it stole eggs and even devoured chickens and doves. When it was hungry, it would gnaw through the door of the cupboard. It chewed shoes and slippers. Once it had carried away an entire fried fish, left on the altar. It had clawed out a hole behind the wall in which it lived. It was like the devil of this house.

"Go away!" Lit screamed at it, frightened.

The old rat bared its teeth. "Give me your kitten."

"Never, you damned murderer!"

"Give it to me!"

The old sewer rat charged at Lit. Nhit fainted between his mother's paws. The situation was desperate. Lit bent down and laid her kitten out in front of her. Nhit was as limp as a piece of cloth. The rat was pleased, and stroked its whiskers, thinking that Lit was obeying him. How could the kitten escape becoming his prey now?

"Look, you damned old sewer rat!" Lit cried, her voice filled with pain and determination. Then she bent over and, howling bitterly, opened her mouth and bit through Nhit's neck. She bit into her kitten, held his tiny body by his front legs and clawed *him into pieces and swallowed him. His blood ran out of the two corners of her mouth. In an instant, Nhit was back in his mother's womb, as safe as he had been when he was a fetus. Lit sat motionless. She had integrated her child back into herself to keep an enemy from devouring it. Tears ran down her cheeks, but she felt strong.*

The old sewer rat was dumbfounded, and then it turned to run away. It was suddenly very frightened. For the first time, it had encountered a love so strong it would consume what it loved in the most terrible way in order to defend it.

The second story was called "Mr. Tue's Garden:"

One afternoon when the southern breeze was blowing gently and I was wandering in his garden, I heard Mr. Tue call: "Khiem, can you find me?" I was ten years old then and like a small bird that hopped around the garden, searching for him in every corner. Where was he? Behind the trellis of betel leaves? Up in the jackfruit tree? Finally, my eyes fell on the newly dug well. I looked down into its depths, my gaze traveling along the layers of stones, spiraling down and down and down. And then stopping at the bottom. A strong laugh drifted up to me: "Khiem, I have discovered water here!"

In my native province, water is usually found in the valleys, at the base of the hills. Since he had built his house on the crest of a very high hill, Mr. Tue had been determined to find water somewhere below its slope. For three months he had been jumping all over like a cricket. Hoe, dig, drill. He had to go nearly eighteen meters deep into the hill until he forced the underground dragon to release its water. That well seemed to be a combination of the three levels of the universe: heaven, earth, and hell: it was the road of life that linked the heart of the earth to the sky.

Human beings are the miracle of the world, a combination of the five elements. But Mr. Tue, our neighbor, was beyond most people. He once said: "Water that lies under the ground is useless. When it moves up and becomes water in a well, it becomes useful. Every part must be useful to the whole."

Mr. Tue's clan settled here at the time the country was founded. Both history and legend tell that this clan has produced many people of extraordinary talent; they were intelligent, courageous in defending the land against invaders and in conquering new lands, yet at the same time were generous and refined. Many of the heroes from his clan are still worshiped in the pagodas here.

When I left my native province, I always held Mr. Tue in my mind as a part of the legendary sky that had sheltered my childhood. I would remember the story of his well.

And the story of how he had fought with his jackfruit tree. He had put me onto his shoulders and asked me to climb to the top of that ancient tree. I did what I was told and when I looked down, I saw that he was dressed only in a pair of shorts and was performing the martial arts Tiger movements. He stopped abruptly and cried out, like a clap of thunder: "Hey, jackfruit tree!" From the top, I called down timorously, "Yes, here I am." I saw then that he was holding a sword. He began to attack the tree like a warrior on the battlefield, slashing it mercilessly. Its sap streamed out of a myriad of small wounds. And I understood that I was the jackfruit tree, my soul as green as its leaves, but ready now to bear fruit in the coming years, to offer and devote myself to the common good, as all things must, even plants and trees, to their utmost ability.

Now and then, over the years, I would visit my mother and sister, but after I'd grown up I hardly saw Mr. Tue, since he had been assigned as Party secretary of the district committee and at the same time as an executive member of the provincial committee. Now thirty years had passed, and when I came back to my native province to rest and recover after an illness, I met Mr. Tue again. He had retired early, when he was only about fifty, but the people around here say that when this century ends, the one person who is likely to have his named inscribed *on a stela or his visage sculpted on a statue is Mr. Tue. He rescinded the regulations which had limited agricultural production in our district for years. The people said of him: "A good brain is more precious than great wealth." Pretending to be a beggar, Mr. Tue had gone on an investigation of the way people lived in this area and had found that most were poor, oppressed, and not being given the chance to use their natural abilities. He and a few other comrades formed a working group of talented people and produced a new plan. But it was rejected by the upper levels; whereupon, Mr. Tue began to secretly implement the family-farm contract system in his district. Believing he was working only for the good of the people, he never thought he would be attacked when, as a result of his policies, food production soared like a kite in the wind. From the very old to the very young, after only one harvest, people had enough to eat and to buy clothing, and morale was high. But someone used Mr. Tue's unauthorized decision as a weapon against him, a way to get promoted.*

So it was that Mr. Tue lost his position and had to retire at an early age. When I asked him how he felt about that, he just laughed. "I've been lucky. If one struggles for a just cause, one can be either victorious or go down in defeat within two weeks. That's normal. And being ensnared by one's own colleagues is also normal, has been since ancient times. But remember—if Heaven causes harm to you, you must accept your suffering. But if man harms you, you must prevail against it and move forward!"

Time has brought several unexpected talents of Mr. Tue's to the surface. He has been a success in well-digging, in gardening, and in helping poor peasants to prosper. People regard him as a gift from Heaven. Stories spread about his accomplishments after his forced retirement. As soon as he put his knapsack down, he began to dig fishponds, bake bricks, and reorganize his garden.

That garden has become a legend. He has grown a fence of

rattan and other trees around its two thousand square meters: "a toad's skin covering the eggs (treasures) inside," he says. It is true. There are numerous kinds of fruit trees, medicinal herbs, plants, and flowers, most of the seeds having been given by friends from everywhere.

He begins his working day at dawn by talking to the trees and plants, praising them, weeding them, asking them to give him their fruit and flowers. The garden is healthy and clean; it is his friend and part of his life. The eternal cycle of nature in it demonstrates the failure of those who have wanted to ruin him. A man's true strength is marked by the desire he has to offer himself to others.

I asked him, "Mr. Tue, if you were to choose one line of one poem, which do you like the most?"

He replied simply, "I would choose this line: 'I have wronged the one who loves me.' It is a line from The Tale of Kieu that a teacher once quoted to me, and it stays in my mind."

I have wronged the one who loves me! The worst fear is to be unworthy of the one you love. As for the people who are bad to you, they are not worth mentioning. I listened to that line and I meditated on it until the tears came to my eyes.

* * *

Tears ran from Hoan's eyes as well. The author of both stories was "Thinh Luong." She had found him. The two stories were the goosefeathers dropped by Princess My Chai for Prince Trong Thuy to follow. The commitment they had made to each other at the beach that day had been realized. She had found her Khiem. She read the stories in her own way, seeing in "The Love of Lit" how she had wished to swallow Khiem and possess him forever, seeing the bitterness of his situation. But "Mr. Tue's Garden" was more direct: his real name was used for the protagonist of the story. After his

illness, he had gone back to his home earth to rest: Co hamlet, Thanh Hoa commune, Song Thao district, P province,
all of it noted at the end of the story, his guide to her. Live
peacefully and calmly, follow the example of nature, the
example of the garden. Love human beings and live for the
ones who love you. Overcome your fate, because tragedy has
become so vulgarized it is no longer of any significance.
Again, she felt that Khiem was invisibly supporting and
guiding her, waking her from the unconscious drift of her
life.

Giddy with happiness, Hoan neglected to read the
newspaper, and so didn't see either the article about the corruption scandal at General Department T, or the account of
a woman from Hanoi who had died during the course of an
illegal abortion.

The bus turned onto Giang Vo road, and stopped at the
Kim Ma bus station. Hoan stood. She had come to a decision
and she would act on it immediately. She would leave the
two baskets, and the nineteen kilos of opium hidden under
the peaches, right where they were. She would cut herself off
from this period of her life. As she started forward, the short
man with the bag of cassava sprang forward and picked up a
peach from one of the baskets. "How much are a dozen of
these, madame?" Hoan ignored him. She calmly took her
handbag, and tried to push past the two policeman, a
sergeant and a senior sergeant, who had boarded the bus just
before the short man had grabbed the peach.

"Where do you think you are going?" one said to her.

"What kind of question is that? I'm getting off the bus."

She tried to slip by them on one side. But the sergeant, a
dark-skinned man wearing sunglasses, moved his stocky
body to block her.

"What are you doing?"

"Pick up those two baskets and come with us, please."

"Which two baskets?"

"Over there. The red one and the blue one."

The senior sergeant stood near the baskets. Hoan looked at them and shook her head. "Those aren't mine."

"Whose are they then?"

"How should I know?"

The sergeant took off his sunglasses and peered back into the bus, seeming to look for someone. Immediately, the man with the cassava walked up to them. He grinned at them and laughed rudely.

"Try hard to remember," he said. "If they're not yours, whose are they?"

"What are you saying?"

"Stop pretending." He reached into his pocket and withdrew a red peach pit, then smacked it into the palm of his other hand. "At Luong Nhan market, you took one peach from the red basket, split it in order to eat it, and threw the pit down. Here it is. It is the pit of a longevity peach, a fairy peach. It comes from the peach tree of the Western Fairy Queen in China which gives fruit only once every three thousand years. If one eats it, one might live forever."

Hoan tried to conceal a shiver. She laughed coldly. "That's not enough to prove anything."

The two policemen were still chuckling over the description of the longevity peaches. They looked at Hoan and nodded. "You seem to be very experienced. But please come with us to the police station anyway. Longevity or a short life-—by and by we'll see which it will be."

They picked up the two baskets and began walking out of the bus. Hoan stood motionless for a moment, then, a silent sob shaking her heart, she called to Khiem in her mind: *Darling, please protect me.*

Chapter Twelve

THE HORSE

Vang had been arrested in Lang Son. U escaped to Hong Kong. A dealer named Thuy sold some "product" to a pock-marked driver named Khieu who afterwards gave her a lift straight to the police station in Ha Dong. When they got there, he lifted his leg and kicked her out right at the front gate of the prison. Chang, a teacher from Quai To, who after being released cut off one of his fingers to prove he would never testify, was rearrested in Thai Nguyen with three kilos of opium hidden in a sack of dried tea leaves. Pham, about to be caught, wrapped some opium he was carrying in plastic and stuck it up his anus. He was arrested and the opium found anyway. Twisted Ngo, the chief trafficker in Pho Cuu, was in prison, along with all his couriers.

Hoan heard all of this in the district prison where she was sent after being arrested in Kim Ma. Many visitors came there to see newly arrested prisoners and, intentionally and unintentionally, she overheard their conversations and pieced together a picture of what had happened.

But she felt numb and indifferent to everything, even when she was put into her cell. It was only about nine meters square, and there were already about two dozen women inside when she arrived. As soon as she sat down, the three or four closest to her asked what she had done. When she didn't answer, they chorused: "Opium smuggling, eh?" and then seemed very respectful. They knew the traffickers had a strong organization that would take care of anyone arrested, and they hoped Hoan would share some of the food they knew she'd be given.

By the end of three days, she knew most of the names, crimes, and life stories of the other inmates. By coincidence, except for one woman named Loc, everyone else had a given name that started with "H." Hoan, Huong, Hoa, Hao, Ha, Hoi, Hong, Hung, Hien, Hoat, Hang, Hieu... More than half of them were in their fifties and had been officials and bureaucrats in the economic and financial sector. There was the director of a credit cooperative, the head of a fund, a department director, an accountant, a cashier. Two business-women in for tax evasion. A boiled-shrimp seller who'd insulted the police who had searched her shop. And seven or eight cold-faced young women in their twenties and early thirties who chatted together as casually as if they were sitting at home. She met them one by one.

Huong, called Fat Huong, was plump, charming, white as powder, and introduced herself by saying casually, "I killed someone."

"Who?" Hoan asked.

"The man who betrayed my boyfriend." He had been her boyfriend's deputy and had created false documents making it seem that Huong's boyfriend had taken a bribe of $130,000. After his arrest, he'd hanged himself.

"I swore to his soul I'd avenge him," she told Hoan. She'd hired gangsters to stab the deputy. "Sister Hoan, to be cruel to a cruel person is kindness, isn't it?" she'd said, laughing innocently.

Since Huong came from a privileged family—her father was a colonel—she was well supplied with good food. She and the others from rich families, Hoan noted without surprise, had fruit for dessert, and were able to wash themselves with La Vie mineral water, while the ordinary prisoners ate poor quality rice and a few vegetables.

Among the unprivileged was Hoi, a twenty-year-old half-Chinese woman whom Hoan found quite lovely. But when she praised Hoi, the younger woman squeezed her arm. "I'd rather have your beauty—you're in your forties and still lovely. If I were a man, I'd fall in love with you im-mediately—your kind of beauty persists. Don't worry, sister, prison will just preserve your looks." Hoi had already been in prison three times. In spite of her youth, her life had been turbulent. She had fallen in love with a married en-gineer whose wife had caught her and cut off her hair. As a result, she'd left home and gone to work as a maid for an old Chinese man in Tuyen Quang, who raped her and got her pregnant. She had had an abortion, stolen twenty ounces of gold from him, and wandered the streets ever since, living by her wits. She'd been arrested this time for swindling a sticky rice seller in the Hang Da market out of her jewelry. She'd rented a room from the woman for an ounce of gold every month, and when she'd moved in had deliberately let the rice seller see the twenty ounces of gold she had. Soon after, she had gone to her landlady. "Madame," she had said, seem-ingly agitated, "my friend is getting married at the same time her family is having a funeral, and I haven't had time to offer gifts for her. If I can just borrow your necklace and ring for token offerings, I'll bring them back, and I'll give you half an ounce for interest." The old woman knew Hoi had twenty ounces of gold in her room and felt secure letting the girl borrow her jewelry. Hoi took the necklace, the ring, and her twenty ounces and promptly disappeared. Shocked and heartbroken, the old woman had a stroke and dropped dead. Her son, a soldier, had chased Hoi down and caught her as she was boarding the train to Vinh.

Hoi's best friend in the cell was Hien, a twenty-five-year-old forestry worker who'd been jilted by her boyfriend. After he'd told her he was marrying someone else, dazed and lovelorn, she'd wandered off alone and been taken in by the head of the sawing section, who'd gotten her drunk and taken her virginity. When she'd awakened and realized what had happened, she grew furious and killed him with an axe. Her main fear in prison was of being put into an isolation cell. She was terrified that the souls of executed prisoners haunted those cells as headless ghosts.

"When I first met you," the next H, Hieu, said to Hoan, "I was sure you were an undercover cop—you look too refined to be here." Hieu's nickname was Crocodile, after the emblem she'd embroidered on her t-shirt. She advised Hoan to get out of opium trafficking. "If Buddha and Heaven pity you and you're released, come into the 'gather and share' game with me. It's much better." But when Hoan asked her what she meant, she fell silent. Her friend Hoat, a seventeen-year-old—she had stolen $200,000 and tried to escape to Hong Kong—explained: "She rented a shop and hired an honest girl to work there, for about 300,000 dong (approximately $20) a month, and registered the shop in that girl's name. Then she invited suppliers to bring or ship their products to the shop—clothing, electronic products, cosmetics. Since she had a shop address, they automatically gave her credit, and she didn't have to put up any money in advance. She resold everything she received to other small retailers, for two thirds the wholesale price. After she'd made over a dozen million dong, she ran off to Saigon, leaving the straight girl she'd hired to take the blame."

These were the lives intersecting with Hoan's life now, cursed by bad luck, bitter situations, horrible sins, dark desires, and cruel natures. But was she any different? She'd had her face slashed, she'd been discarded, cheated, humiliated, pushed into insane situations. She had ruined her life looking for revenge. She'd wanted much, wanted money to prove her worth to herself, to humiliate those who had humiliated her. She'd wanted to make them crawl before her money. She had planned to plant a kilo of opium in Pho's house, in the houses of his colleagues, ruin their reputations. She'd wanted to throw shit and mud into their faces, those who had attacked the man she loved. Being cruel to cruel people was a kindness, wasn't it? How was she different from Fat Huong or Hoi or Hien the Crocodile? Perhaps only in the regret she'd come to feel before her arrest.

She knew, accepted, that she was guilty of everything she had been accused of. But the road she had chosen for herself led to Khiem, and she would do whatever she had to in order to come to him again.

On the ninth day of her detention, her interrogator came. He was in civilian clothes: a young man with an oval face and liquid, romantic eyes, his mouth as pretty as a young girl's. He glanced at her, his gaze distant yet soft as velvet.

"You said you went to Lai Chau to buy medicines. From what illness are you suffering?"

"Post-delivery sickness."

"I see. But why did you have to go all the way to Lai Chau?"

"Perhaps you don't recall that there are different qualities of traditional medicine, depending on where the plants they're made from are grown. The ones from Lai Chau are better than those from Sa Pa or Da Lat."

"Thank you for reminding me of that fact."

"Not at all," Hoan said blandly.

"But tell me, along with the two packets of medicine, how many kilos did you have in the two baskets?"

"I don't know what you mean by kilos. And which baskets are you talking about?"

He was silent for a moment, then sighed. "Look, I know you're not a professional smuggler, or someone who truly wanted to be involved in trafficking. Probably, for one reason or another you had no choice; perhaps you suffered some crisis. We identified you, you know, by the scar on your right cheek—your description was given to us by your office. And it was your colleagues who sent someone to follow you, through all your trips to Hoa Binh, Son La, and Lai Chau."

"I haven't worked in any office for a long time now." Hoan shook her head slowly. "And I haven't done anything wrong. What right did they have to follow me? What right do you have to keep me in jail for nine days, without any proof? You're the ones breaking the law."

"Enough," he said, standing. "We'll stop at this point today." He looked gloomy.

Back in her cell, Hoan said nothing to her fellow prisoners. As for the interrogation—she knew of course they were aware of her activities. But they had no proof. She thought about the policeman. He seemed kind. Perhaps he suspected that her ex-colleagues, who had hired the man with the bag of dried cassava, were acting malevolently. She remembered, clung to the memory, of how he had grimaced ironically when he had mentioned the man.

She didn't know what the young policeman knew: that the man with the cassavas was Khoai's brother and that he'd been promised a job as a guard at the cultural affairs division if he pointed the police towards Hoan.

***

It is a flower with a special and rare beauty. Its colors turn and change from one hue to another, and its fragile petals blossom against scenes of dew-heavy mountain meadows and clouds.

The beauty of the opium poppy is mystical, but its flowering form conceals a devil. The fairy of opium, as in the tale by Nguyen Ngoc, still flies over remote jungles, and remains beautiful, and has no intention of taking her own life.

248

In late summer and early autumn, the local people clear the jungle with their slash-and-burn methods. Their fires burn arrow-shaped clearings on the eastern slopes of the mountains, and smolder down finally to a layer of gray ash. When they have gone out, the opium seeds are planted in the softened ground.

The plants germinate and grow no differently than any other crop. The opium looks like any other plant. Its leaves are green and lush and edible as lettuce. Chew it. It's a little bitter at first, but later leaves a sweet taste in your mouth. But its vitality is stronger than any other plant's. By winter it is a meter tall, and without any aid from human beings, it blooms beautifully, its blossoms strange and lovely. They glitter from clearings muted with mist, like dreams of the jungle. By spring, the flowers grow pods as big as betel nuts, and the sap is ready for harvest. The locals say that whenever the opium starts oozing sap, a storm—thunder, lightning, pouring rain—strikes the mountains, as if even heaven and earth tremble at this arrival.

Hoan didn't know if it was true, and she wasn't an expert in the botany of the plant, but in her travels she had learned to tell the difference between the various types of opium. The first grade came from a yellowish sap, the color of condensed milk—out of the four kilograms of opium usually harvested from a field, only two hundred grams would be of that quality. It would be twice as expensive as the second grade, which came from honey-colored sap, and three times as expensive as the third, made from dark brown sap. The mountain people would collect the raw sap, condense it into pieces the size of squares of chocolate. When she smelled it, it would shoot straight to her brain, then leave her with the warm, flushed feeling that she associated with the smell of the milk flowers at night, in autumn, in Hanoi.

The first time she had come to the mountains and had seen a flowering opium field along the slopes of the high mountains, she had been transfixed. The country had seemed like a paradise. Then a Hmong woman had jerked at her sleeve and told Hoan if she wasn't going to buy, she, the woman, would leave. Hoan snapped out of her reverie, took the money from her bag, and paid the woman. Money was always paid first, that was the rule. There were so many rules to remember. The trade had gone on for a long time, was governed by thousands of unwritten, unspoken, strictures and customs that everyone knew and followed. They controlled the minutest details, relationships, styles, language: they controlled lives. Hoan knew, for example, that to say anything openly and directly was regarded as clumsy and dangerous. If you said you would come today, it meant you would come tomorrow, and if you said tomorrow, it meant you would come tonight. You never told anyone your schedule. You said you were going to Pho Lu, but you really went to Dong Mo. You stayed in one house, but the owner wasn't the dealer. You never met as a threesome for an opium deal. Only the seller and the buyer. You only knew your own contacts, no one else's. There were many gangs and networks, some of them international. The gangs could kill each other's members but could never raise or reduce prices as a way to destroy or compete against one another. The price of opium was agreed upon and fixed for the entire region.

Hoan had learned the slang the gangs used. "Mor" meant cop. "Meter" meant kilogram. "Do you have some flower design cloth?" meant "Do you have high quality opium?" "Did you bring a lot of paddy?" meant "Did you bring a lot of money?" She had learned that the trust among the traffickers had to be absolute and unquestioned. You never counted the money when you were paid. You never checked the quality or quantity of the goods after the dealer had told you what and how good it was. Trust was essential. Betrayal was the worst transgression, the most feared action. Better to lose money than to lose trust.

She had been smart and aware, had become experienced both in purchasing and in overcoming all the risks and dangers of the job. She had learned that wrapping opium in an old Hmong skirt would mask its smell even from drug-sniffing dogs. Her own sense of smell had become keen enough to discern the quality of opium and where it came from. She had been cunning enough to recruit her own team. She had been tough and yet likable; she could win over people, and she had learned to enjoy risk. She had even learned to use the womanizers who pursued her, accepting lifts, moving her opium in the cars of provincial chairmen, heads of customs units, even police colonels and army commanders. She had wanted to do something that would shake the earth. But she had also looked at it as a mysterious game, unknown to outsiders, and after she had played it, she would return to her other life, would make all who had harmed her pay for their arrogance and egoism.

The first time she had come up to the opium-growing regions, her guide had said, "You're here," and then had disappeared. The heavy mountain mist surrounded her, chilling her skin. Suddenly she saw two beams of light undulating in the mist like silk ropes, then converging on her face. She had bent down, broken off a branch, and whipped it back and forth in that direction. The lights disappeared, and she heard a burst of laughter. A young Hmong, riding on a white horse, appeared out of the mist, right next to her. A second later another Hmong, middle-aged, also on a white horse had ridden up also.

"We're just teasing you," he said calmly. "It's rare that a Vietnamese woman dares to come up here alone."

This Hmong was Giang A Dua, a clan chief and opium lord who controlled three Hmong villages on To Bo Mountain. It was said there weren't three square meters of flat land in his whole territory, nor three sunny days per year. But the soil grew huge ears of corn and large opium poppies.

Giang A Dua was forty-five years old, a seductive man, tall, with a square face, a high Western nose and blue eyes under long eyelashes. His mother had been a very beautiful Hmong girl who'd worked in the Lao Chai church; she'd been impregnated by the French priest who'd been assigned to the area from 1945 to 1949. Giang A Dua had been sent to the provincial school for minorities and had become a district youth secretary and, later, a judge in the district court. But when a young girl was brought before him for opium trafficking, Dua, struck by her beauty, had released her and then quit his job and returned to his home territory. His adoptive Hmong father had been the eldest son of the chief of the mountainous region, and upon his death, Dua had inherited his opium fields and had consolidated the Giang clans. The young opium lord had become very powerful, very wealthy, though he continued to live in a simple and traditional way. His family owned a herd of a hundred buffalo, a hundred cows, and other livestock, and had ten large earthen jars filled with "white" silver. Dua surrounded himself with five bodyguards and often dressed in expensive foreign clothing. His connections extended to the Golden Triangle, and he was known and respected even by the greatest opium lord, Khun Sa. The local authorities couldn't touch him. Instead they had decided to use him to help pacify the region by paying him a salary to be a member of the Provincial Fatherland Front, an umbrella organization for ethnic and religious minorities in Vietnam.

At their meeting, Hoan had offered him a piece of red cloth and five eggs, a gesture of trust and serenity. He invited her to join him in a meal of rooster blood pudding with red wine. Hoan downed three full bowls of wine, an act which shocked and impressed him. She watched closely as he ate, then carefully imitated the way he would sip a little water after eating a mouthful of food.

The Hmong, smitten by Hoan, taught her more of the

lore of testing and mixing opium. If flame was put to it and it reddened quickly, its quality was low, since opium must burn slowly. If a drop of liquefied opium was drawn into a hypodermic, the best quality would form into a fragile thread. But if the thread broke in the middle, its quality was inconsistent. He taught her the skill of cutting and mixing the opium for more profit. Hoan had been a quick learner.

Just before her arrest, Dua had given her nineteen kilos of good quality opium and escorted her down his mountain. When he'd said goodbye, his eyes had been bright. "The first time I saw you drink wine, I thought you were beautiful. After you've finished your business, come back to me. There's something I wish to talk to you about."

He bent down and kissed her hand, trying to conceal his desire. He wanted her, and he would have her. But he knew he couldn't rush her. This one wasn't like the other beautiful women he'd had. She was distant, and there was always something elusive and lonely about her. A coolness. She risked her life to make money, but seemed detached, as if she were playing a game.

If she could have known what Dua was thinking, Hoan would have agreed. She did what she did, proved what she had to prove to herself, with an indifference that allowed her control, kept her anger in check. It was a means. A horse for her to ride to reach her destination. But Dua had no idea what that destination was.

Chapter Thirteen

HEADLESS GHOSTS

It was the same interrogator. Young, handsome, smooth, understanding. His voice soothing. Van Nhan's lips were beautiful and his eyes were kind. But they were also very sharp and seemed to see everything.

"What you've told us was very interesting and you told it so well," he said, not unkindly. "You're clearly an educated person. Of course, all of the information you gave us about the secret lore of the opium trade and so on is very commonplace. But any added knowledge is useful, and we thank you for it. However, there is something we still need to clear up."

"Oh? What's that?"

"The main thing."

His gaze slowly traveled over Hoan's face, inch by inch. She felt the edges of the scar left by Thoa's razor grow cold. He leaned forward slightly on his chair, then suddenly shrugged.

"I still don't understand why you didn't take the two baskets with you when you left the bus."

"Which baskets?"

"The red basket and the blue basket and the Meo peaches you used as camouflage. How many kilos did you put under them again?"

"I repeat, those baskets were not mine."

"And the peaches?"

"Nor the peaches."

"Then why did you take one when the bus stopped at the Luong Nhan tax-collection station?"

"What if I told you they looked so nice and I was so thirsty I stole one peach?"

"Very well." He smiled. "But..."

"I repeat: I know nothing about the so-called nineteen kilograms of opium on that bus."

"How would you explain that the opium was wrapped in an old Hmong skirt and tied with the same black twine that you had in a roll in your handbag?"

"If that's all you have on me, then everyone on that bus with the same kind of string should have been arrested as well."

He smiled, with what seemed like admiration. Then turned serious. "You should be more sincere."

"But I have nothing else to say."

"You know very well that the possession of nineteen kilograms of opium is considered trafficking. That amount can mean the death penalty for you. But if you are honest and sincere and confess now, you might be saved." He stopped. When he spoke again, his voice was lower, kindly again. "I understand you, Miss Hoan, believe me. Please don't misunderstand me. I've read the poems in your diary; I know the sincerity of your love. Your behavior has not been consistent with your nature."

Hoan turned to the window, feeling a trickle of doubt. Van Nhan was a policeman, fulfilling his duties. But perhaps he had recognized some of the complexities of her motives.

Van Nhan glanced quickly at his watch, and began to ask Hoan about her life and her job. She replied, wanting to think she saw pity in those beautiful eyes. But she held her tongue. After half an hour, he stood up.

"You may have to suffer terribly, Miss Hoan," he said, almost in a whisper.

***

Was this what he meant? The darkness surrounded her. She felt there wasn't enough air to breathe. Echoing from somewhere she heard a man's derisive laughter, a voice that sounded as if it came from a fat man: "End Miss Beauty's life."

But the laughter jarred her from her frightened numbness. She sat motionless, trying to calm herself. After a moment, she began to feel around herself, trying to get a sense of the dimensions of this place. The Special Cell. The Death Cell where the condemned waited for execution. The dark cave to bury the criminal who didn't confess sincerely. It was just high enough for her to stand up in, and she could feel its walls by stretching out her arms. Most of its floor was taken up by a cement platform, which she was to use as a bed. It was like a stone coffin.

She had never felt so terrified. Being thrown into prison had been nothing compared to this confinement. There was no day here, no night, no difference between life and death. An unending nightmare. She was buried alive in a tomb. She was surrounded by her own death.

Hoan sobbed. But then stopped immediately, horrified by the sounds that had come from her. It was like an echo of a soul crying from hell. She tried again to calm herself, pressed her hands against her chest as if to slow the beating of her heart. Her trembling subsided. Everything will pass away, she consoled herself. She'd suffered many tragedies, one more meant nothing. It was her fate. She shouldn't complain but accept.

She finally fell asleep. But immediately woke. All around her was an icy coldness. She shivered violently, cried out,

"Who's there?" A headless shadow flitted across the ceiling of her tomb-like cell. She sat against the wall, drawing her legs up, trying to make herself small. The thing that had terrified Hien the Crocodile was appearing to her now. She could see the shadow of a headless, skeletal body with bare feet; it was waving its disjointed arms at her. She screamed with all her might: "Oh, Khiem, save me, Khiem!"

Her voice splits the darkness. Then, strangely, she has left the cell and is flying up and she sees that Khiem has heard her and is waiting for her. She stops sobbing, and she can even smile now. He holds her hand, and they walk on the dike at Thinh Luong and down its slope, and they enter Old Tuy's house. She is amazed: it has been a year, more, since they were here, and yet everything is exactly the same. She closes the door and she undresses as she did before. But this time Khiem seems more experienced, and he kisses her breasts for so long that she pushes him away and tells him, "Darling, I can't take any more!" And the storm begins again, and she is like a ship that doesn't have enough time to let its anchor down, shaking, quivering, tossed up and down on the waves. Oh darling, oh darling! Her thighs feel swollen, her nipples hard, her belly heaving, she on the verge of orgasm. She holds back, she has to enjoy it to the utmost, enjoy what belongs only to her, make this first time of theirs that had finally opened her sexuality fully last forever in her mind. She has to drown herself in this dreamy lovemaking with Khiem. She burns. She screams. She is turning into Lit the mother cat, she will possess him fully, totally, eat him up, absorb him, make him part of her body. She will preserve his semen this time, keep herself part of the circle of life, fight against Death and the headless ghost.

> *Sleep well, sleep well, darling*
> *Sleep in my arms, in the soundless lullaby*
> *I want to sing*
> *The storm has passed, but the whirlwind comes*

The rhythm of life continues
Sleep well, my darling
The ocean is calmed in the circle of my arms
I am here, don't be sad
Sleep well, darling; in your dreams you'll see
The rhythm of life continues

She sings it for Khiem, and he looks down at her lovingly, his eyes fixed on hers, his lips pressed on hers, and she whispers, "Do you see, darling, you criticized my poetry unfairly; I don't want to be a poet, only to prove my love to you." Yes, he nods, but he says nothing, only caresses her hair with his fingers, which have pillowed her head, and his stroking is signaling her to read more of her love poem.

It is you, the only one I think of
You are in my mind all the time
and I tease you that you look like the
director of a farm commune
with your thick scarf and your careless way of dressing
How can a proper writer go around with his
shirt never properly tucked in, wearing
trousers which are never ironed?
Oh my darling, whenever I see you
Forever I follow you in my dream
to the bright ocean...

His fingers pinch her shoulders and she stops. They sit and hurriedly dress, shivering in the cold. It is stormy outside and she knows they both share a vague feeling that something horrible is going to begin, or to end. Then they see Old Tuy walking towards them. He is dressed as the chief of the ceremony honoring the Princess My Chau. But he is wet and bent over, and, as he comes closer, she sees his face is wrinkled and shrinking like a rotting lemon.

"*What's wrong with you, uncle?*" *she cries. She is very worried. Old Tuy takes off his coat and lies down.*

"*That crater filled with water poisoned by Agent Orange has claimed its fifth victim now,*" *he moans.* "*Oh, the triangle of those three C130's moving across the sky...*"

The headless ghost floats out of Hoan's tomb.

Hoan was in the cell for ten days. On the tenth night, she woke at midnight, the nightmare she'd been having about the ceremony of the Princess My Chau lingering in her mind, disturbing her. It seemed to predict her separation from Khiem. Just as the separation between Thuy Kieu and Kim Trong in *The Tale of Kieu* had been foretold by Dam Tien passing through her tomb. Did the tragic end of My Chau's life tell what would happen to her and Khiem? No, she thought, Old Tuy had always said the princess was killed in error; she had been innocent and hadn't intended the consequences of her actions. Khiem had once read her Anh Ngoc's poem about My Chau:

> *If there was ever another My Chau*
> *Who loved so passionately and yet vigilantly*
> *Who never made a mistake*
> *Who never fell*
> *for the enemy's trick*
> *A My Chau such as we have often dreamed of having*
> *Then Princess My Chau would not live forever*
> *Faithful with a love that has lasted*
> *for more than two thousand years*

No, Hoan thought. Princess My Chau was beheaded by her father, but she was not dead. A perfect pearl had formed itself around her love. Literature was the thirst for love described through the pain of life. She also would use her death to prove her love for Khiem. The purest love was death.

That was her situation now. She would achieve the fulfillment of her love in this death cell.

But when the jailer suddenly called out, she was terrified.

Death, foretold in her nightmare about My Chau, had arrived and was calling her name. She steeled herself, tried to concentrate on only one thought: what could she leave for Khiem to show him how much she loved him?

"Are you awake, 212?"

It was her convict number. She crawled to the door. The jailer unlocked it and pushed it open, its rusty hinges shrieking. The morning light poured into the cavity of the cell, and she had to put up her hands and shield her eyes.

When she could see again, she made out a plastic basket on the floor. It was not a red one, nor a blue one. It was yellow and filled with food. Bread, roasted chicken, sausages, and pork pâté. Three bottles of La Vie mineral water, and some clean cotton cloths. She could clean herself finally. She hated to be dirty. When she was a kid her grandmother had always helped her shower. She felt very alone. She looked at the food and water again, knowing it had been sent by the Network. Knowing everything must have been checked over thoroughly to prevent any messages from getting in to her.

But on the label of the bottle of mineral water, she could see the code that spelled out: "Be calm. Everything will be OK."

Chapter Fourteen

TRAVELING BY HORSE-CART IS FASTER THAN TRAVELING ON FOOT

Khoai laughed, baring his even teeth. "For nineteen kilos of opium, she'll get the death sentence for sure."

"They shouldn't wait to sentence her—just tie her to a pole, blindfold her, and shoot her," another voice said. "I'm talking about Hoan, the woman you admired so much—get it?" he added, as if afraid he wouldn't be understood. They were all sitting around a long table laden with food and drink.

Chuong folded her arms across her chest, shrugged, and said nothing. The man who'd spoken, thinking she was frightened, chuckled, a silver tooth gleaming suddenly from the left side of his mouth. "She who dares to steal must be beaten," he said. It was Quan, Khoai's brother, the man with the bag of dried cassava who'd followed Hoan and turned her in. Khoai and Quanh had arranged this party to introduce him to the staff in his new position as a security guard: Quan, a provincial hoodlum who'd wheedled a position with the tax control authority and become an official thief, would now join the Division of Cultural Affairs. He had found out just before he started following Hoan that he was about to be arrested for corruption. Now his brother, the soon-to-be deputy director, had set him up with this great job in the capital.

It was true—Khoai was cheerfully certain that Quanh would promote him now that Hoan had been arrested with his brother's help. At the party, he was loud and garrulous, an endless stream of filthy jokes spilling from his mouth. "I don't agree with the old saying 'One can be clever for three years and stupid for an hour,'" he said to the women. "Who can last for an hour? Who is that strong? Me, I get it done in a few minutes!" His brother, his odd-shaped body made even more grotesque by a secondhand suit, nodded eagerly. He didn't know how to speak to anyone, so he kept his attention fixed on Khoai, occasionally exclaiming, "How funny! How interesting!"

"Please, Big Brother, have some *guator*," Tiny Hoi said, tilting the teapot and pouring tea into Quan's cup, her eyes narrowed and gleaming, as if to show how funny she found Khoai's jokes.

She was wearing a red miniskirt, silk stockings, high heels, and thick makeup. It was her birthday, and she'd been appointed full-time staff and keeper of the seal, a reward, everybody understood, for inciting Thoa to come and slash Hoan's face and for denouncing Khiem. Quan stood and gallantly pulled out a chair for her. "What are you saying? Today you are our honored guest. Let me be the one who serves you. We are a cultural affairs division, after all!" He took the teapot and circled the table, cheerfully serving tea to everyone.

"I wonder what we'll be tomorrow," Chuong whispered to Tam.

Tuyen came into the room. She had just come back from the storage room and looked angry. Quan placed himself in front of her. "I am honored to serve you tea, my dear younger sister," he said. Staring at this strange man, Tuyen muttered, "Thanks, but my father never ate salty food."

"What!"

"I said my father never ate salty food—do you understand?"

Quan was taken aback: he had no idea what she was talking about. Convinced that she was somehow insulting his father, he put the teapot down and rolled up his sleeves. Chuong, sensing he was about to scream at Tuyen as if they were at a bus station, stepped up next to him and murmured that it was only a customary way of saying one wasn't thirsty. At that moment, Quanh, wearing a faded old short-sleeved shirt and slippers, shuffled into the room.

He had not changed much since becoming acting director. His squint was a little more pronounced, but otherwise he seemed healthier than he had ever been. When he was deputy, he'd often pretended to be ill in order to take days off. But now he had to demonstrate his dedication in hopes of getting a permanent appointment and keeping his title. Since he had taken power, in fact, he was proud to say that everybody had a title. Thong, the division's only driver, for example, had become Director of Transportation. Meanwhile, with the help of Khoai, Phu, and Lieu, the Cultural Affairs Division was grinding out regulations and policies and new rules as relentlessly and regularly as birthdays, and with as much celebration and fanfare.

"Is anybody absent?" Quanh scanned the room. Phu reported that Thong's wife was ill and had to stay home. Quanh nodded, and was preparing to say something to welcome Quan, when Khoai suddenly shot to his feet. "I have something to report to the director! According to a source I trust, the prisoner Hoang Thi Hoan has been placed in the death-sentence cell and has confessed to her crimes."

"Bravo!" Quan shouted, and Phu and the others around Quanh beamed at him approvingly. But the rest of the staff remained silent. What was Quanh cheering? The arrest of a criminal? The purification of society? Or was he yelling 'bravo' for opportunism? Three cheers that we've relegated to history the comradeship that had been the essence of the struggle for independence and freedom! Hooray for the opportunists who took advantage of their opportunities, tricked the unwary, slandered their comrades, and grabbed power for themselves! Bravo to the filthy and ruthless competition for individual gain! Long live the vulgar rule of the mob that had locked Khiem's novel into dusty storage! *Viva* the rule of the hooligans!

"I'm frightened, Chuong," Tam whispered loudly. "Surely this place is haunted by ghosts and devils!"

"Shut up and listen to what our director has to say, please!" Phu exclaimed, raising his hands and bringing them together in a loud clap.

Quanh smiled thinly at the women. "I smell the stink of incense-sticks around here, even though Phu has told me he tore down the altar behind the stairs. I welcome his action. We have to put away superstition. We have to be optimistic, right?"

"Right!" Khoai agreed. He stood, glanced sharply towards the women, and raised his voice. "If you please, Mr. Quanh, we'd like to hear a poem from you now. We know that it isn't only Mr. Khiem who has literary talent! Our director, Mr. Quanh, is also a poet. As you know, he has recited poems for us recently, but I happen also to know that he has written poetry from an early age."

Tam whispered into Chuong's ear: "The Venerable at Ha Van pagoda told me that he has noticed a new phenomenon—worms, dogs, foxes, and leopards are turning into human beings. That's why we are seeing so many people around us who look and act like those animals."

"Leader, please read your poem!" Tiny Hoi shrieked suddenly. Quanh stood, complaining that he had been working too hard, reading too many manuscripts, and smoking too much to keep himself awake, and his throat was sore. But it was true, he had been writing poetry for a long time, though he'd never published any. To prove it, he wanted now to read a poem he had written while back in school in his province:

> *I remember the cassava mixed with rice and the big bed*
> *In the complimentary class we have been together*
> *sharing a book and a kerosene lamp*
> *Now we have separated and you can't find me any more*
> *Search for me, I am like a bird flying away*
> *Now I am a leader, now I am writing a poem*

Tam and Chuong looked at each other and made no comment. The other, older editors, clenched their teeth and pretended to pick at the bowls of candy in front of them, trying to keep from bursting out laughing. Only Quan, Phu, and Khoai applauded. It was true, animals were turning into human beings. Yes, Quanh looked like a toad. And Khoai used to be good-looking, but now, as he stood next to his brother, the women recognized for the first time that both looked like monkeys. As for Phu, Mr. Thunder, the ex-carpenter would fit himself into any role he needed to assume. Since striking Nghiem—who had subsequently returned to his depression and become silent and withdrawn—he had presented himself as a serious person. He had destroyed the altar someone had built under the stairs. He'd do whatever he needed to do to assure his appointment as deputy director.

Both he and Khoai had drawn ahead of Lieu in that competition. Lieu had remained quiet during the party, keeping himself aloof from the others. It was a sad thing for him to be in such a weak position now, especially since the three of them had all started from the same point, as section heads.

Meanwhile, unlike Quanh, he had kept away from writing any more poetry. He'd finally acknowledged to himself that writing was as difficult for him as driving a cart with a lame horse. Besides, a literary reputation, while putting someone in the spotlight, had its disadvantages. It could easily put someone in danger, make other people jealous. You only had to look at what had happened to Khiem and *The Haven*. No, he had tried instead to please Quanh, Phu, and Khoai by giving each of them a pet dog. He had figured that giving would be more profitable than selling in the long run. Everybody likes to get gifts, and even though the price of dogs was going down, his puppies were still beauties. But he still felt shaky about his chances. He hadn't taken any concrete action, like Phu, Khoai, and Tiny Hoi. Khoai's brother had managed to get Hoan arrested; he couldn't duplicate that. Nor could he be as crudely blunt as Tiny Hoi or as cold as Phu. Why? He needed to coolly calculate the best course for himself, follow the example of his brother. Was he going to let himself be affected, all of a sudden, by a nagging sense of shame? The thought troubled him.

"Are you sleeping, Mr. Lieu?"

"What is it?" He looked around, startled. The party was over. He looked up. To his shock there was Quanh. Staring up into the acting director's squinted eyes, he saw something horrible, and turned away. The skin on his face began to itch, as if fleas were crawling over him.

"Mr. Lieu, do you think you still have your former skills?"

"Dear boss, what do you mean?"

"Listen closely. Can you still drive a horse-cart?"

"Yes, of course." He hesitated, then said, "Whatever you need, I'm ready to do."

Quanh turned toward the door, cupped both hands under his buttocks, hefted them. "It's very simple. But you need to keep your mouth shut about it. We have two thousand copies of *The Haven* down in storage, and they're causing problems. Ms. Tuyen has been complaining that the rats are eating them. Besides, the newspapers have been hunting for news about the novel: they've made accusations that Mr. Pho has violated the law; some have even written that he was engaging in an anticultural activity by destroying books, like Tang Tsui Wang. It's nonsense. I myself have been a poet for a long time. What worth does a poem have? It's only words on paper. Nothing more. Those reporters are always causing trouble. Mr. Pho has also been charged with corruption and tax evasion too, so he doesn't need any more trouble. He told us to act immediately. But you have to do it skillfully and secretly." He looked out the door, and even though there was no one in the hall, Quanh bent down and whispered into Lieu's ear. Lieu's eyes sparkled. When he spoke, his lips trembled. "I swear to you, if I can't fulfill this duty, then a half hour later I'll resign and go home to help my wife breed and sell dogs."

As soon as the words were out, Lieu regretted them. How stupid! How could he say something like that? But Quanh only clapped him on the shoulder. "Lieu, you're always joking!" he said, smiling.

***

Where could Quanh have found such a beautiful horse? It was as beautiful as the horse in the paintings of the famous Chinese artist Tsu Bihong. Also, this horse looked very much like the one he'd had when he worked at the print shop. He felt suddenly nervous, seized by a gloomy feeling of premonition. The horse had always been a symbol of power, always linked with great men. But at the same time, he couldn't help remembering how his father-in-law had humiliated him by telling him not to be so stuck up—he was only a horse-cart driver, a slave for his bosses.

The horse was a small, long-legged black, with a white star on its forehead. It seemed haughty, but Lieu didn't mind: he knew how to deal with it, turn it to his purpose, as he could deal with everything, everyone. Quanh thought he was using him. No, dear boss, I'm using you. Mr. Khiem's unselfish and honest ways are out of style—it's every man for himself. And who knew who was enslaved to whom?

The horse and his cart, he learned, had belonged to a funeral company that had thought it would be profitable to offer old-fashioned horse-drawn funeral processions to people for whom cars were no longer luxury items. Maybe Quanh had the idea that he was organizing a funeral for Khiem's novel. Or maybe he wasn't that subtle. But it was a sure thing the reporters would never suspect that the books were being hauled in a hearse. They'd be watching for the regular transport truck.

"When will you get it done?" Quanh asked him.

Looking at Quanh's face, Lieu could see that the old toad was nervous, so he pretended to answer reluctantly. "I'm not sure, dear boss."

"Why?"

"It's necessary to take some time to train the horse. It's healthy, but it only just completed its training in pulling a cart and hasn't made its acquaintance with city noise. It has to get to know me and my voice—that's not easy, you know."

"I'll give you a week! Just one week, understand?" Quanh said firmly, and turned away, unaware of Lieu grinning behind his back. Got you. He didn't need a week. He knew how to use the whip. The way you beat a horse let it know immediately who was in charge. It would run as far as he wanted, just like the gentlest horse in the world. It would look at Lieu, his tough face, his eyes, his muscles, and know to take him seriously.

He really would take a week though. Take his time, earn some money with the cart. Maybe he would even drive it the thirty kilometers to his brother's house. It would take, what? Only three or four hours. That was all. It wasn't necessary to do what he'd heard during the traffic jam at Tam Diep, that guy who'd run home to kill his father with a pestle, erase the black mark on his biography. He'd tried to train himself to run, but it was tiring. And why shouldn't he be able to write in his dossier that his brother was dead? That curse on his life. It was his fault that he, Lieu, had had to watch and plan every step he'd ever taken in his life. To always calculate. And his brother was still his weakest point, wasn't he? Khoai and Phu must be using him as a weapon against Lieu, keeping him away from the deputy directorship. That was it—they must be! There was no way they could ever match his intelligence. It was his damned brother again.

***

As the cart left the Center, Lieu, trembling slightly, felt as if he had come home. The horseshoes clopped regularly against the pavement. Crossing Nguyen Thai Hoc street, he turned left to West Lake, then across the Long Bien bridge to Thanh Tri. He hadn't driven a horse-cart for seven years, but after half an hour, all his old skills came back to him. This was the way he had demonstrated his membership in the working class, that had led him to Party membership and promotion. He was still a horse-cart driver; it was in his flesh and in his blood.

He drove to Dai Co Viet Avenue, then on to Cong Vong, enjoying himself, feeling relaxed and in tune with the horse. But as they reached the Vong railroad station, he suddenly began whipping the horse frantically. He didn't believe it! Hoan! But there she was, walking out of the railroad station. Thinner, paler, but still with her unmistakable style. Had she been released from prison? How had she avoided the execution Khoai had been so certain about? Had she escaped? Been released through the influence of some important relative? Been found to have been unjustly accused and freed?

The enjoyment he'd been feeling evaporated. He turned around and took the road to Ha Dong, then to Ngoc Khanh, where his house was. By the time he pulled the cart into his yard, though, he was feeling cheerful again. Khoai, you just lost your opportunity—your brother lost his prey. I'm right behind you now, but traveling by horse-cart is faster than traveling on foot, my dear colleagues.

***

Hoan took a taxi to the Sword Lake Post Office. As soon as she had reached the city, she'd bought a copy of *Art and Literature* and seen that Khiem had a new short story, still published under the pen name Thinh Luong, with the same address. Certain it was the goosefeather he was leaving for her to follow, she went to the post office now and sent him a telegram. "I'm safe. I'll be waiting for you in Hanoi, in three days."

Walking down the post office steps, she thought she saw Lieu, driving a black horse-cart.

***

After his rest, Lieu had sprung up, ready to act. He searched for and found a pestle, then drove the cart to the south side of the city. Life is short, he told himself, and I must act quickly. What better time than now?

A person can make four to six kilometers an hour walking. Running, his speed can be the same as a bicycle, ten kilometers an hour. A marathon runner can do forty-two kilometers in two hours. But a horse, even with a cart attached, can go twice as fast as that.

It was a time when force won over everything. Neither Pho nor Quanh could compare with Khiem in talent. But they had gotten him fired and had detained his spiritual child, *The Haven*. And Phu's power lay in his fists, in the blows he had inflicted on Nghiem to shut him up. The three won their way with blows and curses, by acting like gangsters.

A horse runs faster than a human being. The person who killed his father with a wooden pestle had to be as fast as a marathon runner, and had to plan his crime thoroughly. Crime? If he was not caught, then there was no crime. He was just acting as he was supposed to act, as everyone around him was acting. How could that be a crime? Didn't history demonstrate that using violence as a means to an end was not always a bad thing?

Lieu's horse galloped across Giai Phong road. Then to Quan Ganh. Then to Thuong Tin, twenty kilometers south of Hanoi. The rice paddies were filled with water for the spring crop, buffaloes, and the shapes of the plowmen working in the mud mirrored in their water. He remembered how he and Khiem would talk, and how sometimes he would be distracted for hours by their conversations. Khiem's life had been so straightforward and selfless, so driven by ideology and faith. When he was eighteen, he had joined the army and fought to rid the mountains of bandits; when he was thirty, he re-enlisted and fought in the South. He was a bullet that, once shot, flew straight, without hesitation or calculation. As for him, Lieu, even when he'd been a full-time horse-cart driver, he had never been selfless, always schemed and calculated which action he should take according to how it would benefit himself, just as he had deliberately gone about establishing his working-class credentials to demonstrate his rejection of Chuong Kien, his traitor brother. He never had a peaceful moment; all of his time was taken up with weighing his next move, and the young boy who had once helped his classmates to copy a missing textbook or lent them his eraser or fixed their bicycles, was long gone.

It was dark now. Lieu reined in the horse, slowing down. The road had turned into a rough village path, too bumpy to allow the horse to gallop. A shiver passed through his body, as if his nerves were attached to the trembling and jostling of the cart. Sweat ran down his spine.

He had arrived at the hamlet where Chuong Kien was living with his mistress. They had been here ten years now, and the war was long over, but his brother's sins during the time of the French were still haunting Lieu. He was certain that was why he wasn't getting the promotion. His brother was always there, in his mind, tormenting him. But he was suddenly unsure about just what he was doing here. He had never actually named, even in his own mind, the reasons for his urge to train himself, to run every morning. Traveling by horse-cart is faster than traveling by foot. But either was only a means. What was important was the end, and right now the end was unclear in Lieu's mind. He couldn't let himself name it.

He got off the cart and tied the horse's reins to a tree. The narrow, muddy lane was embedded with sea shells that cracked under his step and smelled like land newly reclaimed from the sea. He had been here once before, when his brother had been released from the reeducation camp and had come back to stay with his family for a while, before disappearing. Kien had come here to be with the businesswoman who lived near the reeducation camp, instead of staying and taking care of his family responsibilities, or even his own children from his first marriage. Lieu's mother had told him to come here and teach that woman a lesson. When he'd arrived, Kien was away in Nam Ding, and Lieu had pointed at the woman's face, told her he would smash her into mud. But that was all.

A crescent moon was shining over a row of bamboo. He stopped for a moment, seeing something white flit by under the banana palm near the lane. But it was only a white dog. It sniffed the air, and then ran away. Lieu let his breath out and rested the pestle on his right shoulder. The weight and touch of it startled him, and for a second he thought: why am I here with a pestle? But he rubbed his eyes, clenched his teeth, and kept walking.

It grew darker. Mud stuck to the soles of his shoes. He wanted to spit, but fought down the urge. He must remain silent. Oh, Chuong Kien, why didn't you end your own life when you were doing forced labor in Upper Laos? Why didn't you die when you were suffering in the heat and humidity of the reeducation camp?

"Don't leave yet, Mr. Tan," his brother's voice said. "Stay for a few days—we have so much to catch up on, and time passes so quickly. No, you must stay and have another drink."

The house in front of Lieu was lit up. Lieu was shocked to see the stout man with the hat, the one he had met in the traffic jam coming back from Thinh Luong. But his brother, sitting face to face with his guest, seemed smaller than he remembered him.

"This is the third time I have come North," the man said. "Each time, I've tried to find you. Once I went to the address you'd written down for me, on Ly Cong Uan Street. A young woman there—I assume she was your younger sister—told me very coldly that no one named Chuong Kien lived there, and if he ever had, he'd passed away a long time ago."

"Forty years have passed..." his brother said wistfully,

"From 1953," Tan finished. "Do you remember the Rue Catinat and the Café Givral? '*Ho, we soldiers, marching forward to the far battlefield...*'"

"What happened to you after graduation? My mistake was failing to go South after the Dien Bien Phu defeat."

"No, you were lucky."

"Lucky? What do you mean?"

"We were passed from French hands to American hands.

It's the tragedy of a small nation, to have to depend on foreigners."

"I'd thought by now you'd be living in America, or France, or England..."

"No. I didn't want to live with any of them. The French are too volatile. The English are too cold. The Germans always make me uneasy. And as for the Americans, they're too pragmatic."

Kien chuckled. "Pragmatism and profit are the watchwords of our time now, Tan. People live only for their own gain, and do whatever they have to for it."

"You remind me of a conversation I once had when I came North the first time, and was stuck in traffic at Tam Hiep pass..."

"Tan, you faulted me for disappearing into this small village. But you must understand that I just want to be left in peace. I'm afraid of everything in this life, and I'm afraid of myself as well. I feel we're all victims of some global delirium. I just want to forget. I want not to be me anymore. I want to escape. I want to be alone. I've come to this far corner of the earth, so that only someone who truly loves me would bother to come and look for me. Either that or someone who hates me so deeply, to the bottom of his heart, that he would come here to kill me."

Lieu's grip opened and the pestle fell. He tried to step back, avoid it. At the same time, he felt something sharp and thorny penetrate his trousers below his knee. Looking down, he saw he was being bitten by the white dog. He raised his foot and kicked it hard. The dog howled and rushed into the bushes. "Who's there?" Chuong Kien shouted. Lieu retrieved the pestle, turned, and ran, full of shame, as if his most secret thoughts had been announced to the world.

Chapter Fifteen

I HAVE WRONGED THE ONE
WHO LOVES ME

Life is always a question, but who knows where to find the answer? Khiem had tried to live his life in such a way that his day-to-day behavior was the answer. But life had offered too many contradictions. He recalled a poem by the Russian Andrei Voznesensky, *The Monologue of Marilyn Monroe:* Living without love was unbearable. Yet suicide was unbearable. Yet living was even more unbearable. And living without thinking was unbearable. But thinking constantly was even more unbearable. And to commit suicide was to overcome it all. But to commit suicide was to embrace it all as well...

Right.

But contradiction spurred movement, and the answer to life grew from the contradictions of life. His time in his native Midlands had strengthened him, allowed sadness and joy to leave sediment inside him, the foundations of the person he was now becoming. He had met Mr. Diep and Mr. Tue and had seen how they had learned how to stand against the flood of betrayal, degradation, and greed sweeping over the world by simply declaring it as unworthy of their fear. Coming here had brought him closer to the memory of his father as well, the legacy that had been given to him by his manner of living and dying, the understanding of what it meant to be a hero in this time. *Comrades—don't sleep in the cave!* He had lived and would live like a soldier on the battlefield, like a bullet from a soldier, flying straight at its target. He thought of Hoan (he was certain she would read his stories, recognize his pen name, find him) who had become for him both a purpose and a way of moving towards that purpose. He had passed through his despair and doubt and was in balance again now; the stone was in his hand and it was necessary to throw it. The thirst to live had to be slaked now by living.

At the ceremony to invite his mother's soul into the pagoda, the altar was set high, its red lacquer and gold leaf glittering in the candlelight, incense sticks diffusing the scent of burning sandalwood into the air. Offerings were laid before the statue of Quan Yin sitting on lotus petals, and the statue of the reincarnated Buddha, one hand pointing to heaven, the other to earth, the eternal points of existence. Surrounded by goddesses and disciples, shrouded by the smoke of the incense sticks, the perpetual metamorphosis.

His sister Nguyen sat on a mat in front of the altar, he and the other member of the family and villagers behind her. Her head was covered by a scarf of red silk. The offerings were removed, leaving only the candles glowing on the altar. The Venerable handed a long green bamboo shoot to Nguyen, a symbol of the Buddhist tree branch.

The clacking of the wooden fish, the tinkling of the temple bells, the chanting of the nuns entered Khiem, filled him with a strange and sacred emotion. His soul seemed to be lifting from his body, separating, rising to a different plane. He was aware of faint, floating presences around him, saw the bamboo shoot in Nguyen's hand trembling slightly, as if touched by a breeze, then begin to shake violently, as if surging with a universal energy. It began to spin.

"Madame, are you in need of anything? Why are your hands so cold? What's happened to you there? Madame, your son has returned here to pay tribute to you. Please bless him and bless all your children and grandchildren—oh, Madame Teacher."

The brown-robed Venerable asked each question in a sweet tone, all the while holding Nguyen's hands. When she had finished, she embraced Nguyen, who was weeping and trembling violently as the shoot whirled; she could feel the presence of her mother's soul, hear her mother's voice speaking to her. She felt she had returned to her childhood, to the sanctuary of her mother's arms.

***

In the late afternoon, the smoke from the incense sticks swirled around the two tombs of their parents, warming the cool autumn air. Water lapped against the banks of the marshy pond. Gray clouds lay motionless and melancholy in the sky. A flock of ducks swept in to land on the surface of the pond.

Khiem stood, his eyes embracing the scene to the furthest horizon. The foothills and mountains seemed at once gentle and majestic, filled with a strength and sweetness that swelled in his chest. But he had to leave. All he had seen and remembered and learned in this place was pushing him out of it now, and into his life.

Nguyen placed a tray of pamelo flowers in front of their mother's tomb and turned to Nghiem, her eyes red. "Brother, at that moment I couldn't say a word to our mother. All I could do was cry."

"I felt as if you were speaking to her."

"She spoke to me. She said she was not sad and didn't need anything: she was with our father again. She only felt sorry for you and me and her grandchildren. But for you the most, my brother." Nguyen's voice caught. "She told you to go, that one is waiting for you. She wanted you to remember the sentence: 'I have wronged the one who loves me.'"

Khiem burst into tears. *I have wronged the one who loves me.* He wept as loudly and as naturally as a child, kneeling in front of his mother's tomb.

***

Mr. Diep and Mr. Tue had already decided to accompany him to Hanoi, in case he needed friends around him. But, as if Heaven wanted to second their decision, Mr. Tue suddenly received an invitation to appear before the Central Party Committee to discuss both his dismissal and the death of Khiem's father. "I've sensed that there would be big changes before the end of the century," he said to Khiem. "But I'm going to make sure they hear about what has happened to you before anything. Everything else will come out eventually, but your suffering is today's story. What happened to me already happened." Life was corroborating Mr. Tue's faith that truth would eventually be made known.

Similarly, Mr. Diep also found that he was being called to Hanoi for other, worthy, reasons. The fabulist and humorous poet was a man of strong humanity: he had understood and deeply appreciated Khiem's "The Love of Lit, the Mother Cat," for, as Khiem had intended, it was his story. For Diep, family was the basis for society and community, and children were the continuation of family. In short, he learned that his daughter was pregnant and he would soon be a grandfather. Since she had been sickly as a child, he was worried about her now, even more worried than her mother, or husband, or in-laws. He had bought piles of books about pregnancy and maternity for her, and even planned to name the child. He was concerned now about reports of some problems with the development of the fetus and decided to see his daughter at the OB/GYN hospital in Hanoi.

They planned to leave at five in the morning.

That evening, Nguyen's husband Khuong returned from Hanoi and his regular checkup. He asked Khiem to come for a walk with him—there were several things he had to tell him. While he was in the city, he had taken the time to see what he could find out about Khiem's situation. He'd learned that dozens of letters expressing concern about Khiem's safety had been sent to the authorities, from both other writers and his readers. Pretending to be a buyer, Khuong had gone into the Cultural Affairs Division office and asked where he could purchase a copy of *The Haven*. As soon as he had spoken, a skinny, dwarfish woman had rushed, as if panicked, to fetch a short, squint-eyed man and some others. They began firing questions at Khuong, asking him where he had heard about that book. He heard other strange bits and snatches of conversation whirling around after his question: the squint-eye asking a bearded man how long it took to train a horse, a heavy-set woman grumbling that they were going to destroy the books and weren't they afraid of being punished by spirits?

Khuong clasped Khiem's arm with his good hand. "I'm afraid they're hurrying to destroy the copies of your book. But they seem very disorganized, and ashamed and nervous as well. The squint-eye particularly looked very unhealthy."

Walking beside him, Khiem said nothing. When they were almost back at the house, Khuong told him to wait for a moment before going in. As they stood there, he told him two other pieces of news. He had checked with Thinh's family, as Khiem had requested, and had been told that Thinh had been killed in a car accident in Angola. Secondly, his wife Thoa was also dead. She had gone to Saigon for an abortion, and had died during the procedure. Worse, she had taken Hong Ha with her, and now nobody knew where

Khiem's daughter was. Khiem stood motionless, unable to move, as if he had turned into stone. It wasn't until Nguyen called his name that he was able to make himself walk into the house. She handed him Hoan's telegram, but he held it in his hands, unable to open it, until Khuong helped him. After he read her message, he covered his face with his hands and wept.

That night he couldn't sleep, but lay in a kind of waking nightmare. His sister and brother-in-law also lay awake, until finally Khuong said he would accompany Khiem back to Hanoi. As Nguyen and her daughter helped get his things packed again, Nguyen said: "When your grandmother came back to me, I was crying so hard I couldn't say anything to her. It's better to be calm."

***

Another person in the hamlet who couldn't sleep that night was Mr. Tue, a man who understood calmness. He had accepted the unjust way he'd been treated with equanimity and had put his energy into rebuilding his life by digging canals, making bricks, constructing houses, and planting his orchards. Nothing made him nervous, which made his sleeplessness exceedingly unusual.

Perhaps, he thought, his decision to become engaged in clearing Khiem's name signaled a new involvement in life for him. Certainly that was it. He'd worried about Khiem from the day he met him again, had immediately empathized and wanted to share Khiem's difficulties, fight the injustice of his treatment. He'd wondered at first if the person who was responsible for Khiem's mistreatment had been acting out of some specific revenge or whether this was simply another case of ordinary jealousy, during these times when people seemed to be struggling only for their own benefit.

Later he'd come to understand that Pho, Khiem's former pupil, a bad student, a mediocre cadre, had schemed to eliminate Khiem not only to cover his own past misdeeds but also because the two men were natural opposites. A former high-ranking cadre himself, he understood quite well the great hatred that base, uneducated officials had for literature. Artists and their work uncovered and helped their readers see clearly the degradation of human beings and the decline of the quality of existence. Those who opposed Khiem and Diep and himself did so not because of individual issues, but because they were on opposite sides of history. The first law of modern history was: the more you thought about it, the worse you felt. Baseness and cowardice were everywhere so strong, and the individual was so weak. Even though he was retired, Mr. Tue was aware of everything going on around him. He knew that life in this country was changing radically, that production was increasing rapidly and with it and the new policies, there were new problems. Many were getting rich; corruption and class divisions, the gap between rich and poor, were growing. Khiem's tragedy, though stemming from a clear case of personal revenge and ambition, had to be seen against the background of what was happening to the whole country. The thought reminded him of what he had read in the newspaper yesterday, though he hadn't yet shown it to Khiem. Nguyen Van Pho and his circle had been arrested and charges of corruption had been filed against the upper echelon of General Department T.

And so, restless, Mr. Tue went to his garden. It was still dark, and the stars were shining over the mountains, but he could feel the faint coming warmth of the dawn on his skin. The heavy scent of the flowers pervaded the air like a vital force, drawing man into nature. He felt his garden take on the serene aspect of a great temple, a place for meditation and the development of mindfulness.

So Pho, Duc, and Hien would be put on trial. He had

read that the total amount involved in the corruption case was two hundred billion dong. Pho had received five billion dong, and Duc and Hien had each been given a villa, as bribes. The details of the article were not only simple facts and amounts. They were numbers that represented darkness, as Khiem represented the aesthetic side of life.

Life in his garden was endless, though filled with difficulties. But the garden survived, and with the work of his good hands, it was beautiful. It was the same with the process of history. Each period needed good, talented, kind, honest people who dared to offer their own lives to defend justice, to defend the people's happiness.

Mr. Tue had done his best, worked with the peasants, pretended to be a beggar to find out what would be best for them, to liberate them from stagnation. Now he was old and soon would leave this life. But he had never lost hope. Khiem had once told him that he felt surrounded by Pho, Quanh, Lieu, Tiny Hoi, and Moc as if they were deformed symbols of the alienation he saw everywhere around him; they filled him with disgust and horror. Mr. Tue understood, had felt the same, yet looking back now, he understood that these people were guilty, yet at the same time to be pitied. It would take a long time for human beings to become human. And perhaps, he thought, he was wrong about everything, but at least this line of thinking was not pessimistic. Life truly could be like a well-organized, well-cared-for, and selected garden. Fruit trees and flowers were both ordinary, but when cared for by human beings they were elevated, existed both materially and spiritually. Human beings turned the water running useless under the earth to water used on the earth. Human beings created beauty and would create joy as well. How beautiful people are, he thought, and how they have loved me. *I have wronged the one who loves me.* I have not been worthy enough of them, he thought.

He saw the light from the stove fire glowing in the kitchen. His wife was preparing morning tea for him.

"Will you be going to the Central Committee meeting today?" she asked him.

Gripping the hot cup of tea, Mr. Tue looked at her. They had been together for fifty years now, sharing hardship and sweetness, suffering and happiness. Her hair had gone completely white. But she, like him, had never lost hope.

"Yes," he answered her. "But I want to bring up the issue of Khiem first. He's a talented man, and he's like his father, and..." He stopped himself from uttering the words that would have come out next: like me. "...And he has enemies," he finished lamely.

He put the cup down and took her hand, as if he wanted to share her calmness. Then he walked to the garden again. The sun had risen. He passed the jackfruit trees heavy with fruit, the other fruit trees, saying goodbye. Finally, he walked over to the well to get some water. He could see his square blunt face staring up at him from under the rocky ground of that mountain, as if he were reflected in a mirror.

Chapter Sixteen

TRAFFIC JAM

The souls of the people killed at that place on the road were still angry. They refused to leave, go where they belonged, and instead stayed here to take their revenge by causing more accidents.

Two shrines had been built to commemorate the two unlucky drivers killed last year on the twisting road that snaked through Tam Diep Pass. Now, again in late summer, two IFA trucks smashed into each other and flipped over, blocking the road. Once more the two drivers were badly hurt, lying unconscious on the road and covered with mats while the ambulance came from Dong Giao state farm.

The yellow van had left Hanoi at 8 a.m. and it was now noon. The traffic had been stopped for over an hour, and the backup from the north side stretched for more than a kilometer.

"Let's take a rest here," the woman said. "Maybe we won't have to wait until we get to Thanh Hoa to catch up with him." She and the three men left the van and began walking towards the tea shop at the side of the road. She was an elegant woman, dressed in a dark blue blouse and wearing a mourning band. As they approached the tea shop, she suddenly took off her sunglasses and stared at the cart at the front of the queue. "Heaven has helped us," Hoan said, smiling.

At dawn on the day she thought she would die, she had heard someone call her name. She had been told that condemned prisoners were shot at dawn, after hearing their charges read and having a good meal, and she was certain that the final moment of her forty troubled years had come. Since death seemed inevitable, she decided not to cry. She would not cry. Her only regret was that she couldn't live so she could keep loving Khiem, though in the last letter she had written to him, she'd told him she would love him even after death.

She had prepared herself, was ready to welcome death: she had lived a full life. But then that life had surprised her again. Her belongings, including her journal with her love poems to Khiem, were returned and she was told to leave. She felt like someone leaving hell for paradise as she left the prison, ordered a cyclo, told the driver to take her to the railroad station. She bought a ticket to Hanoi.

Throughout the journey, and even when she had walked out of the station into the streets of Hanoi, she still felt she was moving in a dream. How could someone condemned to death suddenly be declared innocent? Had her arguments made the investigators look foolish? Were they finally simply unable to prove she was connected to those nineteen kilos of opium? Or maybe the opium itself had been stolen on its way to the lab, magically transformed to tar or clay. The Network was skillful at such tricks. Perhaps they had used their hidden influence to rescue her, threatened or bribed the necessary officials, maybe offered a piece of the profit from the heroin, enough to buy a three-story house for someone. Was that it?

But life is like that. Sometimes there are no answers or explanations. Life is messy and murky and some things never balance out. You shouldn't expect everything to be explained in life. Nor, reader, should you expect it to happen in this novel. How can we understand why Lieu drove to Dong Van with a pestle? Was it some passion that seized him on the spur of the moment, or had he planned and calculated the action? Who knew? One shouldn't ask, any more than a lover should ask of his or her beloved, "Why do I love you?" and expect a response, as if one's beloved were a student answering a teacher. Once Hoan had swum in the ocean and emerged just at the point where Khiem had come out of the chaotic crowd on the beach, without either of them planning it. Her love for Khiem was not based on reason. It flared the day they met each other for the first time. It was decided by Heaven. And now Heaven didn't wish them separated any longer. Heaven had set Hoan free.

She had come back to life. Last week, walking in Hanoi, she had felt like a child seeing the streets for the first time. Every once in a while she would stop, stare at everything. It all astonished her, had become fresh and new for her, even though she was walking down the same streets, seeing the same people and trees and flowers that had always been here. How beautiful and sweet freedom was. It was life; it was eternal love.

In a happy daze, she had gone shopping, keeping at it until she had spent all the money the police had returned to her. She hadn't had a chance to spend money for a long time, and she had never bought clothes for a man before. Remembering the poem she had written, teasing Khiem for his casual way of dressing, she went to the most expensive shop on Hang Trong Street and bought two suits for him. When the shop owner asked if she knew the size of the person, she found herself visualizing Khiem's body as they were making love. Then she bought some things for herself and for Old Tuy. She was still haunted by her dream of seeing him die from the U.S. Agent Orange he had drunk, and planned to go to him as soon as she could.

After her shopping spree, Hoan had dropped by the Central Post Office, thinking to search for Khiem as she had near the Luong Nhan tax collection station—in the newspapers. She found short stories in nearly a dozen newspapers signed with the pen name Thinh Luong: the goosefeather trail of love. This evidence of a burst of creativity must mean, she'd felt, that her lover had regained his spirit and inner force.

But suddenly her heart had frozen. On the front pages of all the newspapers was another headline, the same from one paper to the next: Typhoon Olga had struck the central coastal area. At its peak, it had had Force 11 or 12 winds and had deluged the area with nonstop rain for days.

Its center was Thinh Luong.

Thousands of hectares of paddy, jute, and salt had been washed away. Over two thousand people were missing, along with hundreds of cows and buffaloes. The disaster had affected millions of people along the coast, causing unimaginable harm to them and to their property.

She had read everything she could find about the storm, shivering as she thought about the nightmare about Old Tuy she had had in her cell. She sent a telegram to Khiem, saying she would meet him in Hanoi in three days, then found a taxi that would take her to Thinh Luong.

She'd arrived the next morning. When she got out of the car, she was trembling so much she had to lean against its side for a moment to regain her composure. The entire landscape, which had been so green and lovely, was stripped as bare as a no man's land. Rivers and canals had overflowed and split the land into islands. Where there was no water, the land was covered with mud. Sluice gates had been smashed, bridges had collapsed. Roads and lanes had all disappeared, and downed banyan trees lay everywhere. She saw a ferry boat lying upsidedown on top of a hill. The sea pines lining the shore had been torn, twisted, uprooted. Houses had been blown away as well, leaving only their broken foundations. And the beach, the beach where she had swum straight to Khiem, guided by love, was a reeking trash dump of broken boats, debris, contorted branches, and human bodies. Bodies still floating in the sea, bodies recovered and laid out in straight rows and covered by straw mats.

There were about fifty corpses. Around each one were gathered exhausted women and children, too tired and terrified to weep any more, moaning softly.

Trying to keep calm, Hoan walked down the row, looking at each face, seeing in each a lifetime of pain left for the survivors. Why did people have to suffer like this?

"You look familiar to me," a man said to her. "Who are you looking for?" But Hoan was looking at a woman standing ankle-deep in the water, motionless, staring at the sea. She had to shake the woman's shoulder five times before she would turn and look. Her cheeks were hollow and her eyes were empty. She was looking for her husband, had been looking for weeks, would stand there until she turned to stone, the man who had spoken explained. He was a district cadre, sent to help the people here. Hoan told him Old Tuy's name. But he just shook his head and, pointing, told her to try the young man staggering along the edge of the water. He was pale, with protruding eyes, and didn't respond to Hoan's question. He continued to walk back and forth, staring out to sea: looking, the cadre said, for his father's sail.

Hoan thought of the joyous festival, with its colorful flags, its palanquins of the God and Goddess, of the parade, the beating of drums, the solemn speeches, and the rhythmic and lovely flower dances. Where had it all gone? Death covered the earth, the sea, the faces of the people. She felt completely alone.

It wasn't until late afternoon that she ran into a man in his mid-forties, with a shaved head and a stricken face, but with eyes that were somehow not as empty as the others she had seen.

"Are you looking for your uncle?" he asked. "Sit down, and I'll tell you about him. We were in the same boat...but I'm the only survivor. I shaved my head to thank Heaven and my spirits."

"Oh, uncle," Hoan said, and immediately collapsed. The realization hit her hard. Her uncle would never be back. The war veteran, the chief of the ceremony, the brave fisherman—he would now stay forever in the ocean. But it was a death worthy of him.

The man told her that Old Tuy had started feeling ill about three months before, and had told him then that he would be the fifth and last of his group to die from the Agent Orange poison the Americans had left on the land. "'What will come, will come,' he said, but he told me not to say anything to anyone. He didn't want to go to the hospital. He wanted to continue fishing, facing the hardships and risks of the sea. It was the way he had always lived, and he was proud of his skill and courage and wanted to live that way until the end."

Fifteen days earlier, he and the owner of his boat had gone out to sea. Old Tuy had made the normal agreement for 40% of the catch. They received information about the coming typhoon, but thought it would only be a Level 4 or 5 wind, which they knew they could easily handle. That kind of atmospheric pressure was excellent for catching squid. They did, and then spotted a school of ocean horse mackerel. These, the man explained, run about one hundred kilos and are much more valuable than other fish, since they're thought to cure obesity. Both men had searched for years for these fish. Finally, one had struck their hook, but it slipped itself off and swam away fast. Old Tuy laughed and yelled, "Let's race." He laughed with delight as a pod of whales frolicked alongside the boat. He had hooked the mackerel again and had it lashed to the oarlocks when the wind hit. They had won. They had won, which is what human beings want. They had won, just as in the war, in spite of the loss being so dear. They had won. That's all they needed to know. That was their business; the typhoon was the business of Heaven. It raced them in, but they couldn't match the speed of its winds. The sky fell dark as night. Waves rose above them and rocked them violently. It was far more terrifying than the typhoon when Old Tuy had been among the eight survivors out of 140 fishermen.

They couldn't see more than ten meters ahead. The bow sank and the stern rose, as if they were being played with by the sea goddess. What would come, would come. There was a huge cracking noise and the boat split in half. All that was left on the surface was a large plastic marking buoy they had carried. "Hold on to that," Old Tuy had said to the owner, pushing him forward to the buoy. "Get home, say farewell to the villagers, and to my niece as well." Then he released his grip and sank without a trace.

**

So her uncle would remain forever in the sea. Yet before his death he had remembered and planned for his unlucky niece. In his will he had left her all his property, worth about twenty ounces of gold, and had deposited money in her name in the Credit Fund.

Hoan prayed for his soul. She was two days late for her meeting with Khiem now, and so telephoned for a taxi to pick her up in Thinh Luong and take her straight to his house in Hanoi. Her leaning tower of Pisa, directly under the constellation of the Great Bear. When she arrived, the door was wide open.

She walked in without a second thought. She felt directed and powerful: she knew she loved Khiem with all her heart, and now she had money. She would give Thoa all her gold, ask Thoa to forgive her, to let her continue to love Khiem. She loved him completely, loved him physically and spiritually. They had become one person, subsumed into each other; he filled her, her love for him was pure carnality and it was sacred and elevated. She had suffered, been betrayed, enjoyed the peak of love. Yet the past year had proven to her that the more bitterness she experienced, the more sweetness she would taste. At the core of what she had learned was the knowledge now that beauty was to be found in living bravely, and it was that bravery which was the soul of Khiem's writing, that had somehow linked her to Khiem, that had turned them into a single entity.

But inside the house was neither Thoa nor Hong Ha nor Khiem. Instead she found herself shaking hands with a tall old man with a square face, big nose, and large forehead. She instinctively thought she recognized him. "Are you Mr. Tue?"

The old man embraced her, his strong arms wrapping her like eagle wings, his hands flapping against her shoulders. "And you must certainly be Hoan."

She noticed the smaller man standing near him. He smiled, pointed to his chest. "As for me, this ordinary citizen standing before you, I'm Diep, also called the Plow, which means I'm good at both tilling and weeding. But let's talk about me later. May I ask if this is the first time the two of you have met?"

"I read Khiem's story "Mr. Tue's Garden," and felt I had known him from a previous life."

"As for me," Mr. Tue said, "I'm simply sure that this is Khiem's true woman."

They drank tea, and Mr. Diep filled Hoan in on Khiem's family issues. He had been here, and had asked them to tell her not to worry: the most important things he had to do now were to find Hong Ha and to visit Thinh's family.

Is it my destiny to sit for the rest of my life looking at a horse's behind? Lieu asked himself. He had been sitting there for over an hour, the whole line of traffic stopped dead. He was very nervous. So was the horse, who twitched and strained against his harness.

It was almost dusk. The sun was setting behind heavy gray clouds. It wasn't very hot, but the air was heavy with humidity, suffocating. The stink of his own sweat, mingling with that of the horse, made Lieu even more uneasy. It had been a difficult journey, right from the beginning, and today was an inauspicious day, the seventh of the lunar month. Quanh had been insistent and had started to fault Lieu for being too hesitant. But Lieu was a fervent believer in omens, and when he was loading the books into his cart, Tuyen had warned him that his behavior was unlucky. Knowing the books were going to be sold in order to be pulped and re-cycled in Thanh Hoa, Tam and Chuong had both reminded him of what Nghiem had said, and had built an altar under the stairs again. Phu had ordered it dismantled, but no one had dared to do it, not even Phu himself.

Lieu had also been irritated by Thuc, who'd kept nagging him that morning about not getting promoted to deputy director. "Forget that squint-eye," she'd whined. "Stop daydreaming. They were generous enough to let you into the Party, now stop trying to climb up that slippery pillar and concentrate on making money. That's all that's important—money. That's all I need—just money." He had unzipped and pulled himself out, screaming at her: "Don't you need this too?" Last night, he'd pleased her; in the morning it was as if she'd forgotten all about it. What a woman.

As he looked back over the events of the last year, Lieu realized that he had gained little and lost more. He had always considered himself superior to Khaoi and Phu, and

even to Quanh. He had put himself into the working class
when he was sixteen, and had become an acclaimed worker-
poet. Khoai had been a carpenter. Phu had worked with his
hands as well. Pho, Duc, Hien were no different; they all used
to be laborers. What had made them do better than he? Why
had they gotten so much, he so little? Compared to them, he
was a person who knew how to plan, calculate his moves,
weigh advantages and disadvantages before acting. Sure, his
brother had ruined his own life, but his advice had not been
wrong. He'd followed it, and he wasn't a stupid man. He
admired Khiem, had sworn to be faithful to him, but he
hadn't wanted to be brought down with him. Better to let
Khiem despise him. The time when people lived together in
harmony was long past. It would have been better, wiser, for
Khiem to try to flatter Pho a little bit—he was good for
nothing, but he had power, and power should be obeyed.
But Khiem hadn't. Quanh also was a terrible person, it was
true, but he also had power, and there was nothing that he,
Lieu, could do but betray Khiem and follow him. It was so
hard to plan one's life! Everything was moving so fast,
changing so rapidly. Just look around: here he was, stuck
behind his horse, in a queue of hundreds of cars, all kinds of
cars, stuck here in a traffic jam when a moment before they
had all been moving rapidly down the road. In the last
century, people would have traveled here only by horse or
palanquin. How different everything was. Couldn't Khiem
see that the definitions of loyalty and betrayal had changed
as well? Why did all the writers like him have to identify with
the Le dynasty? Why didn't they adapt to the period they
lived in now, adapt to modern life? Why was life so
complicated? Why was he so confused?

As he moved up towards the front of the line of cars and
trucks, he kept thinking about all of it, and from time to
time, tears ran from his eyes.

***

The scene looked just like the traffic jam he had been stuck in the year before, in this same place. The traffic was backed up on the right side of the road. There were the same company trucks: Vietnam Airlines, Vietnam Textiles, the Youth Theater, a Trade Union Department of Tourism, a Forestry Products truck, its bed packed with bamboo, a Kama loaded with cement from the Bim Son Factory. Again, most of the queue was made up of private cars: Nissans, Toyotas, Dawoos, Mekong Stars, Fiats, Peugeots, Mitsubishis...all of them colorful and luxurious looking to Lieu.

He held back the reins, trying to control the nervous horse, wondering what he was doing here in a horse-cart. But looking more closely at the traffic, he could see more differences among the motor vehicles as well. More often than not, they belonged to either foreign-owned or joint-venture companies, and the vehicles belonging to the domestic social and economic organizations paled next to their sleek, modern attractiveness. Breweries, cookie bakeries, companies selling shoes, glutamate, electronics, gas stoves, thermos bottles, toilet equipment, and washing machines had bright ads painted on their sides, turning the whole line into a commercial festival. And making his cart look like a beggar in front of elegant gentry.

He noticed that more cars than he'd ever seen before had white plates, indicating they were privately owned. He knew they belonged to the directors of the limited and trading companies: the *nouveaux riches*. He could suddenly hear Thuc's voice, nagging him to make more money whenever she saw his face, and looking around him now he understood how right his wife was: the differentiation between classes was growing clearer and clearer every day. He felt suddenly nervous, leery of speaking to anyone, and began to turn the cart around. A man crossed the road towards him, passing the horse.

"Hi there!" The man looked like someone coming into town from a small village in the countryside: he had a big bag on his shoulder and was fanning himself with a palm hat. His eyes sparkled joyfully in his little face. "Do you own this horse-cart?"

"Yes," Lieu said, "but my cart is full of goods; I can't take any passengers. What do you want?" He propped one foot up casually on the cross bar of the cart, and rubbed his palms together, as if he were cleaning oil off them, his face cold and expressionless. He was sure this guy wanted some favor from him.

"Look, I don't want a lift," the man said, shaking his head gently, "or to disturb you in any way."

"Then what do you want? Who are you?"

"This is the first time we've met."

The guy seemed to be all right. Lieu scratched his nose. "Do you know my mother?" he asked, keeping his voice low.

"No, nothing like that. I just want to discuss...." He glanced over at the grassy lane alongside the road and said in a voice just above a whisper, "Why don't we go over there to talk?"

"Sure."

Lieu smoothed his hair, let out a breath, and willed himself to relax. There was nothing to worry about. He glanced at the villager again, trying to assess the man, then asked, feigning indifference, in case the man really was interested in buying the books he was hauling.

"Let me explain." The villager took off his palm-frond hat and slid it over the brown bag he had slung on his chest. "There is a legend which goes like this. Once upon a time, there was a beautiful princess who was hated by her step-mother, the queen. That woman ordered her soldiers to take the girl to the forest, kill her, and then bring back her heart, as proof. The soldiers brought the princess to the forest, as ordered. They all felt sorry for her: she had committed no crime, and yet what could they do? At that moment, a deer ran out of the woods and said to them: "Kill me instead, and take my heart back to the queen."

Lieu smiled. "Very nice."

"Thank you. So, you see, the soldiers were able to fulfill their duties, and the princess was able to live happily ever after."

"I get the point," Lieu said. "So?"

"Sorry to be so roundabout. In short, I'm a trader in scrap paper. I saw you were transporting paper to be recycled, and I wanted to buy. The only question is, what's the price?"

Lieu nodded, looking at the man. "You want to buy it right here?"

"Why not? The road is going to be jammed up for a long time, and my factory isn't far from here—only about a kilometer from Bim Son factory."

"I planned to take this scrap paper to Thanh Hoa. They have a shredder, and they throw everything into acid before recycling it."

"We do the same."

"There they would pay...but look," Lieu raised his voice threateningly, "Are you putting me on?"

"Do I need to show you my i.d. card so you'll believe me?" The man put his hand into his pocket. "I used to be head of the district cultural section, but now I've retired, and I purchase old books for recycling. I can show you letters of introduction from both the province and district levels. Understand?"

Lieu nodded. He understood. He would bring the princess' heart, the money, to Quanh. He could feel something relax in himself. He wouldn't have to commit the sin of destroying the books himself, an act the spirits would never forgive him for. More important, he would make some money as well! A horse's yoke wasn't as heavy as people thought. Maybe this was Heaven's way of evening things out for him.

A thought occurred to him. "Look, are you sure you have enough money to make an offer?" he asked the man, his eyes narrowing. "What I have here isn't going to be cheap."

"You think I'm fooling around?" the man chuckled. "I'm a serious player. How much do you want—ten million?" He patted the brown bag.

This is one big fish, Lieu thought cheerfully. "Great— let's get something to drink, sit down, and talk. Where are you from anyway? How long have you been in the recycling business?"

They sat on the grass and Lieu ordered drinks from a passing vendor. If he took the books to Thanh Hoa, he would only get a million dong. Now, piled in front of him in 50,000 dong banknotes, was ten million dong. He couldn't believe his good fortune.

The man went back to his vehicle. A few moments later, the drivers who'd been sleeping on the grassy strip along the side of the road with their hats on their faces, began sitting up and shouting: "Hey, stop that van—he's jumping the queue. Who let him in there? Somebody stop him!"

The van stopped and the driver explained what he was doing, then continued to drive slowly along the edge of the road, until he drew up to Lieu's horse-cart. Lieu pulled up the rear cover. The horse, thinking it was going to be let loose, neighed excitedly. The piles of books in the cart were revealed: the word *Haven* in blue, the faint brown trace of a river bank on each white cover, the design of the young artist Van Sang. Lieu took the ten million dong, and began loading the books into Mr. Diep's van.

Hoan, who had spotted the author's name, Dinh Van Khiem, printed on each book, willed herself to keep calm, keep out of Lieu's sight until this battle was won. It was a battle between occupied and occupier, between those who used power as a weapon and those who lived as honest people. It was a small battle, but it was a link in the chain of tumultuous moments and crises that had led to so much tragedy. But what she was seeing was surely occurring by Heaven's will, and thinking this, Hoan now began to cry, to cry for everything that had happened, for all the suffering, for her uncle's death, for everyone who had been hurt so badly.

At the same time, Khiem and Hong Ha stood in the waiting area of Noi Bai airport. Hong Ha had been staying with her maternal grandmother, and had come home with Khiem as soon as he'd found out where she was. Both of them were wearing mourning armbands and standing next to Thinh's wife and two children, waiting for his body to come home from Angola. Another casualty, Khiem thought bitterly: an intellectual living in times so impoverished he had to focus his intelligence and strength on finding work abroad so he could send money back to support his family. Thinh's wife had told him that his friend had saved every cent in Angola, lived on tomatoes and bread, worn the same poor clothing, and gotten involved in exchanging dollars on the side. The town of Sumbe is located about 160 kilometers from the former slave market of Luanda, and the exchange rate of local currency to the dollar was considerably less there than in Luanda. Every month, Thinh exchanged dollars to kwanzat in Luanda, then took kwanzat to Sumbe to buy dollars. He had saved more than $2000, a small fortune for a poor doctor. He was taking all his money to make one last exchange before coming home, when the taxi broke one of its front axles and fell into a chasm next to the road. His tall, healthy body lay smashed at the bottom, the dollars he had with him covering his body, sticking to his blood.

A great talent, a great intellect, a veteran who had never gotten over his fear of death on the battlefield, had died because of a petty scheme. The man who had saved Khiem's body and spirit had died in a senseless accident.

Holding the jar of ashes, Khiem's vision blurred with tears. In his mind's eye he saw again his strong, innocent friend, scolding him, advising him, carrying him to the hospital.

"Hong Ha, this is your Uncle Thinh," he sobbed. "Ah, Thinh, Thinh, I never thought that what you told me at Tran Quy Cap railway station would come true. But you predicted everything. You were truly a man of this century. But how can I live on earth now without your friendship? How can I show my gratitude to you now, my dear friend?"

Coc Mountain, 13 October 1991
Sam Son, 11 August 1992
Ha Noi, 1998

AFTERWORD

"In Vietnam, I learned of Thuy Kieu and began, at last, to understand how the Vietnamese perceive suffering and sacrifice and sorrow, and why so many of them are able to bear so much of it."
　　　　—Gloria Emerson on *The Tale of Kieu*

Against the Flood presents a very modern love affair between two middle-aged professionals: the plot centers on the relationship between Khiem, a married writer and editor, and Hoan, a proofreader who works in his office. Yet despite the novel's contemporaneity, and its unusually frank (for Vietnam) eroticism, at its heart is both the ancient legend of the Princess My Chau and Nguyen Duy's epic poem *The Tale of Kieu*, written in the nineteenth century. Thuy Kieu, separated from the man she loves and forced into prostitution in order to save her family, is a well-loved character in Vietnamese literature, and any reader of this novel familiar with *The Tale of Kieu* can see its heroine's strength reflected in the travails and triumphs of Hoan's life. That My Chau's story is also a coda in the novel, as it is in Vietnamese culture, may seem somewhat stranger. In love with a Chinese prince, My Chau inadvertently allows him to steal her country's secret weapon, and then, as she flees with her father the king after the Chinese victory, leaves a trail of goose feathers from her cape for him to follow. Thus she tragically betrays both her father and her country's struggle for independence—violates both Confucian fealty to the paterfamilias and loyalty to the cause of national liberation. Yet, in a nation that fought for a thousand years against foreign domination, people still worship at My Chau's shrines and celebrate her life. Perhaps she is so revered because the other side of her betrayal was her loyalty to her own fierce, misguided love. If My Chau were to see her lover clearly as the enemy he turned out to be, she would not be the human, passionate woman she was, and if she were not that woman, so strong in following the passion of her heart, she would be somehow less Vietnamese.

As the Vietnam scholar Neil Jamiesen notes: "One of the broadest and most fundamental oppositions in Vietnamese culture...has been that between *nghia* and *tinh*. While *nghia* is about morality, ethics, and duty, *tinh* is about feelings. *Tinh* is spontaneous, subjective, intuitive, unpredictable, emotional. *Tinh* is often used to refer to 'love,' but it is also used to signify passion, sentimentality, desire, or emotionalism, what we might call the dictates of the heart. *Tinh* was always subordinated to *nghia*, however, in folklore and in literature..."

Perhaps it is true then that My Chau's story appeals to many Vietnamese because of its very ambiguity, because it raises questions rather than providing answers, because it speaks to a hunger to acknowledge the complexity of the human heart in a land that has been shaped by the dichotomies of struggle, by the need to take sides, to become completely subsumed by national purpose. As they have defined Vietnam, the priorities of war and survival after war have also conscripted modern Vietnamese literature: as a result it has often been peopled by characters who are embodiments of ideals, good or evil, rather than multifaceted, fleshed-out human beings. Perhaps a people involved in one of the most costly and vicious wars of the century and its aftermath could not afford the luxury of ambiguity. But perhaps the need for paradox and complexity seen in the story of My Chau is tied inextricably to the struggle for freedom; perhaps the freedom struggled for is ultimately the freedom to be paradoxical and complex. To be, in a word, human. And to see one's humanity and its concerns reflected in literature.

The question revolutions must eventually raise is not only what one will be free to do, but what one will be free to be once liberated not only from one's oppressors, but from the need to hone oneself into a weapon, simply a weapon, nothing but a weapon. The truth is, of course, that such clarity can be comforting, and the protagonist of *Against the Flood*, Khiem, a dedicated communist and a war veteran, yearns for it—though his lover, Hoan, knows that clinging to such singular moral certainty is like bleeding from an open wound in a tank of hungry sharks. Khiem at first tries to maintain a touching and naive faith in the essential goodness of his co-workers and they in turn attempt to destroy him. Khiem's masterpiece, his novel *The Haven,* is banned, and he loses his job: the vengeful fury of his colleagues and superiors is stoked not only by their own greed and insecurity about their ignorance and incompetence, but also by the nagging example of Khiem's trust and virtue. The bleakly comic backbiting of office politics, the depiction of the serious writer in a culture that has elevated ignorance and cowardice and devalued learning and integrity are trends not unique to Vietnam, and will resonate as much with readers in the West as in that country.

On one level, then, the novel fits into the genre of sharp social criticism that has emerged since the policy of *Doi Moi,* Renovation, was adapted in the nineteen eighties. Yet *Against the Flood* goes further than social satire. At its best, it poses one of the basic questions modern novels have to pose: what is the best way to live our lives on these turbulent waters in which we all find ourselves adrift and rudderless? Hoan and Khiem attempt to create a haven for themselves, an island in the raging flood of greed, betrayal, and corruption all around them. What they want to find, finally, is a life of meaning, a life that is about more than an endless and vicious scramble for money, power, and hollow recognition, that allows for individual joy as much as for collective good. In their love for each other, in their belief in art and literature and the culture and traditions of their country, in the strength of the people who till its soil and fish its waters, in the love and loyalty of a small and ever-smaller circle of seekers like themselves, Khiem and Hoan search for what each sees as the lost idealism and sense of purpose of the war years, and the lost or battered virtues of traditional Vietnam.

Their quest brings them together—and then drives them apart into separate journeys that allow us to see the complexity of choice offered them...and modern Vietnam. Khiem's journey brings him back to the rural roots which are often seen as the source of renewal and strength in Vietnam. The physical geography of his past, in the midlands, the heartland of Vietnam, remains intact: he can go there and find who and what he has missed and come back renewed. But Hoan's return to her birthplace takes her to a place already eroded by the people and values she has fled, contaminated by hotels and brothels for the privileged few, by a rapacious greed. Her loss of balance, and her desire for revenge, drive her into the world of drug smuggling and prison. While Khiem is portrayed as a man of pure motive, a man all of a piece, Ma Van Khang's true triumph in *Against the Flood* is realized in the creation of Hoan, with her sharp tongue and her gentleness, with her sophisticated intelligence and her superstition, with her love and her lust for Khiem, with her virtue that refuses to ask favors and her passion for revenge. Hoan reaches a level of complexity that is rare in the way contemporary Vietnamese literature depicts female characters—yet that stems directly from the tradition of My Chau and her passionately wrong choices, of Thuy Kieu and her strength to suffer and overcome, to be blindly romantic yet ruthlessly pragmatic, to be chaste and demure and yet to revel in her sexuality. Like Kieu, Hoan must attempt to fit herself to the values of the place where she finds herself, and yet must struggle to remain herself. Her road back, to Khiem, to love, to herself is marked by tragedies and transformations which can only be overcome by her strength and adaptability, which like Thuy Kieu's, like Vietnam's, allow her to endure and prevail.

Wayne Karlin

A Note on the Translation

The translators have edited portions of the original Vietnamese edition both to clarify the plot for western readers and to correct several inconsistencies. All such editing has been done in collaboration with the author and with the deepest respect for and adherence to the spirit and intent of the novel.

Born in Kim Lien Village near Hanoi on December 1, 1936, MA VAN KHANG, the pen name of Dinh Trong Doan, is a veteran of the people's Army of Vietnam who saw his first military service at the age of 13 during the resistance against the French. A graduate in Literature from the Hanoi Pedagogical University, he was the headmaster of a high school in Lao Cai Province, and Deputy Editor-in-Chief of the Lao Cai newspaper. Since 1976, he has been Editor-in-Chief of the Labor Publishing House and of the Foreign Literature Review section of the Vietnam Writers Association. He is also on the Executive Committee of the fifth session of that Association (1995-2000). Ma Van Khang's novels include *The French Silver Coin* (1979), *Summer Rain* (1982), *The Athlete in His Arena* (1982), *Border Area* (1983), *Young Moon* (1984), *The Garden in the Season of Falling Leaves* (1986), *The Lonely Orphan* (1989), *A Marriage Without Certificate* (1989), *Bi, the Wandering Dog* (1992), and *Against the Flood* (1999). He has also published nine collections of short stories: *A Beautiful Day* (1986), *Ripe Fruit in Autumn* (1988), *The Strong Breeze* (1992), *Moonlight on the Small Yard* (1995), *Suburb* (1996), *The Classical Circle* (1997), *Lotus Marsh* (1997), and *A Windy Afternoon* (1998). He received the Vietnam Writers' Association prize for best novel of the year in 1986 for *A Garden in the Season of Falling Leaves*, and the Vietnam Writers Association prize for best short story collection for *Moonlight on the Small Yard* in 1995. In 1998 he received the ASEAN Literature Prize.

PHAN THANH HAO lives in Hanoi. She is Assistant Editor-in-Chief of *Education and Times*, published by the Ministry of Education and Training, and General Secretary of IOGT-VN. She has translated *The Class* by Eric Segal and *Evening News* by Arthur Hailey into Vietnamese, and is first translator for Bao Ninh's novel *The Sorrow of War*, published in England in 1991. She has also translated *The Virgin Fairy, The Land of Many Ghosts and Many People*, and *The Cattle Station*. Her poetry appears in the anthology *Visions of War/Dreams of Peace*, and her short fiction has been published in Australia.

WAYNE KARLIN served in the Marine Corps in Vietnam. He is the author of five novels: *Crossover, Lost Armies, The Extras, Us*, and *Prisoners*, and a novel/memoir: *Rumors and Stones*. In 1973, he contributed to and coedited, with Basil T. Paquet and Larry

Rottman, the first Vietnam veterans' anthology, *Free Fire Zone: Short Stories by Vietnam Veterans*. In 1995 he coedited, with Le Minh Khue and Truong Vu, and contributed to *The Other Side of Heaven: Post-War Fiction by Vietnamese and American Writers*. He has received a fellowship from the National Endowment for the Arts, four individual artist awards in fiction from the State of Maryland, and the Paterson Prize for Fiction.

ABOUT THE SERIES:

VOICES FROM VIETNAM, a series of contemporary fiction from Vietnam, is a long-term project of Curbstone Press edited by Wayne Karlin. Over the next decade, Curbstone will publish some of the best contemporary writers of Vietnam, including (as of press time) Le Doan, Ngo Thi Kim Cuc, Nguyen Minh Chau, Nguyen Khai, Nguyen Manh Tuan, Nguyen Khac Truong, Nguyen Thi Minh Ngoc, and Vu Bao.

#1: *The Stars, the Earth, the River*, short fiction by Le Minh Khue.

#2: *Behind the Red Mist*, short fiction by Ho Anh Thai.

#3: *Against the Flood*, a novel by Ma Van Khang.

CURBSTONE PRESS, INC.

is a non-profit publishing house dedicated to literature that reflects a commitment to social change, with an emphasis on contemporary writing from Latino, Latin American, and Vietnamese cultures. Curbstone presents writers who give voice to the unheard in a language that goes beyond denunciation to celebrate, honor, and teach. Curbstone builds bridges between its writers and the public – from inner-city to rural areas, colleges to community centers, children to adults. Curbstone seeks out the highest aesthetic expression of the dedication to human rights and intercultural understanding: poetry, testimonies, novels, stories, and children's books.

This mission requires more than just producing books. It requires ensuring that as many people as possible know about these books and read them. To achieve this, a large portion of Curbstone's schedule is dedicated to arranging tours and programs for its authors, working with public school and university teachers to enrich curricula, reaching out to underserved audiences by donating books and conducting readings and community programs, and promoting discussion in the media. It is only through these combined efforts that literature can truly make a difference.

Curbstone Press, like all non-profit presses, depends on the support of individuals, foundations, and government agencies to bring you, the reader, works of literary merit and social significance which might not find a place in profit-driven publishing channels, and to bring the authors and their books into communities across the country. Our sincere thanks to the many individuals who support this endeavor and to the following foundations and government agencies: Connecticut Commission on the Arts, Connecticut Arts Endowment Fund, Connecticut Humanities Council, Daphne Seyboldt Culpeper Foundation, J.M. Kaplan Fund, Eric Mathieu King Fund, Lannan Foundation, John D. and Catherine T. MacArthur Foundation, National Endowment for the Arts, Soros Foundation's Open Society Institute, Puffin Foundation, and the Woodrow Wilson National Fellowship Foundation.

Please support Curbstone's efforts to present the diverse voices and views that make our culture richer. Tax-deductible donations can be made by check or credit card to:
Curbstone Press, 321 Jackson Street, Willimantic, CT 06226
phone: (860) 423-5110   fax: (860) 423-9242
www.curbstone.org